S(H)ELF HELP GUIDE

A PULP NON-FICTION BOOK

S(H)ELF HELP GUIDE

THE SMART LIFTER'S HANDBOOK

BY

GABRIEL CAIME & GABRIEL GHONE

If you paid for this book, you might learn something!
If you did not, take it back. You do not need it.

TriX Publishing

Although the authors and publisher have extensively researched all sources to ensure the accuracy and completeness of the information contained in this book, we assume no responsibility for errors, inaccuracies, omissions or any inconsistency herein. Any slights against people or organizations are unintentional or done in good faith.

 Published by TRIX Publishing, 2255B Queen Street East, #249, Toronto, Ontario, Canada, M4E 1G3. First edition. ISBN: 0-9680761-0-6

Canadian Cataloguing in Publication Data

Caime, Gabriel, 1952-

The S(h)elf Help Guide: The Smart Lifter's Handbook: A Pulp Non Fiction Book

Includes bibliographical references.

ISBN 0-9680761-0-6

1. Shoplifting. 2. Retail trade-Security Measures.

I. **Ghone**, Gabriel, 1953- II. Title. III. Title: Self-help guide.

HV6652.C35 1996 364.1'62 C96-900341-2

PRINTED AT: **SHARON EXPRESS,** Toronto

EDITED BY: **GLORIA FROST**

ATTENTION COLLEGES AND UNIVERSITIES, CORPORATIONS, RETAIL ORGANIZATIONS, RETAIL ADVISORS, AND OTHER PROFESSIONAL ORGANIZATIONS: Quantity discounts are available on bulk purchases of this book for educational or training purposes. Special booklets or book excerpts can also be created to fit your specific needs. For information contact:

TriX Publishing, 2255B Queen Street East, #249,
Toronto, Ontario, Canada, M4E 1G3,

Phone:1-416-531-5928 Fax:1-416-531-8276

E-mail: caime@trixnet.com
ghone@trixnet.com
publisher@trixnet.com

Web site: http://www.trixnet.com/front.htm

TABLE OF CONTENTS

FOREWORD

"The real risks for any artist are taken . . . in pushing the work to the limits of what is possible, in the attempt to increase the sum of what it is possible to think. Books become good when they go to this edge and risk falling over it-when they endanger the artist by reason of what he has, or has not,* artistically *dared."

(Salman Rushdie)

This book is about shoplifting. Boosting. Snitching. The "five-finger discount." Writers of hundreds of articles in trade magazines and scientific journals have tried to get a grip on this important component of the underground economy, but like most authors of entire books on the subject, they have yet to succeed because they **moralize**.

Why we embarked on this trip

We offer a different perspective. Our book is a self-help guide, a manual for the hypothetical would-be shoplifter. We present every aspect and facet of shoplifting **objectively**. Casting ourselves as **amoral** advisors, we talk about such things as "the best of times and the worst of times" to do shoplifting, the different types of stores a thief encounters, the laws he violates, and the training given to the security personnel who try to catch him. We reveal strategies for defeating security devices and show the best and worst techniques lifters use - the ones that work and the ones that do not. Although we marginally touch on issues of morals and justification, the issues facing retailers, and the past and future of shoplifting as we see it, our main thrust is an objective look at shoplifting without moral considerations.

The art of shoplifting

We do not deal extensively with theories and issues arising from statistics, sociology, and psychology. When we do touch on these matters for practical reasons, we promise to be brief. This book is about the art, ***not*** the theory.

To be funny, not ridiculous

Our first and foremost goal is to entertain you. We want you to laugh and shake your head in disbelief. We are willing to take the risks inherent in humor because we realize, having researched the literature on this subject extensively and thoroughly, that being "serious" often leads to being ridiculous. While doing our research, we ran into dated attitudes, useless information, self-serving trade literature, and, perhaps most ridiculous of all, academic literature which had little to do with reality.

The butcher, the baker, the candlestick maker...

Our target audience is everybody and anybody. The public at large may derive great satisfaction from this book as a catalyst for fits of moral outrage. Teenagers may learn in these pages that shoplifting is not an adventure. Middle-class housewives may find out that they should drop a few bad habits next time they go "a-thieving." Even professional shoplifters might be able to pick up a few pointers and some new methods.

Teaching aid

And let us not forget about the security folks. Although their first instinct will be to damn us for this book, we hope that curiosity nudges them into giving it a chance. Where else, we ask, can they find a concise, systematic analysis of shoplifting methodology? We sincerely hope that our book will become required reading for all store-security personnel.

The folks we won't make happy

The only group of people we cannot even hope to make peace with are security consultants and their comrades, the 'gizmo' manufacturers. Although theirs is a multi-billion-dollar-a-year industry (and growing), most of their wares are useless, and the statistics they use to peddle them are bogus. Our book is very likely to upset these folks, but we hope that their anger won't make us feel compelled to move in with Salmon Rushdie! - Then again, who knows? This guide's publication might lead to another boom for them. By proving their current wares useless, we could give them an opportunity to make still more very big bucks pushing new, improved gadgets that the Joker himself might envy.

Key word: buy!

To any and all moral-mongering zealots who find our book totally offensive, we can only say, Good for you! Make a statement! Buy a few more copies and burn them!

Our sources

Our sources include active or 'retired' members of three distinct groups of shoplifters: professionals, experienced amateurs, and booster-gang members.

No career criminals

We excluded criminals for whom shoplifting was either a step on the way toward becoming bank robbers, drug dealers, etc., or just a sideline to their more serious criminal activities. We also left out what the literature sees as the backbone of the shoplifting crowd: middle-class housewives, juveniles, retired people, and all other impulsive lifters who do not have methods, getaway plans, or schemes worth investigating.

The smart lifter

The literature defines professional shoplifters as those who steal for resale. Because we were trying to concentrate on methods and not motivations, our most valued sources were articulate, intelligent, skilled professionals and experienced amateurs who consider shoplifting to be an 'art' and are able to describe it as such. We refer to them as the 'smart lifters'. We look upon the information gathered from these smart lifters not as a collection of statistical, psychological, or sociological data, but as information on the practical aspects and elements of shoplifting.

Although it definitely did not dazzle us, we also made good use of the limited information we were able to find in the 'literature.' We found very few good books on the subject, and we can confidently say that anything that appears in the trade magazines is rubbish.

Educational fallout

Common sense suggests that books written about shoplifting (or media exposure given to any kind of crime for that matter) will invariably supply criminals with advice. However, to attempt to reduce the impact of this educational fallout by moralizing in a book about crime serves no practical purpose except to reassure the prudish reader.

Everybody according to his ability

Throughout history many writers have positioned themselves on the 'wrong' side of the moral divide. We are proud to be in the company of such literary figures as Jonathan Swift, William Makepeace Thackeray, Bertolt Brecht, Jean Genet and, Lo and Behold! The Marquis De Sade. Also, let us consider the fact that time-honored lectures, if not slide-shows, are being offered continually in crime's postgraduate institutions of higher learning, our prisons. Anything we say here can be picked up in jail from the masters of the art. Some might argue, by the way, that these imprisoned professors of boosting theory and technique are not real masters. They are currently cooling their heels in the hoosegow, are they not? However, it seems to us that anybody can get caught without his rubbers on a sloppy day.

Teaching the thieves teaches the thief-catchers

Common sense also suggests that books like ours which either deliberately or inadvertently educate criminals can serve as a teaching aid to enforcers of law and order. For example, the chapters in Abbie Hoffman's *Steal this Book* which describe shoplifting techniques have been used to train security personnel.

Security personnel are very unlikely to take courses from 'masters of the art,' and so we sincerely hope that our book ends up on the mandatory reading lists of their training courses. We honestly believe that our approach and attitude will make this book more useful for these particular teaching applications than anything else we saw while doing our research.

It is more fun to have an attitude

You could ask how we can excuse ourselves for writing a book which might promote crime. What about our morals? Our reply would be that we enjoy doing outrageous things. Doing outrageous things requires a cynical attitude, and we love being cynical.

Anything goes

Indeed, basic cynicism helped us to identify other attitudes as we did our research. Books and articles on shoplifting written in the fifties were paternalistic. In the sixties, ideological. In the seventies, 'psychologistic.' In the eighties, plain frustrated. Now we are in the nineties. Utter cynicism is the order of the day. Anything goes.

No answers

Whenever criminologists, sociologists, and psychologists get busy trying to understand the motivations behind shoplifting, they tend to find excuses. We ourselves are far too cynical about shoplifters to excuse them for any reason. The above groups of worthy investigators also ask questions about crime which boil down to one very basic philosophical query: "Who is the true victim?" Is 'honest' society a victim of the criminals, or are criminals victims of social inequalities, their upbringing, or their own psyche? The books and articles we looked into could be more or less evenly divided according to their answers to this question. We don't even ask it.

The amoralists

We are amoral, not immoral. We could try to make the point that being amoral makes us unbiased, in turn helping us to be objective and factual, thereby gaining insight that leads to a better understanding of the phenomenon which may suggest to us more effective methods of prevention that could lay the groundwork for some fundamentally moral changes in the world of the five finger discount - but to say such a thing is to moralize, and we don't moralize.

Nor do we apologize.

Stealing is a trade

We do not personally condone shoplifting, but for the purposes of this book we pass no judgment on it either. We toss morals aside and focus on the nitty gritty details of the 'trade' - because that's what shoplifting is: a trade. It has rules, methods, and trade secrets. It gives a return on time invested. It involves certain risks, but if you can be successful at it, it also has benefits. If you are not disturbed by the fact of its immorality, it can be made into a full time profession, but we do not ***advise*** anyone to do so.

We cannot emphasize enough that our book is not intended to promote any criminal activity.

No leads, no distance

We had many discussions about the format of the book. Our concerns included how much of what we had heard from lifters (our primary source; the 'literature' is our secondary source) should be quoted directly and what formula we should use for identifying these helpful folks. Should we use tags like "according to J., a 25 year old legal secretary"? - or should we give our sources more colorful identity tags, i. e., "says Joe, the leader of a booster gang" or "concedes Harry 'The Finger' Wishbone". We decided to avoid any tags at all.

The essence of these questions of format was whether we should distance ourselves from our primary sources by identifying them, or setting them apart from us, in some specific way. Because we found keeping our distance to be both cumbersome and condescending, we chose an informal style, one that you would expect from a teacher of any subject who has filtered knowledge from primary sources through himself, playing fast and loose with it.

We just descend, not condescend

We quote directly from the 'literature,' but when it comes to our less 'respectable' sources, we flow freely in and out, quoting them directly only when appropriate. (They tell great stories.) Having said that, we also have to say that we were quite liberal with our interview material. The 'direct' quotations from it are likely to be rewrites - capturing, we hasten to add, the gist and the truth of what each person told us.

A 'politically incorrect' note: We always use 'HE' in the third person singular unless the gender of the subject is clearly female. We sincerely hope that our politically sensitive readers will understand that we mean 'he' to apply equally to either gender.

Why 'HE'?

As we were writing, we happened to think of a few famous quotations which fit our subject amazingly well. Having been thus inspired to search our minds and libraries for more such quotations, we decided to select one for every little passage in the book. The result is that in some cases we use famous or infamous words which fit like a glove. In other cases, however, the fit is less apt. Even in these latter cases, we hope you will forgive us for retaining the looser fits simply because they were fun to read. Some chapters have no quotations at all. If you think of one, write it in!

We started to write this book for the fun of it. Our expectations were met. Now we can only hope that you will have as much fun reading our book as we had writing it.

You should have fun too.

ATTITUDE DISCLAIMER

We have to point out that, regardless of the style of presentation, all the information, ideas and methods that we offer in this book are hearsay. We couldn't possibly 'guarantee' that any of the methods described are practiced or would work in real life. Although we have tried to analyze the practicality of some methods, we have never actually tried them. Of course we ***would*** say that even if we had verified them scientifically and made millions using them. Another of our formatting decisions is to cover our derrieres. **You will never know!**

WE DIDN'T DO IT!

We can hardly emphasize enough that no matter which side you are on, **THERE ARE NO GUARANTIES!** No place is absolutely safe from shoplifters or for shoplifters.

SHOPLIFTING IS A CRIME! WE URGE EVERYBODY TO REFRAIN FROM DOING IT!

SPECIAL THANKS TO OUR CONTRIBUTORS

A special place where the authors decided to be a hundred percent nice

Our special thanks to Tom for his contribution to the title, R.B. for his stories and information on internal theft, K.T.G. and Sz. P. for introducing us to the art of fencing, A., R., R., K., Cs., J., and all the others, who insisted that we refrain from citing their full initials in this book. Our thanks also to the few 'anonymous' retailers and security experts who helped us. Thanks to Jake and Cynthia for bailing us out many times when we were stuck for a synonym or an idiom. Thanks to the lovely Gloria, our tireless editor. Thanks to the countless writers from whom we learned a lot. Their due credits are given after the quotations and in our bibliography in the 'Appendices' of this book. Thanks to Prozac, the 'wonder drug' of the nineties without which we would probably have strangled each other. Many thanks to the only women in our lives, Bobo and Renata, for their support, and for providing us with the space we needed to make this book possible.

And last but not least, thanks to the Academy, and its members....

“

. . .

PART ONE

ASSUMPTIONS

MORALITY

"I never approve, or disapprove, of anything now. It is an absurd attitude to take towards life. We are not sent into the world to air our moral prejudices. I never take any notice of what common people say, and I never interfere with what charming people do."

(Oscar Wilde)

THE MORAL STANCE OF SOCIETY

> ***"The moral virtues, then, are produced in us neither by nature nor against nature. Nature, indeed, prepares in us the ground for their reception, but their complete formation is the product of habit."***
>
> *(Aristotle)*

The Greeks knew something!

Thieving is a 'time-honored,' ancient art. One could probably call it the 'second oldest profession' in the world. The caveman was not above stealing the stash of his luckier fellow hunter. The Ancient Greeks worshipped the delinquent god Hermes, son of Zeus and Maia, who, besides being the official messenger of the gods and the god of commerce and young men, was the god of cheats and thieves. The first deed of his life, only a few hours after he was born, was to steal the cattle of Apollo.

Stealing the thief

The Romans understood the appeal of such a divine creature. They praised the god Mercury, alter ego of Hermes, whom they 'borrowed' from the Greeks.

Adoption and redefinition

In the Middle Ages, guilds of thieves had patron saints. After all, the merchant guilds had their patrons, and so it was only fair that thieves be accorded divine protection, too. It is amusing that the Christian protector, Saint Nicholas, patron saint of children, scholars, virgins, sailors, and merchants, was also the patron of thieves. The Greeks, the Romans, and the Church of the Middle Ages all gave thieves some sort of heavenly recognition!

Throughout most of history, until very recently, thieves were not thought of as 'specializing' in specific property crimes. Thieves, pick-pockets, burglars, robbers, con men, tricksters and highwaymen were all lumped together, and their underworld activities during the Middle Ages are well-documented. From the early fifteenth century to our times there are numerous literary references to thieves in the works of François Villon, Henry Fielding, Alexander Dumas, Victor Hugo, Emile Zola, Charles Dickens, Jean Genet and others.

An outdated definition...

The lack of differentiation between property crimes is still reflected in the law today. Many states still sentence people under charges of 'petty larceny,' a legal label derived from English common law. The two core elements of the definition of petty larceny are the lack of force and the value of the gain. Beyond these distinctions, however, the term covers "...the picking of another's pocket, ...the embezzlement of funds by a bank employee, ...the conversion to one's own use of personal property belonging to another, ...or obtaining property by fraud or false pretenses."

...and an unappealing new

It wasn't until a few years ago that a proposal called the Model Theft by Shoplifting Code was created by the National Coalition to Prevent Shoplifting. While an increasing number of states use this proposal as a model for their shoplifting laws, the 'Code' is still far from being universal.

The history of shoplifting is closely related to - Wonder of Wonders! - shops.

A contemporary vice

Theft has as long a history as property itself does, but shoplifting as a separate category of endeavor must be defined as a modern-day phenomenon.

"...the shoplifting that emerged at the end of the nineteenth century represented something entirely different: its context was the department store, it was a pervasive phenomenon, and it demonstrated, quite dramatically, a form of deviant behavior by a new group, the middle class." (Abelson, 1989)

Shoplifting is born!

Modern-day shoplifting was born with the modern-day shopping experience, and a new phenomenon, the department store, was at the center of it. Emile Zola in his book *Au délice des dames (The Ladies' Delight)* graphically illustrates the process through which department stores became so large and grand that they achieved the distinction of being the most important tourist destinations in many world capitals.

Department stores created a culture of consumption and were also the catalysts of many other significant changes in society.

"With the ability to exploit a vast array of goods, the large stores educated people to want things, and they played a crucial role in determining the essentials of middle-class life and aspirations. The stores themselves served as showcases as they became part of a new urban, public culture. (...) The central focus of the department store was the creation of desire. How well the stores succeeded was amply demonstrated in the increasing incidence of shoplifting." (Abelson, 1989)

Seduction, impulses and privacy

Department stores were designed to seduce shoppers into making impulsive purchases. They generated the desire to go far beyond actual needs. To insure the success of this new, seductive environment, store managers had to make fundamental changes in the way potential buyers made contact with the merchandise.

The notion of 'shopping' was born. The floors opened up, everything was displayed, and gradually, over the century, most items became touchable. At the same time, there was a considerable reduction in the number of sales people tending to the needs of shoppers. Seduction is a lot more effective if it can happen in privacy. Browsing alone amongst the goods became the typical way of shopping. Indeed, the word 'shopping' itself became a synonym for browsing. Stores succeeded in creating an environment where people could freely select what they needed - and even what they did not really need but were suckered into desiring. According to several statistics, about 40% of all consumer purchases are made on impulse.

A matter of survival

Department stores started the trend described above, but in time almost every other type of mercantile establishment was obliged to jump on the bandwagon. Making everything accessible to the shopper became a necessity, a matter of survival.

A requiem for Pete's Music Emporium

"I can still remember the record stores of my childhood. I couldn't even touch a record without asking the salesman to hand it to me. I had no way of browsing, and, beyond the few records displayed, no way of knowing what they had on their shelves. I had to go there with a specific request, and if I was lucky, they had it. If they didn't I couldn't just make up my mind to buy something else instead. I can't imagine such an old fashioned music store surviving today."

The cost of success

As we mentioned above, by opening up their floors, the 'shopping freedom' stores successfully seduced the public into buying on impulse, thus generating sizable profits for themselves. Being able to sell goods with an ever-decreasing sales force resulted in sizable savings as well. Unfortunately for these progressive retailers, however, the new benefits came at a cost. The more convenient it became for shoppers to buy, the more convenient it became for shoplifters to steal.

Striking a balance

Ever since stores first made their goods so temptingly accessible, one of the greatest concerns of any mercantile establishment has been the question of how to strike a balance between effective marketing and reasonable safety from shoplifters.

Alienation

As the stores opened up to the shoppers, the people 'closed down'. They needed and asked for less help. Through this independence they also became more alienated from the sales folks. Surely you have occasionally seen two shoppers asking each other for help. It is, after all, easier to find another customer on the floor than it is to find a clerk. Quite often, too, another shopper may know more about the store than its rare, elusive personnel do. Shopping in big department stores has become impersonal.

The function of the salesperson has been reduced to stocking the shelves and ringing up the purchases.

Shoplifters do not make headlines

The evolution of retail marketing coincided with rapid urbanization and increased mobility of people. Both of these developments made people more faceless. Getting caught shoplifting in a small town where everybody knows you might still be stigmatizing, but in a large metropolis, nobody who counts has to find out. Quite a few of our interlocutors shoplift regularly without most of their friends even knowing about it. As long as you are not condemned for a 'heavy' crime, you can easily pursue a criminal career without losing other social or career opportunities.

Mobility equals anonymity

Cars give shoplifters mobility and a safe place to stash their loot. They also permit their owners to lift more often at more places so that shoplifters need not call on the same establishment over and over again. The greater number of stores accessible to lifters with wheels helps them stay faceless in the crowd. If they commit their petty crimes out of town, they further increase their anonymity.

Theft has been with us since the dawn of civilization. Shoplifting as such appeared in the middle of the Nineteenth Century, but the kind of retail theft which is the subject of this book developed its present shape in the second half of this century. Retail establishments had been encountering problems with theft for quite some time, but the real blows begun to fall in the Sixties, provoked by the changing attitudes of society.

The forgiving society

Society's attitude toward shoplifting parallels its attitude toward poverty. When the poor are seen as victims of life, of circumstances, of needs and desires, as opposed to being seen as lazy, irresponsible bums, then society tends to be more forgiving. It is interesting that this attitude manifests itself whatever the social level of the perpetrator. If shoplifting is 'absolvable' because by definition it is caused by a fundamental social injustice, then it is 'sort of' absolvable even if it is done by someone who has not been wronged by society in any way. What happened in the second half of this century, that is to say a change in attitude from total condemnation of the act to an attempt to 'save' lifters from themselves, echoes the invention of an affliction called 'kleptomania' at the turn of the century. In both cases, theoreticians tried to find an external cause (i.e. an excuse) for the deviant behavior.

The perception of immorality

The perception of shoplifting by society is integral to the perceived seriousness of its immorality. We should talk about the degree of immorality perceived in any era under discussion because it constitutes the primary influence on the laws, social policies and processes of that era. In the second half of the Twentieth Century the attitude toward shoplifting followed closely the changing attitude of society toward delinquency in general.

Leave it to Beaver

In the golden days of the Fifties people still knew right from wrong, Morals were fairly simple and clear; "Thou shalt not steal" still rang in people's ears. John Wayne was a star. We learned from Jimmy Stewart that life is wonderful, and moral problems were left to 'The Beaver.' Failure to live up to a moral standard was punishable but correctable. If you did something wrong, you had to pay for your mistake, but you must also be given the opportunity to rehabilitate yourself. Books and articles from the era were paternalistic and condescending, but they did hint at both the possibility and the desirability of rehabilitation. Authority and the law were respected more than they are today. Fear of exposure and its resultant shame still worked as a deterrent. The attitude of merchants, especially in the case of juveniles, was different. Calling the parents was seen as a viable alternative to prosecution. Even adults were often let go with a lecture.

Those colorful little books

Then came the Sixties: 'Flower Power,' Little Red, Green and Black books. Sit-ins and riots. Anarchists like Jerry Rubin and Abbie Hoffman.

Let's focus for a moment on just one of these Sixties symbols of revolution. Proponents of the 'Great Society' heralded the idea that criminals are the victims of society and that society owes something to its 'less fortunate' members. This new view of 'social justice' resulted in more cumbersome criminal procedures. The perception of immorality, especially regarding petty crimes such as shoplifting, changed. Shoplifting did not become 'right,' but it did become more excusable if not outright acceptable.

Disco Democracy

A laborious process of change in laws, attitudes and behavior characterized the Seventies. The social revolutionaries of the Sixties found sympathetic ears. Collective wisdom suggested that if criminals of all types were victims of their circumstances, it was obvious that society had an obligation to change those circumstances.

The new social theories on crime were not truly satisfactory, however, because they did not explain why only certain people affected by bad social conditions turned to deviant behavior. Scores of studies were conducted in an attempt to understand that strange creature, the shoplifter. As if they had not discredited themselves enough by inventing a disease called kleptomania seventy years before, psychologists rushed into the fray again, eagerly seeking to define and alleviate one of society's woes. The titles of their articles show them running amok:

Those Wonderful Scientists and Their Jaunty Ideas

"The Influence of Psycho-Social Factors on Non-Sensical Shoplifting"

"Absolute and Restrictive Deterrence in a Panel Study of Youth: Explaining the Onset, Persistence/Desistence, and Frequency of Delinquent Offending"

"Toward Revitalizing the Group Premise in the Sociology of Deviance"

"Contrast and Complementarity in Three Theories of Criminal Behavior"

"Theft groups for women: a cry for help."

"Criminality and Homeless Men: An Empirical Assessment."

"Deterrent and Definitional Influences on Shoplifting."

Mission Impossible

Confused and confusing titles, eh? You should have tried, as we did, to make sense of the ***contents*** of these ambitious essays!

The lean Eighties

The Eighties was a decade of disillusionment and prevention. It slowly became evident that leniency, reforms, group therapies and support groups didn't work. Later on in the decade when retailers began to encounter leaner economic times, they felt an ever-increasing pressure to control their losses. The Eighties was the real boom decade for security devices. Gizmo manufacturing grew into a multi-billion-dollar industry.

The mean Nineties

And now, we are in the Nineties. The decade of cynicism. The decade of 'Gangsta' Rap', Reservoir Dogs and Pulp Fiction. We can still hear some fading voices of morality, but it is becoming increasingly common to think of crime as a game of tag, a 'Catch Me If You Can.' It is hard to detect even the pretense of morality anymore. Risks assessment on one side. The Neo-Conservative 'morality' of retaliation on the other. New prisons. Tough sentences. Three strikes and you are out.

The real danger for boosters

Luckily for shoplifters, the current approach to crime is that of an all-out war with clearly set priorities, and eliminating shoplifting is not one of them. The biggest danger to boosters could be the legalization of recreational drugs. If hash-smokers came out of jail in droves, shop-lifters might be invited to move in to fill all those empty cells.

THE MORAL OF THE PASSAGE

We've come a long way, Baby. It seems that we have seen everything, tried everything, experienced everything. Where we go from here is anybody's guess. The 'Post-Caime-and-Ghone' times could still hold surprises.

THE MORAL STANCE OF THE ACTORS

"It is certain that stealing nourishes courage, strength, skill, tact, in a word, all the virtues useful to a republican system and consequently to our own. Lay partiality aside, and answer me: is theft, whose effect is to distribute wealth more evenly, to be branded as a wrong in our day, under our government which aims at equality? Plainly, the answer is no."

(Marquis de Sade)

We found an amazing array of rationalizations for this obviously illicit and immoral activity. Some of the mind games we discovered were apologetic in nature. Others were defiant, articulate, fuzzy, philosophical, and even practical. Most of them came from our sources, some came from quotations in the literature, and a few sprung unbidden from our minds while we were trying to assess certain 'scientific theories' found in the literature. These worthless excuses invariably reminded us that there is no substitute for facing facts squarely and objectively.

In this connection, we offer you the fable about the Elephant and the Owl.

The Elephant and the Owl.

"The Elephant is walking up and down in the forest slowly shaking his head in puzzlement, murmuring to himself: 'I don't understand! I don't understand!' The Owl lands on his head and says: 'Slow down my friend, I can explain it to you!' The Elephant stops and says: 'Explain? I can explain it myself! I just don't understand!' "

KLEPTOMANIA

"This is adding insult to injuries."

(Edward Moore)

The female problem

We have already quoted from *When Ladies Go A-Thieving* by Elaine Abelson, quite possibly the best book we came across in our research. Abelson's book is not so much about shoplifting as it is about the birth of consumerism and the resultant changes in the social status and image of women around the turn of the century. The kleptomania diagnosis is cited therein as an excellent example of the general attitude toward women which was in vogue at the turn of the century and still, to a more limited extent, prevails.

"In the study and treatment of respectable thieves, the role of physicians (and scientific medicine) in developing categories of behavioral irregularity become vitally important. Women of the middle class took merchandise from the dry-goods bazaars, and doctors explained their actions not in terms of what the women were doing - shoplifting - but in the language of physical and mental illness.

The female imbalance

(...) Labeling many of these women 'Kleptomaniacs,' doctors judged them to be fundamentally irrational, testimony to the 'natural' constraints of the female sex. The result of the popular medical response was the creation of a new, representative female figure - the middle-class shoplifter - and her inclusion in the prevailing cultural definition of women.

The female disease

(...) Lumping together a variety of physical and mental ills, they described much of what they could not understand as the consequence of the imbalance of nervous energies." For women, the imbalance was located in the stress of monthly menstruation, which exacerbated the effects of the so-called critical periods in a woman's life: puberty, pregnancy, and menopause. These natural processes of the female life cycle became the explanatory model for behavior. Was shoplifting without obvious indication of material need a disease? The answer for several decades was 'yes'." (Abelson, 1989)

The diagnosis of kleptomania has been largely discredited. Nowadays, no judge would accept it as a waiver of personal responsibility.

The more everything changes, the more everything remains the same

"The medical image (...) has undergone substantial modification. In the nineteenth-century definition, any middle-class woman was susceptible by virtue of her sex; in the late twentieth century definition, the middle-class woman who shoplifts IS a woman with a problem." (Abelson, 1989)

We would like to point out that the idea of 'kleptomania' was an imposition. It was not an excuse which shoplifting women invented but rather an escape hatch that was provided to them. It wasn't a justification to explain away the immorality of shoplifting but a way to get around it. Although no self-respecting psychologist would diagnose kleptomania today, traces of the idea that people can be victims of an uncontrollable urge to boost still linger. The word 'kleptomaniac' is still in common use.

THEY ASKED FOR IT

"What is a man if he is not a thief who openly charges as much as he can for the goods he sells?"

(Mohandas K. Gandhi)

Who created the monster?

There are a few books on consumerism, written by social scientists and their ilk, which point out the inherent contradictions in the goals of the retail industry. The argument of the authors of these books is that the retail industry should not complain about the 'monster' they themselves have created. The business of the retail industry is not simply to satisfy needs, but to create them as well. What they have to create first is the perception of need, and then the habit of using whatever merchandise is supposed to satisfy that perceived need. Once the habit is established, the need will not be questioned. How can one question, for example, the need for computers, birthday candles, diamond engagement rings? Isn't it obvious that writers must have computers, kids must blow out birthday candles, and only a cad doesn't give his fiancé an engagement ring? This common sense theory of need establishment is not just the province of the social scientist. Smart lifters share its wisdom, too.

The corrupting power of television

"The ads on TV play with your mind and desires. They push that new shampoo or some useful- looking kitchen gadget and usually succeed in arousing my curiosity. I want to try the new thing out, but even if I have the money, I hesitate spending it on something that I have never tried. Lifting it doesn't seem to be such a waste. Sometimes it works, sometimes it doesn't. I mean, sometimes I like the shit and eventually start buying it."

We are not exactly sure what our interlocutor means when he says he starts 'buying it,' but we certainly see how advertisements on television (and elsewhere) alter people's perception of need.

"They advertise that new and improved stuff on TV, and when you see it on the shelf in the supermarket, you have this urge to try out that new coffee in that improved packaging. Spending my money on it, that's another question. (...) Most of the stuff these stores sell you don't even need, and I ask you: Why should I pay for something that I don't need?"

The impulse to possess might override the impulse to buy

There is no way to separate the impulse to possess from the impulse to buy. That separation takes place on a psychological plane, where the retail industry doesn't seem to have much clout. Retailers wish only to create the impulse to buy, but to their great frustration they can't help feeding the fires of the desire to possess as well. The function of their 'loss prevention measures' is to undo some of the harm caused by the success of their very own marketing efforts!

"The big [department] ***stores sell a lot of garbage. I'm sure that they make more money on selling the garbage than they lose on the stuff I lift."***

A hard sell

What can we say to this guy? Should we try to extol the virtues of the 'honest' marketing efforts of the retail industry?

Let's see what those efforts are: To create the impulse to buy, merchants offer their wares abundantly and accessibly, thus creating an environment for shoplifting as well as a climate which stimulates the desired impulse buying. The retail industry puts up with a 2-3 % inventory shrinkage due to shoplifting in exchange for an extra 40% in profits which results from impulse buying. Very virtuous.

SOCIAL JUSTICE OF THE ROBIN HOOD KIND

"What monster have we here?
A great Deed at this hour of day?
A great just Deed — and not for pay?
Absurd, — or insincere."

(Elizabeth Barrett Browning)

Self-help is helping the poor

Remember him? A romantic, adventurous, and very moral figure, this green-hooded hero who stole from the rich to give to the poor! We thought that we would see more references to him in the literature about shoplifting, but we were wrong. In the welfare society, the government is doing Robin's work. Among our interlocutors, we could not find an altruistic thief. Oh, our lifters are very charitable people, but in a utilitarian, self-help way. They steal from the rich (the stores) to give to the poor (themselves). The only trace of the noble ideals of Robin Hood is that most smart lifters avoid hitting on small stores (the poor).

SOCIAL JUSTICE OF THE ANARCHIST KIND

"Mere anarchy is loosed upon the world,
The blood-dimmed tide is loosed, and everywhere
The ceremony of innocence is drowned."

(W.B. Yeats)

This book you should pay for!

At the end of the Sixties, Jerry Rubin proclaimed that shoplifting was a legitimate act against the capitalist establishment. Abbie Hoffman advocated shoplifting as a political act in his notorious and controversial publication, *Steal This Book*. (Original copies of *Steal This Book* have become collectors' items. For obvious reasons, libraries have been unable to keep copies on their shelves.) Rubin and Hoffman were not concerned with 'justice' as such. They advocated shoplifting as a tool to destroy the very structure of society. Shoplifting for them was simply a means to an end, and that end was the creation of anarchy.

SOCIAL JUSTICE OF THE CAPITALIST KIND

"Two wrongs don't make a right, but they make a good excuse"

(Thomas Szasz)

"Shopkeepers and retailers are always whining. They try to picture themselves as poor innocent victims of that bloodsucking predator, The Shoplifter. Let me tell you, they are just as much bloodsuckers as I am. Whatever I take away from them illegally, they take back from me and others legally a hundred times. They are thieves just as much as I am."

They have profits, I have profits

An articulate explanation of the attitude of some lifters might be: Let's face it, you are defenseless when stores steal from you. They can arrest you, charge you, sue you for damages when you are caught, but if and when they rip you off there is not much you can do.

Shoppers have no defenses

Follow patiently this long rant of a friend:

I went to buy some meat once. I asked for 3 pounds, the price was $2.99 a pound. The guy gets a chunk of beef, throws it onto the scale. The scale swings up to about 2 and 3/4. The guy doesn't let the scale settle. He picks it up on the first rebound, packs it, and writes the price on it: $9.74.

I am no Einstein...

Nothing pisses me off as much as someone taking me for a fool. I'm no Einstein, but I am able to multiply three by three in my head. Even if it was three pounds which it wasn't, it couldn't cost more than $9.00 The guy puts a figure on it that makes him look like Einstein. The amount sounds so precise, everybody is thinking, hey, he must know what he's doing. His self-assurance is so intimidating that most people wouldn't dare to question him.

It happens to me all over the place. I go to a store specifically because they advertised some cheap wrapping paper. It turns out that the specs in the ad were wrong. Or when I went to this other place to buy some clothes that are advertised as 75% off the sticker price. Looks like a good deal, although you could already at this point question the honesty of the merchant because 75% off would mean that before discounting he was selling them with a 300% markup, but never mind that now. I try on a jacket, reach into the pocket to find a price tag indicating a price that is only twice the marked 75% off 'sales' price. The cunning

..but neither are they!

cheats. I got into an argument with the salesgirl, till she advised me to leave. I am serious, there is this question, who steals more? The public from them, or 'them' from the public?

The butcher with the meat, even if I accept the marked price as fair, was trying to steal from me about 15% of the value of my purchase, and what can I do about it? Not much. I can go to another store. The point is, you see, that they can do it, but you cannot. With the exception of some very serious cases of very obvious frauds, you can't even sue them. Even then, even if you can sue them and win in a civil court, they have no criminal liability whatsoever. No retailer has ever gone to jail for stealing from a customer. No matter how seriously they !@#$ you they don't face any real risk in doing so. I hope you understand why I cannot feel sorry for those guys."

Need we comment?

The Luck of Joe, Or How to Get Ahead In the Retail Business

"In this beautiful town where I live there is a very successful discount store, Honest Joe's. It is a disgusting place, it makes me puke when I have to go there (I haven't been for years.) Everything is cheap there, and I mean cheap, as in shabby. When you consider the actual value of the garbage they sell you, it could be easily one of the most expensive shops in town. But never mind that. The founder of the store published his biography. Picked it up in a bookstore and flipped through it. It talks about the early successes of his store. He tells a story about buying some little whatever from a bankrupt company, or something like that. He made a huge sign, dumped the gadgets into a bin and sold them for the 'very special price' of only 99 cents. It cost him 9 cents a piece. He makes an 1,100% profit, brags about it and has no shame calling himself honest.

I personally wouldn't touch anything in his store, but I couldn't think of anybody who deserves to be ripped off more than he does."

Again, no comment. We just move onto the next excuse.

THE PERSONAL REVENGE THEORY

> ***"If you prick us, do we not bleed? if you tickle us, do we not laugh? and if you wrong us, shall we not revenge?"***
>
> *(William Shakespeare)*

Our sources told us that whenever they were treated particularly badly or were over-charged in a store, they returned to get even.

Many scenarios from ordinary life illustrate this feeling of resentment. In the simplest and most common, the disgruntled shopper is made to wait too long. Have you ever been forced to hunt for a salesman in order to pay for your purchase? Did it cross your mind that you could just walk away without paying?

You did think of it, didn't you?!

"For a long time, this buddy of mine and me, we kept referring to our 'shopping' as 'punishment.' If we didn't like anything in a store, we said that we would 'punish' them... we wouldn't buy the shit. Eventually the expression came to represent lifting in general. If they didn't have what we were looking for we would 'punish' them and take something else. If we found a store was an easy target, or even if we liked their stuff, we would say: Let's 'punish' them!"

THE CLEAN-UP-YOUR-ACT THEORY

This is a variation on the above. Many of our lifters told us that, in a way, they were keeping the retail industry on their toes. They kept the merchants honest and the prices fair. They were not very clear on how exactly their actions achieved that noble goal.

Cleaning up by cleaning out

"I had my regular 'little guy' computer store that I was dealing with. I never lifted anything from them. At some point I needed a piece of software that somebody asked me to get. Eight-hundred-dollar stuff. I bought it from them, installed it and didn't like it. It was a little embarrassing, as if I'd given the wrong advice to my friend. Half a year later it turned out that what the store sold me was four years out of date. When I bought it, I even asked them if it was the latest version and trusted them enough not to double check. They sold me something that had been sitting on their shelves for years, at full price. They made me look like an idiot in front of my friend. I always followed the principle of not hurting the little guys, but this one pissed me off so much I made an exception. Since that time, I have gotten my money's worth back from them."

The $800.00 rip-off

We are not sure whether the merchant learned a lesson from the above experience, but we can definitely appreciate the personal satisfaction felt by the lifter.

ECONOMIC NEED

"The seven deadly sins.... Food, clothing, firing, rent, taxes, respectability and children. Nothing can lift those seven millstones from Man's neck but money; and the spirit cannot soar until the millstones are lifted."

(George Bernard Shaw)

Hunger and morality

Some of them can be lifted, but what did Shaw know about lifting? The oldest of the justifications for theft is need. "What I did was not immoral, because I needed it more than them." Or, "What I did was immoral, but I'd rather be immoral than hungry." Sometimes we find that defining need is not so simple:

What is need indeed?

"It is a funny thing when people talk about need. They think that it is more excusable to steal bread than caviar. Or food than a watch. It is always a matter of priorities. For a long time I had arguments with my wife, who was not particularly keen on the idea of me shoplifting. "We can afford to buy this," she used to say. I had to explain to her hundreds of times that there are things that I cannot steal. I can't steal a movie ticket, or the cost of the car insurance. Taking the things I can means that we have the money for the rest of the things we need."

The puzzled retailers

The above opinion strongly echoes a recurring theme in the trade literature. The articles never fail to mention that in most cases shoplifters have enough money on them to pay for the goods they steal. The implication is that theft in these circumstances is an irrational act.

ADVENTURE AND PEER PRESSURE

I am not an adventurer by choice but by fate.

(Vincent Van Gogh)

"We used to have contests. We started out on a street and set a finish line a few blocks down from there. The goal was to snatch as much stuff as possible before we reached the line."

Up for adventure! Very frequently the literature cites two undeniable reasons people shoplift: The quest for adventure and pressure from one's peers. The source we quote above is a mother of three who shoplifted only when she was a 'wild' teenager. The central element of teenage shoplifting is bravado, not need. Because the excuse - teenage bravado - is almost expected by the thiefcatchers, it is used quite often. Probably too often.

SUCCUMBING TO TEMPTATION

"I can resist everything but temptation "

(Oscar Wilde)

Sometimes even smart lifters shoplift impulsively because they like what they see and must therefore have it. The inability to resist temptation is a holdover from childhood. It is an excuse which should only be accepted by indulgent parents who wish to assuage their guilt for being unable to provide their offspring with designer sneakers.

BEING OUTSIDE THE MORAL FRAMEWORK

"Ordinary morality is only for ordinary people."

(Aleister Crowley)

The Cat and the Mouse

"Morals only work if you accept their framework. When a cat catches a mouse, morality is not an issue. If a cat society passed a law saying that catching mice was illegal, that would still not make it immoral. If every cat understood that mouse-catching was bad for cathood in general and therefore bad for each individual cat, then catching mice would truly be immoral. The law of the jungle knows no morality, and it is my choice to see this society of ours as a jungle. As long as I can get away with it, I steal. To stop, I would have to accept the idea that it is wrong. Convince me. So far nobody has been able to."

THE SOFT CRIME THEORY

"About morals, I know only that what is moral is what you feel good after and what is immoral is what you feel bad after."

(Ernest Hemingway)

It's better than robbing people

"I'm not gonna walk up to someone and put a gun to his head and rob him. If I get caught, that's armed robbery. Means maybe six years in the joint on a felony. Who wants that?"

It's hard to see it as hard

He prefers to go to a store where the merchandise is waiting to be taken. He can make $1000 a week doing that. And if he gets busted? He will get a slap on the hand. Nowadays shoplifters are encouraged by a society that perceives, judges and punishes shoplifting as a very soft crime.

THE MORAL RELATIVITY

> ***"A system of morality which is based on relative emotional values is a mere illusion, a thoroughly vulgar conception which has nothing sound in it and nothing true."***
>
> *(Socrates)*

The Big Guys deserve it!

This excuse could be the most often heard justification for shoplifting. It is made on the assumption that the only real crime is a violent one. Non-violent theft of business property is placed in a different category which might be labeled 'Mildly Offensive Behavior'!

"Sometimes I look at my adversaries, the sales girls and the young security guys and... I feel sorry for them. I never hurt them, I am sure. They chase me, and they have nothing to show for it. After a good trip, I have... believe me.. I do have a lot to show. Meanwhile, they're making six bucks an hour. Whether they catch me or not, they get big zilch, nothing!"

A difficult mental exercise

It is indeed very difficult to conceptualize the owners of a department store as people whom you do not want to hurt. Especially when you see the people working there, who are obviously not the owners. They do not behave like people who really care about the place. For all we know (and we do know) they are responsible for more inventory shrinkage than the lifters.

Our sources would never think of stealing from friends, relatives or individuals. Each and every one of them steals only from big businesses, preferably from large chain or department stores. They accept the morality of not stealing from an individual while refusing to draw a parallel when it comes to businesses. Being impersonal seems to be very important to them.

GRANT

> ***"A frenzied passion for art is a canker that devours everything else."***
>
> *(Charles Baudelaire)*

Our sources included a few artists. Although they did not make excuses for themselves, they did attempt to justify their actions as an issue of priorities.

Those immoral Bohemians

"My theater and my artistic integrity are very important to me. You have seen some of my plays. You know I'm good. But it's a fact that you can't make a living with theater. In Prague maybe, but even there, who knows, maybe you can build something on the tourist trade. Anyway, here the only thing I can count on are the grants. And on my fin-

gers. Believe me, I can have far more trust in the latter. In a way I see my shoplifting as an extension of society's support for my work. "Shoplifting is a crime everybody pays for," they say. In my case, they pay for my theater this way. I support myself. I never shoplift for straight profit, but giving it up at this point would mean that I have to give up on my dreams as well."

COMPETENCE

Most of our subjects took pride in their ability. Some saw their lifting skills as the only marketable expertise they had. To be competent at something is extremely pleasant. The tangible benefits of successful shoplifting are gratifying. We can understand why is it so hard for a master of the 'art' to quit.

It feels good to be good at something

IT'S TOO EASY NOT TO

It is just too easy. Dozens of wide open entrances and exits. Self-help shelves. Gondolas reaching to the ceiling. Nobody in sight. Even when there is someone, he is too busy to care. It is just too easy.

"Sometimes I have the feeling that they want me to do it. I am left alone in these big places surrounded by those wonderful things. No other shoppers. No salesmen. No one to stop me."

They must want me to do it!

Merchants offering their goods bluntly and openly to the shopping public create the illusion that the only thing their customers have to do is pick up the article and it is theirs. The ultimate feeling of everyone in such an environment: "They want me to have it!" The ultimate feeling of the lifter: "They want me to take it!"

EVERYBODY DOES IT

Several studies in the literature quote surveys wherein a noticeable percentage of the respondents came up with the above 'reason.' We assume that the answers came from a homogenous group of shoplifters, most probably teenagers, whose incidence of shoplifting is much higher than it is in the general population. On the other hand, over sixty percent of all people admitted doing it at some time in their lives. We assume that half of the remainder were not honest enough to admit having shoplifted, whereas the other half did at least think about doing so. There are many forms of stealing which people do not even consider as such. Taking a pen from the office, for instance, or sampling the fruit at the supermarket. If we are strict enough with our definition, we have to

Birds do it, bees do it, even educated thieves do it...

agree with the statement - everybody does it. Not that this makes the act right, but it seems to be the truth.

SELF RELIANCE

The freedom of movement is the freedom of the spirit

Self-reliance is a motive that came up in several of our interviews and discussions. Our interlocutors do not want to depend on anybody or anything. Their desire is to live on minimal amounts of money without worrying about when the next cheque comes in.

"I work like everybody else. I make more than most of them and spend less time of my life doing it. They do it from nine to five. I do it a couple of hours a week. I go when I want to. I stay home when I feel like it. Beat this, brain-boy."

NO WELFARE FOR ME

Libertarian pride

"Never went on welfare. I don't like to beg for help. I help myself. When I walk around downtown, seeing the filthy, drunken panhandlers, it makes me angry. Especially when they bug me. I don't have any more money than they do, but I won't humiliate myself as they do. I'd much rather go to jail with my head high. But I'm good, so I won't."

MORE WELFARE FOR ME

"Nobody can live on the money they give you. Maybe if the government wasn't so stingy, I wouldn't need to do it."

It is never enough

She went on saying how much farther she can stretch the little money that she and her daughter get monthly by doing some lifting. She said that sometimes she feels almost like a 'normal' person. They live in a decent apartment. There is always good food on the table. She can get nice clothes for her kid. She has never been caught, and she knows that even if she should be caught, she would get ***only*** a small fine. She seems to understand the facts.

THE TEN COMMANDMENTS' OF SHOPLIFTING

One of our interlocutors couldn't resist the temptation to doctor one of the most basic codes of human morality. He shared his wisdom with us. We figured that when this book appeared, accusations of blasphemy would be one of our lesser worries, and so we have decided to share this revision of basic morality with you.

I. I am the Lord of Retail, your God of Desire, who brought you into the Land of Plenty, out of the bazaars , into the age of large department stores. You shall have no other gods before me.

We pray for our Lord's forgiveness for this

II. You shall not let them make a graven image of you or your fingertips. You shall not bow down to them or serve them.

III. You shall take everything but the name of the Lord of Retail in vain.

IV. Remember the Sabbath day, keep it holy by lifting diligently.

V. Honor your father, your mother and your fence by giving to them a part of your loot.

VI. You shall not kill, rob, mug, or deal drugs so that you can have a long life of stealing.

VII. You shall not commit adultery on the Retail Battle Grounds. Take her home.

VIII. You shall steal.

IX. You shall not bear witness against your partner.

X. You shall not covet. You shall just take it.

THE MORAL OF THE PASSAGE

There isn't much left to say. About morals, that is, not excuses. Excuses go on ad infinitum. Anything goes. Anything can be rationalized. If you are clever enough, you can even show that stealing is an act of philanthropy.

THE MORAL STANCE OF THE AUTHORS

"The only immorality (...) is not to do what one has to do when one has to do it."

(Jean Anouilh)

Make no mistake about it: If you steal, you will be treated like scum. No explanation will change that fact. Nobody buys the social justice bullshit anymore. In the welfare state that we are living in neither the Robin Hood theory nor the victim-of-poverty excuse will cut the mustard.

In the list we presented to you in the previous chapter, there are plenty of excuses and explanations. Quite a few make sense, but none, we repeat, ***none*** provides grounds for absolution. Some of them might soften the heavy blows of the law, but none of them furnishes a valid moral justification for shoplifting.

The moral framework again

On the other hand, as we have already said, and will say again, morality only works if you accept its framework. "Locks are for honest people!" said a renegade thief in an interview printed in one of the security magazines. If you do not care about morals, if you do not care about the consequences, there is absolutely nothing to stop you.

We wish to emphasize that there are three distinct questions here:

Do you know that stealing is wrong?

Do you care that it is wrong?

Do you do it or not?

We assume that everybody knows that it is wrong, and in case you personally didn't know, we are telling you now. Yet we are not here to give your life a direction. What can we say to the thief who doesn't care about getting caught? To illustrate what we mean, here is a little story:

"Awhile back I was talking with a couple of friends. One of them was planning a trip to Northern Africa. The other one, who has been there before, was warning her about sanitary conditions, especially about the quality of drinking water.

"It will make you sick," he said.

"Surely one can get used to it after awhile," she answered.

"Nobody can get used to that!" he replied.

"But what about the locals?" she asked.

"They are used to it," he said. – "Not to the water, but to being sick."

That is how we see this to be with our sources (excuse the pun) as well. They all know that it is wrong, and that it might make them 'sick.' They have simply gotten used to the idea that they are petty criminals and have learned to live with it.

[The hidden moral of the story, in case you missed it, is that you'd better steal some bottled water if you are in North Africa.]

You doubt the credibility of our morals? You ask, "Why do the writers of the book, who say they are not themselves shoplifters, refrain from lifting?" Indeed, based on the knowledge of the 'art of lifting' we present here, we could make a fortune. (That's a joke, folks.) If we are as cynical as we claim to be, what is there to stop us? Could it be that deep down we do have the morals that we say we don't care about? - Or are we chicken? Would we be embarrassed if we were caught?

It's not our morals...

While we were on our 'field trips' to check the credibility of the assertions of our sources, we indeed experienced temptations. Seeing the lack of security or knowing what needed to be done to defeat it was, ...well, tempting. So why didn't we do it?

..we felt the thirst...

The answer is simple. After making our own risks and benefits analysis, we decided that it would be far more beneficial and profitable to write a good book about what we had heard and observed, and that is exactly what we have done.

..but we wanted a big gulp...

THE MORAL OF THE PASSAGE

Your morals are nobody's business but yours. You are the only person you have to face every morning.

THE ECONOMY

"The art of losing isn't hard to master;
so many things seem filled with the intent
to be lost that their loss is no disaster."

(Elizabeth Bishop)

THE IMPACT ON SOCIETY

"Get your facts first, and then you can distort them as much as you please."

(Mark Twain)

THE SIZE OF THE DAMAGE

The Cookie Jar

We promised you at the beginning of the book that we would not bore you with the statistical results of sociological and psychological research which purports to explain the 'what,' 'who,' and 'why' of shoplifting. However, we have come to realize that we must do so. We will try to keep it brief. We hope it will seem important to the 'working men and women' both that they understand the nature of the 'cookie jar' and learn what the 'wise guys' on the other side seem to know and think about them.

The Wise Guys and what matters

In the next few chapters we will give you a short summary of what we found in the literature. First we will tell you what the 'wise guys' think they know, and then we will share our reactions to this 'wisdom.' (You may already suspect what those are.)

There are two kinds of statistics about shoplifting. The first kind describes losses, and the second kind studies the thieves themselves. The only common characteristic they share is their absolute unreliability. The trade literature tends to show more interest in economical and legal aspects. The 'scientific' writings deal more with sociological and psychological aspects.

The types of statistics

It seems to be a tradition that every year around Christmas time, a few major weekly magazines print articles about the economic effects of shoplifting. About the terrible toll it takes on the retail industry. About unscrupulous shoplifters and the valiant efforts of the industry to fend off these predators. Heroic stories of success enliven these articles, as do sensationalistic figures - billion dollar losses causing skyrocketing loss-prevention expenditures.

How much?

The economic losses, the dollar figures per year (month, week or day) are high, and yet the truth is that nobody really knows how high. Neither do they know how these losses occurred. Estimates on yearly losses go anywhere between two to twenty-four billion dollars. The range of these estimates should give you an idea of how much these trade statisticians actually know. The large discrepancies in the estimates are due to the variety of methods used for estimating losses.

Mystical numbers dividing the pie

The main reason for this uncertainty is that inventory shrinkage consists of four distinct elements: Shoplifting. Employee theft. Vendor fraud and errors. Bureaucratic errors. The proportioning of these factors to the whole of the inventory loss is anybody's guess. We came upon colorful and impressive pie-charts with widely varying figures on them.

Uncertainty

In one of the more interesting studies it was pointed out that the assumptions retailers make have no grounding in reality. They expect the employee theft and shoplifting ratio to be 30% and 60% respectively, when in fact the opposite may be closer to the truth.

The truly serious literature on the subject always points out both the wide variance in study results and the fact that shoplifting losses are impossible to separate from the other factors in the equation.

The only thing of which we may be more or less certain is that losses among the different types of retail establishments vary. This is still not reliable information about shoplifting, but we can assume with a moderate degree of confidence that the proportion of shoplifting to other shrinkage factors is not different in different types of stores.

Numbers mean little

"Department stores account for 41 percent of the total retail sales in this country but experience 61 percent of the retail crime losses. (...) Drug stores account for 6 percent of all retail sales and suffer 10 percent of all losses due to crime. (...) Grocery stores account for 42 percent of retail sales and experience only 21 percent of all criminal losses. (...) Figures pertaining exclusively to shoplifting are not available." (Baumer and Rosenbaum, 1984)

Baumer and Rosenbaum go on to point out that the size of the business seems to make a difference, only to conclude at the end of the passage that what they said actually means diddly squat, because they have no way of knowing.

Speculation about speculations

"The size of the business establishment is another factor suspected of having a substantial impact on shoplifting rates. Smaller stores generally do not have developed security systems or the personnel expertise that one finds in larger department and chain stores, and therefore they are more susceptible to shoplifting losses. The U.S. Department of Commerce speculates that small businesses with receipts under $5 million suffer 3.2 times more crime, including shoplifting, than those with receipts over $5 million (Morton, 1975). Since many smaller establishments have a

profit margin of only 3 or 4 percent, shoplifting losses could conceivably cause a business to fold. In one report, however (Small Business Administration, 1969), small businesses reported relatively few losses due to shoplifting. In contrast, larger businesses are generally able to document a portion of their losses through apprehension statistics and shrinkage rates. Certainly, the large retail stores in the major metropolitan areas are heavily hit by shoplifting. Unfortunately, we cannot ascertain from the available data whether small businesses actually suffer greater losses from shoplifting because their profit margins are small or if they are in fact disproportionately victimized in comparison to larger retail establishments. (Baumer and Rosenbaum, 1984)

This quotation is from one of the best books we came upon. We learn from this passage that the U.S. Department of Commerce **speculates**, lumping every kind of crime together, and **contradicts** the Small Business Administration report. The authors then **speculate** that the contradictory and meaningless **speculation** of the Department of Commerce is actually relevant to shoplifting. Next, based on that **assumption** they make their own **puzzled conclusion**, cleverly presented in the form of a **poetic question**.

Puzzled puzzlement over puzzling puzzles

Dealing with numbers is quite frustrating for everybody, and yet there is a tremendous drive and desire in the retail industry to quantify and categorize the nature of their losses.

Some of the methods for calculating damage (estimated shoplifting losses) are seriously off the wall. Let's look at a proposed 'calc-sheet' we found in an issue of *Security Management:*

Indicate the percentage of total inventory losses you believe the following factors contribute:

If you like math, this is the time to have fun

Shoplifting	______%
Employee Theft	______%
Vendor Theft	______%
Good Faith Undercharge	______%
Inventory/Accounting Errors	______%
Other	______%"

After you have filled in these percentages the 'calc-sheet' offers the next mathematical 'easy as pie' step:

$	x	%	= $
Total inventory shrinkage	***Attributable to shoplifting***		***Estimated loss***

Presto! You have a totally unreliable guess on paper, one that is completely useless. Our guess is that if you divide the estimated loss caused by the shoplifters, you will get a dollar amount average attributable to an average shoplifter. But that would not be thorough enough. So, the next valuable part of the 'calc-sheet,' which finally allows you to use what you learned in Math 101, goes on as follows:

$	x	x	x	= $
Average theft	**Number of shoplifters per day per store**	**Number of operating days**	**Number of stores**	**Estimated shoplifting loss**

The article goes on to show how this wonderful algorithm works, using all the supermarkets in the entire United States as an example:

$ 11.61	x 8	x 363	x 37,170	= $1,253,202,905
Average Theft	**Number of Shoplifters per Day per Store**	**Number of Operating Days**	***Number of supermark ets in US***	***Estimated shoplifting losses US supermarkets 1983***

Limp figures

Please note that the figures refer to 1983, but for our purpose here the numbers are irrelevant. The point we are trying to make is that all the results based on these elaborate calculations are meaningless if most of the information is based on guesswork. The sad part is that by the time these numbers are presented to the public, they are accepted as factual figures. When a weekly magazine or a daily newspaper prints an article, the writer, who has collected his data from the 'experts' takes the numbers at face value and uses them in good faith.

An assertive woman

In 1980, Dorothy Brenner Francis, the author of eight published books and a concerned mother of two from Marshalltown, Iowa, took it upon herself to thoroughly research the subject and write a book about it entitled, *Shoplifting: The Crime Everybody Pays For.* Her book contains excessively naive morality tales, but it also presents some sensationalist calculations, the kind the media love to headline.

"A Pennsylvania retailer estimates that prices could be lowered by 15% if merchants did not have to pay for security measures and make up for the cost of lost items. [Then she goes on to help the feeble-minded to understand that complex mathematical concept] **Thus, if you buy a $30 sweater, $4.50 of the price is the 'shoplifting tax'.** [on the very same page we also learn that] **... such passed-on costs add up to a large chunk of the average family's annual budget. It has been estimated that each of the five million adults now** [1979] **living in Florida pays out an average $51.38 yearly in shoplifting tax. An Ohio family supports the shoplifter to the tune of $150 every year." (Dorothy B. Francis)**

A good figure is hard to find

According to Dorothy's wonderful calculations, an average adult in Florida spent $342.53 for retail goods, whereas the yearly spending of an Ohio family on food, clothing, medicine and all else was $1,000. Hmm. We wonder, Dorothy, how much was it in Kansas?

Where are we, Toto?

Fortunately, there are some studies where at least the math is right. The most comprehensive study was conducted by Ernst and Young in 1989, but even that most comprehensive study dealt more with drug testing for employees and methods of physical inventory taking than it did with shoplifting. Again, we have to understand the limitations of the approach dealing with the total amount of losses. It is anybody's guess how much of that is due to shoplifting as opposed to the other factors.

Dorothy, I don't think we are in Kansas any more

	Average shrinkage as a percentage of sales		Prevention expenses as a percentage of sales	Average value of merchandise recovered at retail per apprehension in 1989	
	at retail	at cost		from employee	from customer
All Participants	1.92%	1.20%	0.32%	$1,350.00	$196.00
Department Stores	2.18%		0.54%	$650.00	$165.00
Drug Chains	2.33%	2.13%	0.22%	$349.00	$48.00
General merchandise	1.82%	1.01%	0.33%	$801.00	$87.00
Specialty Apparel	1.84%	1.85%	0.39%	$3,044.00	$225.00
Specialty Hardlines	1.98%	0.70%	0.17%	$2,378.00	$375.00
Supermarkets	0.93%	1.38%	0.22%	$592.00	$107.00

(table compiled from information in the Ernst & Young survey)

With all that in mind, according to them, the average loss is 1.92% of sales, varying considerably between the different sectors of the retail industry. The spending on preventing these losses is about 0.31% of sales.

A hard figure is good to find!

We were desperately looking for some information that would indicate value recovered as a percentage of total loss, a calculation that might not have much value by itself but would indicate clearly the effectiveness of certain loss prevention measures. Our search was fruitless. We are forced to assume that there must be such information, based on numbers found in the research, but that it is not of interest to the security industry, nor to their advisors and stooges.

It's hard all right, but is it big?

Having gotten over these 'shocking' statistics, we can also ask: Are those 'big' losses really that big? The average loss is still below 2%,and that includes employee theft, errors and spoilage as well as shoplifting. If we accept the industry's estimate of shoplifting being about 30% of the losses, then we get that frighteningly gigantic figure of 0.7%

Is Dorothy still with us?

A very conservative estimate!

We do not know about you, but that 0.7% is hardly our idea of a 'big' loss. At an end-of-season sale, stores drop their prices 20-50%. Dropping prices 30% on only 10% of their stock can result in an impact five times bigger than the impact of shoplifting!

There are many things store management can do that would result in an impact on their profits far greater than 0.7%. They could save more than that with improved inventory management, better buying practices, or more effective advertising.

Scare mongering and the margin of profit

This information was one of the few surprises that we encountered while doing our research on the subject. We thought the losses would be much greater. Now we can hardly suppress the impression that the scare-mongering tactics of the retail industry, in concert with the security management industry, arm in arm with the security device manufacturers, may just be a justification for their pricing policies.

Don't feel sorry for them retailers

While all the statistics and research provide reasons for retailers to cry and whine about their losses, you do not have to feel sorry for them (whether you do or do not shoplift). They are comfortably padded for their losses.

TYPES OF MERCHANDISE STOLEN

The list of the lifts.

In this passage we will attempt the impossible. We will try to compile a list of the most often lifted items, combining the results of different statistical-sociological researches. Most of the data in the trade literature shows only the numbers and types of recovered merchandise instead of the actual shrinkage caused by shoplifting. The direct information from the other side (our chats with the successful and professional smart lifters) might be an interesting addition to the information contained in the books and articles. We find that there is no correlation between the type of shoplifter and the type of merchandise he prefers to steal.

The weight of the lifts.

Ladies Clothes	***2.44%***
Men's Clothes	***1.84%***
Children Clothes	***2.65%***
Health and beauty	***3.51%***
Fine Jewelry	***4.71%***
Shoes	***1.84%***
Fashion Accessories	***7.57%***
Toys, Hobbies	***2.10%***
Records, Cassettes, CDs	***4.13%***
Radios, Stereos	***3.37%***
Sporting Goods	***3.44%***

(Ernst and Young Survey, 1989)

A few things have to be kept in mind about these figures. They are quite obviously higher then the 1.92% average we were musing about. The information comes from department stores. The question asked of them was "What is the department with the highest shrinkage?" The answer given is not an average, and it is not representative of the loss of these types of merchandise in retail stores in general. We can also assume that in a department store certain popular items are more frequent targets of 'cross-departmental' employee theft.

Gender bender.

The above numbers indicate that the most preferred (or most likely recovered) items are fashion accessories, CDs, cassettes, and jewelry. It is interesting that the trade literature always insists that gender is not a determining factor, men and women being represented in equal proportion in the shoplifting crowd. However, fashion accessories do stand out, being at the top of the list. You might call us sexist, but it seems that this category covers rather gender-typical, 'unmanly' target items.

Lifter twister

Beauty products, radios and stereos, and sporting goods are also assumed to be prime targets of the 'working men and women.' It appears that articles that are small and easily concealed are on the top of the shoplifter's list. But there is a variable here. Although larger articles are not lifted by amateur shoplifters because they dare not try to conceal them, the bag of methodical smart lifters is full of tricks for concealing and stealing anything, irrelevant to its size.

Budget hatchet

Another researcher found that most recovered articles were luxury items. Articles that the family budget would not be able to cover, including coats, dresses, luggage, radios, cameras, jewelry, small leather goods, cosmetics, and stationery.

Better seller

To the professional lifter, who, it is generally assumed, works only for resale, little things of high value are the most desirable. Such items can be easily hidden on one's person and afterward easily carried to a fence from whom they will fetch larger monetary rewards than most bulky items do. As fans of Deep Space Nine are well aware, this policy corresponds to one of the most important Rules of Acquisition adhered to by the Ferenghi. The Lifters of Earth agree: LIFT LOW, SELL HIGH!

Baumer bummer

"Through an analysis of merchandise recovered from apprehended shoplifters, some of the major studies (Griffin, 1981; Citizens Crime Commission of Philadelphia, 1979; Metropolitan Washington Board of Trade, 1978; Shave, 1978) provided information about the most commonly stolen items in various types of stores. In supermarkets or grocery stores, the results indicated that meat was most frequently recovered. Other commonly recovered items included deli foods, liquor, health and beauty aids, and cigarettes. Among drug stores, clothing was most frequently recovered, but health and beauty aids were also taken quite often. Among discount stores, clothing was the primary merchandise recovered, as it was in department stores, especially men's clothing. Other noteworthy items that are costly to department stores included costume jewelry, watches, and sporting goods." (Baumer and Rosenbaum, 1984)

Lamer brainer

The above quotation proves that most statisticians will single out items which would be obvious to anybody. They do not bother to research less obvious items thoroughly. A number of very obvious types of articles indicated by Ernst and Young, such as tools, batteries, cassettes, CDs, and books seem to be missing from most of the compilations. A very interesting item, the watch, probably one of the most closely 'watched' (excuse the pun) item in today's stores, does show up in the statistics.

On the whole, smart lifters don't single out items. They go for a large variety of different merchandise. Only the single-minded 'money-maker' will develop a range of favorites because his choices are decided by the needs of the fences he works for.

Fishes, brushes!

"One of the men [I knew] ***is retired now. He lives in a $250,000 home and goes to the Bahamas five months of the year. All he ever stole - and I laugh even thinking about it - were paint brushes and fishing lures. Everyone thinks you***

wouldn't want to steal a paint brush, but look at the price of a good one. And they put them in places in the store that are out of the way because they say: 'Nobody's gonna steal a paint brush.'."

THE MORAL OF THE PASSAGE

That everything and anything can be, may be and will be stolen from all kinds of stores is a fact nobody can deny. We strongly advise against stealing the counters or display-cases, the detectives, the salesgirls and the exit signs. Other signs or price-tags might also be passed over. Warning: Develop a wonderfully inventive method before you try to shoplift a whole bedroom set!

THE IMPACT ON THE "ACTORS"

"The man who knows it can't be done counts the risk, not the reward."

(Elbert Hubbard)

RISKS AND BENEFITS

'Soft crime' versus 'Hard crime'

When it comes to analyzing the potential risks and benefits of shoplifting, the first thing that we have to keep in mind is that it is a 'soft crime'. Soft in every respect. It is not violent, and society and the law take a rather soft attitude toward it. It compares quite favorably to most criminal activities. You could make a lot more money dealing drugs, but the risk you ran would be much higher. (Maybe the risk of **detection** would not be higher, but the punishment would definitely be much more severe.) When compared to violent crimes such as armed robbery, or even breaking and entering, shoplifting definitely looks 'positive.'

When we think about the risks and benefits of shoplifting, we should make the distinction between professionals and amateurs. (Or should we?) In this context, we shall use the definition the way it is used in the literature.

The professional shoplifter

The term 'professional shoplifter' means a person who steals for resale. We have to make this distinction because the elements involved in decision-making are different. What matters to an amateur is the value of the item to himself, whereas the professional will consider the resale value of the merchandise.

Calculating the risk

In either case, the 'criminal calculus' has only three main variables:

- the perceived value of the item
- the likeliness of getting away with it;
- and the likely consequences of getting caught

The freedom principle

For professionals the third variable is obviously not a very important consideration. They look at shoplifting as a profession, and they see possible fines as being analogous to paying one's taxes in an ordinary job. They view potential jail terms as time they may have to spend in order to make a living. Any temporary loss of freedom, they believe, is an acceptable payment for the long-term freedom of their lifestyle.

"If you want to earn your living outside the legal boundaries, your best bet is to get into pro or amateur shoplifting. (...) Never do felonies. Felonies send you to jail."

Fuzzy Rules!

We might restate the three main variables in the criminal calculus in this way: What is the value of an item I am considering stealing? How likely am I to get away with this theft? How likely am I to be punished to an unacceptable degree? There are no 'black and white' answers to these questions. They are in a 'gray' area. They are fuzzy. (see Bart Kosko's excellent works on 'fuzzy thinking,' 'fuzzy machines,' and 'fuzzy logic.') Every act of shoplifting is a decision based on fuzzy answers to gray-area questions.

Perceived value of the loot

If the value is very high, the risk will figure lower in your calculation. (One of our contacts was peddling a specific kind of tape player until all the careless merchants in town became familiar with his face and locked the players up in display cases.)

We have used the expression 'perceived value' up to this point, but we should now differentiate between 'perceived value' and 'perceived gain.' This differentiation indicates the fact that the value of an item is not simply determined by the sticker price. Risks and value must be weighed to determine gain. For example:

Perceived gain

Instant film for your camera is expensive, but is also very easy to conceal. Most stores sell it from behind the counter or from closed display cases. The difficulty in accessing it raises the risk, and therefore lowers the perceived gain. One does not take unnecessary risks for a ten-dollar item. Now, if you find a store that has instant film displayed in a reachable place, such as on a shelf, that fact will increase its desirability, hence its value. The fact that it would be more difficult to steal elsewhere also increases the perceived gain. (We have heard from one of our sources that he used to go to a store where instant film was displayed as a bonus with the camera itself. He went there and helped himself to the 'bonuses' to such an extent that the store stopped the practice.)

An experience of our own echoes the one above. We came across a store that had instant film in the open. We were puzzled by the apparent stupidity of the management. It did not take long for them to wise up, however. The next time we went there, the film was under lock and key.

Inhibition, shmin-hibition

Similar examples could be found or simply figured out for the other two rules as well. Finding good 'blind spots' such as a labyrinth of aisles with ground to ceiling shelves will somewhat decrease the likelihood of getting caught, easing thereby the burden of making the decision to act. Tight security and strict prosecution might inhibit the lifter, but won't necessarily stop him.

Deterrence, shme-terrence

When people are arrested and convicted for shoplifting, giving them fines which they most likely cannot pay simply sends them back on the trail to raise money. To put them in jail for a couple of days is expensive when one considers that incarceration will have no effect on their behavior. Recovery laws that allow merchants to claim restitution from the perpetrators are just another way of sentencing them to pay a fine. When shoplifters are sentenced to community service the system gets some restitution, but it is unlikely that such a sentence will function as a deterrent.

"The judge smiles at me and sends me to this community medical center to work. I smile back and go. For three weeks. Every day. Nice place. Blue paint everywhere. Man, I even liked it. There were these nice old farts with great stories. One of them was decorated or something by Eisenhower. He brought this medal in his pocket every day. He showed it to me every day. And all the others. For three weeks I am telling you, it was an experience. (...) Mind you, I still loaded my fridge from the store the same way as I always do, and shame-shame on me, I lifted a bunch of plastic gloves from there for my girlfriend so she can do the dishes without ruining her hands."

Punishment, shmunish-ment

"For my fifth offense this judge, an obnoxious blond bitch, gave me ten days in prison. They take me from right there in the system, man. I really felt awful. Called the woman, my wife, and swore to her that I would not do it again, never ever. You can believe, for a second, I was seriously considering quitting 'the life'. They keep me in this dirty cell for a couple of hours, then load me and the others in this van and we ride. After we arrived, I was just amazed. Nice, clean prison, TV, games, books. They gave me cigarettes, personal hygiene articles, and an okay supper. In about fifteen minutes my cell mate offers to buy my tobacco off me since I will be sent home next morning with time served. I was doubtful. Come next morning, after breakfast they call my name and they send me home. It is amazing how soon after I arrived home I didn't think any more about quitting or any such shit. The funny thing? I also forgot to give them back a pair of very thick gray socks that I still wear proudly. Maybe I should wear them as a lucky charm when I go out boosting. The only real punishment was that the TV was continuously on some stupid sports channel and I can't stand that shit."

"A 15 year employee for a West Coast supermarket chain stole an estimated $300,000 worth of merchandise (...)

Upon his conviction for grand theft the employee was sentenced to three years' probation. He was also ordered to pay a restitution of $10,000 and to perform community service" (Progressive Grocer, June 1990)

Probation, shrobation

He must have had a good lawyer to get that deal. To make the perpetrator pay back less than 3.5% of the damages is to slap his wrist with a wet noodle. And what exactly does probation do? Keep a Sword of Damocles over his head while he is busy enjoying the gains of his activities? Bummer!

Quality dependence

For most smart lifters, shoplifting is a matter of practical decisions. They value their freedom, their art, their independence or their drug dependence more than they fear the risks of boosting. Often they have a lifestyle they can only afford if they shoplift. They see shoplifting as a means of surviving, a necessary 'job' through which they can live for whatever passion - painting, dancing, getting high - consumes them.

"If you add up the time I was arrested or in prison for shoplifting, you won't even come close to the amount of time a normal factory worker spends just on commuting to work and back home..."

THE MORAL OF THE PASSAGE

> ***"The thief. Once committed beyond a certain point he should not worry himself too much about not being a thief any more. Thieving is God's message to him. Let him try and be a good thief."***
>
> *(Samuel Butler)*

Speculation or risk assessment? It depends on your angle. Shoplifting is the crime that pays, and unless there is a major shift in society's attitude, it will always be a good area for the speculator.

THE IMPACT ON THE AUTHORS

> ***"Want of money and the distress of a thief can never be alleged as the cause of his thieving, for many honest people endure greater hardships with fortitude. We must therefore seek the cause elsewhere than in want of money, for that is the miser's passion, not the thief's."***
>
> *(William Blake)*

We most definitely and most sincerely hope that this book's economic impact on our lives will be sizable. If you got the idea of buying our book because you saw it listed on the New York Times' Best-seller's List, then we have probably experienced the impact already.

Sorry! ...or are we?

We want to make it crystal clear that as writers of this book we have neither criminal nor altruistic motives. We wrote the book to have fun. We hope to sell many copies and make money. We hope you understand!

Does fun and money make funny-money?

THE MORAL OF THE PASSAGE

We want dollars and cents, pelf, Mammon, wealth, lucre, filthy lucre, the root of all evil, circulating medium, cash nexus, currency, decimal currency, managed currency, fluctuating currency, hard currency, soft currency, sound currency, honest money, legal tender, money on account, precious metal, gold, ringing gold, clinking gold, silver, bullion, ready money, the ready, the best, cash, spot cash, hard cash, petty cash, dough, lolly, dibs, bread, scratch, wampum, shekels, the green stuff, change, small change, coppers, small coins, pocket money, pin money. We want it all!

In case you are still wondering

WHO AND WHY

"Repudiating the virtues of your world, criminals hopelessly agree to organize a forbidden universe. They agree to live in it. The air there is nauseating: they can breathe it."

(Jean Genet)

THE WAY SOCIETY SEES THEM

"There is no confusion or inconsistency in these results. They prove absolutely that thieves are also not honest."

(James Carolin, Jr.)

Who are the shoplifters? We could find no reliable data or coherent statistics to help us answer this question. The figures offered were confused or contradictory, and they seemed to have been tampered with to fit a particular bias. Typologies of shoplifters should simplify the task of identifying them and should also provide practical guidance for the development of theories about who these people are, but the data on which existing typologies are based is hopelessly unreliable, and therefore any attempt to theorize is always thwarted. Honest work on the subject of the identification of the type of person who shoplifts can be recognized by an open admission of perplexity.

To recognize the type

"The most popular typology (Angelino, 1953) involving the classification of shoplifters into the familiar groups of professionals, amateurs, and kleptomaniacs offers some guidance regarding underlying causes; for example, professional shoplifters are most likely to be motivated by economic gain. The question remains, however, as to what causes amateurs to steal. In general, typologies used in this field have not been sufficiently precise about the underlying causes of shoplifting." (Baumer and Rosenbaum, 1984)

The twenty thousand dollar question

Typologies such as the one above separate shoplifters into distinct groups, but these groups are usually created arbitrarily. They are practically useless.

There are two ways to approach the question of categorizing shoplifters: We can try to determine what characteristics differentiate shoplifters from other social groups. In other words we can try to find the best description of shoplifters as a self-contained group. Or, we can ask whether there are any groups in society who are more or less susceptible to the temptation to shoplift.

Directions the windbags point to

The first approach, trying to describe shoplifters according to basic sociological variables, is usually a failure. Let us examine, as an example, a statistic that appeared in the magazine *Chain Store Age Executive* about the income level and the educational level of accused (meaning: apprehended) shoplifters.

INCOME LEVEL OF ACCUSED SHOPLIFTERS

LOW INCOME	27%
MIDDLE INCOME	45%
HIGH INCOME	28%

EDUCATIONAL LEVEL OF ACCUSED SHOPLIFTERS

COLLEGE GRADUATE	21%
SOME COLLEGE	27%
HIGH SCHOOL	40%
SOME HIGH SCHOOL	12%

(Greater Washington Board of Trade)

Normal distribution

About these numbers there is only one thing to be noted: They represent a perfectly normal distribution, which is, in fact, the same as the general distribution of the entire American population. Because the population profile of the shoplifter is almost identical to that of the general population, these figures simply indicate that persons from every class and condition of American society show up in stores and 'bargain' prices down to zero. We are convinced that similar figures in other countries will show similar distributions. We could hardly believe our eyes when we saw these numbers presented in the magazine (arranged, to be sure, in nice pie-charts) as significant information!

A truly democratic crime

We cannot identify shoplifters by any demographic variable. There are some variations, but they are so small that they cannot be used in a meaningful way. We cannot identify shoplifters by age, sex, income level, or ethnic background. Shoplifting is the only truly democratic crime. The only statement we can make with some certainty is that shoplifting behavior decreases with age. Both apprehension statistics and self-report questionnaires indicate this fact.

The same question sunny-side up

The second approach to the question of categorizing shoplifters runs into the same type of problem, which is not a surprise when we consider that these two approaches are opposite sides of the same coin. How is it significantly different to say that X% of middle-class homemakers shoplift than to say that Y% of shoplifters are middle class homemakers?

No trends!

Both of these approaches could be useful if they showed some strong trends. If we could say that the proportion of those who steal is significantly higher among middle-class homemakers than it is among, let's say, widowed pensioners, we would have meaningful figures. We don't know exactly what the meaning might be, but we are sure it would be there. Also, if we were able to say, for example, that eighty per cent of apprehended shoplifters were under twenty years of age, we could use such information. Security personnel could be instructed to pay more attention to this group, and new propaganda material could be designed that would target it. However, we have never seen results such as those described above.

Although we are uncertain about its usefulness, we will discuss (briefly, just stay with us) the ways social scientists gather the data on which all characterizations and typologies are based. There are three major means for getting information about shoplifters:

Just for the heck of it!

- analyzing apprehension data
- self-report studies
- observational studies

Each of these approaches and methods can be argued for and against, but the advantages of all three are ultimately outweighed by inherent disadvantages.

ANALYZING APPREHENSION DATA

The most frequently used and quoted statistics are numbers of arrests. The limitations of this data ought to be apparent: calculating numbers of lifters by the use of arrest statistics does not work because it is mostly the bad (amateur) lifters who get caught. Also, mere arrest numbers do not reflect the amount of damage the 'caught' (as well as the 'non-caught') do. There are some damage speculations available, based on inventory shrinkage versus recovered merchandise, but we could not find hard figures on recovery as a percentage of loss solely attributable to shoplifting.

Basic limitations

A less apparent, but equally serious, limitation is the fact that arrest information is extremely difficult to obtain. In most places the police or the courts do not keep separate records for shoplifters. Officialdom simply lumps them together with all the other offenders charged with a misdemeanor. In those cases where information is collected about the perpetrators, it is limited to 'just the facts' - Address. Physical description. Gender.

"Law enforcement agencies compile their statistics from people who have been caught, (...) A real professional rarely gets caught and they are responsible for the majority of theft [maybe counted as employee theft] **that goes on. (...) Professional shoplifters** [contrary to certain statistics and beliefs] **are not stupid people. They're some of the most inventive, in-**

The catch of the day?

dustrious, intelligent people you will meet. Unfortunately, they steal. They do it seven days a week and they're very good at it." (quoted in Chain Store Age Executive, February, 1985)

Records have no faces

Early sociological research was based mostly on store apprehension information that was more extensive and reliable than police or court statistics. The limitation of this approach was the fact that only large stores or chains kept such files. Police information on a person or group was easier to obtain, but researchers were usually not privy to those data banks. And even when such information could be obtained it was unreliable because parts of it might have been legally erased by court fiat.

Later, in the sixties and the seventies, new approaches were employed, such as self-report and observational studies.

SELF REPORT STUDIES

A self-report study is based on questionnaires completed by a sample group of the population. The participants, who are assured of anonymity, are asked questions about their own criminal behavior.

Get a pious thief and ask him what he does

Again, as in so many other cases, the problem we have with the results of these surveys is the way the research is conducted. Different studies come up with disparate results. When their results vary from 8.9% to 63% we can only wonder whether any of these numbers are reliable. Also, when we compare results we must make sure that we are not comparing apples and oranges. The question, 'Have you ever shoplifted in your life?' will obviously result in a higher number of 'yes' answers than the question, 'Have you shoplifted during the last twelve months?' Even if the subject is the same, the researcher can expect a lot less cooperation in a shopping mall than in a school. How the questions are phrased as well as the order in which they are arranged, can make double digit differences in the results.

Self-reported criminal behavior is a very sensitive subject, and the variations in the results seem to indicate that not many sociologists are up to the task of obtaining reliable data.

Honesty is bliss!

The half-witted quotation at the beginning of this section comes from an article analyzing a 'study' conducted by an eager beaver loss-prevention officer who decided to play sociologist. He wrote a ridiculous questionnaire that was filled out by apprehended shoplifters while they were waiting for the police. The 'author' seemed genuinely shocked by the fact that his subjects did not incriminate themselves to his satisfaction. They lied. What a surprise!

OBSERVATIONAL STUDIES

Observational studies send out observers to a retail environment to detect shoplifters. Their job is the same as that of a store-detective, except that they do not actually apprehend any culprits. The advantages of this method are that the researchers observe everybody in the store indiscriminately. They do not focus only on people they find suspicious as a store detective would do. They can also record a strong suspicion as a 'base hit'. On the other hand, the shortcomings of these studies are painfully obvious. They are very expensive. They are highly unreliable. The researchers operate like untrained store security personnel. In a study quoted by Baumer and Rosenbaum, confederate shoplifters were sent in to steal, thereby double-checking the observers. Only 45% were noticed. The observers missed the other 55% of the 'home runs' made by the 'ringers.' In another study conducted by security people, none of the confederate shoplifters were observed in action. They went into 'extra innings'.

Take me out to the ball-game

WHY DO THE VOODOO THAT THEY DO SO WELL?

There are as many answers to the above question as there are people tackling it. Nobody can really understand why shoplifters lift, but everybody tries to explain the phenomenon. If one wants to take a 'scientific' approach, the first step toward an explanation is classification.

The 'big' puzzle.

"To use a common example, Holcomb (1973) made ten categories of amateur shoplifters: juveniles, juvenile gangs, housewives, alcoholics and vagrants, narcotic addicts, mentally disturbed people, individuals with deep-seated resentment, those who want to be caught and punished, old people, and psychopaths. The problem with such typologies is that shoplifters are not distinguishable from the general population or from certain segments of it except by the fact that they exhibit theft behavior. Theorizing that shoplifters are 'juveniles' or 'housewives,' for example, does not give us a very precise definition of what is causing (motivating) the individual to shoplift, since most juveniles and housewives are not shoplifters. The explanatory usefulness of typologies is enhanced, however, if they lead us to identify the causes of theft. For example, what is it about being a juvenile that increases the probability of shoplifting for some individuals?" (Baumer and Rosenbaum, 1984)

Holcomb's top ten list

We most certainly agree with the writers of the above passage. Typologies do not provide explanations. We cannot create a link of causality between any of these theoretical groups and the act of shoplifting. As we have already said, the explanations are many, but there are some trends and parallels in them. Most of the theories are variations on three basic explanations: a) the need for economic gain, b) the need for excitement and risk-taking, c) the need to satisfy psycho-pathological motives.

For psychologists, the issue of shoplifting is just another jousting field for the Freudians and the Behaviorists, who never see eye to eye on any delinquency issue.

Freudian obsessions

"In some cases, the theories of shoplifting appear as fragments of more general theoretical models in the fields of psychology, sociology, and criminology. The utility of shoplifting theories as opposed to general theories of criminality or juvenile delinquency has yet to be demonstrated. At a minimum, authors writing in this area are guilty of ignoring many of the variables identified in other disciplines. For example, there are numerous theories of juvenile delinquency that could be applied to this topic area (see Johnson, 1979; and Hawkins, 1980, for extensive reviews). The obsession with virtually untestable hypotheses concerning pathological motives is unfortunate and has probably detracted from the development of alternative models." (Baumer and Rosenbaum, 1984)

Science battle grounds

There are serious works (note the plural) proposing the ideas that shoplifting could be done as a search for sexual gratification or as an expression of the individual's need for love! In this no-win battle, for a long time (as in many other areas) the Freudians had the upper hand, but they are steadily losing ground to the Behaviorists.

The nurture fixation

"While environmental or situational explanations of human behavior have dominated psychological and sociological research in recent years, they have not been fully applied to the crime of shoplifting. The importance of environment-based theories for the retailer is that some of the factors identified are controllable, and can be changed or corrected to prevent some of shoplifting." (Baumer and Rosenbaum, 1984)

In the works of the Behaviorists there are several motives named as possible causes. They can be either temporary or enduring. Let us see them one by one:

Frustration

A psychological term. True for those frustrated for any reason (?) but cannot be generalized for shoplifters. There are some psychologists who are advocates of the principle that every person on this earth is frustrated to some degree.

Opportunity

We have touched on the subject before. There is even a proverbial half-truth about opportunity giving birth to theft. Of course, opportunity is a factor, but this factor is present for everybody and therefore cannot be cited as a cause of shoplifting.

Now that term rings true. Almost all of our smart lifters mentioned something about the risk of getting a heavy verdict being very small. They rarely get caught, but they figure that if they did, society would find it too expensive to punish them with a prison term.

Light penalties

This category would not even come up if amateur juveniles caught boosting did not use it so often as an excuse. Peer pressure exists, of course, but recognizing it as a cause for shoplifting seems too lenient. To do so shields the individual from responsibility for his actions. Can we really say to a young person, 'If your buddies pushed you into doing it, then it is not (so much) your fault'? All societies walk a fine line when they try to decide how understanding they should be of the fierce desire of teenagers to please their fellows.

Peer pressure

We wouldn't touch this category with a ten-foot pole because it is far too general. Every evil, social problem, and crime is rooted there.

Social structure, norms and values

Although it is true that some people steal food and clothing when in need, it is also true that a large percentage of shoplifters (according to all those wonderful statistics) comes from the middle class or higher.

Economic conditions.

"In general, there is a paucity of empirical support for most of the concepts examined, due primarily to the insufficiency and low quality of existing data bases." (Baumer and Rosenbaum, 1984)

But...

Now that we have attempted to demolish certain accepted classifications (a point on which we can be easily attacked, but, then, we welcome friction), we will present some figures to you that we found reasonable enough to recommend to your attention.

We welcome abuse!

Richard Moore in a study conducted in 1984 established the following typology and figures:

Impulsive Shoplifters	**15.4%**
Occasional Shoplifters	**15.0%**
Episodic Shoplifters	**1.7%**
Amateur Shoplifters	**56.4%**
Semi-Professional Shoplifters	**11.7%**

Mary Owen Cameron's classification is far more elegant and simple:

Snitches (amateurs)	**90%**
Boosters (professionals)	**10%**

It's not over until it's over

So, after all this mumbo jumbo, we have finally hit upon a usable categorization. Amateurs and Professionals. Two distinct groups. Finally a categorization somebody might be able to do something with. Slow down, it's not over!

The proportion of the amateurs

Amateurs (ninety per cent) come from all backgrounds, religions, colors, creeds and races. It is futile to try to determine why this 'distinct' group of people resorts to criminal behavior.

The nature of the professionals

With the smaller number of professionals (ten percent) the problem with sociological and psychological approaches is twofold. Researchers can rarely find professionals, and when they do, they do not know what to do with them. Let us present you with a medley of illustrative quotations:

"The need for economic gain is again the basic motive attributed to professional shoplifters, who allegedly choose stealing as a means of making a living (Angelino, 1953). While they are frequently the topic of conversation among security personnel, they are not frequently apprehended, and thus little is known about them. (...) For example, there are at least two anti-shoplifting programs, where shopliftings have been staged on numerous occasions (...) and the acting thief has never been apprehended." (Baumer and Rosenbaum, 1984)

"One thing is clear: Offenders are apprehended at a low rate. A typical professional shoplifter commits an average of ninety-five offenses before being caught." (Uniform Crime Report of the FBI)

And some more from our friends:

"I am over forty now. I read in an FBI report about how they arrest a pro shoplifter, on average, after a hundred lifts. If that were so I would be in prison ten months a year."

The real world has real numbers

"You count twenty years for my working days [shoplifting] ***and count in my very humble estimate of maybe 250 steals per year - and I'd say there were more than that, since I go almost daily and if not, I go out only one day a week but I hit ten-twelve separate stores. They caught and prosecuted me on six occasions, always small stuff, small fines, community service. Nothing big. Go ahead, you do the math! I come out clearly with a one in eight hundred average. And I'm telling you, I am not even a pro. I only do it for survival."***

Finally, here is a list of signs that might indicate a professional shoplifter (compiled by a sociologist). We are tired. Insert your own jokes or sarcastic remarks!

Sociological shopping list

Two or more prior arrests.

Physical injury to staff, personnel, others.

Could not produce proper identification.

Had victimized other mall stores.

Resisted apprehension or arrest.

In possession of contraband.

Sold articles to a fence.

You are probably also getting tired of the stupidity of these lists too. We could ask discomfiting questions about every item on this one. What do these signs indicate to whom? How is such information obtained? When can one get this information? Who can get the information? What does it matter? When does it matter? To whom does it matter?

THE MORAL OF THE PASSAGE

They can make it, they can fake it. They can slice it, they can dice it. They can cook it, they can nuke it. They can spike it, they can spice it. ***BUT THEY CANNOT MAKE US EAT IT.***

No shit!

THE WAY THE "ACTORS" SEE THEMSELVES

"All the world's a stage,
And all the men and women merely players:
They have their exits and their entrances..."
(William Shakespeare)

Shoplifters are people too

What matters to lifters is what matters to most people. Their livelihood, their family, their friends, their work (if they have any besides lifting). When they have to define themselves as shoplifters, the important question to them (and to us in our investigation) is not the why but the how. How did they start? What changed them into what they are today? What was the process like? Who do they work with? Who in their environment knows about what they are doing? What do they tell their families? Their parents. Their children. How do people around them relate to their activities and lifestyle? In this chapter, we will let our sources to do most of the talking.

Every criminal is innocent

"I look at myself and I see nothing wrong. Look at me... I have a nice family, my life has goals and meaning. In a sense, I honor all of the Ten Commandments but the one about stealing. I am a thief... this is my job, my means of survival. Of course... I know 'It's wrong!'. I was caught four times. The shop-owner, the police, the judge... they all told me so. And after them, when I spent a night in prison even some guy.. maybe in for armed robbery... told me that shoplifting is 'wrong', there is no money in it - he advised me - you can make much more if you sell drugs."

People are shoplifters too...

Obviously neither the incompetent nor the smart lifters perceive themselves as serious criminals. Sometimes they even refuse to admit that the word 'crime' describes what they do. Although they may not necessarily be conscious of doing so, they arm themselves to the teeth with excuses. Even hardened criminals - whose crimes justify the label - would very probably be found to have the same arsenal of excuses.

Public rating of shoplifting

While we had no substantial contact with amateur shoplifters, it is safe to assume that they do not think of themselves as criminals. We read the results of a study about the perceived seriousness of crime. The public at large rates the seriousness of shoplifting just a notch higher than the writing of a bouncy cheque, which was the lowest rated crime in that study.

Unlike the social revolutionaries of the Sixties, the majority of contemporary shoplifters do not have 'noble' intentions. They do it for gain and use the excuses provided to them by society whenever they can. They are satisfied that what they do will not hurt anyone and often advise themselves and each other 'Do not graduate!'

Basic rule of smart lifters

"Never did drugs and I would never hold up a store or mug somebody. And I would definitely never kill. I dodged the draft just for this very reason. Shoplifting for me is what social science folks call the 'redistribution of wealth'. And I appreciate the fact that I don't need to organize revolutions or use guns to do that."

The peaceful socialist

"Dream on. When I first stole and my mom found out about it, nothing happened. It was a small woman's wallet, little gray, leather thing. I gave it to her. She knew I stole it. Nothing. Not a pip from her. I was twelve. I guess my mom just looked at that as... I don't know, but definitely not stealing. Later, when I was bigger, it just... you know, it was like with my smoking. She never said anything. Not against it, not for it, she just accepted it"

The understand-ding mother

"How it started? It started with my father's pocket. I don't think that there is a person anywhere, who never stole change from his dad. I did. He used to drink after work with his buddies. Not like an alcoholic, I never seen him drunk, but you know, socially. Anyway, he always kept this bunch of twenties in his breast pocket. Time after time I stole one... then another one. I kept buying these stupid plastic soldier figures, and I always had more money than my friends. I am telling you, he never ever noticed."

The social drinker

"Nobody. Nobody ever told me not to do it. Not many of my friends know about it, but the ones who do accept it as a non-important fact of life. You know what they say? Don't get caught! They care about me not being caught."

The good friends

"As my daughter grew up, I had to tell her. I mean she sees that we have not much money, so where is the stuff coming from? Anyway, I hate to lie, and I wanted to stop these fake explanations. A tale about a deal, that it was on sale - enough.... She was kind of surprised, but her morals were not shaken. I suspect she did it, or would do it. She said: Be careful. I cannot know what she really thinks, but her attitude was about the same as my wife's. She doesn't like it, but she never said to stop."

The surprised daughter

"My dad was tough on me. The police brought me home and told him about me stealing in the hardware store. He

The strict father

looked really angry and told them that he would punish me. He did. I told him that I was trying to steal a hammer, for him. He told me that from my allowance, I had to buy that hammer. I went back and stole it. Never told him about it. But the topic of shoplifting never came up again. Maybe because after that I was never caught. Maybe he didn't want to push it. It's a tricky thing you know. How can you go tough on your kid for shoplifting, when you cheat on your taxes, or if at the restaurant where you cook, you bring home everything that is not chained to something!"

The piano teacher

"My parents made me take piano lessons. God, how much I hated it! I started to steal from my piano teacher. I guess I learned early to compensate myself for unpleasant experiences."

The hypocrite

"I was well over twenty when I really started. I only did it once as a child. When I was eleven, I stole some school supply with my buddy. We got caught and we were both very severely punished. My father gave me this working class morality bullshit talk. He was very strict. But then what did I see? He was bringing the whole !#@$ing factory home! He always tried to make it look that he only took garbage, but once he even got into trouble about it. He was a !#@&ing hypocrite."

The episodic lifter

"I'm an episodic lifter. What I mean is that I never made it into a career or even a habit. You know where I'm from. Back home I never touched anything. I had friends who did it but not me. Then I went to Rome, you know, just waiting to get here. Everybody around me was doing it like crazy. The system was more lenient. A lot less to fear. We were also without any existential status, not much to lose. I started to do it then. When I came here, I stopped. I don't know why, but I did. Then a friend of mine came here who always did it and never stopped. When I went out 'shopping' with him, I felt stupid not to take anything while watching him walk home with several hundred bucks worth of stuff. Then things started to go fine and I stopped again. I haven't done it for years. Not because I have such high morals; I just don't like the hassle."

The music lover

"To me it is always a rational decision. If I have money, I never do it. I mean when I have a good income; but when I'm broke for a long time, I sometimes go wild. Books and music are important to me. I can live on dry bread, but my mind and soul need classy nourishment. I steal books and CDs. Only for myself, only what I really like, and only when I haven't had the money for a very long time to buy them."

"I don't tell it to anybody. Are you crazy? Would you? I don't lift that much anyway. Not any more. My girlfriend knows about it. She doesn't like it, but she knows I'm a grown up and do whatever I want. I get textbooks and I dress on 'discount'. Sometimes I look at myself and say gee, I have nothing on me that I paid for. I'm cool."

The cool dresser

"I started lifting for the kick when I was a teenager, then I got into drugs and shit, I never stopped since. I have a few convictions, but what do I care? I'm not politician material anyway. Well, actually maybe I am, what do you think? I have to be careful, I'm on probation till March but then I have to start 'working' again. I need the money. I want to travel. I don't want to get stuck in this stinking city for the whole summer again."

The politician material

"I was working in this big office. I'm a professional; my boss was a bureaucrat. He understood close to nothing of my work, but I had to take stupid directions and 'help' from him. It was very frustrating. It wasn't a conscious decision, but I did notice after awhile that when I got really frustrated, I brought half the office home. To get back at them somehow. I can imagine that most of the employee theft in department stores works like this. It is satisfying to rip off the boss."

The office worker

"I never lifted as a kid. I don't lift on an everyday basis. It's just work. I used to go out with these few guys; hit the malls; I made about a grand a day. There is nothing I could make that much money with. Maybe drugs, but that's too risky. You see, I don't steal my food at the supermarket. I don't 'work' every day. When you do it, you have to be there. What can I say? It's work - that's all there is to it."

The working stiff

"Sometimes I have nightmares that I get caught with one of my kids. I never touch anything when I'm with them, but I still have the nightmares. I definitely don't want them to do it or to ever even find it out about me. Maybe I AM a hypocrite, but that is the lesser one of my sins. I shouldn't worry about it."

The concerned father

Enough of the confessionals, let's get practical again. What matters most to smart lifters is the way the act is performed. Alone, or with partners?

Only the Lonely

Many of our interlocutors told us that it is good to work with partners. Others like to go at it alone. Some become members of so-called 'booster gangs' and go out in groups. All three approaches have arguments both for and against them. Advantages and disadvantages. The smart lifter will appreciate all these differences. We understand these arguments, but it seems to us that in most cases the decision made is based on personal taste, habit and attitude and not on weighing 'risks and benefits'

WORKING ALONE

"What makes loneliness an anguish
Is not that I have no one to share my burden,
But this: I have only my own burden to bear."

(Dag Hammarskjöld)

No friend, no partner, no snitch, no problem

Many boosters categorically reject the idea that working alone could have any advantages. We found that the ones who like to work alone are the 'skilled amateurs'. There is no pressure for them to make money, to get certain goods instead of others. They can make and throw away plans as the circumstances change. A pro-lifter working on an order of twenty-five jeans from his fence has no choice. He has to go out and steal the jeans. Maybe he even has a deadline. The poor 'working stiff' has to do his duty! He has to pass over some possibilities, a number of more easily obtainable goods, since he has no use for them at that particular moment. Working with partners puts an extra pressure on our 'friends' not to come out empty-handed. The 'skilled amateur' can go out with a plan to buy jeans and come back home with an electric tooth brush. He had never thought he would want one, but it was so easy, that he felt obliged to say 'yes' to the opportunity.

Confession of a 'good guy'

"I have a freezer and a pantry with lots of shelves. I go out for milk.. or dog food.. or eggs, anything that I cannot handle... cereal, laundry detergent, big stuff... that is hard to hide. Every trip I make for those will bring something onto the table. I don't go for certain stuff. I go; I see something... an aisle is empty... you see; I just pick up the stuff. Indiscriminately. Nobody suspects me since I don't have to look for a place where I can hide the stuff.... the place finds me... There is one problem though. My wife seriously gets on my case when I come home with something that doesn't fit her, or she doesn't like.... I take the blame. Send the stuff to the 'Salivating Army'... You see, we are good people..."

That damned freedom concept again!

Shoplifting alone, if you are sure of yourself and you have the skills, sounds like a good idea. Being responsible only for yourself creates the reassuring feeling that you are free to make choices by yourself. The burden of punishment is yours alone.

WORKING WITH PARTNER

***"And so we plough along,
as the fly said to the ox."***

(Henry Wadsworth Longfellow)

"I rarely work on my own. I prefer to work with a partner. We go separately in the store, and both of us keep an eye on the other and what is happening around. We've developed a couple of 'catcher-signs' on our own to warn each other, or simply just show what is where or what is good."

To work with somebody watching your back does have its obvious advantages. It is harder to catch two than one. Remember the cowboy films where our beloved heroes divided the band of pursuing Indians by going in separate directions? If you have a good partner, the 'working conditions' are much safer. Fewer accidents in the 'work place'!? With your buddy covering you from behind a rock, the shooting is just fine!

Cowboys and Indians

A good partner should be somebody who knows at least as much about the 'art' as you do. There must be an agreement, a set of operating rules between the partners. One of our lifters whined about the time when he worked with a partner who kept abandoning him. Eventually, poor him, he got caught. Obviously, the two of them did not set ground rules beforehand. In case of problems, partners usually agree that whoever can get away without implicating the other should do just that. One fine, one record or one court case is better than two.

Compatibility and agreement

It is true that a couple of guys can be more noticeable than a lonely lifter. It is up to the partners to decide whether to work as 'shopping friends,' as a 'family,' or as two separate individuals who may only secretly communicate with each other. Some partners work out signs and signals. It is also possible to engineer the getaway of one's partner by creating some kind of diversion. The possibilities range from making a simple inquiry to occupying the vendor's attention to taking desperate actions.

Family and Friends

In stores or departments with only one vendor, the first partner can easily occupy said vendor's attention while the second partner is working. It is also possible to create a 'fake-booster' partner who will be picked out by store security because of his suspicious behavior. While the snoops are following the one who looks suspicious but does nothing against the law, his partner, the 'normal shopper,' can work unhindered.

Distraction is a method that Napoleon preferred.

The forging of true friendships

"Never had a buddy I trusted enough to be involved in my things. But it changed. About two years ago, at a party, I met a guy. We talked a lot, actually we both got plastered. Then... you know... at the 'confessional' stage of drunkenness, he fessed up that he helps a couple of guys take stuff from the department store where he works. Waboom! I 'took' him. Or he 'took' me? I don't remember. Anyway, it turned out to be a profitable partnership."

Some lifters have partners who may be on any rung of the corporate ladder from simple sales assistant up to manager. If you work with such a partner, you are walking on easy street. Actually, you are in the store, but ...okay... not the best choice of words. The real problem for us comes in categorizing this kind of lifting because we see these partnerships as borderline cases between shoplifting and employee theft. It is hard to differentiate between who is the 'doer' and who is the mere 'helper.' The most typical of these arrangements is what the trade literature calls 'sweethearting.' The cashier rings in only a small portion of the actual value of the purchase.

Love conquers all. Have a sweetheart!

"A girl I used to know was working as a cashier. She had a UPC sticker taped on her wrist. Her boyfriend.... he arrives with a large load of loot. She uses her wrist - with the bar-code of a pack of anti-acid tablets, ninety-two cents, thank you very much - and passes the items through without reading the actual prices. From the manager's pulpit everything looks just dandy. He can see the machine ringing in everything fine. The guy pays for twenty-three packs of anti-acid - that is a lot of heartburn, my friends! - and takes home two-hundred dollars worth of stuff. Like it? It is cute, isn't it?"

WORKING WITH GROUP OR GANG

"Madness is something rare in individuals, but in groups, parties, peoples, ages it is the rule."

(Friedrich Nietzsche)

"A technique frequently used by shoplifters is the buddy system. One or more accomplices act as lookouts while another person commits the theft. Larger cities are plagued with organized gangs of professional shoplifters who operate in these teams. Each gang or team may consist of a set-up person, a lifter, lookouts, and distractors. They can steal thousands of dollars worth of merchandise a day." (Security Management, May 1989)

"You wanna know how I got to court the first time? It wasn't about shoplifting, but it shows you how careful you have to be. We were using fake IDs to rent pretty expensive music stuff. Keyboards, mixers, stuff like that. We paid a small deposit and then took off with the stuff. Musicians, even when they are straight, are a pretty loose bunch, so the store was losing its equipment heavily. They got into the habit of taking a Polaroid of everybody who rented stuff from them. We didn't worry about it much. The pictures were so shitty they wouldn't have found us based on that. We rented a keyboard with my friend who's a pretty good musician and was actually using the stuff. He rented it with his fake ID. We just went together.

Playing the tune....

At the same time, we had a mutual friend who was ripping off UPS. He was working at a warehouse directing the parcels. He was heavily into redirecting, actually. Whenever he saw something valuable, like a computer, he changed the address on the box. He did it for some time and occasionally he used my musician friend's address, who was also selling the goods for him. Anyway, the guy at UPS eventually got caught. They just followed the address on the box and snatched my friend too. They found the !@#$ing keyboard at his place. It was already on the police list as stolen. You know how I got into this picture? When they took the Polaroid of my buddy at the music store, I was standing beside him and half of my face was on the !@#$ing picture! That was enough for them to get a search warrant and they found some more shit at my place. It was a real !@#$ing bummer I tell you."

...and dancing to it.

'Group work' has the advantage of added security. A 'booster gang' can employ several methods of 'catch-prevention.' Because of their 'manpower,' they have an infinitesimal chance of being arrested all at the same time, but this 'benefit' can also be a disadvantage. If one of them is caught, will he spill the beans on the others? How can they be sure? What is there to provide the required discipline? Groups of criminals have no other recourse against a 'deviant' than violence - a course of action which we maintain not to be part of the 'shopping game'. Yet, if they use disciplinary measures against their partners, they will jeopardize the group. One disgruntled snitch, and the whole den of thieves is done for!

A disgruntled snatch blows the gang

There is talk about some South American gangs working in the US and making a multi-million-dollar dent in the profits of the retail industry. We will not get into socio-geo-political explanations. They come. They take. They go. If something goes wrong, North American prisons might provide better conditions than most

Veni vidi voli!

hotels in their own countries. In the case of these gangs, the benefits seem overwhelming.

The decision of whether to lift alone, with a partner, or with a whole group is a personal one. None of the three choices seems better than the others. There is no advice to be given. It is the individual's choice to make. We, personally, do not like gangs. Remember the saying 'thick as thieves'? It wears thin fast!

ART AND DANGERS OF FENCING

"Good fences make good neighbors."

(Robert Frost)

To sell the goodies safely

Wearing the tag 'professional shoplifter' does not mean that someone is good at what he does. He might happen to be a bumbling idiot with amazing luck or a guy so completely indifferent to the consequences that he fools the world into regarding him with no suspicion!. Everywhere in the literature, being 'professional' simply means doing it for the money. It means selling what is stolen to a fence or other acquaintances.

A large proportion of the 'professional shoplifters' admitted to us that they try to get orders from their circle of friends or family. They deflect suspicion by telling these people that they may have some kind of a direct source, or that they know somebody who knows somebody who can get the stuff.

Ripping off auntie

"Of course I sell the stuff when I need cash. Sometimes it is easier than stealing it. Once, a friend of my mother said that she was going to buy such and such a telephone. I said to her that I have a friend who is moving to another town and he is selling all his stuff. He has that kind of a telephone and wants to sell it. My mother's friend can get a really good price. So she said, yes. I went out, stole one, peeled the serial number off and brought it to her. She is not stupid. She saw the serial number missing and asked if it was stolen. I said I didn't know anything, but the guy is only asking seventy bucks for it. She suddenly had no more questions and paid right there on the spot."

Safe fencing

This method that we call 'safe-fencing' seems very secure, almost flawless. You deal only with people you know, and they know nothing about you being a lifter. It is natural that between friends deals can be arranged, and, most of the time, these deals will not raise any suspicions. And even if they do, if the price is right....

Creative fencing

You can tell your friend that you and your wife bought the same thing (assuming there is no serial number involved). You can say you bought the wrong size, lost the receipt, and now you are stuck with it. Explanations? You will find them pretty easy. Creativity is the key.

A fence around the yard

Another method of 'safe fencing' we heard about from a middle-aged woman shoplifter. She combines her knickknacks, useless books and records, plants and old dresses with the stuff she has collected throughout a month, and every first Sunday of the month, she organizes a yard sale - a regular flea market - on her lawn. To confuse (or secure) the situation even more, she asks some of her friends if they would like to have their old stuff displayed at this monthly event.

You can be your own fence (somewhat similar to the above lady) if you decide to advertise your loot in the classified sections of newspapers. If it is 'hot,' meaning it has a serial number, then you wait. Listen.

Classifieds

"Anything will cool down after some time. Anyway, it is safe. The person who bought it will use it instead of flat-footing around to find out the origins of the stuff. If he finds out he got some stolen stuff, I don't think he might be very anxious to reveal that he bought some 'hot' item. Anyway, it is unlikely that he remembers you or your telephone number."

"I used hot computers for awhile. I was a student and couldn't afford a new one (a cool one I should say.) I used them for about a year and a half, then I sold them, even with a little profit. I had three computers while I was in school. Figured that after a year I could sell them without much of a risk."

Pawn shops

When the trade literature talks about fences, it typically describes them as second-hand store owners or pawn-shop owners. Pawn shops, unless you know them well, are risky. They are regularly visited by police. They are asked about suspicious merchandise. The police might actually look for certain items. According to the law, pawn-shop owners are required to demand identification. The only ones that may prove to be safe are the ones who imply their intention of complicity by not asking for your ID.

The Pawnbroker and the Policeman

"I take stuff. Every day some crook comes in with something that is obviously stolen. If it is a good deal, I buy it from him. Jewelry, stereos, cameras, VCRs are good. My other daily visitor is the local cop, who comes in, checks my in-and-out account, and asks if there is something. Sometimes I make up a story about some guy who came in with a VCR or something, but the whole deal looked fishy and I said no. Never-ever he asked me for a description. He just does not care, I guess. But what I buy from the crooks, I take home. If a customer looks for something I have at

home I ask them to come back the next day. You have to look at them and know the types, so you won't be hung by some undercover cop."

The three categories of fences

The first type is the one who suspects that the goods are stolen, but keeps his suspicions unspoken. The second type doesn't pretend and has no expectations. If he can use the goods he might buy them. The third type is the 'real' fence who has lifters working on order. He demands specific items that the boosters deliver for a price, usually 25% of retail. Contrary to common belief, pawn-shops and second hand stores are not the backbone of fencing operations. Fashionable boutiques, music and book stores, hardware stores, computer stores and others might be much safer if one is looking for a place to sell.

Long John Notebook!

"It was a hilarious situation. I had this buddy, a computer salesman. All of his booster friends went to him for appraising their goods and to ask for his help selling them. He sold most of the stuff to a little store he used to work for. His buyers never really met his sellers, but once, when he had one of the computer technicians visiting him, he (the technician) got a glimpse of one of the lifters who was delivering a notebook computer to my buddy. I only know about the story because we went to the store together a few days later. The first thing the technician told us when we entered was that our friend 'Long John' was there. He didn't know that this was the store where his goods ended up and he didn't recognize the technician. He was looking for merchandise. He was told that the store has nothing for sale. He got the message and left."

Fencing relations

Of course, it is hard to find a fence because you cannot go in a store and ask the person behind the counter if the store buys stolen goods. One method that we heard about is to walk into a store and offer something for sale as a feeler. Based on the reaction you get, you can slowly build a fencing relationship.

The dangers working with or for a fence are obvious. In case of arguments both sides have something on the other and can cause each other headaches. Police may discover a fence and stake out his place and identify his clientele. Work with somebody you know and trust, and even then, never identify yourself. Only that can make the relationship moderately safe.

THE MORAL OF THE PASSAGE

Partners and fences can be both helpful and risky. Assessing the risks of your association is just as important as assessing your methods.

THE WAY THE AUTHORS SEE THEM

"To say of men that they are bad is to say they are worse than we think we are, or worse than the ideal man whose image we have built up on the basis of a certain few."

(Jean Rostand)

Money makes the world go 'round...

Our answer to the questions of 'who?' and 'why?' is rather simple. We choose to consider **material gain** as the only causative factor for the act of shoplifting. We do not buy into any of the other bullshit. We went underground, we broke into the heads of smart lifters, and that is what we came back with. We read whatever there was to be read, and we found that everything in the trade literature tries to dehumanize our 'actors,' whereas the scientific literature over-humanizes them. Our impression is that the 'scientific' writers are more interested in finding excuses for shoplifters than in understanding them.

They are only human!

The lifters we met come in all shapes and sizes. Some of them we consider friends. Very good friends. Although we might not necessarily accept their reasons for shoplifting, we understand them. We do not want to change or save them; we can only sympathize with them. We found them trustworthy and reliable people. You know what? We will go out on a limb, and dare to call them respectable. They are truly human. Some others, of course, we would not have anything to do with, or want to be seen on the same street with, but then again, there are merchants, lawyers, pseudo-scientists and other 'respectable' people that we would not want to have anything to do with, either.

They are doing their job

There are a few interesting observations that we made throughout our personal interviews with our small sample of thieves. We talked to a couple of guys who are professionals in the sense that they are stealing for resale. Almost strictly for resale. They both consider boosting to be their job, and the money they make to be money earned. One of these guys lifts hundreds of compact discs a day. After selling them to his fence, he spends his 'hard-earned' money on himself, buying things that he could have lifted with the same ease. They make a fascinating contrast to a couple of artists (skilled amateurs) who would find it deplorable to steal anything for resale. These artists satisfy a considerable portion of their personal needs by shoplifting, but they would not feel comfortable lifting anything for resale. To do so would make them feel as if they were - as one of them philosophically put it - **criminals.**

And a last note. In our opinion the literature puts an undue emphasis on the role of drug addiction. We can certainly understand that the urge for a fix does have a detrimental effect on moral standards. From the last bum on the street corner to the king of Wall Street, hopheads are led by their addiction into the fields of crime. What they need - in our opinion - is money. This need does not change the basic equation: shoplifting or fixing the market equals material gain.

THE MORAL OF THE PASSAGE

Going out on a limb

Shoplifting is a crime, but the lifters are people. We are not looking for excuses but pass no judgments either.

PART TWO

ART

WHEN AND WHERE

"Where force is necessary, there it must be applied boldly, decisively and completely. But one must know the limitations of force; one must know when to blend force with a manoeuvre, a blow with an agreement."

(Leon Trotsky)

RETAIL CHRONOGRAPHY

"A single day is enough to make us a little larger or, another time, a little smaller."

(Paul Klee)

Any time? Any Place?

It may seem pointless to discuss the nuances of when and where to shoplift. After all, everybody believes that shoplifting occurs any time and any place. Well, in a sense it does. Impulsives - housewives, juveniles and others - do it any time, any place. In the case of the smart lifter, however, the situation is different. Although pro lifters may, occasionally, act on impulse, know-how always governs their impulses. They can measure risks and benefits in a split second and change their plans accordingly. They can afford to be flexible because before going to a given store, they have 'cased the joint' and designed a strategy which probably includes a scheme for recognizing and seizing moments of opportunity.

Eager Beavers and Busy Bees

Any loss prevention or security officer will tell you that his work schedule changes according to time and season. Merchants hire temporary store security for certain hours of the day, days of the week, and seasons of the year during which they believe shoplifters do more damage. Holidays also figure in their calculations. The smart lifters know this 'secret' information about security scheduling. Inexperienced shoplifters, on the other hand, are blissfully unaware of it.

Check your assumptions

Indeed, inexperienced thieves would be surprised if they became aware of how much retailers know about when they are likely to show up. In the next passages we will compile a more or less accurate picture of what both sides know about the effect of time, season, and place.

THE TIME OF THE DAY

***"The gates of Hell are open night and day;
Smooth the descent, and easy is the way:
But, to return, and view the cheerful skies;
In this, the task and mighty labour lies."***

(Virgil)

They try, oh, how they try!

Various statistics show the time of the day when shoplifting will probably occur. The only thing a shopkeeper can find out from these figures is when his store is likely to be the busiest. (Useful information, isn't it?) Based on these statistics, security is built up at hours considered to be busy and therefore appealing to shoplifters. We think that, contrary to these statistical findings, it is quite possible, even probable, that the lion's share of the losses occurs at other times, when apprehension rates are low.

Early bird catches the worm

According to one 'valuable' source, only 8 % of shoplifting occurs in the morning. We don't place much faith in this type of statistic, however, because it reflects only the number of people (mostly amateurs) nabbed for boosting at this time of day, ***not*** the dollar value of losses in merchandise. We can tell from this apprehension statistic that during the morning hours, fewer amateur thieves are present in stores, bumbling around and being taken into custody, than come in to 'shop' during other periods of the day. How many smart lifters are also morning people is much harder to determine because smart lifters are apprehended much less often than amateurs are. We do know that they are very likely to be lifting items of greater value than those the amateurs are stumbling after. Statistics for the losses in dollars and cents which our superstars of boosting cause every AM are impossible to find, but we believe the figure is significant. Merchants, lulled by a low apprehension rate as well as the fact that not many shoppers, whether honest or dishonest, drop by before noon, do not engage extra security during this relatively 'safe' time of day. Salespeople are busy setting up their stations, having their breakfasts, or talking over yesterday's TV shows. It's like shooting fish in a barrel for a smart lifter who chooses to hit on virtually empty stores in the wee hours of the shopping day. These very wise morning lifters are the most skillful of their breed. They are arrested the least often, and they probably cause the largest proportion of losses.

An uplifting atmosphere

If you, go out 'shopping' in the morning, you will encounter fewer people to watch for, fewer people watching you, more 'blind spots' and a generally more pleasant 'lifting' atmosphere. Everything will be easier. Listen to a lone professional:

First thing in the morning: a good coffee

"It is better to go out early in the morning. Later, the store gets busy, the housewives start their visits and steal their steak knives, and the kids come out of school and go

for their chocolate bars. Detectives roll up their sleeves and appear by the dozens. In addition, more people around means that you have to look behind your back more often. Go when the stores are empty. Early morning. The detectives are having their coffees or chatting with the sales-girls. You can see them, but they won't see you."

Lunch-time

Between noon and 2 P.M., according to the same source, 14 % of the day's shoplifting occurs. Again, we must remember that this is an apprehension statistic. It is perceptibly a tad higher than the morning figure because more shoppers, including more amateur lifters, are in the stores during their lunch breaks, thus raising the apprehension rate for this period. Smart lifters who have part-time jobs, or who work at home, also make good use of their lunch breaks to do the 'deed'. An advantage for them during this period is that sales and security people have to take time for the noon meal. Staggered lunch breaks usually mean that fewer eyes are watching out for the damage which pro lifters can and will do.

The achalia shade lipstick disappeared exactly at: 14:23

"There is a fair amount of agreement regarding the time of day that most shoplifters are apprehended. According to Griffin's (1978, 1981) multi-year data base, the greatest numbers (approximately one-third) are apprehended during the hours from 3:00 PM to 6:00 PM In the state of Washington, two stores indicated that peak shoplifting hours were between 12:00 PM and 4:30 PM (Shave, 1978). Data from many Washington, D.C. stores show that 65 percent of all apprehensions are made in the afternoon (Metropolitan Washington Board of Trade, 1978). In New York, 47 percent occurred between 2:00 PM and 6:00 PM (National Retail Merchants Association, 1976a). Thus while consensus on specific peak hours would be difficult, most studies agree that the greatest volume of shoplifting apprehensions occurs in the afternoon." (Baumer and Rosenbaum, 1984)

Nobody takes naps

Almost all the 'scientifically' oriented research, often a blatant advertisement for certain security firms or consultants, declares that the retailer is most vulnerable to theft between 2 and 6 PM. This declaration is based on the fact that 42% of all shoplifting apprehensions takes place during that time period. Naturally! The retailer's 'task force' is out at that time of day, sniffing after everybody, following unsuspecting shoppers and thieves alike with the nose-to-the-ground dedication of near-sighted beagles. After crunching the numbers found in apprehension headcounts, the researchers all seem to come to the same conclusion:

"Temporally, the data consistently show that the bulk of shoplifting apprehensions occur in the afternoon." (Security Management, May 1989)

See the forest behind the tree

The bulk of these 2 to 6 PM apprehensions includes, in large numbers, the occasional shoplifter who is easily caught with his small prey of a pen, cosmetics item, or food. On the other hand, the skillful shoplifter can discover a number of new ways of dealing with a situation where the sheer number of legitimate shoppers is as large as it is during this time period. For example, a family in front of you, strolling along behind their cart, covers you perfectly from the front. Other shoppers standing next to you hide you from cameras and detectives.

More people, more distraction

Certainly, the larger-than-usual number of security personnel and the relatively great number of people in the store during this time period, taken together, create a high apprehension rate. These same factors, however, mean that detectives or 'ghost shoppers' have little chance of observing and pursuing real offenders, distracted as they are by so many possible suspects. Perhaps adding on more security services to their stores during this time period does not help as much as retailers think it does. All these security folks may simply be bumping into each other going after, catching, and processing hapless amateurs while our canny smart lifters waltz off with the goods.

Monte chases his tale

One can also speculate that these scheduling practices work as self-fulfilling prophesies. The more detectives there are on the floor, the higher the apprehension rate is bound to be, thus 'substantiating' the theory that more detectives are needed. A similar assumption is made in stock market manipulation: If you buy more, the price will eventually go up.

Crowd is good

There is a special category of pro lifters which prefers crowds and busy business hours. This category is composed of people who work in teams or gangs. The more chaotic movement there is around them, the more delighted these people are. Their first goal is to create a diversion. They can easily direct a frazzled security team's attention to a partner who works hard to attract it. This accomplice keeps the security personnel of the store on his case, diverting their attention from his pals who are working carefully but persistently in the background, hidden in the crowd.

Closing time, losing time

From 6 P.M. to closing time 20% of lifting takes place. This 'useful' figure loses its efficacy, however, when one considers that the smart lifter is out there 'working' diligently during these hours. The number of apprehensions is lower than in the afternoon (most dishonest housewives, juveniles, etc., are probably eating supper at home), but dollar value losses, on the other hand, might be even higher.

"....Closing time can be very profitable for shoplifters, especially. At this time most store employees are burdened with chores such as closing out cash registers, cleaning, restocking, or doing paperwork. Experienced, professional

shoplifters know how to take advantage of the decrease in customer traffic and the scarceness of store personnel." (Security Management, May 1989)

The remaining 16% of shoplifting, according to our doubtful source, happens at night in stores that are open around the clock. All-night stores, 24 hour drug-stores, and large food stores are targeted by those boosters who prefer a calm atmosphere, empty aisles, and scarce security. Indeed, 'security' in these places is mostly composed of part-time workers stacking shelves.

Silent Night, Holy Night

"I was delivering pizza for a few years. I finished after two every night. There was an all night superstore on my way home in a fancy neighborhood. I never missed it. It gave me the most pleasant shopping experiences of my life. No crowd, no line-ups, no fighting over the last chicken. Serenity. Other than the five zombies stocking the shelves the place was empty. My bag was full of goodies, my soul was full of joy. At Christma time, on snowy evenings, I seemed to hear the bells of the reindeers as I left the store."

The above poetic recounting is very moving, but it leaves a fly in the ointment. At night extra attention must be paid to the cashiers, who, because of the calm atmosphere in the store, have plenty of time and energy to observe carefully the activities of people who enter with bulky bags, bulging pockets, coats or jackets. For professional shoplifters, night time means a safer, faster and easier getaway (in a one-horse, open sleigh?) Operating at night is favored by the 'crazies' who prefer the 'Grab and Run' and 'Whole-Carting' methods. Although arrests are scarce and unlikely inside the store, police response, if there is any, may be considerably faster than during the day. "Who knows? A full moon means violent crimes are on the rise, so the police are busy," said one of our 'friends.'

DAY OF THE WEEK

"Anybody can observe the Sabbath, but making it holy surely takes the rest of the week."

(Alice Walker)

Some more worthless information

"The distribution of shoplifting by day of the week is as follows: Saturday appears to be the peak day for drug stores, while supermarket and discount stores experience a more even distribution of apprehensions (Griffin, 1981). Over a twelve-year period, Thursday and Friday were the heaviest apprehension days (Griffin, 1978). Again, department store data are lacking. Retail establishments studied in Washington, D.C. - many of which are department stores-report that the weekends account for 55 percent of all apprehensions (Metropolitan Washington Board of Trade, 1978). Thus

weekends are probably peak periods for department stores, in contrast to stores in Griffin's sample." (Baumer and Rosenbaum, 1984)

The Thursday Mystery and the Sanctity of the Weekend

Most of the available statistics name Thursday as the day when stores are most frequented by shoplifters practicing their art. They have no explanation why. It does not make much sense; does not even seem logical. One would think that after a week chained to their desks at their regular places of work - from Blue Monday to Thank God It's Friday - lifters would be out doing the majority of their boosting on their days off (Saturday and Sunday). Then again, maybe not. Maybe they prefer to stay home and be with their families.

Generally, stores that are open on Sunday reach their highest volume of sales on that day. Department stores with unionized sales forces must cope with a limited availability of bonded employees on Sunday and are therefore forced to use their non-union security personnel as cashiers. Obviously, while these people are busy running the cash registers, they can pay much less attention to the job for which they were originally hired.

"Distribution by day of the week seems to depend on the type of retail store, with department stores experiencing the greatest number of apprehensions on the weekend." (Security Management, May 1989)

Pick a day, any day!

The high arrest rates on weekends and Mystery Thursdays might be explained by the fact that more amateurs steal on those days. Some of them may prefer Thursdays to the weekend rush. Others choose Sundays since they are working on the weekdays. We think the simple fact of which *day* you go out hunting does not change the possible amount of prey or the given risks and benefits of shoplifting.

SEASONS

"To everything there is a season, and a time to every purpose under the heaven ...."

(The Bible)

More then four seasons for retailers

Busy shopping periods such as Mothers' Day, Easter, Christmas, Season End Sales, White Sales, Bankruptcy Sales, and the like, are given special attention when merchants plan store-security. The winter, from October to late February, when shoplifters can wear puffy ski-jackets and long coats, is thought of as a period when snoops need to be out in force trying to detect stolen merchandise concealed in these big, handy garments. Summer seems to calm the retailers. They believe that fewer shoplifters are visiting their establishments.

Outside in the streets, it is teeth-shatteringly cold. Still, people go out shopping. In their large parkas, loose and puffy jackets and long coats, they are all suspects in the eye of a store detective. During the pre-Christmas rush, shoppers are out in enormous numbers, and they are invariably loaded down with bags and packages. Smart lifters float among them, looking just like any other customer. Winter time is obviously an appropriate time to lift, especially if you plan to obtain many items at the same time. Your seasonal clothing will provide several excellent hiding places. However, there will be increased security watching you and looking for the 'bulges of winter' on your coat, jacket, or whatever.

Winter is on your side

"The winter's cool. There are a lot of people in the stores. The girlies are busy. The spooks are running after everybody. Don't use a winter coat. Just stroll in, wearing a snappy leather jacket, open it up and let it hang open, as if you came in from the bitter cold - and now by golly - you feel a little bit too hot. You can take more stuff and safer this way. I usually work like that and pack onto my back, under my shirt, into my crotch."

Interesting advice about the loose, open over-garment. Wearing it inspires less distrust than a bulky coat would and also allows you to secure 'not paid for' items at the door by buttoning or zipping up as you are about to step outside. We also heard from our interlocutors about using the open garment trick with an additional touch of cleverness: Adding a scarf conceals the view of any item that is carried under one's upper arm and hides how much your shirt or sweater bulges.

Take another sweater!

A collective sigh of relief can be heard from shopkeepers on the first really warm day of summer.

"Summer I fear shoplifters much less. Even the lightest jacket or pullover will expose the shoplifter, and what else can they do? Put the staff in their pockets? Bags, handbags? We always had a policy against carrying bags into the store. Will they hide something under their rags on their head? Ludicrous. We have it easy." (Anonymous Shop Owner)

Easy does it!

Not so fast. In some ways, for the smart lifters, summer is an even better 'hunting season' than winter. Although it is true they are not able to 'rescue' larger items, they ***can*** go for the smaller stuff - they just have to do so more often. For the ladies, a tight pair of workout pants under a short skirt provides a secure holding place for goods. Male boosters use tight briefs, or, if they are more experienced at the art, bicycle pants, under their shorts. In both cases with the addition of a comfortably hanging shirt or blouse, or T-shirt, they look as if they came straight from the beach.

Summer-time, summer-time, sum-sum summertime

Summer is your friend, too

Almost all store-owners assume that there is no way crooks can conceal anything on their bodies in summer. Suspicion and surveillance are at their yearly low. A little bit more work, a couple more visits to the stores per day, could bring large profits for the smart lifter.

Be outstanding by not standing out

Spring and autumn are very similar to each other in one respect: the weather is changeable. People dress in response to each day's forecast.. The smart lifter does the same. On a warm, summer-like day, he dresses for summer. On a nippy, early winter-like day he brings out his jacket. If he consistently follows this rule, he will be unnoticeable in a crowd. There are no great advantages or disadvantages either for the security folks or the lifters during spring or autumn. According to the weather, both groups follow either the winter or summer rules.

HOLIDAYS, AND OTHER SPECIAL SEASONS

"From a commercial point of view, if Christmas did not exist it would be necessary to invent it."

(Katharine Whitehorn)

We've already said that: more shoppers, more lifters.

"Even if apprehension figures can be accumulated that show increases at Christmas, we must remember that additional security personnel are usually on duty and customer traffic is much greater than at other times of the year. There is the possibility that more apprehensions are made due to extra security guards yet the absolute number of shoplifters had not increased, but this seems unlikely. The added volume of shoppers leads one to believe that regardless of security, the total number of shoplifters increases during this season." (Baumer and Rosenbaum, 1984)

Does any special day of the year hurt?

Retailers are particularly alert during the shopping days that precede the gift-giving seasons of the year. Although Valentine's Day, Mother's and Father's Day, Easter, Back To School Days, and the like, are equally dangerous for both lifters and merchants, the most troublesome period is the Yuletide Season. As the humorous host of a nighttime variety show used to warn his viewers: "There are only seven shoplifting days left till Christmas!".

Christmas in September

"Always stop at Christmas! You would think that the crowd helps. Maybe you think so, but I don't. You have more detectives and the sales people are on the look-out. It lasts for two weeks, three weeks. I consider it as my vacation. And my own Christmas 'shopping' I already did in September and October. It's a small price to pay for feeling secure."

Fish in the snow?

Other lifters, however, prefer to dive into the large crowds and the enormous amount of merchandise displayed at Christmas time. Indeed, there are groups or gangs who feel like fish in water when a store is full of customers. They never really worry about security. They have very 'secure' methods of fooling the snoops. Christmas is, for most people, a time to buy presents for others. For many lifters, however, it might be more tempting to save money on presents for others and spend it on themselves.

THE MORAL OF THE PASSAGE

> ***The advantage of time and place in all practical actions is half a victory.***
>
> *(Sir Francis Drake)*

You can go at dawn, morning, day, dusk, evening, or night, but take into account what time is best for visiting the type of store you have in mind. Also, consider your own skills, desires, and needs. Ask yourself what precautions you need to take. The articles you plan to lift, and the place where you plan to obtain them, may somewhat determine the best time-period for your 'shopping.' You should also listen to the weather report before you go out lifting so that you can dress to be invisible in the midst of the legitimate shoppers. Do not arouse suspicion with out-of-season fashion choices.

It is all up to you, just don't arouse the guards

RETAIL CARTOGRAPHY

"Everybody ought to have a lower East Side in their life."

(Irving Berlin)

NEIGHBOURHOODS

"The composition of some neighborhoods or living environments may be such that they encourage or discourage shoplifting among local residents. Very little information is available as to the volume of shoplifting per neighborhood or area; there have been some comparisons of urban versus suburban chain stores, but even these results are not consistent." (Baumer and Rosenbaum, 1984)

Shoplifters are also not 'politically correct'

Our smart lifters expressed the 'biased' opinion that in better neighborhoods the going is easier and more profitable. They usually do not frequent the so-called 'dollar stores' or cheap department stores. They are after bigger profits than can be made in such junk bins.

The Yuppie Mall

"There is this mall, out in the suburb. Only rich, young people live around the area. I call it the 'Yuppie Mall' If that place has any security, then I haven't seen them. A couple of mall-cops, that's it. No buzzers, no tags, no nothing. It is never a good idea to lift in shabby clothes anyway, but for 'shopping' there, I dress up extra dandy. Put on this pair of glasses with window-glass in them, comb my hair neatly and there I am, the upper middle-class yuppie husband looking for a present for the wife or the little ones."

We don't believe (or pretend to know), that all better neighborhood stores operate with less security than do stores in less affluent neighborhoods. It seems to make sense, however, that they experience much lower inventory shrinkage and their apprehension rates are lower. Hence they probably do put fewer dollars into prevention. The authors have come across several malls similar to the one described by their source above.

The other 'hoods' and hoodlums

The 'have-nots' definitely have more 'reasons and excuses' to shoplift, and security personnel working in inner-city discount stores therefore expect more shoplifters. The security folks may be guilty of making unfair discriminatory assumptions about poor people, but they usually manage to 'prove' themselves right. They catch many poor guys or gals with some cheap stuff. The shrinkage is comparable to that caused by other 'hoods,' but apprehension rates will be higher. The smart lifter never, or almost never, goes into stores that cater to the poor.

SEARCH AND DISCOVERY

"Data is what distinguishes the dilettante from the artist."

(George V. Higgins)

DO NOT GRADUATE! KEEP IT SOFT!

These are the most basic things to keep in mind: Know your store. Experiment. Try not to hurt yourself or anybody else in the process. Remember, shoplifting is a very soft crime for which the punishment is soft. Keep it soft and do not 'graduate' to 'harder' criminal activity.

Trial and error

If you face a new electronic buzzer system with a tag, or magnetic sticker, go ahead and remove said tag or sticker. Throw the device through the 'buzzer gates' to find out if it works at all. You can do something else, too, when confronted with magnetic or radio stickers. Put one on the sole of your shoe and get caught. Either they will find nothing on you, or they will find a sticky magnetic strip you have stepped into 'accidentally.' Embarrassment for them. Fun for you. There is also a ruder method you can experiment with. You can find yourself an unsuspecting victim, put a tag on him, and watch what happens. Make sure your victim has only the strip thrust in his bag or stuck into his pocket. Do not make him suffer by loading him with stolen merchandise so he will be caught! You are above that sort of thing.

Be a good scout; keep your eyes open

Whenever you visit a store you know little about, it is a good strategy to buy something and observe the tag removal method at the check-out counter. Really wise stores locate the counter inside the gates. The clerk gives you the merchandise only after you have passed through the gates, hence revealing nothing about their system. In this case either leave that store alone, or work on discovering and cracking their method. Sometimes, these stores cunningly hide EAS stickers inside the packaging. Perhaps you might investigate a legitimate purchase or two to ferret out this hiding place. The money you spend on 'search and discovery' will pay for itself many times over.

The thin magnetic line between me and the books

"I had this book store. Everything was fine. I really liked their selection, but I couldn't figure out why they had those gates at the exit since on the books there was nothing. They weren't packed, they weren't tagged, big nothing. One day I was browsing for a book, just wanting to know if they had it. What do I see? Two babes, maybe students on a part time job, working at a counter, placing thin metal strips in

the books. I tell you, that store became my favored bookstore. The only confusing thing is that sometimes I cannot find the little thingie, but then I leave that book alone..."

THE LAYOUT OF THE STORE

"The physical design or layout of a store is believed to be an important contributor to theft. It may affect perceptions of the risk of apprehension and accessibility to merchandise. Security personnel are aware of the problems associated with placing high-priced items near exits or out of employees' visibility. In addition, areas of the store offering seclusion and non-surveillance are believed to invite shoplifting. Although little research has been conducted to assess the impact of various retail environments on shoplifting (and employee theft), much effort has gone into proper environmental design in recent years." (Baumer and Rosenbaum, 1984)

They actually make designs?!?

The layout and design of a store can tell a lot about security in that particular location. If its interior is spacious and well-lit, there might be more eye surveillance. Large, bulky, floor-to-ceiling shelves might indicate hidden security devices and detectives. A lack of anti-theft devices and methods might or might not mean light security. It may simply say: We do not care! or We are so good that nothing shows! or We have a zillion ghost shoppers spying on you! On the other hand, the more gadgets you see, the less you have to worry about human surveillance. As long as you know how to handle the technology, these stores could be the safest ones.

Are they pondering what I am pondering...?

"I walk into this trendy fashion boutique. Imagine. Men's fashion. Okay, let's see. Walking past their fitting rooms and seeing that the empty ones are full of tried-on and left-there stuff I knew that the security was non-existent. That is a rare find, I am telling you. It means that nobody cared about real shoppers going in and out the fitting rooms. Instantly, I took a couple of jackets, expensive ones, over two-hundred bucks instant profit. I walked in, undressed, put one on under my shirt and pullover, put on my jacket and went out. A couple of minutes, that's all. I smiled at a sales-girl, asked her if they have this jacket (showing her the second one) with pockets on the side... she said no... I put back the second one, thanked her and left, baby... that was a good one."

Do they reckon as I reckon...?

"Retail space, that is the proximate environment that surrounds the retail shopper [and shoplifter], **is never neutral. The retail store is a bundle of cues, messages and suggestions which communicate to shoppers** [and shoplifters] **Retail**

If you are really in the mood...

store designers, planners and merchandisers shape space, but that space in turn affects the and shapes customer [and shoplifter] **behavior. The retail store (....) does create mood, activate intentions and generally affect customer** [and shoplifter] **reactions." (Markin, Lillis, and Narayana, 1976)**

Information, data and knowledge shines through

We use this quotation (with our additions in square brackets) not only to show how the actual layout and store-design affects the activities in a store, but also to show what the smart lifter looks for. We explained earlier that the trade literature gives the same amount of advice to thieves as we do. (It's not the approach but the information that counts.) The above passage is a shining example of our assertion.

The 99% safe store is within reach

To design a completely secure store which would be safe from shoplifters is the easiest task on earth. Let's see. The store has large shelves all around the store, aesthetically and invitingly displaying all the merchandise. Also all around, in front of the shelves, display cases or counters are placed, manned with an adequate number of sales help. There you go. Except for the occasional con-artist who might fool your staff members and magically make something disappear from the counter, and except for the violent 'grab and run' artist, no shoplifter will bother your merchandise. Yet, as we all know, security is always hanging in the balance and found wanting. To run a secure store, the owner would have to hire more vendors to serve the customer better, thus sacrificing a larger portion of his profit than the portion he presently loses from theft.

Checks and Balances

No matter who designs the store layout, and no matter the how or why of that design, it will prove impossible to create a truly safe store if hunger for more profit governs what is actually built. If the urge to sell in large quantities, entice impulsive shoppers, go gung-ho and sell!-sell!-sell! holds sway, such matters as the position and height of the gondolas and shelves and the position and type of gates and cameras will always be of secondary importance.

SHOPLIFTING IN A FOREIGN COUNTRY

Keep your hand to yourself

Most countries have relaxed laws and punishments for shoplifting. Most 'civilized' countries, that is. There are still some countries, however, who go after lifters in a barbaric manner about which we have no solid information. It is possible that you will find that the punishment in certain countries does not fit the crime, manifesting itself in some kind of Medieval method such as caning, whipping, cutting off of hands, long prison sentences, or other similarly unsophisticated tortures. Do not go to such places, and if you do, do not do the deed!

If you 'work' abroad, know the country. The advantages of 'working' in another country are numerous. The most obvious is that lifting on tour reduces your overall travel expenses. Those souvenirs can add up! The other is the language advantage. A language totally foreign to security officials creates a solid barrier between you and them. (The advantage obviously shrinks in English-speaking countries. Pretendez-vous d'être français! Legyetek magyarok!) It is so frustrating for them to try to communicate with you that they are very likely just to kick you out of the store. For the shoplifting-traveler from North America, gallivanting around Europe provides a wide range of opportunities as well as added safety from punishment. And vice versa: the European shoplifting-traveler enjoys the same advantages when visiting this side of the planet.

The shrinking world

"I am an immigrant. My mother often visits me, and she just loves the stores here. She buys stuff. She also lifted once and they caught her. Now, I am called into this drugstore where they are holding her in the back. Since she speaks only enough English to understand that they wanted somebody she knew, she gave them my name and telephone number. Of course, she is ashamed and frightened, but they did nothing. She only had her passport, no residence, so they didn't do anything. They asked me to lecture her. "

The story of the naughty mother

If you have carefully researched the habits and laws of a foreign country, you may be in a safe position. The worst that can happen to you is that a shopkeeper may hold you for awhile in the back room of his store. The police, if called, will say that they have enough trouble without bothering to make a report on a stupid tourist who has tried to lift a CD, a book, or a bottle of whisky.

They don't understand you, you don't understand them

THE MORAL OF THE PASSAGE

Try to find the place, store, neighborhood, country where the return on time and effort invested is the greatest. Know your stores, know your territory! The basic rule to follow once you do know your territory is to keep your eyes open and use what you have learned from your research (whether you cased the neighborhood comic book joint or went to the library to look up the laws of Upper and Lower Bangatook).

RETAIL BATTLE GROUNDS

"Modern man, if he dared to be articulate about his concept of heaven, would describe a vision which would look like the biggest department store in the world, showing new things and gadgets, and himself having plenty of money with which to buy them. He would wander around open-mouthed in this heaven of gadgets and commodities, provided only that there were ever more and newer things to buy, and perhaps that his neighbours were just a little less privileged than he."

(Erich Fromm)

IF THIS IS A WAR, WHO'S WINNING IT?

Fingers against eyes, tact against vigilance

The 'fight' for profit on both sides of the war between merchandisers and smart lifters is waged with different armaments depending on the layout of a specific store. As regards security, any trick, layout ploy, or surveillance level works until the shoplifter has figured out how it works and can evade or overcome it. The retailer cannot trust any defense strategy which has remained the same for a long time because the smart lifter researches his 'battle ground' relentlessly and ultimately learns it by heart. Battles are being fought this very minute. Who is winning? It all depends on the current preparedness of the opposing camps. If we were bookies, however, we would give pretty good odds on the smart lifters. Of course, the 'bad guys' will win a battle or two, but we think that the deck is stacked against them.

We have to admit that we cannot describe all the retail battlegrounds in the world. Stores come in countless shapes, types and sizes. Describing them all would probably fill a multi-volume encyclopedia. We only have space to include a few of the store-types targeted by boosters. Freely admitting that our list is not nearly complete, we offer for your consideration ***The Top Ten Stores Most Loved and Frequented by Lifters.*** We shall pull a David Letterman and begin at the bottom of the list with Store Number Ten.

BOOKSTORES

The love of learning the sequestered nooks,
And all the sweet serenity of books.
(Henry Wadsworth Longfellow)

Books don't bark, so you can walk them

Books are man's second best friend (the dog comes first). Many of our sources admitted going to bookstores to satisfy their intellectual needs by acquiring books for themselves, but we talked to other lifters for whom books are just a commodity, another easy-to-sell item. Although the resale value of books is relatively low, this group frequents bookstores for the purpose of acquiring cash.

The Lifter and the Innocent Bookseller

"There was this special bookstore in the basement of an office building. They had expensive textbooks, rarities, lots of fine art books and tons of expensive paperbacks. Four or five all around my waist easy and presto, I made out with about four-hundred dollar worth of books. This second-hand bookstore owner happily bought all of them from me. I told him I have a large library and serious cash problems so he would not get suspicious and ask himself, "Why the heck is it that fellow keeps coming, almost every week?" He never asked; I never told. He maybe knew that something was rotten in Denmark, but didn't seem to care. The money was not fabulous. He paid like maybe a little less than a quarter of the original price, but it paid the rent and my car loan for awhile."

There is a buzz about some books

Many large bookstores have installed an EAS (Electronic Article Surveillance) system. An interesting and quite-often-used type of EAS involves a slim magnetic wire embedded in a long, thin, paper slip. If you find this slip and remove it, you are safe, but not finding it can be frustrating. You don't know whether the slip is really there hiding from you.. Stay on the safe side. The only book that is a safe 'kill' is one from which you have personally removed the EAS slip or tag (see below). If you can't find such a device in a particular book, no matter how attractive that book may be, leave it alone. There are other books and bookstores.

Another type of protection is the magnetic or radio tag, either paper or plastic, disguised as a price tag, with or without barcodes. It is usually a thick, square-shaped, easily removable paper sticker. (You will find these stickers in record stores as well.)

Books don't have to 'go', Take your time before you walk them

It never intensifies security's suspicion if one spends a long time browsing in a bookstore . Use this fact to your advantage. Browse a lot. Even the best-organized bookstores have 'blind spots' somewhere between their shelves. Use those blind spots. To hide a book is the easiest thing in the world. It slides nicely under your arm inside your shirt. It fits in your crotch, covered with a loose T-shirt or pullover. It can be hidden on your back, partially tucked into the waist of your pants and held in place by suspenders. over which you wear a loose-fitting jacket or sweater. Some times even a simple pocket will do.

Think twice about stealing from small bookstores. Many of our sources told us that they do not feel comfortable hurting small book shops owned by real book enthusiasts who make very little or no money. Go for the big ones. Special, rare books can also be taken from libraries. Their security systems usually suck and are always easy to circumvent. Again, use your 'moral standards.'

It is not nice to break the little guy's neck

Note from the authors: While doing our research, we tried very hard to find Abbie Hoffman's infamous *Steal This Book*. It seems the title has worked extremely well. We could not locate a copy anywhere. Our knowledge about his opinions had to be built on word of mouth or other literary sources that mentioned him. Had he been wise enough to give his book a different title, it could still be educating the 'interested public.'

Do not steal this book.... from a library!

One more thing. Many bookstores have office supply or cassette sections. Because these items are not their main merchandise (or profit makers), they watch them with less diligence. On the other hand, for some strange reason, they are always out to get the guys who loiter around leafing through the magazines (checking out the 'skin'). Maybe they assume (and by now, we know that security experts assume a lot) that a magazine is easier to steal than an eighty-dollar college textbook. Or perhaps they believe that a guy who ogles skin pix has such low moral standards he cannot be anything but a thief.

Tail wagging is for Fido, not a book aficionado!

DRUGSTORES

"The desire to take medicine is perhaps the greatest feature which distinguishes man from animals."

(Sir William Osler)

Your everyday-use items are there. Hardly anything to make a profit on, but to shrink your budget to the minimum, it might worth the trouble. Shampoos, combs, brushes, toothpaste, make-up - if you have to buy them - do add up. A general piece of advice is that you buy whatever you cannot possibly steal, and conceal whatever you can.

Bear necessities of life

Drugstores are usually crowded. They are watched with cameras and very often have store-detectives or 'mystery shoppers' (mostly minority women. - nobody told us why).

Kaa of the Rock is trying to see you!

The experiences of our sources tells us that drugstores almost always prosecute for shoplifting, exasperated as they are by being the target of a great many non-professional shoplifters. Almost all of these stores are, as we mentioned, very heavily policed by plainclothesmen. This formidable presence should deter the budding, inexperienced shoplifter, but the real, smart lifter need not worry.

You don't want to be taken to the Council Rock!

We cannot say it often enough. Be careful. EAS is being used more and more in drugstores, but you will find that they tag only special items like expensive make-up or small appliances. Other expensive items such as cigarettes, films and cameras are usually kept out of reach on shelves behind the cashier's counter.

Drugs are easy, Man cub. Do drugs!

"You remember the Tylenol scandal. Since then any over-the-counter medicine is free for the taking. The stores don't dare to tamper with the original packages."

Many items like over-the-counter drugs cannot be tampered with, and so if they have any kind of devices attached to them, said devices will be on the outside packaging and therefore visible.

Don't go with the Pack(age)!

Most of the articles you might bring home from a drugstore are very easily concealed. Their only protection is some fancy or extra-large packaging. If it is possible, remove the packaging and take only the item itself. The box and/or any other removed packaging can be easily discarded behind, say, a row of soap or detergents. Some expensive articles that are kept strictly behind the counters may sometimes seem within your reach, but you ought to go for them only if the coast is clear. It is not the best idea even then, however, since the same articles might be found on display in large department stores. Drugstore sections in big department stores or grocery stores are very rarely watched.

Shere Khan says: Do you like gum? Chocolate?

One more thing. Just as gas-stations do, drugstores keep gum, chocolate bars and other small goodies right at your fingertips at the cashier's counter. While you are paying, why not load your pocket with something to chew - or some sweets for the road?

FOOD STORES

"Let the stoics say what they please,
we do not eat for the good of living, but because
the meat is savory and the appetite is keen."

(Ralph Waldo Emerson)

"My buddies always kept laughing at me because I kept going out to boost in the supermarkets. They were working in video cassettes, music CD's, and expensive clothing. But I

tell you, those little one-thirty-twos and four-twenty-fives add up."

Supermarkets have the lowest 'shrinkage rates,' and therefore theirs is usually the most relaxed security system around, but you never know! They might have cameras or EAS. Or detectives. Even 'ghost shoppers'! Case the place and deal with them accordingly.

Skimpy security

"Food stores are usually good, but there is a No-Name chain store I know in a poor neighborhood where they protect the onion as if it was Russian caviar. They have EAS on the bean-cans! I prefer to go to the better stores anyway."

The corner stores aren't likely to have any technology better than convex mirrors, but if you can avoid it, do not hurt these little guys even though you might feel that some of them deserve it for their inflated prices.

Ma' and Pa' 'disrobed' in front of the mirror

Electronic devices are usually attached only to those items that the store deems to be popular with shoplifters because of their resale value. If you know your store, you will find these devices easy to remove. EAS is usually found on extravagant cheeses, cold-cuts, meat, or other somewhat expensive stuff. Many times selected items will change according to shopping trends. Follow the trends.

Always look for the 'blind spot' (By now you've heard about it, and you'll hear more.). Pack and conceal only when you are absolutely alone or very well covered. Isolation or a very good cover is also required when you are busy cracking the plastic packing on those items that you suspect may have EAS stickers. Sometimes you cannot see these stickers because they are hidden under the meat or stuck onto the plastic tray from the inside. These stores always provide you with plastic bags for fruit and vegetables. Use one to re-pack the merchandise, and you are home free. The discarded packaging will only get the janitor caught. (Advice to janitors: Check the garbage before walking the meat!)

Strip the meat!

As a rule of thumb you should always buy something: milk, bread, cat food, whatever you need and would never 'collect.' If you are planning to take some meat, first get it into your cart and then continue shopping. Later, when your cart (use the child seat if you can) has a large number of other items (some of which you can discard later), the meat and other stuff can neatly disappear.

Where is the venison!?!

"I was kind of green-eared about large food-stores and very inexperienced when this happened. I packed my cart, the child seat... you know what folds back, so, okay... packed it with meat. I was walking calmly in the empty aisles... I'm telling you I checked very carefully; they were empty.... Anyway, I was certain that nobody watched me

The vanishing venison!

packing them away one by one. Okay. I never thought that one of the spooks picked me out from afar when I was collecting the meat into the cart and later he saw me again with the empty cart. He was waiting for me outside. You see, if I'd had the cart packed full with cheap and bogus items, it would have spared me a conviction and a hundred-dollar fine..."

Delicious ideas

Food stores usually have only one exit. Frequent those that have two or more. It is also good to be there with a car (a car, by the way, is probably the most important tool of a professional shoplifter). A partner (preferably one about your age and of the opposite gender) is invaluable in food stores, providing both of you with the cover of being a couple out doing the marketing. It is a nice touch to have a shopping list in hand to convey the impression that a real shopper is wandering around the store. To stop in a good 'blind spot' can be even more secure if you use the time to look into the store's pamphlets, clumsily trying to remove some coupons they have there.

MUSIC AND VIDEO STORES

"Music for the neck downwards."

(Keith Richards)

The Music Makers. Ode from the Enigma Variations

Unlike supermarkets, music and video stores are hit the heaviest by pros and amateurs alike. In the war against shoplifters, they are probably the best-protected stores (well, best-equipped anyway). There are some that are impossible to 'crack.' The ones, for example, where everything is on display but every plastic box is empty and you have to go with the empty sleeve to ask for the CD or cassette at the counter. Ugly.

"I know a couple of music stores where I never go. They have these big plastic boxes with the radio alarm inside. I say why bother?"

Aluminium Fandango. Opus 6

A short note. This shoplifter has probably never considered using an aluminum-foil-lined bag or pocket. The real 'heavies' are not flummoxed by unbreakable plastic boxes with buzzers inside. They know that aluminum foil foils the system. A real pro lines his pocket or a bag with foil and then plunks in the article.

As we will discuss in detail at another place in our book, one good method is to ask a question you know they can't answer. Asking whether they have *Výlety Pana Brouèka* conducted by Domenico da Nola in stock will humble any salesman. If you are not looking for a specialty item, and only work for resale, it is a good bet that in department store music sections you can find what you want in an atmosphere where security is more lax. Same goes for videos. You have to experiment to find the best source stores, but never get too comfortable. The set-up can change from one day to the other - fast.

Der Fliegende Holländer, Mondestrunken, Saudades das Selvas Brasileiras, Der Dandy, Výlety Pana Brouèka Orlando finto pazzo, L'inconazione di Dario, Eine blasse Wäscherin, Der kranke Mond, Rote Messe, Geimeinheit Parodia, Il cimento dell' armonia e dell' inentione, Der Mondfleck und Serenade, Heimfahrt, O alter Duft....

Music and video stores have various security devices. Cameras are often employed. The most utilized anti-theft device in these stores is EAS. Surprisingly, some of the larger 4-6 CD operas or other CD collections are without tags or stickers because the security people have been 'thinking' again: "Oh, they will be too bulky to conceal, and who would want them, anyway?"

Generally, it is easy to remove the EAS tag or sticker if the store provides good blind spots. With a small penknife, or an old-fashioned razor blade, you can smoothly remove the cellophane together with the EAS tag stuck onto it (the noise will be less noticeable than it would be if you ripped the tag). You have to discard the cellophane cautiously, and with the least possible noise (do not crumple it). In a store you don't know well, it is advisable to open the item and thoroughly check its contents. You might find another device cunningly hidden under the covers.

Smaller, second-hand stores might be a good place to hunt. If one still 'collects' LPs, the right way of hiding them is to put them behind a back suspender (women can wear suspenders, too, these days), sliding one corner partially into your pants and then covering the deed with a loose jacket or coat. Since that fateful day when LPs disappeared from the music market, their prices (sometimes they are sold in their original jacket, unopened) have sky-rocketed. For the money-oriented pro shoplifter, boosting LPs has become a very profitable new venue because some of them are priced at over a hundred dollars. The one mentioned in the above side-note is definitely priceless.

The original LP of Mario Lanza and Maria Callas in The Velvet Underground

Video stores are similar to music stores. The only difference is that the manufacturer does not allow retail outlets to tamper with the original packaging of videos offered for sale, so finding an EAS tag would be a real surprise.

No hidden surprises....

"It is for promotional reasons. They might have a coupon inside, or for pure copyright conflicts. Also because they fear pirating. 'This-and-that' (I am not authorized to name them) company will forbid us to open their original packaging..." (A Security Manager of a Large Music Chain)

..but anything can happen in the moving pictures.

However unlikely it is, do not get cocky about it! It might happen against all odds that there is a device inside a video offered for sale. If possible, cut open the cellophane and check inside.

Unlike music CDs and cassettes, videos are rented as well as sold by stores. Most rentals are not available on the shelves, but there might be some rare stores which display their rental tapes, trusting the almighty EAS tag or sticker, which is always easily removable. Although the sales section is likely to be equipped with an EAS system, most stores rarely use any surveillance in the rental section, giving the lifter an excellent opportunity to browse aimlessly after lifting a new tape.

CLOTHING STORES AND CLOTHING DEPARTMENTS

"People ask how can a Jewish kid from the Bronx do preppy clothes? Does it have to do with class and money? It has to do with dreams."

(Ralph Lauren)

The hardship of picking cotton

Clothing is the most profitable merchandise for the professional shoplifter. He frequently harvests it for resale to a fence. Sometimes, however, he simply reduces his living expenses by 'shopping' for himself or his family. Security devices vary from store to store and must be checked out thoroughly beforehand.

Jack and Jill went 'round the store to fetch a...

High fashion, classy stores are best hit with a partner, if possible one of the opposite sex. Their sales people will come straight up to you and help you until you buy something or die. Their attention, however, leaves your partner free to graze the field. In these stores there are so many methods to use and so many types of articles to bamboozle 'em out of, that it would be impossible to cover them all. The golden rule: know your size, know what you want, and then be comfortably fast. But where, you ask, can you pack away such large items as pants and dresses?

The folding and piling of the sheaves

"There is something to be said about how you walk - how loose, how your hands move; it is something you have to learn and experiment with at home in front of your mirror. And the absolute skill. The fold. Everything is in the fold. How you fold them shirts, them pants and dresses."

You can hide articles safely, provided that they are neatly folded, almost anywhere. You can put them behind your back (suspenders). You can hook them under over-garments. You can stick them in your crotch with a comfortably large pullover. But never forget that to hide an item of clothing effectively, you must be able to fold it into the smallest and flattest shape possible. After proper folding, concealment is almost as easy as falling off a log.

A particularly efficient way to do your folding is to use the fitting rooms. Stores have different policies about their booths: One can take only a certain number of articles. One has to be accompanied by a sales clerk. Only the sales clerk has the key. One has to be given a tag with the number of articles taken in. And there are other 'cool tricks.'

Guarding the silo from the rodents

"They give you this ridiculous numbered tag. If you take two pants, the tag says '2'. They feel safe. Dandy. None of them know that I already packed away the third pair of pants, tidily under my arm. The one that fits me. The other two are just for cover. I'll go in the fitting room, cut the tags and all other stuff from the pants I'm gonna liberate... When I come out I give the woman the tag that says '2' and give back the two pairs. If I feel like chatting, I tell her about how they didn't fit or how the style was not me, or ask her if she had it in purple or some other nonsense. No way I will pick up a tail after that!"

A barn trick

It is one elegant and refined strategy! You do not steal an article from the store but rather from a fitting booth, using polished concealment methods and skills. All rules about 'dressing up' apply here as well as at any other place. You cannot look much bigger when you come out than you did when you entered. If you wear the stolen article, pants have to be folded inside socks, skirts pinned up to underwear, shirts' collars opened and folded back. The article has to be checked for any EAS tags before you leave the booth, or even before you take it in there (sometimes there are buzzer gates on the booth itself-watch out!). The privacy of the booth insures safety for carrying out these concealment procedures.

Roll up your sleeves to do the milking

One must be wary, however, of an annoying policy followed at some stores. They advertise it on the fitting room doors and inside as well.

"This fitting room is under the supervision of our Security Department. Our fitting room inspector may enter unannounced from time to time to check merchandise." (SECURITY MANAGEMENT, 1984))

Laws change like the wind, and so there may have been some kind of privacy challenge before the courts at some point in time since 1984. We do know that most legislators consider video surveillance or two-way mirrors in fitting rooms to be an invasion of privacy, and we agree.

Keeping the peeping under control

SHOE STORES

> ***"Boots and shoes are the greatest trouble of my life. Everything else one can turn and turn about, and make old look like new; but there's no coaxing boots and shoes to look better than they are."***
>
> *(George Eliot)*

Where is the right shoe?

Many stores display only one shoe per pair. Unless you go with a partner and do some serious acting to create a diversion, these stores will not provide you with a complete pair to lift. Smaller discount shops, or larger department stores, on the other hand, display shoes in pairs or boxes.

In with the old, out with the new!

A somewhat risky but workable method is to wear an old pair of rejectable shoes, try on a couple of pairs, keep the pair you like on your feet, discard the old shoes, and leave. If you work fast, and if you are in a large and busy store with no sales people in sight, chances are above par that nobody will notice. (Remove all tags; a penknife could help to cut the plastic strings.) We read about a man who did this and, when caught, talked his way out of a charge by saying that he was only going outside to look at them in the sunlight. There **is** something new under the sun - this guy's story!

If the shoe fits!

Another procedure is to hide the shoes on one's person. One good hiding place is the crotch (the shoes' soles facing out). You could hang the shoes on a hook under your skirt or coat. Or you might put one under the right arm and the other under the left arm. It is important to realize that this 'underarm technique' requires experience and a certain amount of training in the art of mime. After you have trained for awhile, you will be able to maintain a firm hold with your upper arm while the lower arm is swinging along naturally. If you have a partner, one of you can leave with the right shoe, and the other can carry off the left one.

HARDWARE STORES

> ***"But lo! men have become the tools of their tools."***
>
> *(Henry David Thoreau)*

Tool time!

Hardware stores are similar to drugstores in the sense that they provide you with your daily, "simple, bear necessities... of life." You, like everybody else, need tools, batteries, electrical supplies - in short, almost everything that they sell there. They rarely use EAS as a security device, but if they do, the tags are placed only on small, very expensive items such as batteries, which with their high prices tempt even the most honest shoppers. Management might chain any unboxed appliances to the display shelves, annoying you with the task of having to remove the boxed ones from their packaging. However, they are kind enough to leave the boxed appliances in handy locations.

Hardware stores differ from drugstores in one important aspect. They have a very polite and helpful sales force. Because the mandate of a good hardware store is always to be of help, ready to answer the questions of amateur handymen and women, help will always be available. Don't turn it down. Let them help you. Ask for something unusual - something analogous to the rare opera recording that humbled 'em in the music store.

Sticking to you like glue

"In a hardware store, you can ask a lot. You can even tire the guy, so he will leave you alone. If you can find something, that he has to look for in the storage area, you are free of him for awhile. Sometimes I just tell them I'm here to check out their prices..."

Because of the statistics compiled by those wonderful scientists, hardware stores expect the average shoplifter to be a middle-aged male. If you fit that description, your best bet would be to show up as a teenage female (expected in drug stores). Could cross-dressing be the answer?

The sexist disadvantage. Male bashing!

These stores confront you with another annoying tic besides sexual stereotyping. Most of their merchandise comes in some kind of special packaging such as a box, a paper-plastic combination cover, or a large plastic bag. The rule of thumb here dictates that you are better off if you leave the packaging material behind, taking only the actual article. Remember, though (in case you are thinking of opening your own hardware store), that unpacked hardware items have almost no resale value.

Joe's Janitorial Supplies

COMPUTER STORES

"Man is still the most extraordinary computer of all."

(John F. Kennedy)

The adventurous and trendy lifter will find two types of computer stores on the 'information highway'. The first type is the small, independent computer store - slash - service-provider, usually operated by one person alone. This kind of store is of a very modest size, hence easy to supervise. There is usually a poorly stocked inventory, and they will only obtain expensive items from their suppliers if you place an order with them. Anyway, if you have the same soft spot for small businessmen that most of our smart lifters do, you would not want to hurt one of them. Even if you are cruel, considering the empty shelves in these one-horse stores, you have no business being there.

To get the chips, don't go to the cheaps

Because they are in the electronics business anyway, these small operators are likely to use video surveillance, which in most

Little Bro's growing pains

cases serves only one purpose (as in many other small stores of other types): to record on a videotape, in a loop or in intervals, the history of the day. If there is a hold-up, armed robbery, credit card fraud, assault, or injury, it is sure to be recorded. At the end of the day the store might have your nimble finger movements somewhere on the video (if you were careless). Not to worry. If the manager has neither watched nor suspected you, the next morning the tape, and thus the evidence, will be erased.

Kilo chairs, mega chocolates and giga chalks

The other type is THE PLACE. The Gigantic Super Store, where they try to sell you everything you might need. Anything that you have ever wanted, don't need, or didn't even know existed. The whole shebang. From erasers to furniture, ink to modems, tacks to full multi-media computer systems. There are pencils and telephones, loads of outdated, unusable software packages and books, a pile of CD-ROM's priced at a quarter - the list is endless.

Since their size is enormous, with floor-to-ceiling shelves and a big labyrinth of aisles, the opportunity-seeking smart lifter can easily find 'blind spots' and corners where he can open packages containing computer programs or CD-ROMs, remove the software and instructions, and conceal these items on his person.

Dumbness is the wisdom of the smart lifter

Preparing specific questions beforehand really works well for computer store boosting. Knowing about some novelty that is not out on the market and asking for help finding it in the amazing maze of aisles always proves useful in creating some space for yourself. Long browsing is accepted as the normal behavior of legitimate shoppers, so you can spend as much time as you wish. Knowing exactly which item you have come for and where they keep it enables you to find the merchandise fast and then spend all the time you want doing 'legitimate' browsing or diffusing suspicion with your prefabricated inquiries. In a word, spend some time and energy on 'catch-prevention'.

IF, ELSEIF, THEN, GOTO,

These large computer stores have either video or EAS. They also have a large number of helpful salesmen (deterrent), who are kept really busy with other customers (encouragement). If you were a legitimate shopper, you would still have to wait a long time until one of them became available to help you (open invitation).

These stores trust the deterrence value of over-sized packaging. They put a small computer disk or a CD-ROM in a large, usually very attractive paper box sealed in plastic. It is your task to free those itsy-bitsy items from their large prisons and take them home.

DISCOUNT STORES

"Everything can be had so dirt cheap that one begins to wander whether in the end anyone will want to make a bid."

(Oliver Wendell, Sr. Holmes)

Discount stores occupy their own uniquely tasteless category. Because their patrons (in large urban areas) are likely to be from ethnic minorities, so are the shoplifters they catch. This fact reinforces social and racial stereotypes in the mindset and ensuing policies of security personnel. They pursue members of these groups with special vigilance.

Don't bother to bid, brother!

At first glance, these stores appear to be easy targets for smart lifters. Yet, in reality they are not. Only amateur shoplifters choose to steal there, and, as the data show, large numbers of them get caught like clockwork with their under-a-dollar items. Statistics on the sizable number of thefts which occur, and on the very high number of apprehensions, show a disproportionate social picture, further reinforcing stereotypes.

Don't bother to lift!

Like poor folks who think they can find something at an incredible bargain price in these stores, shoplifters who hunt for bargains there are bound to be cheated out of their 'money.' It is a waste of boosting energy to snatch such incredibly cheap, useless and low quality merchandise. You are better off not going to these places at all. Simple, down-to-earth logic dictates that there is no difference in the risks (in any store by the way) of stealing a cheap, low quality item or a more expensive, and probably more enduring, higher quality article. About that, one of our shop owner sources had this somewhat twisted question in his head:

Don't bother to go!

"I understand that they steal because they are hungry. I even pity them sometimes. The thing what makes me angry that those bums come in and steal my best, most expensive stuff ... then I really hate them." (Anonymous Shop Owner)

We did not tell him so then (note: as anybody can see the guy is seriously infected with hatred against the poor), but we can tell you now that he is completely out of touch! Is the punishment for stealing a pound of chicken-bologna with pasta and processed-cheese pieces different from the one doled out for lifting a pound of black forest ham? - No! - So, why in God's name would any hungry shoplifter go for the stuff that makes everybody puke?

I am hungry, not stupid!

"I used to steal only what I really needed. I didn't go for quality. Then I started to think. Does it really matter if I am caught with the ninety-nine cent chicken wieners, or the more then three dollar quality all beef hot dogs. Be reasonable. There is no difference. If they caught me, which I

doubted would happen, I would be still in the 'theft under a thousand dollar' category. And stores that sell higher quality are expecting much fewer shoplifters, than the ones with the cheap stuff."

In closing, let us say once more that no smart lifter should ever darken the door of a discount store-and neither should anybody else!

MALLS AND DEPARTMENT STORES

> ***"The new shopping malls make possible the synthesis of all consumer activities, not least of which are shopping, flirting with objects, idle wandering, and all the permutations of these."***
>
> *(Jean Baudrillard)*

Ambience? Make it so!

At the malls - unless you are ready to walk in for one special item and then go home - you cannot shoplift effectively without a car. Another potentially unfortunate fact about mall boosting is that malls have added security, but since these professional spooks are in the hallways and not in the stores, 'shopping' may actually be easier for you. The choice of the mall is crucial. We don't advise working in downtown malls or those in poor neighborhoods. The best ones are out of the city, in the suburbs, in a smaller town, or a wealthy neighborhood. A little research goes a long way. You want to find malls with very well-known, reputable stores in them. The prices charged are a good indicator of what kind of neighborhood they serve.

Ten Forwards, Promenades, Hollow-Decks and Replicators with little short-order cooks inside.

Of course there are hundreds of stores in a mall. The really good targets there are the department stores (see more below) and the smaller, overstocked little stores where one can hardly move. The great advantage of a mall is that it has several exits to facilitate your getaway. Malls also provide comfort stations for worn-out 'shoppers,' enabling them to fix a weakening hold on the merchandise or just change the 'diapers' on it. Be careful with the disposal of packaging materials. Somebody might be in the next stall. The best place to chuck them is in one of the large garbage bins in the restaurant areas.

Find parking, Spock!

If you arrive at the mall in a car, do not park close to the entrance in the vain hope of making a quick getaway on wheels. If you have to run away (Beam me up, Scotty!), you cannot head for your car, anyway, or they will get your license plate number.

Bioenergy contra fossil fuel!

Never think of a car as a good getaway. If the security people are behind you, they will call the police to give them a description of your car and report the direction you are headed. Trust your running shoes. Always leave your car alone. You can send back a friend to retrieve it. If the lot is big enough, and you have parked reasonably far from the store you hit, you can even go back for it yourself.

"Three of them were running after me. Steady, strong fellows. I had only a couple of things, which I dropped, but one of them kept coming after me. I passed my car; ran some more. He kept coming. I had to scale a fence at the highway before finally he gave up. Believe me, I was out of breath. Totally. It took me a good twenty minutes to compose myself. Later, around six o'clock, I sneaked back for my car."

Tractor beam, counter measures

Always pay strict attention to your surroundings before leaving. Check carefully, on the sly, to see whether you are being followed. Even if you have passed the store's exit, security can still be in pursuit of you. Check again before you leave the mall, but never turn back to look without miming a credible excuse. Try to find an article to check out in a shop window. Hunt for your wallet or car keys. And while you are taking one of these evasive actions, search for any possible pursuers from the corner of your eye.

Evasive action Gamma Three!

The large department stores are very similar to the malls. They provide you with many exits. They are usually multileveled, sometimes eight or nine stories high. They have escalators and elevators, both being somewhat adequate places for packing away. Look out, though, for the extra gates that buzz when you leave one floor to go to another. An unfortunate interpretation of the law allows their personnel to apprehend you upon leaving the floor where the item is sold.

yolpa'Daq yIjaH

The levels have different departments designed and built as small separate stores. Modern department stores, as a matter of fact, have created mini-malls which contain these mini-stores all on one level, with walls and separate entrances. Sometimes there are even separate anti-shoplifting systems.

The great thing about modern department stores is their enormous size, offering countless hiding places and 'blind spots'. And they have departments! Furniture. Linens. Office Supplies. Toys! Often, these divisions completely lack any traffic. They have restaurants for sitting down to secure some hastily concealed item. They provide rest-rooms for your convenience. Sadly, they also have the latest security systems, EAS, CCTV and Ink-Tags. (Don't fret, we will address these 'dangers' later!) The experienced and skilled lifter can spend a pleasant time learning the place. In fact, only after he has done so should he start 'working'.

Several places to cloak!

THE MORAL OF THE PASSAGE

Very funny Scotty, now beam down my clothes!

Know your store better than the 'bad guys' do. If possible, try to shop, even if only for little items. Don't just steal things. Hang around the store only as long as the type of store allows. Ask questions, be friendly and humorous with the sales help. It is good to know what they don't have, so you can ask for it (over and over again). Follow the trends. Cautiously go for the item everybody buys (or tries to lift).

WHAT AND HOW

"An ounce of action is worth a ton of theory."

(Friedrich Engels)

METHODS AND BEHAVIOR

"For every flowering thought there will be a page like a wet and mangy mongrel, and for every looping flight a tap on the wing and a reminder that wax cannot hold the feathers firm too near the sun."

(John Steinbeck)

Methods. Our sources (ex-pros, pros, skilled and unskilled amateurs) described many good, bad, brilliant and worthless schemes to us, each requiring knowledge, confidence, experience, and/or guts. None of them is foolproof.

Guts 'n' brains!

As we evaluated each method, we had to keep all the other components of the lifting process in mind. The different methods described in this section of our little 'chef d'oeuvre' never constitute complete and safe formulas by themselves. Shoplifting is a complex practice. Every time one lifts, the circumstances involve many elements. That is one reason why we have coined a new name for those shoplifters who distinguish themselves from the rest of the pack. These superstars of lifting are talented, experienced and cautious. They are truly 'smart' lifters. Whether they work for fences or steal only for themselves, they are rarely caught because of their cautious assessments of different scenarios. They continually and almost automatically analyze the risks and benefits of any lifting experience.

Instincts 'n' reflexes!

Many times we do not comment. Let our 'friends' 'do the talking.' At other times, when, for example, a 'friend' was fairly inarticulate or several sources described the same method, we have taken the liberty of rewriting what we heard. We comment on the brilliance or stupidity of a given scheme whenever the spirit moves us to do so.

Let them talk! They did the walk!

THE BIG SWITCH

Partners. A pair of shoplifters goes out together. They have agreed upon methods of concealing loot, packing at the right time in the right place, visiting a fitting room, etc. The most artful partnering scheme has one of them just waiting. He walks around behaving like a regular customer, or he simply sits in an empty

Simulated weakness postulates strength

fitting room. His partner works, hides stuff, and 'furtively glances over his shoulder,' directly inviting the attention of security.

The 'lifter' (the decoy) might also carry a large bag, wear a coat on his shoulders, or dangle other suspicion-raising items in front of security's nose. His job is to make sure that he will be picked up as a suspect. If he does his job well, security will either follow him or wait for him at the exit. After suspicion has been created, at an appropriate moment the 'big switch' takes place. The decoy leaves the stuff he has openly collected at a foreordained location in the store where his buddy can smoothly pick it up.

Then, still drawing store security's attention with his 'clumsiness,' the decoy leaves and is apprehended. While the spooks are dealing with him - taking him back into the store to search him - his carefree partner waltzes off with the loot.

THE CIRCULAR DISPLAY RACK

A boy-girl team told us about this scheme. We find their tale a bit on the fantasy-fiction side, but here it is.

Even the most unwieldy strategy triumphs sometimes!

"Frankie, at a good moment when nobody was around, climbed under a pants-rack. You know, those round ones with a hundred pants hanging all around them. I just kept on looking for jeans. Time after time I went over with a pair - we had a fence for jeans - and dropped it onto the floor next to Frankie, between the pants. He just picked it up and packed it away. In his ski-jacket, three pairs went on his back, two on the side, one in his crotch. Really, Frankie looked like a balloon when he came out. Went straight to the exit. I knew I could not have a tail since nobody seen me around packing. (...) We made it with six jeans in every turn, so at the end of the week, we delivered fifty-four pairs of jeans to the fence. He didn't even have enough money to pay us right away."

THE RECEIPT

The bold shall inherit the inventory!

Go to the store early in the morning and choose four or five things whose resale value you can calculate. Pick items which you can store easily and which will be of use to you later on even though you may be over-supplied with them at the moment When the cashier offers to put them in a sack, open your sports bag and ask him to place the items in there - or just do it yourself. It's good to make sure he notices that you have used your bag. After leaving the store, discard the items either in your car or at home. Keep the receipt.

Return and lift the same items over and over again, concealing them in your bag at a good 'blind spot' to avoid detection. The only soft spot in the scheme is that somebody might see you slipping the stuff in your bag, so be careful. Next, choose and buy some small item. After paying, once more refuse the store's bag and use your own. Of course you can also follow this plan without the extra shopping.

In case you are stopped, you have irrefutable proof that you have paid for those items. You have the receipt. You can say that you forgot to buy something and have returned to do so. Your chances for repeating this 'act' are in direct proportion to the number of exits and cashiers. You can repeat the scheme until you are stopped for the first time.

Unbeatable proof

If you are shameless, brazen and audacious enough, you can also, as a last blow to the store, return the original selection of items and ask for a refund.

THE RECEIPT, A SEQUEL

Another, seemingly very tall tale. It is about receipts found on the floor.

"You just look for receipts - everywhere. I got the habit when I was working as a buyer for a company, and I was able to make some extra money with extra receipts. Like I was buying them - tools, coffee and sugar, drinks, office supplies, everything. I added a couple of extra receipts from the floor and part of the petty cash was buying me a couple of bottles of booze. Anyway, you can find even receipts for TV's and stereos and refrigerators stapled onto the boxes the guys put out for garbage on the curb. Then you only have to find the store, stick it on a box and walk with it. If they stop you can scream at them: "What the @%?! you mean, stopping me! I got a receipt you bum!"

A laborious idea for the meek!

Note: Never scream at a security guard! They won't take it kindly. They will make every effort to provide you with a hearty breakfast in the canteen at the county jail as soon as possible.

BUY THE STORE

Really? Not really. Almost, though! The idea is that you will seem to be a less suspicious person if security sees you apparently doing some real shopping. There are two slightly different ways of executing this clever scheme. The first way is to start doing some real shopping after you have finished your boosting. Select anything at all, regardless of whether you want it. Your loot is concealed. You are ready to leave. Your shopping cart is filled with goods as if you were shopping for a family of four for

What do you mean, buy!?

a week. Go to the check-out counter and let the cashier start ringing up your purchases. How long you let him work really depends on how cruel you are. Anyway, at one point you 'realize' that you have no money. Never had it, it is in the car, in your other pants, it went up in smoke when you lit your cigar this morning - make up your excuse as you go. Now, tell the cashier that he should keep your purchase for you until you get money (from your bank, from home, from the moon...). He will be more than happy to do that for you, especially if you let the whole purchase be punched in. Security's suspicion level plummets close to zero, and you are safe or safer to leave with the plunder.

Yes, we do mean buy!

A slightly different take on this method is to enlarge your 'cover shopping' and mix in articles which you are actually going to pay for. (In this 'variation on a theme,' you don't leave the store without making a nice, friendly purchase.) At the check-out, you pull out your money and 'realize' that you do not have enough. (You have prepared your cash beforehand, putting in the exact amount for the couple of items that you actually need and will really buy.) Finally, you 'choose' the items that you deem necessary and give back all the 'cover' stuff. To make matters even friendlier, you offer to take the items you cannot buy now back to the shelves. Once in a blue moon they may accept this offer, but most of the time they will not. In any case, you have avoided suspicion and gone down in their books as one of the good guys.

You must not fight too often the same enemy, or you will teach him all your arts of war

This method is one you seldom use in the stores in your own neighborhood. You should make a list of the stores you do hit with this method, writing down the precise date of every lifting visit. Avoid each of them for quite awhile afterward. Remember, as far as the personnel there know, nothing 'criminal' has happened. They do not suspect you of shoplifting, but if you are caught short of money too often they are likely to catch on.

Excessive knowledge is an impediment to effective action

Another warning: Because security professionals keep trying to upgrade their skills, they do eventually learn (or at least they are told [we are telling them (and you) now]) that a full cart does not always mean an honest shopper. But, then, these earnest souls are continually being hit with new information which tends to contradict their cherished principles of operation, thus badly confusing them. (In this respect, they are like the general public, which keeps hearing that something it loves is bad for it, gives it up, and then is informed that the original warning was based on silly research.) The final attitude taken by professional spooks toward all the contradictory knowledge which is hammered into their heads, and which ultimately tells them to suspect everybody, is to flush out the whole lot of it as basically bad and return to their own flawed assumptions, usually based on that most comfortable of psychological assets - instinct. A poor thing. A flawed thing. Maybe sometimes a racist or sexist thing. But their own.

THE REFUND

You ***almost*** steal a smaller electronic or household appliance, value irrelevant. You go around the store a couple of times with the item concealed on your person. Then, at an appropriate moment, it 'appears' in your hands and you go straight to the refund counter to request a refund, or, even better, an exchange for it. You tell the cashier that you tried it at home and it did not work, your wife didn't like it, you have found one of better quality - what have you.

Fastidious preparation is half the battle won.

This scheme might also work with larger items such as VCRs, stereos, phones etc. The only problem is that you have to open the packaging, get rid of some stuff (the Styrofoam or carton parts wrapped around the thing), and maybe rip open the plastic packaging inside. Place the manual in your pocket! You must create the illusion that you have opened the box at home and then packed it back up. To do this, you have to be in a true 'no-see zone,' or find a great cover - large shelves; a bunch of boxes. You also have to be 'tooled' (knife, scissors, etc.) to be able to do the unpacking. If you are unlucky enough to be caught opening the box, you can play the 'idiot shopper' who wanted to see the stuff before buying it. In any case, opening a package does not constitute shoplifting.

Okay. So, now, after you have told your little story, they give you the exchange or the money. If not - if they want a receipt (and in most cases nowadays, they do), you tell them you lost it, your daughter bought the item, your wife threw it out, or the dog ate it. Any excuse will do.

Inspired performance brings the victory!

Some stores, as we all know, have a policy of 'no receipt, no refund'. Big deal. If they are reluctant to give you the refund without the receipt, you can start to huff and puff (and blow the house down), then angrily agree with them, saying that yes, you will go home and look for the damned receipt! Put the stuff under your arm, on your shoulder - even on the top of your head - and storm out of the store. If somebody else at the exit stops you, just tell him to go to hell. It was only a screwed-up attempt to return the thing. If your performance has been captivating, you will by now have gathered plenty of witnesses to back you up (and give you a hand.)

Capturing the loot with a captivating show

To sum up: Do research on the store layout, know it very well, and use your acting talent. Also, do not try this scheme at the same store more than once in a year. Stay on the safe side!

The Handyman's Off-Broadway gig

"Once we had a real beaut'! With a friend of mine we invented a scheme. In a building material store my buddy put two expensive doors on the cart, put it close to the counter, and left. Nobody seen him or bothered about him. In a couple of minutes I go in. Push the cart straight to the return counter and tell them a sob story about how my kitchen and part of my bedroom burned down and, since I didn't have no insurance, I was in trouble. I tell'm about these doors I had in my garage and thought, 'Might bring'em back and raise some extra cash money for the repairs I will have to make.' They asked where was the receipt. Told them.... it burned with the kitchen. They really felt sorry for me. We made about fourteen hundred dollars that day."

PRICE (TAG) SWITCHING

Can you teach a new bar code old tricks?

An age old trick. But safe. Nobody can prove that it was the lifter who switched the tag.(Look for more than one tag. There are clever store owners who tag some expensive articles twice or even more. One tag is visible; the other(s) is tucked in there somewhere.) Price tag switching is a scheme so old and safe that it is the one most often used by amateurs.

The 'merits' of tag switching have secured a prominent spot for it in the Proposed Shoplifting Code, which we shall discuss later. Unfortunately, the increased use of point-of-sales devices (bar code readers) is slowly rendering this method obsolete.

An inventive lifter couple uses a price-tag-printer to 're-price' articles. They remove all the old price-tags (which these days are composed of umpteen little parts to discourage tag switching) and then 'price' the item with their machine. One of them uses the machine; the other one actually lifts. The point of their method is not lowering the price, but creating proof - in case the actual lifter is caught - that the article has been bought in another shop. Remember, the retailer is required to prove that the item comes from his store. This method is labor-intensive, but apparently safe.

Prices of second-hand books might be lowered nicely with an eraser and a pencil. Also, with the same color pen and a bit of talent at graphics, you can reduce the price on any item. This ploy works very well where the price on the tag has already been reduced, in handwriting, a couple of times.

A somewhat cumbersome method, often used by housewives when out shopping for groceries, is to glue the bar code of a less expensive item to a more expensive one. If the perpetrator happens to be checked out by a bored and tired cashier, the deal may go through. Of course, there must be a large number of items legitimately purchased at the same time, making this method not only cumbersome and expensive, but also rather silly.

CHASSÉ

"When you are young and giddy you do a lot of goofy things. Once I bought something small like a set of steak-knives, and at the same time I was pushing a couple of sleeping bags together with my backpack through the checkpoint in an army supply store. While I was doing my little ballet exercise I involved the cashier in a very friendly conversation. After I paid and nonchalantly picked up the plastic bag she gave me, I picked up my backpack and my two brand new sleeping bags.. We were on our way to do some camping."

Pas de deux! Exeunt!

PREPARED QUESTIONS

A very useful method of 'catch-prevention' is to arrive at the store with the right questions in your head. Better yet, take a shopping list! Questions provide a cover if a vendor approaches you while you are browsing. With the right queries you can tire him out, send him looking for something in the store room, or just make him leave you alone.

Make them dance to your music!

"An excellent question is the one about a special item. You ask the guy how it works, how much it costs. You can ask about something you know they don't have. You can ask about which aisle you can find this or that. Ask about if he might have seen the wife or kid you lost. Ask about if they have it in another size, shape, with or without pockets or in another color. Where is the washroom, if they have one? Is the price right and can you expect a sale soon? You don't have to be a writer, and you don't have to act too much. Make up stupid questions...appropriate and simple..."

Remember the music store section?

MAKING FRIENDS

You can make friends either with the sales-help or another customer. The more relaxed you seem, the less suspicion falls on you. Make the folks around you laugh. Look like a normal person happily out shopping and enjoying himself. Being buddy-buddy with the cashier gets you out of the store with gratifying ease.

Win over the foot-soldiers and thereby achieve great results!

"Tell a joke. Give'em small talk. It is great to be able to pick out a 'ghost shopper' and involve him in a conversation about how ridiculously high you find the price of something. You tell him that he should not buy it here, because you saw it in another store for much less. Play him a little. It will be fun. He will get embarrassed and try to get far away from your annoying chit-chat. After all that, he's never gonna follow you. You can get on with your business..."

RUNNING

A battle won is a battle which we will not acknowledge to be lost

The shoplifter can be noticed and tailed inside the store, but he is usually apprehended outside, after the fact. There are several ways of dealing with the situation if one is caught or about to be caught. Running away is an option. Not a sound one - but an option. (We have heard about a case where a couple of eager security persons used handguns to shoot a shoplifter who was trying to run away. Not nice!) If you know the store and the surrounding neighborhood well, you should run. If you have a car parked somewhere close, you will have to come back for it later to pick it up. However, if you have dropped all or part of your loot and ran away, the security people may settle for recovering the merchandise and give up the idea of chasing you. If they do not abandon their pursuit, the one who is better prepared physically and mentally will win the race.

THE INSIDE RUNNING

Cool running

This is another type of 'running'. It happens inside the store. You have been made. You know it. A store detective is following you. You have spotted the tail. This is the time to give up. Until a shoplifter has left the store, or the area where he still has a chance to pay, nobody will or should attempt to apprehend him. You must simply get rid of what you have hidden on your person. Remaining calm is imperative. If they stop you, you can easily claim absent-mindedness and the willingness to pay. (Worst case scenario: You have unpacked the item. Improvise! Find a nice place for it on the display rack!) Otherwise, just walk around and put everything back. Nobody has ever been arrested for putting stuff back on store shelves. If you choose to be bold, you can even smile at the person who is tailing you. Leave, and for awhile you had better not visit the same store again. Next time

they might recognize you and wait for you outside.

FALLING DOWN

London Bridge is falling down, falling down, falling down...

"I had a list of twelve different large stores in the city and a couple more close by. Okay, I am just 'visiting' this one. All right. I pack away onto my back this package of this CD-ROM. They put them in these book-like boxes, it is too much trouble to open them...anyway.. I am walking out. Safe, I think. After a couple of steps, just before I reached the exit, somehow the damned box comes loose and I feel it is falling out. It was an on-the-spot invention, I swear I never heard of it before. As the box was falling, I dropped with it onto the ground like a sack of potatoes. Two girls from the checkout came over. They were very worried, and asked me if I hurt myself. I told them I was fine, when one of them handed me the CD-ROM. 'Sir, you dropped this..' It was really cute. They handed me my stuff as if on a silver platter."

Bordeaux wine is falling down, falling down, falling down...

"We were out to get some classy booze with my buddy from a wine store in a downtown mall. We were on foot and already packed with some stuff from other places. I gave him my stuff to hold and went into the store alone. I packed away three bottles and went to pay for the fourth. When the cashier was handling my plastic, I felt that one of the bottles began to slip. My buddy was standing outside, just in front of the door. I made a step toward him to 'give' him my bag. I was already outside the gates when the bottle did slip. It fell onto the marble floor and broke. I promptly dropped the bag with the other bottle, and told my buddy to pick up the first one and scram - drop it in the garbage. It was a nice store. Nice enough to replace the broken bottle. No charge. When I went back to the shelves to pick up my free replacement, I also loaded in another bottle of the other kind I so haplessly lost. I just secured it better. There is no decency left in this world."

GRAB AND RUN

Grab and grabber

The least intelligent, but sometimes workable, way of shoplifting. Take it literally. Grab the stuff and run out of the store. If you are in a good physical condition, you are an exercise-oriented lifter, by using this scheme, you can do your jogging on the job. Naturally, the spooks might see you, and if you have any brains he will never go back to that store again. So, really, it is just a waste of resources. Many amateurs must be doing it though, because if you look around, you will see that most stores feature barriers, labyrinths, double-doors on and around the exit, doors that open inwards, and other tricky devices to stop the 'grab-and-runners'.

WHOLE CARTING (A.K.A. DUCKING)

Grabbiest

Very similar to grab and run. Only very desperate, bold and violence-prone gangs of shoplifters do it. They fill the shopping cart to the rim with stuff and run out (or, to employ hood terminology, 'cart out' or 'duck out') from the store with it. Security advisors warn store owners that they should not pursue these guys, who are prone to be violent. Of course, they have a getaway car, most often a flat-bed truck, maybe even a stolen one, waiting outside. They dump all the stuff into the trunk of the car or onto the bed of the truck and speed away.

We consider this method a borderline case. It is shoplifting in a sense, but it can also be seen as robbery. There is no class, no finesse, no 'artful dodging,' about it, but it does have abhorrent aspects of violence. When we discussed it with our professional acquaintances, they invariably said that they would never go that low. We understand that desperation can make people do crazy things, but graduating to hard crime is beyond the pale.

BUZZ THROUGH THE GATE

Gates that have red lights and sirens work most of the time. If you forget to remove, or cannot remove, the radio, magnetic or audio tag, you will definitely activate them. If you have forgotten your aluminum foil at home, what can you do?

To boldly exit...

"With my friend we used to go out from the store together, exactly at the same time. I took the bag full of CDs while he stayed completely clean. Of course, the buzzer went off. I kept walking. My buddy played the amateur shoplifter who freezes at the exit. They came and asked him to go back with them. By then, I was out on the street walking away. They very quickly found out that it was some kind of error in the system and let my friend go. He got great apologies. I was sitting safely in the car by the time he came."

Where all others exit with you...

There you go. Another (dare-devilish, mind you!) way of beating the system. If you are not feeling bold, and are somewhat uncertain about whether you are carrying something that might set off the buzzer, there is a variation on this method. We heard from other sources who, when they are in the same situation, use legitimate shoppers as decoys. They wait for the right moment and then go through the exit together as a couple of regular people. When the buzzer goes off, the honest shoppers in the line are likely to stop, but our canny lifters just walk on as if nothing has happened. If this trick is too hot for you, do not touch it, but if you like some excitement, go ahead and try! You can still run if it goes wrong.

RUIN THEIR GATES

Break them!

We met a couple of 'desperados' who told us about disabling the gates themselves. Their method was to fall on a gate and break it. It seems a rather clumsy, if not violent, method, calling to mind the ploy of another lifter who spoke about setting a display rack of shirts on fire. But to each his own!

Cut them!

There are simpler and less aggressive methods of rendering the gates useless. If you follow the cable leading from the gate, you might be able to cut the wire. Some stores cover the wiring for exactly this reason, but only close to the door. We can say it has been done, since we were told so, but 'individual results may vary.'

Confuse them!

An even gentler and rather clever method is to get the security person to turn off the system. Of course, you cannot ask him to do it straight out, but you ***can*** put a magnetic sticker on the sole of your left (or right, we are not picky) shoe. Better yet, put it on your socks after trying on some shoes. Now. Walk through. The alarm goes off. They come to investigate. There is nothing on you. Just as they would do in an airport, they might ask you to empty your pockets and walk through again. Brungg! If you are indignant enough and they are puzzled silly, they might decide (or you might even ask them at this point) to switch off the system. If you do it with a couple of your buddies to back you up, it is almost certain that they will. Call the service department. Meanwhile their store is defenseless. (For good measure: you can go through once more to check if they have really made the disconnection.)

USING EMERGENCY EXITS

To an adventurous type of person, setting off an ear-splitting alarm by barreling through the emergency exit door and then sprinting off on a planned escape route - or jumping into a waiting getaway car (wow!) could be the day's - or his whole life's - greatest thrill. It is too desperate for our taste, but it does sound exciting...

Go ahead. Make your day!

Professional shoplifters told us that many stores (mainly big ones) have the alarm disconnected because of the disturbance it can innocently cause. Old ladies might mistake those secured doors for normal exits. (Their glasses are not with them. They decide to leave the store. They set off the alarm.) To check whether an alarm works, by all means open the door when nobody is around and then disappear fast inside the store. Do not go too far. Wait and enjoy the show. If you have found an exit that does not wake security, the store becomes your playground. If the alarm works, you can watch the show, acquainting yourself with store security while measuring their response time for a future thrill. Like pulling the emergency breaks on a train, opening an emergency exit door is an adolescent, childish prank, but if it works, you may have found the yellow brick road! Go ahead. Make your way!

BUMPING

Bumpers and droppers!

A very simple and boring scheme for creating a diversion is bumping into something or somebody and then using the temporary confusion to pocket or conceal the item you plan to 'acquire.' The level of suspicion this ploy focuses on you, however, will be in direct proportion to the confusion it creates.

We also heard from our sources about 'bumping' in a different sense, meaning a situation where you 'clumsily' drop a bunch of items or dump a myriad of articles onto the floor. While you are helping to put all the stuff back on the shelf or into the display (being the helpful angel that you are), one or two pieces of merchandise ends up in your pocket or in whatever place you have chosen for concealing your 'purchases.'

We find both bumping schemes very unimaginative, dangerous and unnecessary. This kind of 'attention- diverting' invariably directs a dangerous amount of attention to yourself. Read on about an accident:

That just goes to show...

"There was this pyramid made of cans of coffee. Accidentally, really... I bump into them. I am putting them back sending apologetic glances towards a stacker guy. 'Look how nice a guy I am!' I was already 'packed full' and ready to go. Okay, I go to the checkout. To my surprise as I was paying for my little 'cover article'... it was a bag of milk as a matter of fact... the cashier asked me about a can of coffee on the low shelf of my cart. Boy, my face was red... my heart stopped.... I honestly never noticed it. It turned out okay. They didn't stop me, but they could have..."

THE DISTRACTOR

The skilful attacker whose opponent does not know what to defend.

We have already told you about how partners and gangs divide and distract the attention of security officers. Another type of distraction scheme, also involving a partnership, has as its goal diverting the attention of a vendor. Security might see the scheme from afar, and in that case the partners are goners. Nevertheless, in a small store with one sales person, this is the way to go. The 'distractor' deals with the vendor by pretending to be a legitimate shopper (in other distraction methods, you remember, the distractor was blatantly pretending to be a crook). The 'distractor' asks legitimate questions, tries on clothing articles, asks for an explanation of how the camera works, and makes other very believable inquiries. In the meantime the lifter browses and 'works'. The partners can either come into the store together and pretend they are friends or a couple, or they can come in separately. Pretending to be, or simply being, a 'couple' has an extra benefit. The opposite sex partner can always pretend to be bored and out of place, desirous of nothing more than to leave and go home.

THE DIVERSIONS

Close Diversions of the Third Kind

Shoplifters working in pairs or in groups are likely to use some kind of diversion. The kind selected varies from store to store. We have mentioned many types of diversions in other chapters. Here we would like to discuss a new one: serendipity. Lot of things can happen that you have nothing to do with but can use to your advantage when trying to slip away with your loot. (Note: The word ***loot*** suggests those riots where thousands and thousands of frustrated amateur shoplifters loot hundreds of stores in one night.) But the distraction does not have to be a riot.

Simulated or existing disorder postulates perfect discipline.

There could be a fire alarm, for instance, or someone might fall ill. As the fire trucks roar toward the store or the ambulance comes for the stricken person, naturally everybody will be enjoying the newsworthy event, including you. If you are not in immediate danger (for instance, the whole store is burning and you have to save your skin) you can shoplift as much as your heart desires and your concealment method allows. Another natural diversion could be the arrest of one or more of your colleagues. Very probably the full store security will be out there dealing with them, which in turn will create an excellent opportunity to do your job.

Any event in a store that diverts everybody's attention gives you an excellent opportunity to come out with an even larger amount of goodies than you planned to.

USING SHOPPERS AS COVER

Don't take candy from a stranger

"You look and look... and there isn't one empty aisle. In another store the salesmen see the whole store. At these times I always use the other shoppers as cover. I like old ladies, fat people, families with kids. You just have to make sure that they don't suspect you. Sometimes, those old ladies could be pests, shouting at you that you are a no-good tramp, or they go like kids and tell on you. Once I had to get rid of a shitload of stuff because of one. But sometimes I meet fellow shoppers. Maybe they are colleagues... who knows... who just wink at me, as if they were approving that I do what I do."

Using other shoppers as a cover is a good idea, but you should never allow them to see what you are doing. Never expect complicity from a stranger.

DROP AND COLLECT (THE HIDER)

Drop-shipping to yourself

It is an age-old method, one which security is well aware of, but which is nonetheless difficult to detect. You choose what you want, put it into your shopping cart, walk to a safe section of the store where there is no traffic, and hide the item behind, let us say, a tall stack of towels. After that you do some browsing or actual shopping, using the time to make sure nobody has 'made' you. When you feel secure, go back to the empty aisle of linen, cushions, and towels, pick up the item, pack it, and walk out of the store without further delay. If you have hidden the article well (the type of shoplifter who uses this method regularly is called 'The Hider') you can, alternatively, come back the next day. Knowing right where to find your stash increases your speed, thus lessening the risks.

Pick it, pack it, pock it....

It is perhaps important to remember that security advisors tell their clients to look out for 'customers' who walk up and down with an item they have not paid for. What can we say? How about, 'Put it down now, and pick it up later'?

THE SHRINKER

Taking a bite out of their profit!

It is an absolvable sin for poor and hungry people to walk around in a food-store eating and drinking as much as they can or want. Or so we have heard. Such behavior simply gets the 'rude' rating from store security, who invariably put an end to it by kicking the perpetrator out of the store. The homeless wanderers who exhibit this behavior keep looking for a new store where they are not known because if they are recognized, they will be kicked out before they have had their breakfast, lunch or supper. In a worst case scenario, one of these poorly clad scavengers might be beaten by a fed-up manager. Sometimes an 'honest' shopper drops by to eat on the sly, too. He does not think of this behavior as an illegal act. 'Just taste this.' 'Just try that cookie.' - and so on. Owners are not willing to complicate the situation by calling the cops and prosecuting anyone because the damage is usually minimal. There ***is*** such a thing as a free lunch!

THE DOG FOOD METHOD

When the dog food is gone...

You buy a 25 pound bag of dog food (or any large-size, heavy bag - cat litter, potato, etc.). You take it out to your car, empty it into the trunk by cutting an approximately eight-inch-long opening at an obscure part of the bag. Put the bag under your jacket and return to the store (maybe the next day would be even better) and begin shopping. At an opportune time, at the appropriate 'blind spot,' you start filling up your bag with expensive items (meat, cheese, cold-cuts, etc.). When the bag is full (weighs approximately the same as before), you repair it with transparent tape.

It is up to you whether you choose to pay for all your cover articles (including your bag of goodies), at the check-out. Before you visit the cashier, however, you should probably spend a little quality time establishing your 'doggie bag' acquisition in the dog-food section (potato, cat-litter, etc.). Maybe you pretend to choose another brand. Put your doggie bag down, pick up another one, hesitate, reject that one, and then pick up your own 'ringer' and go. Be careful. Quite often, employees at the check-out know the shape and weight of large items like these so try to make the bag appear similar to the original. You can line it with something before you come back with it - rubber or plastic sheets, extra paper, or some of the original contents - so it will not have strange bulges when you collect your booty. Good luck!

... you can prepare your 'doggie bag'

Some of our 'friends' expressed skepticism about the value of this method. It is difficult, cumbersome and risky. Filling the bag right is complicated and most of the 'concealment' has to be performed in the open. 'It's always better to work onto your body' we were told.

THE DOUBLE RULE

"It is true: If you feel like you can walk out of a store with something, everything is going fine, safety is established - then don't hesitate: Take two or more! Of the same. Either you've saved yourself a trip, or doubled your profit."

Two is DEFINITELY more than one!

Another interpretation of the 'double rule' is that you always take two of anything from a shelf. You can never be sure who is watching. Anybody who notices you taking something from a shelf expects you to put it back if you do not plan to buy it. The hand is faster than the eye. One hand can slide one of the two items into a temporary holding place (pocket, shirt etc.), but the 'twin article' has to be carefully put back on the shelf whence it came, avoiding mistrust or detection. Quite often the article you want will be in a visible place. While you are examining one of the items, you can put the second one in a less visible place where you can pick it up later.

Two is DEFINITELY safer than one!

DRESSING UP

There are a number of practices that fit under the heading 'dressing up.' The simplest is to exchange an item of clothing - a

Old lamps for new lamps!

coat, jacket, or pair of shoes. You stroll around and choose an item. Take off the one that you are wearing. Eliminate all tags and stickers from the new one, and try it on. Check for security, then put your worn-out piece back in the place of the new one (or just drop it somewhere) and continue your shopping trip. In the case of a coat or a jacket, the exchange may be superfluous. The new article might just fit perfectly over the clothes you are wearing.

Old shoes for new shoes!

"In the fall, when the weather is.... you know... so-so - not too cold, not too warm - I go out to buy my coat or jacket for the winter. I usually choose a large store that sells coats, also. It is important to choose one which sells other stuff, too, like a department store, or a men's fashion store. I just put on a big warm pullover, or a very light jacket, or I guess you could go in your old coat that you don't need anymore."

The Turncoat Tale

"Anyway, since it is warm inside, and outside the weather is so ambiguous, they won't get suspicious. I find my new coat. I check the size; try it on. Then a little browsing, meanwhile freeing the new coat of all the price-tags or alarms, if any. Still more browsing. I cannot choose, oh my! This is the time to put your keys, valet, comb, glasses, change, a couple of crumpled receipts inside the pockets of the new coat. After everything is done, you put on your new coat - with all your old stuff in the pockets and walk. I guess you need your cool, and it is better if you do it in the morning, when the store is empty and nobody is watching yet. Gadgets might be working, but if you know the store well, this little detail should not stop you."

Oversized underwear or undersized overwear?

One of the safest practices falling under the label 'Dressing Up' is to wear the item (shoes obviously excluded) under existing (loose) attire. The lifter chooses the item he wants, plus a couple more 'cover' items, and takes it and them to a booth. Inside he puts the item on and then puts his own clothes on over it. He takes back the ones that were used for cover and tells the clerk they do not fit or they do not look good on him. Maybe we are repeating ourselves, but here are a few reminders: the stolen article has to be cleaned of tags, magnetic devices etc. If store policy requires customers to register the number of articles being taken into a fitting room, you must temporarily conceal the article before going into the room.

SELF CONCEALMENT

Properly dressed for uninhibited exhibition!

Dress up as an employee. For example, wear a shirt and name tag similar to that of a proper 'insider.' Create a disguise - the perfect cover. Do not dress up as a policeman. It is a federal (serious) crime! If they catch you, it will be pretty hard to say that you lost your head and it was the first time and you are never going to do it again and please let me go!

"Once, it was a sorry, bitching December, I ain't had not a !@#$ing dime. I always considered December the month when I could not work, since millions of !@#$ers are out there to catch you. Okay, I hate !@#$ing panhandling more than work, I mean take a !@#$ing job, so I decided to try out for a Santa job. You see me, I am !@#$ing fat enough and that's all the skill you need to be a !@#$ing Santa Claus. Man, the wisest choice of my life. I had this big !@#$ing red suit on, with the bag on my shoulders and as I was distributing merrily candies to the !@#$ing kiddies, I robbed them !@#$ers blind."

Gutsy Santa Claus is coming to town (and it has a dirty !@#$ing mouth)

"I had this girlfriend. She worked in a discount store. They sold everything from sardines to stereos. Once she went to visit her parents or something, and I was staying at her place. So, this one morning I am looking for a towel and what do I find? Her uniform from the store. The shirt, the jacket, they both fit me. There is the name tag, too. Her name was Kim. That's just dandy. I went down to the mall, and in the washroom I changed into her uniform. With my black pants I looked just like one of their guys. I went in and walked around. Nobody even looked at me. An old lady asked me something. I told her that I was new, and I didn't know... (...) Finally, I walked out with this six-hundred dollar mini stereo set in a box. Right through the check-outs. There were a couple of girls, but they didn't even peep. They probably thought I was helping someone carry the stuff to the car."

You need the proper girlfriend!

POCKET AND PURSE

"You never work in the pocket. It is like a principle. Amateurs do it. It would be degrading and anyway, what can you lift in your pocket? A comb? Candy? No, clearly that is not my cup o' tea."

Most of the serious lifters who take pride in their 'noble' profession look down on the pocket as a hiding place. Some, however, dismiss such a snobbish attitude. They admit that in loose pants or skirts a deep pocket can work, and they use it. Lot of small stuff fits there: over-the-counter drugs, cheeses, make-up, pens, pencils, CDs, pantyhose - the list is probably endless.

"The Aristocats"

Sometimes pro shoplifters sew extra pockets into the lining of their coats, providing added space for packing away the goodies. This scheme is probably not immensely clever or even fabulous, but if the circumstances are right, and you are certain that you are in a 'no-see zone,' go ahead and fill those spares! As

The plebes

we said earlier about small, inexpensive stuff - low prices can over time add up to considerable sums. There is also talk in the literature about hooks secured to the inside of a coat for hanging stuff on. Maybe this is a good device to use. Maybe it is not. Maybe it is simply unnecessary.

Not where to conceal, but WHEN to conceal?

According to the trade literature, most female shoplifters hide stuff in their purses. Female professional shoplifters did not tell us that there was anything wrong with this practice. They seem to be less proud than many of the men for whom shoplifting has Marquis of Queensbury rules. The purse might work well if you combine its use with 'The Receipt' method. It goes without saying that you'd better be in a 'blind spot' or otherwise covered.

THE BOTTOMLESS INSIDE POCKET

It is the inner pocket of a long winter coat, cut open inside to provide access to the space between the lining and the stronger outside material. It lets the loot slide down while permitting you to move freely without having to worry about unsightly bulges. Any extra bulk lands inside your coat at the level of your knees or lower.

A practical coat is always in fashion!

"That was a long time ago when I used to go out on these one-day trips to load up the fridge and the shelves with food. Used this long thick black coat. It was the time we wore maxi skirts, maxi coats, maxi everything. It was a good, hand-made coat and it had an inner pocket on the wrong side. On the right. I guess the logic behind that is that pick-pockets don't look on the right side. I don't know. But I slit that pocket's bottom part open and used to shove everything there. After each thing I shook the coat, the stuff moved over, there was more place. From the outside you saw nothing, only the inside lining was bulging. But inwards, you know, around where my ankles are. Unless somebody climbed inside my coat the stuff was invisible."

Preparing for the next fashion cycle?

To show that sometimes the guys on the 'bad side' learn stuff too:

"Shoplifters continue to use some old methods to conceal stolen items but have also proved rather innovative... (...) Any coat can be inconspicuously altered or may have hidden pockets in the liner to hide lifted items." (SECURITY MANAGEMENT, MAY 1989)

Considering the great age of this method (hiding stuff in coat linings dates to the days when coat linings were first invented), and being well aware of the fact that most smart lifters abandoned the practice decades ago, we really must give credit to these managerial geniuses for finally catching on. They remind us....

"The Deepsea Doozle is an amazing learner. The experts recorded the following observations to demonstrate this fact: They observed the Doozle as he kept going home on the same route every night. In the middle of the road he traveled, there was a pot-hole. For a long time the poor Doozle kept breaking his leg falling into it. After a mere ten years, he suddenly started to walk around the hole. While it is true that in the same year the hole had finally been repaired by a city ordinance, the observers still felt that they had successfully established the Doozle's amazing ability to learn how to cope with painful problems." (Loosely translated from a story by Lajos Nagy, Hungarian writer)

The Tale of the Deepsea Doozle (Buvarus Henche-ricus)

THE BAG UNDER SKIRT

Gypsy shoplifters favor this trick because their women wear large skirt-on-skirt combination ethnic outfits. On their waist, the women hang a bag which is long enough to fall between their legs. The skirts provide an excellent cover.

"I never done it for obvious reasons [he is a man] ***but I saw a report on the TV about these Gypsy or South-American shoplifting gangs. The men were doing the diversions, making all the store security busy like hell. Meanwhile, the women were packing away. If not for the security cameras, even the store guy admitted it, they would have never been able to catch them. There were three women. They had a couple of video cameras. One of them had a VCR tucked in the bag in between her legs..."***

They must have had a funny walk

SOCKS AND COWBOY BOOTS

Also, a comfortable hiding place could be your socks under your pants. The elastic in the socks keeps certain items secure, and the pantleg will hide them fabulously, leaving you free of arm-stiffening burdens as well as suspicious bulges. Also a wide-mouthed cowboy boot will allow its wearer to slide in numerous smaller articles. We heard of someone who used his leg cast to pack pens for a fence during the six weeks it took the leg to mend.

Ever thought about it?

"I know it sounds kinda dumb, but I hide stuff in my socks. I don't do it all the time, but, man, it's the safest place. Once they caught me with some stuff. I had it in my shirt, on the side, under my jacket. Lots of stuff. I was so full that I used my socks to keep a pair of sausages. Okay, I give myself up. I give them the meat from under my arm. I empty my

Where is the pepperoni?

pockets of cheese and stuff. The guy searches me, feels me around, checks my crotch... and that's it. The sausages never came out. Don't know if they were just bored, fed up, or simply it was store policy, but they told me to scram and never show my face in their store again and kicked me out. With the sausages."

We were also told that women use their panty-hose or stockings to secure stuff. Elastic is the shoplifter's best friend.

THE SPORTS BAG

A new bag is a good bag.

On several occasions, a sports bag (with a couple of towels and some half-used toilet articles inside), or a store shopping bag might be used. Unfortunately, very few stores have no policy about handbags, and it is always suspicious to walk around with a bag. Nevertheless, official store (brand name) bags, even the ones that bear the mall or department store's name and are available in dispensing machines for a quarter or two (or more), could provide good cover in large establishments. Don't use a 'bad' bag, i. e., the crumpled, used one you brought home from a previous trip during which you actually paid for something. Security is on the lookout for wrinkled plastic bags with the store's name on it.

The 'good bags,' the new plastic ones, help the lifter who has no car and therefore no trunk in which to stash his booty. You can play with those stores that have a policy about leaving the bags at the checkout. You can make an obvious show of leaving your bag at the counter without anybody asking, just to show that you know the rules and are harmless.

A guarded bag is a safe bag

"I always use my bag as a cover. In bookstores, record stores, places where you browse. The point is, you see, that a bag is in your way anyway! You have to put it down if you want to pack away, it could be too obvious to open it, maybe even noisy. Whenever I have a bag or briefcase with me, I always ask the cashier if I can leave it with her. It's the same with cons. You establish the trust, then !@#% them."

A healthy-bag is a wealthy bag.

When security is loose and you are dressed like you just came from the gym, you will arouse no suspicion by carrying a tote bag. If the store has carts, put the bag in front in the basket and after you have found an empty aisle or a safe corner, zip open, slide in, and zip up fast. Buying something after packing is a good idea. When they offer you a bag at the checkout counter, you just say no and use your tote bag. It will not occur to them that you could be shameless enough to open a bag full of loot right in front of them.

THE "BOOSTER BOX"

It is imperative that we describe this outrageous method because it is so well known to all security staffs. It seems to us that modern professional lifters would prefer other, less bulky methods of concealment, but the 'box' is mentioned as a method in every book in the trade literature. None of our interlocutors talked about using it. Maybe in the past it was more popular. Today's stores have pick-up areas, and they also deliver, giftwrap and place other similar obstacles in your way.

After you read it, burn it!

We do not think the 'booster box' is safe. 'Au contraire.' We say that it is pretty risky, but it could be worth considering. If you used it at top speed in a crowded shop right before a holiday, it might still work.

It goes like this. You have to find a legitimate box (TV, microwave, etc.), preferably with a receipt. A trap door might be built on the bottom, or you might cut a secret slit on the side or on the top and cover it with something inconspicuous. You then fill the box (given that you are safe from cameras and such) and leave. If anybody checks you, you are carrying a legitimate purchase. You even have the receipt. Security could ask, 'Where the hell did that receipt come from?' But that's the smaller problem. The major risk of the method is the unnecessary attention a large box draws from spooks and clerks alike. The receipt, the crowd, or your speed are the only things that can save you if you are challenged.

Security Consultants' Pet idea

WASHROOM PACKING

Most stores provide shoppers (and lifters) with the convenience of 'comfort stations'. The 'dressing up' method works very well in these washrooms, provided that entering them is safe. The washroom also provides a safe place to 'tog' (conceal in your clothing) anything lifted in a hurry. 'Going to the washroom' cannot be done unless you are sure you have not been tailed at any time since you entered the store. It is also prudent to take everything that is not flushable (packing material, magnetic alarm, tags and stickers) out of the washroom and dispose of it in a safe part of the store. Also, it doesn't hurt to be careful to hide your actions from others who are using the facilities. They might hear or see something and report it. Indeed, they might be snoops themselves.

Comfort Stations!

PACKING ELSEWHERE

More of a 'havenly' rule than just a method!

It is very dangerous to conceal or wear an item at the place where it is sold or displayed. Amateur shoplifters tend to commit this basic mistake. They think that the moment they lift anything, they must hide it. They also choose this particular moment to shoot those 'furtive glances' around to see if anybody has noticed them. Slow down. You have time, don't you? Just continue shopping and browsing like everybody else. If there is a cart or basket provided by the store, put the goods in there and walk a little. Find the most suitable place to 'tog'.

The gates of New Haven.

There are safe havens (low traffic areas) in all department stores where bulky or non-expensive items like furniture, frames and pictures, pillows, bed-liners, and books are sold. Also, in some department stores they still allow shoppers to use the stairs. That's a safe zone, isn't it?

Pick a place in Haven before you pick'n'pack.

In food stores the best bet is the produce section or the aisle that is least frequented by other shoppers (hygiene products or bulk articles). It is sound advice to tell you to remember that in every store, no matter the kind of merchandise, it is imperative to find the safest place to pack away before you start to pick. In music stores the empty section is usually the classical music department. It is also safe because the detectives or 'ghost shoppers' will assume that snobbish, intelligent classical music lovers do not steal. No way. It is those damn kids, going for the pop and rock best-sellers.

Be a lifter, not a leader!

You have to be certain that you are never followed. That is the second part of the 'havenly' rule. Stop at another section, look at another thing, and instead of turning your head use your peripheral vision. If there is an escalator, use it to see if some eager-beaver is on your tail. It is best to do this checking several times. After all, it's better to waste a bit of time riding an escalator than sitting in a holding cell. Elevators are useful for losing a tail.

THE SPECIAL ORDER

"In this hardware store I used to buy parts for my car. They don't have any of the parts out on the shelves. You have to stand in line - a real piss-off long time - to talk to a clerk, who will send a note down to the stockroom and get the part to you. Like an hour, you have to wait! Then you have a walk to the check-out through this huge store with shelves to the ceiling, no one in sight. Cool. Unpacking the boxes and packing away the parts is a snap.

They robbed me of my method!

"Then I go back a few months later. They probably found the empty boxes that I left behind and in response they introduced a strong prevention measure. When you buy

something, the clerk puts the stuff into a strong burlap bag with a zip-lock top. He zips it in, and locks it, then the cashier unlocks it when I am to pay. I was robbed of my method! I genuinely felt cheated. How dare they not trust me? But the disappointment didn't last long. I soon realized that next time I want a part for my wheels, first I have to walk over to the tool section and get a knife or a pair of scissors. A strong one."

'SHOPPING' FROM A DISPLAY CASE

Danger! Man at work!

Once in a blue moon at an unattended clerk-station you can acquire some articles (watches, jewelry, small electronics etc.) that otherwise are only available through asking for them. A display case may be defective or left open by accident. Expensive electronic appliances, computer parts, watches and other little things are sometimes left in an open case while the sales person is busy serving another customer. The fast and bold seize the opportunity to do some improvised lifting.

Here might be the place to mention that the most important item you can ever lift from an unattended clerk-station is a tool which removes electronically read tags or ink tags.

WALKING OUT

Walking out on the 'wild side'!

This method is used for stealing items that are too large to hide, or too difficult to unpack. It requires only one person (but a backup never hurts anybody). It is best executed in large department stores near the exits. You have to be pretty cool and self-confident to try it. It is not for the nervous type (shoplifting in general is not a profession for people with unstable nerves).

Okay. You choose the item, pick it up and walk out. And afterward, you ask yourself, 'Now that wasn't very difficult, was it?' If you are unable to reply in the negative, you are probably in the wrong line of work.

"I was selling cameras at a department store, right next to the television sets and radios. Once we caught a guy. He always came at the time when the secretaries regularly sneaked away from their jobs. He came to catch their 'stories' in the afternoon. He excused himself to the ladies, picked up a TV set and walked. After we caught him we also found out that, right outside, his van was packed with televisions. The shameless bum was selling them right there from the back of his van." (Former Employee of a Large Department Store)

Once you are out it is easy to get 'in'!

A 'walk out' cannot be easily explained to a store security person if you are caught. You could try to make up a tale about your wife - that you thought she paid for it, for example - or you might claim you were just going to another cashier and there you were definitely going to pay for it - but any excuse is hard to bring off in this situation. Maybe dropping the merchandise and running is your best bet.

The 'slow' walk is the safe walk! But do it steady and fast!

Notice that while you are following the above method, the item is not concealed. In a way, every shoplifting trip ends in some kind of walking. Let us say that you are ready. Everything is tucked away and neatly concealed. In large stores, of course, you have several exits. Not using the first exit and checking one's back is, in general, sound advice. Still, there is the case where you suspect that somebody has seen you or that you may have been caught on camera. You are not certain about your 'security,' and you don't feel adventurous. In this case the best idea is to leave the store A.S.A.P. because the reaction from the security personnel takes time. The clerk has to notify store security on the phone. A radio must be used to alert them, and it is very unlikely that the store has a sufficient number of detectives to send one to each and every exit. Fast 'walking out' might just save you a trip to court.

HOW TO CATCH AN ELEPHANT

Q: How to catch an elephant?

A: Catch two. Then let one go.

The Tale with an Elephant and the Two Hunters

It is an obscure method even in the world of professional shoplifters. We admit it sounds a little like a fairy tale. It helps lifters to obtain large items such us televisions, refrigerators, and the like. It requires two people and some seed money and is done in department stores where they store several very large boxed items on the floor. It won't work in big city department stores which limit you to the options of home-delivery or picking up your purchase with your car at a designated area. Many small town department stores still let you leave the floor with the stuff in tow if you're strong enough, however, and this method works in such places. Anyway, it goes something like this:

Lifter Number One, after a lot of questions and inquiries, buys the item. The clerk fills out the papers and provides him with the sales slip. Either the vendor or Lifter Number One puts the sales slip on the box. At this point Lifter Number Two non-chalantly steps in and takes the item. If he is questioned about it right there, the partners can claim to be together and this trip will become an empty run. Otherwise Lifter Number Two walks straight out of the store. Lifter Number One still occupies the vendor with something or hangs around browsing. If Lifter Number Two is stopped at the exit, he can easily prove with the sales slip that he has a legitimate purchase.

Now. Back to Lifter Number One. After some mumbo-jumbo for the clerk's benefit, he picks up another box containing an identical item. Or he shamelessly asks what has happened to his purchase, pretending to be genuinely shocked by its disappearance. After obtaining a 'replacement,' indignant Lifter Number One leaves with his 'legitimate' purchase. We might add that it is a good idea to pay with a credit card when you use this method. You will have an extra proof of purchase, signed and sealed. They cannot refuse to give you a replacement.

Gosh! Was it perhaps stolen? Where is my wallet?

The next day Lifter Number One can either return the clean item for a refund (my wife did not approve, my kid got scared, the other being stolen was an omen since the cat went crazy when it first saw it - you know, one of the better ones) or find a buyer for the brand new article Just make sure that you sell the legitimate one.

OUTRAGEOUS IDEAS AND METHODS

At first we thought that the following idiotic ideas should be thrown in the garbage can, but then we decided that you might find them entertaining. You may think of them as funny because they are so ridiculous, or you might derive horror-movie type thrills from the thought that there are people out there with such ideas in their heads.

Kamikaze 'no-brainers'

"You work with a partner. Okay. You do zilch. He does the stuff. You just hang around and watch out for him. You can look. It's okay. If they make you, all the better. If my pal has been made... Then I run. I simply start to run past the undercover. I knock him over. Okay. He is pissed, he forgets about my pal, who was only suspicious, and now he is after me. I am running straight out to my car, or, if it is a mall, to the washroom. He is screwed either way. I have nothing on me. He has nothing on me. We are even."

Run to be caught!

"Use a wheelchair. Alone or with your buddy, who will push you around. You will be absolutely above suspicion. Or even better, get your grandma' or Aunt Jamie to sit there. If they are old enough... (...) My mother used to smuggle stuff, liqueur and cigarettes mainly, through the border from the states. She always took my ninety-two year old Granny as cover. Custom guys took a look at fragile old Granny who was quietly snoozing on the stuff and they just waved them through..."

Politically correct

"You go in a bookstore and dedicate, date, and sign a gigantic dictionary for your friend's birthday. In case he

Birthday present

has one or just had one. Some time later he walks in the bookstore, puts the dictionary under his arm and straight walks. They dare to stop him, he just shows the dedication. If they become picky, he shows his driver's license and that's it. Shut up! They have to let him go!"

Lights out or lights up!

"I don't care. If the situation gets 'hot' for my partner I make it even more hot! Diversions. I can fall and start shouting that I hurt myself. Oh, oooh, I broke my leg! It will be more important for the store guys then my partner. I go farther if nothing else seems to work... I just put my lighter to a rack-full of garbs and .poof! There is their hot situation!"

Baby sitter

"Borrow a baby, or, if you have one, take him in your arms. You can then easily hide stuff under your arm. Nobody will see it...(...) you can have him in a stroller and fill the stroller with the goods..." [some might consider this child abuse]

Go blind!

"You know, it's not bad... you are ready to go, everything is A-okay.... you are full... Here you go - you pull out a pair of round black sunglasses. You open a white collapsible blind stick and start with the show. You find a good Samaritan or a salesman and tell him that you have lost your way. Pretty please, with whipped cream on top and a cherry, would he be so kind as to direct you towards the exit.... The best joke is if you choose the plainclothes and ask them for help."

Break a leg!

"When I had my ankle broken and in a cast, and I had to use that pair of crutches I kept lifting stuff and it was easy. You can hold anything under your upper arm, plus crutches. It gives a good hold. Plus, everybody, including the 'smokers' will just pity you...."

And now that we have taken a look at some of the more ham-handed boneheads currently plying their trade - a drum roll please! Introducing! The Prince of the Art:

THE INVENTOR

The Royal Council

The trade literature is constantly trying to define the main types of shoplifters and shoplifting methods in an attempt to make the security professional's job somewhat easier. However, this effort is useless. The frazzled snoops they would like to help are slowly coming to the realization that everybody and anybody is a potential lifter. When our book lands in their hands, we hope that they will read it and notice that it explodes what myths they have left. Perhaps they will re-evaluate their tasks and approaches. But then, the lifters who read our book might do the same thing- and maybe just a tad faster.

The problem will always be there until the retail industry faces the fact that making products easily available makes them easy to steal. We refer them to our description of what a secure store would look like. Some catalog stores go even further, keeping their stock in a warehouse behind the main counter. The shopper sees only the item he asks the clerk to bring to him.

Of all lifters, the inventor is the one most feared and respected by the security industry.

The Archduke of Invention

"A couple of years ago they introduced that pesky little gizmo - the ink tag. It bugged the hell out of me. I couldn't figure any method to crack it. As a matter of fact, if you do 'crack' it, it spills colored ink and spoils the clothes. Ugly!! After a couple of frustrating months, I decided that I had to figure out a way. Especially since they replaced all the old buzzer tags with this 'harmless' little thingamajig. I took home a blouse and conducted my first experiment. It was a disaster. I cut a slit on a plastic bag. Covered the blouse with it, tightly strapping the plastic around the pin. Broke the vials; ink splattered; the blouse was still okay. So far so good. But as it broke, a large plastic chunk still stayed attached to the pin. When I tried to remove that, I lost the hold on the plastic, it moved, and the blouse was a goner."

The Crowning Achievement

"Then, almost accidentally, I glanced at the plastic button on the other side and it hit me. You have to open or destroy this little plug. I heated up a knife on the stove and cut into it. Eureka! I found the guts of the plug. Cylinder, spring, ball-bearings, and all. It slid off the pin like a dream."

The Emperor of New Ideas

To invent a new shoplifting method is not easy, but it isn't impossibly hard, either. An idea just hits someone. We have interviewed several smart lifters who, as they were telling us their stories, suddenly hit their own foreheads and came up with a scheme. There, in front of our eyes, they crafted it, promptly measuring the risks and benefits of the new scheme. They also told us that it would have to be tried and tried until it worked seamlessly. It was exciting, nevertheless, to witness how these smart lifters think and 'create.' They all agree, however, that behavior, even more than inspiration, is the crucial element of any method.

Marketiquette

We hope that these descriptions of methods have given you some new ideas. When you try them out, don't forget about the established rules of good behavior! No method will succeed without proper execution. "Prèsentation, mes amis, une élégance non-challante!"

GENERAL BEHAVIOR

Nothing so much prevents our being natural as the desire to seem so.

(François, Duc de La Rochefoucauld)

Miss Manners says... Do not be immature in mature company!

Showing extreme nervousness through facial expressions or body gestures raises suspicion. Constantly looking around, aimlessly walking up and down the aisles, loitering in any way, or acting fussy or giddy might get you caught.

Respect your host's time as if it were your own!

Spending an unnecessarily long time inside a store (barring situations where the type of store calls for it, i.e. bookstores, computer stores, music and video stores) is a dangerous tactical mistake. Speaking of time, adding the mistake of walking around with something in your hand (provided there are no carts to fill or baskets in which to carry stuff) increases the risk of being caught.

Do not take your leave sans proper adieu!

If you concentrate too much on getting to the exit, not even looking around as one would when calmly leaving a store, and if you then rush through it, you signal the snoops that something is wrong. Send a polite smile to the cashier - perhaps a ta-ta to the goodies you are leaving behind.

Many of our sources said it was not advisable to return soon after boosting in a store where you are not a regular customer, unless, of course, you are using a special scheme, in which case returning a number of times is the core of your method. Otherwise, remember that personnel in a store new to you often notice a new customer. If you return too soon, they might remember that you (the new guy) were around the day the silver candlesticks disappeared.

Be tactful in declining invitations!

Establishing yourself as a regular customer in certain stores, and knowing the personnel, allows you to visit more often. Remember that if you are known to a sales clerk of the eager and educated kind, he is bound to pester you with offers of help. To refuse it is not only impolite but also draws unwanted attention to yourself. Just be a pleasant part of their routine.

To fake interest is better than being rude!

While choosing the merchandise, handle only the items you are really interested in. The moment you know exactly what you want, start checking out something else with 'real' interest. The key, as we always say, is to act like a real shopper.

Never make a mess while on a visit!

Other than the contents of your wallet, or change from your pockets, dropping anything (any merchandise from the shelves) on the floor puts store detectives on the look-out. They are trained to be suspicious of what they call 'the dropper'.

You also arouse suspicion if you conspicuously place your bag or shopping bag on the floor. If you do so, do it as a distraction. Put your bag down in the open, close to a salesman - anywhere, actually - but then walk away from it. You can turn around your bag's negative effect by disassociating yourself from it.

Do not be a glutton at the buffet table!

Today the merchandise in shops is out in the open. You can take it, examine it, walk with it, or place it in your basket. Idiotically covering something on the spot with anything, or hiding a piece of merchandise behind a purse or a package, gives security or the 'mystery shopper' a reason to suspect you and pay close attention to you. Removing price tags or labels, or taking an article of clothing off its hanger, if done in the open, is a dead giveaway.

POSTURE, STANCE, DISPATCH AND PACE

The other shoplifting guides

Anthony J. Faria's article, 'Minimizing Shoplifting Losses: Some Practical Guidelines' could be used by smart lifters as a guide or manual on what not to do. His categorizations not only appeal to other experts in the field. They are the foundation for most decisions on 'the retail battle grounds,' as well.

The information contained in these categorizations (as introduced in practice, at seminars for employees, and as advice from store-owners) boils down to racial, social, and ethnic stereotyping, an all-too-easy way of getting across information to students of the trade. Considering the questionable value of this kind of categorization, we decided to compile our own behavior list, describing how smart lifters would never behave or what they would very rarely do.

Faria presented categories which we follow although we add additional information that comes from the 'catch-prevention' people, the shoplifters themselves. Let us examine the question from their point of view, translating the security manual written for store employees into a security manual for boosters.

EYES

Easy with the eyes...

In case somebody looks at you, look straight back and smile or ask a question. Looking away, shying away from personal contact, or turning your head frequently and redundantly to the left and right arouses suspicion. If you are looking at the merchandise, ***do*** look at it. When holding an item in your hands, do not spark up the spooks by looking around to check who might be watching you.

HANDS

...softly with the hands....

Oh, that magic that you do so well. The magical fingers. The eye is slower than the hand. We are not trying to say that you have to be an expert magician to use your 'sticky fingers' but it is advisable to borrow one basic principle from the magician: Use your hands while the audience is looking at your nose!

Holding your hands down and hidden, below counter level, is not a good idea. Follow Miss Manners' advice: Do not keep your hands in your pocket! Do not try to conceal the stuff the moment you pick it up. If you try to acquire some gum or chocolate at a checkout counter, you have to be sure that the clerk is busy with your purchase or money, and that nobody else can see you (that no one is 'crowding around' you and him).You achieve nothing by putting your palm over something or closing your hand over something . This tactic might work when you are playing with a three-year-old, but in the real world it's an infantile effort.

...then, your work is easy!

Folding or crumpling the merchandise while you are examining it, out in the open, is a simple sign to the sales force that you may be a thief. Folding must be done in a safe place. Crumpling should never be done. It is a ridiculous procedure (everything is in the fold) and potentially dangerous (noisy). Avoid it.

BODY TYPES

"I don't mind that I'm fat. I still get the same money."

(Marlon Brando)

Although security forces and the trade literature never make the distinction between obese and thin shoplifters, there are advantages and disadvantages on both sides of the scale.

Obese lifters

The overweight person inspires pity rather than suspicion in those around him. And he packs well. Think about it. When you look at a fat person, you can never ***really*** know how heavy he actually is or what exact shape that weight on him takes. After the act of concealment, a heavy person, fat with a pot-belly, does not look fatter or much larger than he was before.

"I am a big fat pig. Everybody wants me to lose weight, even myself, sometimes, though, I don't know what I would do if I lost weight. I'm used to my weight, and I like the magnitude of the packing space in my crotch. I can put about 8-10 pounds of meat there, and it changes my shape very little... then when I come home it is an instant gratification to lose that extra 8 to 10 pounds."

Thin boosters

To be thin has only one small advantage. In the wintertime you can dress to be a little more on the heavy side by using a coat or jacket a size larger. After you have packed quite a few items, you will look fatter than when you came in, but the clothes will still fit you. No bulges, no danger.

BEHAVIOR AT COUNTERS

When you face the clerk

Any smart lifter will laugh in your face if you tell him that you steal costume jewelry by trying it on and leaving it on as you nonchalantly walk away. Speaking of nonchalance, do not take articles from one counter to another. According to smart lifters, this action makes you an instant suspect. The same thing happens if you try to 'sashay' the item from the counter towards the edge, or if you perform the 'Turning Away' trick. You may think you have won, but if you have tipped your hand, the magic is gone. Sales folks are people too. Be polite with them, talk to them, crack a joke, ask questions, complain about the weather. Show them that you are a nice person. There is no reason to be rude just because you want to screw them. Au contraire!

BEHAVIOR IN FITTING ROOMS

The thief is not sneaking anywhere!

We have to talk about the etiquette of fitting rooms. The most important rule: Never try to sneak into a fitting room. Always make contact. Ask the sales clerk some questions about the rules, and follow them to the letter. Sending the clerk away to get you more merchandise, not just in this case but at any other time, is not only rude but may be looked upon as suspicious behavior. If you have previously packed something and plan to wear it, try to divert suspicion from yourself. You can, for example, find something in an 'empty' cubicle and return it before you enter. Make small talk. Ask a clerk to guard your bags or packages, or to give you an opinion on how the outfit (the one you use for cover) looks on you. Make up your own routine. There are other simple rules of etiquette to follow. Be polite, inquisitive and funny. If you are able to charm the store clerks in any way, they will like you, and therefore you will not be suspected of wrong-doing.

RECOGNIZING AND DEALING WITH DANGER

"My centre is giving way, my right is in retreat. Situation excellent. I shall attack."

(Ferdinand Foch)

How the rivers flow

Even though we say that you can steal almost anywhere (providing that circumstances are favorable), it is always advisable to go with the flow. Be like water and follow the path of least resistance. In this chapter we have compiled some of the pet peeves of our sources - warnings and warning signs that tell you to push the panic button. Not in haste, though! As the good French general suggests: Attack! If you think somebody suspects you, walk up to him and 'make friends.' From his behavior you will be able to detect what his intentions are.

Leave a few minutes before high noon!

"I went into a computer store with my partner. A big nation-wide chain store that has just opened an outlet in our town. It felt like marching into the middle of a battle zone. Buzzers, chains, magnetic stickers, locked display cases, cameras, mirrors, you name it. What turned me off, you see, was not the difficulty, but their wild west, cowboy attitude. These guys were serious. I had the impression that they would lynch me on the spot if they caught me with anything. Who the !@#$ needs that? We left Dodge City, right away!"

You yourself have never given a thought to what can be seen through shop windows, have you? One of our 'friends' did.

"When I am on the road boosting I rarely worry about people in the store ever telling on me. They generally won't because they don't want to be involved. But people outside parking their cars or walking in the mall, if they see you through that window, will tell on you in a New York minute. They'll run to the telephone and describe you down to the color of your socks."

We have to add a brief note here. Very few security officers will apprehend somebody because of a bystander's testimony. Hearsay doesn't count. The officers must witness the concealment themselves. However, you should never count on them to follow the letter of the law.

Sometimes, it is possible to figure out who the 'ghost shopper' or security person is and avoid him inside the store. However, it is certainly much easier to see the warning signs at the exits. Any unnatural movement around exits and checkout counters tells the smart lifter that it is time to give up. When the girl at the counter picks up the phone, or when there is a guy or woman who has already passed the check-out but still loiters around the exit and keeps shooting 'furtive glances' at you, you have been spotted. If, in a mall-store, a uniformed mall cop suddenly appears at the exit, become a model citizen at once. In fact, any suspicious movement around the checkouts is a sign to stop 'working' at once.

When the Moon is in sextile with Mercury, the thief-catchers gather.

"Dangerous? I tell you what. If I am full of meat and cheese, I weigh like twenty pounds more than when I came in and you cannot see it on me. I am not bulging. My partner checked me out and said that I am A-okay. So. I am standing in line with this large bag of milk. I look, and suddenly everybody starts gathering at the exit - suits, salesmen, other men in running shoes and jackets. A curious group. It is time to go back for that bottle of ketchup I forgot to buy and systematically get rid of the stuff. In these cases, they have made you, no question. They might even see you packing back the stuff. Still, they cannot do anything, only to try to remember your face for the next time. You walk! They might give you those moralistic looks. They might even say something to the effect that they saw you, and that you are a bad boy, but they are powerless to do anything more."

Notice when the 'personnel' constellation is in opposition with your ascendent.

"It happens every now and then when you shoplift: You did not see anything or notice any suspicious character with a walkie-talkie on his belt, but you still feel that you are in danger or somebody is watching you. You know that feeling; those eyes on your back; that feeling of somebody watching you. If I ever feel like that - call me superstitious - I always leave instantly. If I had something I leave it back there and disappear as fast as I can..."

When your astral body pats you on your shoulder!

"Nerves, man, it's the nerves. If you are nervous, you are in danger. I'm telling you, some times for no reason I get nervous, I become paranoid. Everybody seems to walk behind me, everybody I see looks as if he was watching me. Salesmen scurry who knows where and I am certain they are going to call somebody to arrest me. When I get in this state, I get the hell out of there, and even if nothing happens, I give up for the day. There will always be a tomorrow, I say..."

When you seem to know that the sun sets in the East, and the Moon is retrograde.

TURNING DANGER INTO AN ADVANTAGE

Let us consider the 'almost-caught' case. Our lifter has noticed that somebody has apparently seen him and is following him toward the exit. There are calls being made at the cashier's station. Somebody is waiting outside and looks suspicious. Heed these warning signs. Go back, empty your pockets and what not. And then just leave.

"I was packed up pretty well. I had extension cords and power bars, a couple of watches and an electronic travel iron neatly stashed under my arms. I'm doing my little walk around in the furniture department when Lo and behold! this yuppie-looking detective shows up behind me. I make him, but I am not sure. I take another walk around. He's still stuck on me. Now I know that he knows... Start back through the maze of shelves. The iron ends up on a shelf with plant-food. The electric cords meet running shoes for the first time. The yuppie keeps coming, and he sees me packing out. I walk on, look back, the shithead is picking up my stuff. But I am empty now. I smile at him and shrug my shoulder, letting him know that he has won. The cat. Next time it's mouse-time!"

Cashing in the chips is even more methodical in the next case.

"I walk around the store, spot the cameras, if I can, find the detectives and start my little acting job. Pick up something in plain view of a camera; walk a couple of steps; then drop it on another shelf. I get the detective's attention. Pretend that I am nervous. Look around several times. Pocket something very clumsily, then discard it later. As soon as I am certain that they have 'made' me and are following me, I leave fast. They jog after me and stop me outside. I am caught!"

What is the point? Has this booster friend of ours completely lost his mind? Not at all. The 'almost-caught' is a very successful method professional shoplifter teams use. They set up circumstances in which one of them will definitely be caught (or at least strongly suspected and closely followed) - with nothing. The 'stool' makes sure he is seen 'on camera' looking really suspicious. He tries hard to make the thief-catchers apprehend him on suspicion. In a medium-size store, this operation will involve and occupy the entire security force. They arrest the 'stool', take him back inside the store, search him, etc. The store is temporarily rendered defenseless. The partner can walk with anything he is not ashamed to move. Our 'stool' has to be let go because he has stolen nothing.

"Man, you should look at their faces when they find nothing on me. I make them grovel. They apologize a hundred times and they understand nothing. Pure joy!"

MORAL OF THE PASSAGE

The methods are countless. There are at least as many as there are smart lifters. Anybody who decides to take a chance on a journey into the wonderful world of shoplifting should develop and use schemes and methods most suited to his own personality, social status, and physical persona. If you invent your own method, think it over to be sure it doesn't break any basic rules of the art and then try it out. If you face any danger during that trial or at any other time, abort the mission. There is no glory in being caught. Better safe than sorry! What else can we say? If any hint of danger presents itself , leave the place and leave the stuff! There are other stores, and you can even come back to this one at another time. It is your call and your skin. If anybody calls you chicken, send him shoplifting and let the courageous idiot be caught.

SECURITY DEVICES (GIZMOS)

The latest refinements of science are linked with the cruelties of the Stone Age.

(Sir Winston Churchill)

Every gadget there WAS, IS and WILL BE, shall be cracked, beaten, and ultimately rendered 'ridiculous' by the professional, proficient smart lifter. What other famous thinker said: 'No lock is unbreakable and no safe is safe'?

How safe is a safe?

As we look through the different old and contemporary devices designed and employed to dissuade the potential lifter, you will observe how true that statement is, whoever said it first. Most of these devices work to some extent against the amateur, who does not avoid or defuse them because he does not know about them. By trapping amateurs, these sometimes very high-priced gadgets manage to provide an increased number of apprehensions when low-priced items are the target of shoplifting, but none deters the smart lifter, who takes the larger piece of the pie. And, obviously, they do not minimize inside theft at all.

Lifters lift

"I don't care about locks. Locks only keep honest people honest (...) I don't care about chains or wires. I can cut them. (...) I don't care about mirrors. If I go into a store and there are only two salesmen on the floor, are you going to convince me that they are paying someone $8 an hour to stand behind a wall and peek through [a two way mirror] ***(...) at me. I know there's no one there. (...) I don't care about electronic devices because I can beat or remove any of them."***

Honest people are honest

SECURITY DEVICES FROM THE PAST

Some 'theft-eliminating' contraptions have been used by clever shopkeepers for hundreds and hundreds of years. The medieval merchant tied his merchandise to the table, to his tent-pole or in some cases to himself. (Remember the landlord in Dumas' "The Three Musketeers" who tied a string to his big toe to prevent Planchet, D'Artagnan's servant, from stealing the ham from his chimney?). The shopkeeper used chains to tie down his goods,

Planchet and the Ham

locks to close off access to his inventory, mirrors to look at other parts of his store, and small brass bells as an 'early warning system'. We (the writers) remember that when we went to the store as kids, the bell over the door alerted the owner that somebody had entered. At the same time, the sound of the bell alerted the customer that somebody knew he was there. One can still find this gentle device in a few Mom and Pop stores. In the following short section, we deal with other medieval devices which are still in use.

CHAINS, CABLES, RINGS, LOCKS AND MIRRORS

Chains and cables have to be cut before you can get to the concealment part of your deed. Our professional sources told us that the large department stores provide the necessary tools for every kind of removal.

Mirror, mirror on the wall...

In the case of mirrors, always remember your Physics 101. If you look in the mirror, you have to see the person who is looking at you. Try it. You do. Convex mirrors provide a largely distorted image for the snoops. The only thing they are able to see is that there is someone in an aisle. Better yet, you will see them trying to see you. The more desperately they try, the more noticeable their effort becomes. What they cannot see in these mirrors is the lifter in action. If you have acquired even just a mediocre level of skill in article concealment, their eyes will fall out of their sockets before they see you actually doing something.

Jose, can you see?

Two-way mirrors are a touch trickier. Sometimes, though, they are of cheap quality. Even the fairly good mirrors can be seen through if there is a light on the 'viewing' side. If the 'viewer' doesn't like to sit in complete darkness and so has a lamp on - or, to fight boredom, is watching the game on his portable TV set - you are more or less able to see him. The simplest way of dealing with a two-way mirror is to pick up the merchandise casually and, if you are certain that you have not raised suspicion, move to a safe corner to do your packing. Two-way mirrors are unlikely to show up in fitting rooms. Their use has been challenged in the courts.

Jose, can you hear?

The little brass bells are still found in stores for sentimental reasons or reasons of Mom and Pop practicality. In a small repair or barber shop, they summon the only person available. Some owners try to create an old-fashioned image for their stores by using these quaint little bells. They do no harm.

VIDEO CAMERAS, CCTV

The use of Closed Circuit Television (CCTV) surveillance is a modern strategy that employs recent and trendy technologies to battle shoplifting. CCTV provides a vigilant 'electronic warden' which expands the visual field available to store and security personnel. Closed circuit systems are designed to allow visual contact with the floor. A store detective can follow the movement of shoppers through specific areas. Sometimes his view is severely hampered by quite old and fuzzy B&W systems. The wealthier stores, of course, may use high-tech, high-resolution cameras which turn out better action footage.

Smile! You are on camera!

"To catch a thief, whether it's an employee or a shoplifter, retailers may spend a lot or a little. Camera surveillance systems, for example, may cost $50,000 or more per store. And usually there are related expenses, such as cost of hiring and training people to use the equipment. Without the personnel to make the fullest use of [any video] **technology, all the retailer ends up with is an expensive videotape showing how he got ripped off." (PROGRESSIVE GROCER, JUNE 1990)**

Expensive training films? No kidding!

Yes, indeed! It is not just the cost of equipment but also the expenses involved in operating it! All that high-tech gadgetry, which, by the way, costs the shirt off the store-owner's back, 'works.' It makes apprehension rates rise in the short run, and store owners are thus satisfied that they have curbed their losses effectively. The literature written and published by self-promoting trade experts is filled with these statistical miracles. Because the system seems to show results by raising apprehension rates, it comes off with flying colors right after installation.. We have yet to see any data, however, on the long term effect of the changes. As everybody gets used to these systems (lifters included), the situation changes. Store personnel delegate their responsibility to the technology and become complacent.

High budget productions, unpaid extras expensive actors

In a report on high-tech surveillance which ran on a weekly TV 'news magazine,' we learned about fantastic cameras the size of a thumbnail which could be hidden in the eyes of mannequins or behind pictures, clocks or mirrors. The program showed other cameras installed on a display rack, in a fire-alarm on the ceiling and - would you believe it? - in the merchandise itself! Most of these cameras turn in all directions and zoom with the help of a computer which also switches lenses or cameras when desired. The 'cameraman' sitting somewhere in a booth is able to follow a 'suspicious character' with incredible ease from the moment he

Zoom in on that suspicious cleavage!

steps into the frame. The report showed a 'bum' (our wording) and a 'suspiciously black' (also our wording) shopper stealing something. No other description was made of the typical suspicious character. Security 'recognized' the suspects at the entrance, and with the chain of cameras was able to follow them everywhere.

Second camera units 'for show'

Some stores are satisfied with the deterrence value of a 'show' of force. They hope that the very presence of large multi-lensed spheres announcing 'Smile! You are on camera!' will deter lifters. They often have one or two such cameras which actually work alongside some fakes added to impress the dishonest shopper. You can sometimes detect the fake ones if the installers have not attached (fake) cables leading into the ceiling. Other stores have working cameras but only one display screen showing four miniature pictures at the same time. There are other systems where an electronic timing device periodically changes which cameras are working. That picture will be seen for a couple of seconds on the monitor (there is only one) at the check-out counter or in a back room.

Low budget movies

"Sometimes I go in a store, you know, and they have this camera watching the entrance and right next to it a monitor, to announce 'We are watching you closely'. Amateurs might fall for it, but I consider this type of video surveillance to be an announcement that says: 'We have only one camera, go ahead and rob us'.

No matter whether cameras are real or ringers, effective or useless, staying on the safe side when you are out 'shopping' is always a good idea. All cameras must be looked upon as real. Never trust them not to work. Rather, try to discover how they work, and if possible, find out what they show and how clearly they show it.

Color coding and focus

"I know this store with maximum video coverage. One aisle, one camera. But, I can see that little coop where the guy is supposed to be sitting and watching the screens. It's empty. There is nobody... Your call! At another store I see the black and white picture of myself on a monitor as I enter the store and look up. I cannot make out if I am a boy or a girl. What the heck will they see? Nothing."

Of course there are the real ones. Those high-tech, high-quality cameras that are able to turn and zoom. They operate very well, hidden under little black hemispheres on the ceiling (probably half of them are fake, but because you cannot see the equipment, you can't tell which ones).

There is always a way to deal with would-be film-makers. The most obvious one is to stand right under the camera. The laws of optical picture reproduction by lens dictate that you will be in a perfect 'blind spot'. If there is another camera in the other corner of the store, it will show you reduced to the size of an ant.

Off camera action

Let us consider our usual routine of picking up the plunder, walking along browsing for more, and packing away only after eliminating suspicion. Walking into a 'blind spot' (some stores cover only certain areas with video and leave the rest unprotected) and concealing the merchandise there, out of the range of the cameras, or simply hurrying out and away fast, are both effective methods. Never forget that if security has seen you on their expensive toy and decided that you are a suspect, they must follow a somewhat time-consuming procedure. As we said earlier, they have to radio or phone down to the floor to instruct somebody to pick you out of the crowd (using their hastily compiled description) and follow you. In case of multiple exits they have to (in an optimal case) cover all the exits with security people, who have been given your (many times very inaccurate) description. Moreover, they can only apprehend you after you have passed the check-out. All that takes manpower, time, accuracy and planning. And those things, my friend, are usually too expensive.

The size of the crew

"Cameras? That's crazy. They're not manned properly. I know half of them are blanks and aren't taking pictures of anything. And those that are - who's watching the monitor? It's generally a high school girl who also has to do homework, answer the telephone, receive packages, let people in and out the back door, and fend off the advances of the cop who's trying to get a date with her."

How many eyes does the camera-man have?

"Of course anybody can decide to avoid the well equipped stores and steal from unprotected ones, but their chances are diminishing as all the better places with better merchandise will sooner or later use these devices." (A security advisor)

Send them to the other studios

In other words, install expensive, subtle, tasteful security devices in your store (because it belongs to a 'better' class of retail enterprises) and dispatch the thieves to less high-toned joints.

In closing, here are two other uses for CCTV. The first one is to record the activity in the store and/or at the check-out in order to obtain evidence in cases of armed robbery, fraudulent accident claims, and credit-card fraud. Many advisors praise the second use, monitoring employees to find out whether they are having long coffee breaks or are filching items from the store. Some se-

Private screenings, dailies and directors' cuts

curity personnel find it fun to watch their coworkers in the locker rooms undressing or taking a shower. We know of at least one lawsuit presently pending in the US involving an employee who was photographed taking off his clothes. For some reason or other he didn't like being congratulated by his fellow employees on his choice of underwear.

Where do they get those wonderful toys?

Video surveillance systems (those wonderful, expensive toys for security managers) can be your friends if you know where they are and how well they work. After you have learned everything about them in a given store, you can pose the question: Are they worthy of my attention? The answer is a resounding yes, but they may also provide you with extra security, natural hiding places, and slower spook-traffic on the store's floor.

ELECTRONIC ARTICLE SURVEILLANCE (EAS)

Investing in their stock was a good idea at the time...

"These systems represent a rapidly growing industry. Since they were first marketed in 1971, sales have steadily grown at a rate of 35 to 40 percent per year in the United States, with even greater increases being shown in the European market. This places sales for 1980 at a little over $70 million for the industry. With an estimated market penetration of only around 5 percent and recent developments that promise to expand the applicability of these systems continued growth seems assured for the next few years." (Baumer and Rosenbaum, 1984)

...investing in their technologies is still not.

Since the book by Baumer and Rosenbaum was published, the industry has developed still further, making what its publicity people might call 'giant technological strides.' Because of these 'wonderful breakthroughs,' EAS manufacturing has grown into a four-billion-dollar-a-year industry, and it is still growing at an impressive pace. Its sales force has merchants convinced that if they replace employees with high-tech doohickeys, their profits will skyrocket. These wise security councilors peddle their wares with statistics showing that the cost of the equipment will be covered in savings within a couple of years. They even claim that when reliance on personal surveillance is reduced, more merchandise can be crammed onto the floor and displays can be more innovative (They stick them here; they stick them there; those tags can go most anywhere). We've seen no evidence to support those claims. We believe that, rather than replacing people with gizmos, stores should tackle the job of loss prevention by hiring good people, paying them a living wage, and training them to be helpful. .

"One large department store places the sensors at all escalators, stairs, and elevators in order to control the movement of merchandise within the store." (CHAIN STORE EXECUTIVE, 1984)

Electronic article surveillance systems are designed to monitor attempts to remove merchandise from the store, from the shelves, into the fitting rooms, onto elevators, from one floor to another, or to be 'packed away.' The stores tag all the items in the inventory (or sometimes only the more expensive ones) with these little thingamajigs. This method assures them (poor deluded them!) that the unauthorized removal of inventory items from a designated area will be monitored electronically (meaning without using human resources).

Are inefficient gizmos cheaper than efficient humans?

Article surveillance systems primarily address the problem of shoplifting, leaving out a sometimes even greater factor in inventory shrinkage: employee theft. Employees who remove and reuse EAS tags are not deterred. They can still continue to use their 'acquisition techniques'

Uncharacteristic spikes on apprehension charts

EAS tags and stickers are designed to protect the store's most expensive, most popular, or simply most vulnerable articles, which thieves target. They do deter amateur shoplifters, who often try to filch low-priced, popular items and may not notice an EAS device on the article. The merchants, happy and satisfied as apprehension rates shoot up shortly after installation, are deluding themselves if they think that opportunities to steal their best goods are no longer there for the real enemy, the smart lifter, who can darn well tell an EAS sticker from a hole in the ground.

Alluding to delusions

HOW EAS DEVICES WORK

"A deterrent-oriented article-surveillance system is designed to increase both the subjective and objective threats of apprehension. Subjectively, the tags are large enough to be noticed by almost everyone handling the items to which they are attached; thus there is no need to employ signs or lights to draw attention to the system. This high visibility, combined with a widespread belief in the infallibility of modern technology, provides a powerful psychological deterrent." (Baumer and Rosenbaum, 1984)

He who has faith will not walk with full pockets!

EAS systems have two basic components: The sensors that activate the alarm and the gates that sound it. If a tag attached to an article passes through the gate, its mechanism notifies security personnel of the event with buzzers, rings, bells and lights

- whatever is built into it. There are three basic technologies with different types of sensors.

Radio waves

The first type employs radio waves to sound the alarm. The gate transmits waves at a certain frequency, and the tag or sticker contains a semi-conductor which, if in contact with that frequency, reflects it to the transmitter which then jangles everybody's nerves.

Magnetic fields

The second type uses a magnetic field instead of the radio frequency. In this case the gate has a built-in device that measures magnetic intensity. The tag, paper strip or sticker has an embedded, magnetized metal strip. If and when the magnetized tag passes the gate, the alarm is activated.

Doggie whistles

The third and latest electronic gadget uses ultrasound, not audible to the human ear. This sophisticated dog whistle powers up the buzzers and lights on the gate when a stolen item is detected.

Most annoying to a loaded lifter

The alarm may take many forms, but it usually expresses itself in an annoying electronic tone, often coupled with a flashing red light to identify the exit visually. The system is monitored by store clerks who are trained to remove or neutralize all tags upon the sale of an article. Store personnel try to handle the alarms in the best possible way in order to eliminate the chance of a false alarm. They do not like to embarrass innocent customers.

Acquiring peace of mind by 'decquiring' the tag

How do the pesky tags which cause all this trouble come off? Easily. Those large plastic tags attached to clothing articles with a metal pin are removed at the time of sale with a specially designed tool and can be used again. An attempt to remove one of them without the tool is difficult and time-consuming, and also noisy in some cases - or so security managers think. But some of these tags come off easily. If, with a little patience, you can turn the knob on the tag slowly while forcing it outwards, after some time it will come off. Also, the half-way-open pin can be bent or broken. With a pair of nail-clippers or a pair of pliers the removal of these tags is even easier. Sometimes, if security has forgotten to tag one or two items, the 'for-profit' shoplifter can immediately scoop them up.

"The large visible tags are supposed to deter shoplifters, while those who are not deterred but unable to remove the tag will be detected and apprehended." (Baumer and Rosenbaum, 1984)

Another lovable misconception. Only the amateur, who does not even know what the tags are for, will be apprehended. The smart lifter will get the tags off and get off with the goods.

Naturally, the tags have to be removed or neutralized at the time of sale. In department stores the clerks at their stations have removal tools to do that. To obtain one of those tools is every pro lifter's dream. The most often-used type is a small, metal, tubular thingamajig into which the clerk inserts the small knob and removes the pin and the tag. We have heard that tag-removers are hard to lift, but one source told us that he easily picked a tag-remover by unscrewing it from a countertop. He used a stocky little screwdriver to accomplish this lift. Imagine the damage he can cause now! His success is further proof of our theory that no merchant can replace good sales people with gadgetry.

The use of tools makes us human!

The other method of neutralizing magnetic stickers and wafers is to place them on a demagnetizer pad, which is a small rubber pad with a notched or craggy surface. Our sources did not mention obtaining one of these, but we have heard about using an unmanned counter's demagnetizer pad to rape the system.

Demagnetizer pads on the counters...

"I amused myself with this magnetically tagged make-up kit. Only noticed the tag at the check-out. What an ass. I was just about to put it back, when I notice that the lady is half-asleep. I asked her for a pack of cigarettes. She turned away and started to look for my brand. She was slow, man, slow as a three-legged dog. While she was sluggishly decoding the cigarette brand names, I demagnetized the tag on the rubber pad they have."

ABOUT THE EAS SUCCESS

We read countless success stories about how effectively the EAS systems worked for certain retailers, even for some of the larger food chains.

"As a part of our overall shrink management system, EAS tagging has been very successful. In one store in a high pilferage area, for example, fifty alarms were set off by customers walking out the store with tagged items during the first three days the system was installed. That number has now fallen off to four or five a week." (SECURITY MANAGEMENT, JUNE 1992)

Every miracle lasts only three days!

The above quote (like the majority of articles on the topic) describes a substantial success as a result of using EAS, but only for the first three days. After that, what happened? They caught a very small number of would-be shoplifters with the device. The

They wouldn't say, we wouldn't think

article says nothing about the last number - the sad note sounded after three happy days. Was that number higher or lower than it was before they installed the expensive electronic devices? (We think it was the same, but don't quote us on it.) The self-promoting retail security writers never seem to probe much after that third day, or, if they do continue their study, they don't seem to have the integrity to share their findings. Did the shrinkage rate change permanently? Did the crooks just wise up and figure out that they should steal items without tags? Shrinkage must have continued, as we know, because statistics show that employee theft is not affected by this technology, but did the pattern change?

To catch a human you need a human

Although the EAS systems available are not infallible, they do operate at a high level of accuracy, thereby greatly increasing the probability of detection of those 'suckers' who do nothing about them. There are certain instances when the system fails to detect the tag and may also cause false alarms that are detrimental to customer relations. Some stores settle for cheap imitations of the real system. They install gates made of wood and tags with no real function, hoping that they will work as deterrents.

"You can see if the gates are fakes. Even if you can't see the difference you can check if they work. Easy. I use my Walkman radio and earphones. I tune it between two stations and listen to the static. I walk through the gate. If there is any change in the static I know that the gate is for real. No change, no buzz! No big deal."

Knock on the gate for luck!

"We were walking with a friend and my wife on this trendy shopping street. I noticed that all the little boutiques had 'buzzer-gates,' and they all looked alike. First I thought, like... okay, they dealt with the same company. Then I started to wonder how these little shops could afford such systems. I couldn't resist. I checked them out. They were probably sold by the same company, true, but they were fakes. No wires attached. On closer inspection they turned out to be made of wood (some of them were even chipped). I guess they look good."

Stores with an insufficient number of employees are not able to respond in an appropriate manner and time. Apprehension does not take place, and so the system is useless and worthless. EAS does not catch lifters; it makes noise. To catch the thieves, management still needs people, but if they have the people, what's the use of the gizmos? Deterrence; nothing else.

Retailers have said at various times (both to us and to other researchers) that they are not interested in catching thieves. They would only like to deter them. Apprehensions are complicated affairs for the retailer. He needs well-trained, educated personnel. If an apprehension is mishandled, he can expect a costly lawsuit. If a shoplifter is caught and prosecuted, the retailer's employees will miss working days because of the trial. The time and expense will probably not be commensurate with the loss. If the actual catching of the thief could be made into an event, it might serve as a deterrent to other shoppers who witnessed it, but store-owners shy away from creating spectacles for fear of frightening away honest shoppers.

Costs and benefits, and the fear of fret

A NOTE ON EAS EFFECTIVENESS

If you have come this far into our book, you may already suspect that all EAS devices can be defeated by smart lifters. In addition to this fact, there are a couple of other things to stress. EAS devices are not totally reliable. In a small percentage of cases, they go off by themselves or, worse, pacemakers, pager devices, and portable telephones trigger them. Electrical or mechanical failure, sometimes caused by something as simple as a shopping cart bumping into the gates, can render them dysfunctional.

Failure?

PLASTIC TAGS (IN ALL SHAPES AND SIZES)

The plastic EAS tag is visibly (deterrence value) positioned on the article. It is easy to find and, under the right circumstances, easy to remove. Don't forget that the removal must be done in a safe corner or nook of the store.

"I can do a number of things with radio or magnetic tags. I can remove them. I can check if they work at all. I can cover them with aluminum foil and they will not work. I can even walk out sometimes and not give a hoot if the buzzer goes because there is not a soul to stop me. Also, I have already lifted two different tag removal devices, which were left at an unattended counter. So, what do you think about them? Do you think they work?"

They come off now!

Covering the tags with aluminum-foil is said to guarantee that the radio, ultrasound or magnetic tags will not set off the alarm. You can cover the whole article in aluminum foil, or you can line a large pocket in your coat (if not the whole coat) with

Not only for your sandwich

the foil and presto! You have defeated one of the most sophisticated anti-theft devices in use today.

PSEUDO BAR-CODES AND PRICE TAGS

That's the way the plastic crumbles...

Look at those stickers on the backs of books, CDs and other items. They resemble bar-codes, or an actual price tag, and most times they are embedded with a small semiconductor or a magnetic strip which triggers the alarm at the exit. If you are not the 'jogger' type and don't like to run, with the help of a small knife, or just your nails, you can easily remove these stickers. After breaking the plastic wrap, be sure you remove the whole wrapping. Pay attention to the noise. Don't crumple the wrapping! We have already spoken about demagnetizer pads, but here is another quote from one of our 'friends.'

"You know their method of demagnetizing stickers. They have a rubber pad at the cashier's counter. She places the item on it, and that is it. For a long time I removed those stickers with my knife beforehand. One day, I realized that for some reason, they had the same pad plugged in at the pharmacist's counter. After that I did my demagnetizing there. Most of the time he was busy, anyway. When he was not, I asked him to look up something in his computer about my medicine."

LONG MAGNETIC STRIP (WAFER)

Open a book!

Wafers are used mostly in video cassettes and books. They are long paper or plastic strips with a thin magnetic metal foil in them. They can be placed on the outside (simply tear them off), inside (open the box and check for it), or between the pages of a book. In unpacked books you can easily find the strip. The book opens by itself at the wafer as if it were a bookmark. If the item is packaged it can have one, two or even more. If you do not find a wafer, check the item twice; check it three times. If you can still not find one, and you are certain that the store uses them, the best course is to leave that particular item alone and find another one. Just because it looks like it was packed in the factory, do not assume that it has no strip. Security personnel imitate factory-like packaging and cellophaning in many stores. After you have learned their method, make note of it and visit again.

PAINT VIAL TAGS - THE NEW WAVE

PVT a.k.a. OIT

It is the new fad on the security market. Paint Vial Tags, also known as the 'Omnipotent Ink-Tags'. Everybody is raving about them. Several different companies are making them by the millions. Shoplifters, even some professionals or skilled amateurs, are standing with their jaws at their knees. 'What the heck we gonna do?'

The idea behind the ink-tag is simple. If you try to pry it off, it breaks and sprinkles ink all over the article in all the colors of the rainbow, rendering the article useless. The assumption behind the use of this 'low-tech' approach is that even determined shoplifters will refrain from senseless vandalism. Security managers reason that, like everybody else, lifters would like to ***use*** the item. Against amateur shoplifters the ink-tag really is the best deterrent so far, even though it does cause some merchandise to be ruined 'Okay,' say the stores, 'we lose a couple of sweaters, but if that loss teaches those light-fingered louies a lesson and saves us from losing a thousand - great!' They put on warning labels advising shoppers about what will happen if they try to tamper with the tag. Personally, we think a customer in a vengeful mood might make very effective use of this device in his quest to get back at a store where he had been cheated or otherwise angered, but stores don't make their purchasing decisions on the basis of what one or two angry customers might do, and, anyway, a good security advisor" (salesman for the industry) would soon dismiss such an objection by saying that vandalism is covered by insurance.

Put the ink on the sweaters

What we are sure of, however, is what we have learned, and believe you us, in this age of information, even without us it would not stay a secret: The ink-tag is a worthless method of theft-prevention!

"The ink tag is God's little gift to lifters! They trust them blindly. Security is low. You freely take whatever you want. At home a warmed-up thin steak-knife will cut open the plastic knob. You cut the top around about two millimeters down. The little cap, that you just cut away, comes off. A little spring jumps out, and a little metal cup will show. It might be still stuck in the plastic, which can be cleared away in a jiffy. When the metal cup comes out, three or four miniature ball-bearings give - if they do not give, you have to shake the thing a couple times and like in a fairy tale, 'open sesame', it's yours."

Easy as pie! Lots of air and no wind!

We also figure that once you have had enough of this little physics experiment in your kitchen - the knife gets hot, you cut yourself or the lovely pair of jeans you have just acquired -you will simply go to the hardware store to buy (or lift) the hot-wire

Power Tool

electric tool that is used by hobbyists to cut plastic. Once you have it, you can open your own store!

ELECTR(ON)IC WARNING DEVICES

Detected motion or cut current?

These electric cables are attached to small black boxes which are in turn glued to expensive articles or display items in radio-stereo-video stores, department stores, and computer stores. Some little wired boxes are motion detectors. They are sensitive to motion or a cutting of the circuit. To find out if you are dealing with an actual motion detector, not a mock-up, you have only to move or gently shake the item to which it is attached. If the device makes a warning noise, you are out of luck although we did hear one tale about the successful removal of these annoying little traps. If the device is not a motion detector (by the way, we suspect that most of the time it is not), the only problem is that you cannot cut the wire. The wire completes the circuit. To disable the device, you have to cut the casing of the wire (do not cut through), then simply connect the two exposed wires. Another source said that with a thin blade you can cut between the item and the 'whatchamacallit,' that little black box glued to it. Underneath there is a 'spring switch'. You have to keep that switch from springing out with a solid flat object (a knife or blade will do). After the cut has been made, the device can be attached to the shelf and the item is "totally yours" (his words). By the way, although the display item might be connected to this warning system, on the shelves underneath you can often find the same item in a box, ready to be lifted.

PAINTED STRIPS

Magnetic paint?

This device is very rarely used in North America. In fact it seems nobody has ever heard of it, and no literature mentions it. We have very little data ourselves, and so for all we know it may just be a myth, but one of our sources has experienced problems with some kind of white or invisible magnetic paint in a bookstore in Europe. The paint is impossible to detect, but if you should manage to do the impossible, the page or portion of a page is removable. Why magnetic paint is not in wide use, we can only speculate. As we all know, even the so-called experts in the field with their own 'invisible' security elements, are not deterring shoplifting. One wonders why nobody in the industry on this side of the Atlantic has hunted down such an interesting product. But perhaps we already know the answer. When it comes down to it, merchants are interested in keeping their inventory shrinkage to the minimum, not in catching tons of shoplifters.

THE FUTURE TECHNOLOGIES

"The future is made of the same stuff as the present."

(Simone Weil)

In this age of electronic and information revolutions, we may one day see some amazing improvements and changes in tools and tactics. Information chips that trigger silent alarms might be embedded in articles of clothing, and with 'tricorders' (see Star Trek), security could then locate the articles, ergo the shoplifter. There is a spray-paint visible under black light that could put a trace on an article (how they will remove it at the point of sale is another question). We have read about gates that will one day register (like the UPC code at the cashier) all your purchases and 'non-purchases' on the sales-slip as you walk through them. The future could also hold large warehouses, with sample items, where the shopper placed an order through some gizmo and the article was waiting for him at the cashier's station.

Pardon me, Sir, my tricorder has detected an alien object in your crotch!

They could mail you the stuff (mail order, and direct marketing, are booming businesses). They could put a contraption like a back-pack on you that would continuously communicate your actions to the Big Brain of the shop. If you stole something, Robocop would be right there to arrest you. They could introduce nudist shops. Where can someone hide something when he's naked?

Where the sun doesn't shine?

We are sure they will try each and every one of these and more. Technologies do not work without people, and shoplifters always find a way to defeat them. Because lifting is an age-old art, it has a future until the world does away with shops altogether. Then the 'wise-guys' who were shoplifting will have to look for some other way to complement their income and hold onto their freedom and their carefree lives.

Close down all shops!

TOOLS OF THE TRADE

"Man is a tool-using animal. . . . Without tools he is nothing, with tools he is all."

(Thomas Carlyle)

High-tech gizmos are no good to retailers as long as smart lifters have the right tools for disabling them. These tools can also be high tech, but they are more likely to be simple household items. We will give a short description of the use and implementation of those tools.

CAR

Keep on truckin'!

It is at one and the same time the professional shoplifters' storage and transportation. Most lifters like to do 'days' instead of zillions of little jobs, and a car lets them do just that. Everybody except members of some bold gangs on the far side advises against using the car as a getaway. It should be parked not too far from, and not too close to, the store. The trunk is the place to collect the loot. The artful lifter's jalopy allows him to boldly go where no lifter has gone before. He can drive to alien towns where security is in direct proportion to the size of the town and in reverse proportion to its distance from a Metropolitan area.

TOUCH-KNIFE

Make a little cut...

Any thin knife will do for cutting. However, this little knife is the best, most often used, and most often mentioned type. It is called a touch-knife, (maybe because it opens at one touch). It is made in the Far East by several companies. It is a small, colorful, flat plastic half-moon with a small blade inside. It has a (usually black) button that, if pushed outwards, makes a small, very sharp blade protrude. It clicks into position and stays out until a little spring automatically retracts it. Other types of open-close knives used in offices or in print-shops do very well, only they are bulkier to carry and a touch more complicated to use. This little knife removes a lot of cellophane and plastic (together with magnetic tags) that keeps you from the merchandise.

PLIERS (SCISSORS)

Get them in the same store!

There are many different types for many different uses. The ones which enable the user to cut and hold at the same time, used mostly for cutting electrical wires, are best for prying off the little plastic knobs from the inner side tabs. Scissors do the same trick and could also be helpful in opening or cutting the packaging or removing EAS stickers.

OLD-FASHIONED RAZOR BLADE

Same use as the touch-knife. Very sharp. If you put duct tape on one side, you make the razor blade a touch safer. Heated up, it cuts the plastic tips of ink-tabs. Careful, do not burn yourself!

PENKNIFE

A very small pocket-knife, originally named after its use in sharpening quill pens. It is used to cut off price tags, open boxes, and remove packaging. It is also helpful in removing plastic or paper EAS stickers from the merchandise. A cheaper kind of thin, heated knife could be used to cut off the plastic knobs from ink-tags.

To sharpen your image?

SHADES

A controversial tool with serious limitations. You might try wearing a pair in a store or mall with natural lighting. Sources were both for and against using them. The advantage of a pair of sunglasses is about the same in a store as it is on the beach. No, it is not protection against the brightness of those 'murderous' UV rays. The advantage is that you can watch other people without being obvious about it. You can observe without being observed.

Where the sun doesn't shine?

"Yeah, I use sunglasses, but only on the top of my head. If you wear them they will suspect that you are a drug addict and you are trying to cover your eyes. An added advantage of having sunglasses is that you can hold them, fold them, position them. All natural movements of a normal person. You will look more like a real shopper."

PAIR OF GLOVES

If you forget the childish notion that you can hide something in them, a pair of gloves can be useful. In winter it is normal to walk around with your gloves in your hand. The gloves will allow you to keep your arm in a bent position, thus giving you a strong hold on anything you have under your arm. They can also provide cover and some sort of distraction. If the snoops notice that your hand or hands are busy with gloves, it may not occur to them that you could also be using them for something else.

Where the wind doesn't blow?

ALUMINUM FOIL

The normal kitchen type they sell at any corner store. Smaller and larger pieces cut from the roll are useful for covering plastic EAS devices completely. Some lifters use foil to line pockets and avoid the 'dreaded' alarm. We also heard from a source that he had a coat-jacket fully lined with aluminum foil for his gracious exits.

Where radar waves don't ripple?

ELASTIC (TIGHT) UNDERWEAR

After dogs and books your third best friend!

For 'in the crotch' and 'in the back' methodists, tight underwear is a very important piece of attire. Especially in the summer, but any time, really, it will hold flat or folded merchandise straight and tightly in place. Nothing can fall down or slide off. Elastic is a good friend to all of us!

ANY BAG, BACKPACK, TOTE BAG

Carless not careless!

You can use it as a cover by intentionally handing it over at the checkout to indicate that you are an honest and law-abiding shopper. Occasionally, you can pack away some stuff in it, but only in certain circumstances. It can also function as a trunk for the carless user's loot.

Bag it? Not to bag it?

A person walking around in a store with many packages and bags might raise suspicion, except, perhaps, during the holiday season. Just leave your bag at the counter.

A really useful bag for packing away is the one which carries the trademark of the store. You can try to take some of these from an empty counter, or you can use one you acquired with a legal purchase. It is important that the bag look flawless and impeccable. If it looks used or worn you will have no luck with it. If you are carrying your loot in a mall, it is a good idea to invest some small change to buy the mall's large shopping bag. It is displayed in automatic dispensers all around.

STAPLE AND STAPLE REMOVER

Nice try...

Some stores staple the opening of the bag with your receipt on it to show security that the bag is legitimate and to make it 'impossible' for you to put anything else into it. They must never have read this story published in Klemke's book:

> ***"- It's easy to get things. Even like this dress.***
>
> ***- What dress?***
>
> ***- Huh?***
>
> ***She seemed surprised I hadn't known. She opened the bag she had been holding, and there, along with the blouse she had paid for, was a dress.***
>
> ***-But the bag was stapled.***
>
> ***-I put it in the bag in the dressing room. With this.***
>
> ***She opened her purse and showed me a stapler with a staple remover."***

HOOKS AND CLASPS

Old-fashioned shoplifters use hooks, bent wire, or curved metal strips sewn inside their clothes to secure various items. Jackets zipped at the bottom accomplish the same trick. It would be hard to pretend to be an amateur, first timer or 'having-a-bad-day' lifter who had acted on impulse and made one bad move if you had hooks sewn inside your coat!

Peter Pan where are you?

FREEZER

An interesting offering. What can you do with a freezer? Well, you can store meat, cheese, fish and the like. You can load up in a couple of trips, and then you do not have to go back for food for awhile. Time passes; sales help forget. If you show up too often in the food-stores you are stealing from, you risk having them make you.

Keep the cool cod cold!

HOT WIRE PLASTIC CUTTER

You can acquire one in a hardware store. Handymen and hobbyists use this tool to cut plastic. It is essential (although a hot knife or blade works just as well) for removing the tip of the plastic knob on ink-tags. It will pay for itself many times over even if you are not able to get your hands on one for free.

Hot-wiring a three-piece suit

TAG REMOVER

It is a small device the sales clerks use to remove all kinds of tags. They push in the little knob. In the device there is a magnet that holds the little metal balls while the pin is removed. The tag comes off and is reused.

It is, of course, very hard to buy one. Companies who make these tools only sell them with their systems. On the other hand, they are very common in department stores. If a station is empty, look for one. The tubular metal ones are screwed to the table. With a short little screwdriver you can hold onto the screw under the table while you 'remove the remover' from the top. If you have one... the retail battleground becomes your playground.

They live in the wild on counter tops

THE MORAL OF THE PASSAGE

> ***"Oh, all those fantastic new inventions, oh, how they fail their masters."***
>
> *(Anonymous)*

And there will definitely be progress!

There is a skill for every method. There is a tool for every job. You have to be the inventive craftsman who finds the appropriate tool for each lift. It appears that everything has been tried by the security industry. They have curbed a little here, a lot there, but they have never really succeeded. With all of their high-tech equipment, it seems they are catching compulsive shoplifters - housewives, teenagers, old folks - but very rarely any real, professional lifters.

CONCEALMENT AND DRESS CODE

MERCHANDISE CONCEALMENT

> ***"O, divine art of subtlety and secrecy! Through you we learn to be invisible, through you inaudible and hence we can hold the enemy's fate in our hands."***
> *(Sun Tzu)*

Concealment of the stolen article is probably the most crucial moment of the act. There are many different time-honored methods as well as many you can improvise on the spot. The concealment method is the most important component because making a mistake there is the most likely cause of your 'fall'. Seeing through your concealment procedure is the cornerstone of any criminal case against you. Concealment has to be done fast, properly and without any person actually witnessing the act.

The crucial moment

According to sources in the trade literature, in department stores or malls the purse is the typical hiding place for women and for both sexes the plastic shopping bag is a frequent method of concealment. At food stores the purse is used as a method of concealment. Hiding items under clothing and using pockets as hiding places follows closely. These three concealment methods are on the top of the lists in other types of stores as well. In drug stores, our sources have found that placement in a pocket, a purse, and under clothing are the top three methods of concealment.

If they know everything how come there are shoplifters working?

For women the most used concealment method is the purse, or shopping bag from the same store. For men the preferred hiding place was under their attires, shirts, pullovers. Concealment in pocket is used to a significant degree by both men and women but mainly in pharmacies, drugstores, and hardware stores.

Place does not matter! Only if you do it wrong!

We hope that we all agree that this kind of categorization of hiding places is ludicrous in the case of shoplifter-apprehension. It has not much use either in theft-prevention or 'catch-prevention'.

Now we are talking!

"There are probably as many different methods of shoplifting as there are shoplifters. The pertinent literature contains listings of numerous methods for concealing merchandise...." (Progressive Grocer, March 1984)

Successful concealment does not depend primarily on how and where you hide an item. The most crucial factors of concealment are timing, boldness and presence of mind.

Story of the Apprentice

"I am an amateur, and I know that I am. I had a true master who showed me most of the tricks I know. The guy was outrageous. I went to visit him once and stayed so late that I ended up sleeping over. The next morning we went to the corner store to buy some food. It was a small place with the checkout counter in the middle, close to the door. Behind the cashier was a shelf on the desk. That's where they kept the cigarettes. Most of them were exactly at her eye level. Obviously, they knew that they had to watch them. There was another woman in the store, just in front of us at the cash register.

I was holding the basket, my buddy was standing beside me, facing the cashier who was punching in the items for the women in front of us. He reached up, picked up four or five packs of cigarettes and dropped them into his bag. And then another batch. And another. The blood froze in my veins. If the cashier glanced up, she would have seen the whole thing. If the woman in front of me turned her head, she would have seen it, but they didn't. My buddy knew that they wouldn't.

With cold blood

I thought about that incident a lot. I realized that it wasn't as dangerous as it seemed at the time. If she (the cashier) looked up while he was reaching for it, he would have picked one to throw it into the shopping basket. If she did when he was already holding them, he could still have dropped them into the basket and give some back with an excuse when paying for the stuff. The only moment the she was not supposed to see was the one when he dropped them into his bag."

We mentioned many methods of concealment earlier in the book when we discussed, time, place, and methods. Here we will try to compile a list of the ***Ten Most Used and Useful Concealment Places***. Here we go, number ten:

UNDER ARM

Probably the most used and abused method of hiding a stolen item is to shove it under your arm. In situations where the getaway route is secured and fast, packing under the arm works well even for amateurs. On the other hand, if you have to walk a lot, use escalators, or check for a pursuing detective, this method of concealment can be very dangerous. The 'goods' might slide. Using this method requires knowledge of ***what*** can be held under the arm safely.

Thar' she slides!

Thar' she slides!

"It took me some time to get the idea that I can not hold four glossy skin magazines together under my arm. They kept sliding down. I had to press my arm to my side as if I had a charley horse. Now, I shove them under my shirt where they stick to my skin when I'm sweaty, but at least I can walk straight."

They are shiny, they are slimy.

Another problem with this procedure is that the shoplifter's arm often looks disabled and tense, a visible clue for 'thief-catchers'. Our professional sources told us that they rehearsed and exercised a lot to make sure that even though the upper arm was holding something fast to their bodies, the movement of the lower arm seemed natural. 'Take a couple of mime lessons and learn about how to work the muscle groups disconnectedly on your arm,' one of our artist 'friends' told us.

A mime is a terrible thing to waste!

With all its disadvantages, this method remains a classic because of the possibility of smooth execution. When the coast is clear enough, you hold up the merchandise and fold your body 'over it,' meaning that instead of just your hand, your whole body moves, minimizing the danger of somebody spotting a hand movement.

UNDER ARM - UNDER SHIRT

A 'safer' way to pack the 'goodies' than simply under your arm. If you wear suspenders, this improvement on a classic procedure works even better. A loose jacket must cover your shirt (or pullover). A scarf may be added to obstruct the view from the front. There are two ways of executing this method. The first is done when the buttons are opened (and later closed) on the shirt and the loot slides under the shirt, which will hold it without handicapping the upper arm. If a suspender is used, it will provide protection against items slipping back to the front. The second way is to have the upper part of the shirt open under a pullover, and slide the items, from the neck downwards in under the shirt. Both practices will require a secure hold on the shirt, (strong belt, strong elastic underwear) that will not allow the shirt to slip out from pants or skirts.

The new and improved classic method

"I used to work with packing my shirt from the front and buttoned the shirt up before I went to check out. Unbuttoning was always easy, since I did it before I entered the store. But, buttoning back became a nuisance. Then one day I realized that I could slide things straight to the side from my neck. I found the movement of my hand was less obvious, and also I was able to start using T-shirts instead of shirts."

IN THE CROTCH

No not the kick, please!

Another place where 'goods' slide in easily is the crotch. It is a two-handed operation. One hand pulls away the pants, skirt, etc., and the other lets the article slide in or pushes it down. Again, thought has to be given to 'slippage.' Anything that goes down there should be secured. Strong elastic underwear (bicycle pants, firm elastic briefs) holds most objects immobile. It's a good choice any time, but almost the only option in the summer (and in Florida).

Down under, the belly

If you have a little (or big) potbelly, your bodily configuration could be of inestimable assistance. Underneath that walrus tummy is a large space just waiting to be packed. After the region is full, your belly just looks a little more straight, not fatter. A waist pouch is a useful tool for covering or evening out any bulge that has been created in the crotch.

ON THE BACK

Fast and steady wins the race!

A preferred place to conceal stolen items is on one's back. The same precautions have to be taken as with the 'in the crotch' method. Do not allow anything to slip! Naturally, you can put stuff on your back only if it is covered by a loose jacket, coat or pullover. Preferably, you should use this hiding place for flat items, such us books, packaged goods, and the like. You can make your movement look as if you were just tucking your shirt in. You can keep an eye (or two) on the salesman who might turn and see you. You also have to be sure that you are safe from the back. That can be achieved by standing in front of a shelf.

To secure items on one's back a suspender is mighty handy. It will keep the stuff fairly secure from falling out or even making a bulge. If you work with a partner, he can 'cover your back' while you are 'sliding,' and you can also ask him to check whether there is any unseemly bulging.

IN THE POCKET

A pocketful of advice

Use pockets of any kind sparingly. They are not good hiding places. Pockets bulge out easily, and bulges are noticed by security people. You might be politely asked if there was anything in your pockets. And then asked to pay for what was there.. Very small or unpacked articles can go in pockets, but our professional sources, use pockets only if they are also doing real shopping.

The inside pocket of a coat is an excellent place for small items that must disappear safely and fast. Usually, the better coats have inside pockets on both sides. Some of them even have one at the waist (used for gloves). If you pack into coat pockets, it is advisable that the job be done fast and safely at a 'blind spot'. To create some kind of diversion, at the moment of concealment you might want to pull out your wallet, check it, and put it back. This is a mediocre method which takes account of the fact that security looks for people who manipulate in pockets or hold a hand in a pocket.

IN BAGS

We beg you not to bag!

Many stores have policies about leaving your bags at the counter. Sometimes they provide a bag-check clerk who will give you a number for your bag. If they allow bags to be carried around the store, they will look for people who have them. The bag (any bag) might be a diversion measure in stores where they do not have such a policy. You can make sure that they see you as an honest shopper if you make it your business to leave your bags with them and ask them to keep an eye on them.

What a bag can do in the right hand...

"I use tote-bags for stealing shoes and roller blades. I make sure that the bag looks full, stuff a couple of towels in there, so after I packed, it won't change size. But this is an 'in-and-out-in-two-minutes' move. You have to know where it is, what size you want, act fast, and walk out fast. I did this only in big department stores, where you have a lot of ways to scram. Elevators, escalators, stairs. I always check if I am followed or not. If I am, I lose the whole bag at one point and go out without it. They got my two towels, and my worn-out bag, but not me!"

The second run

"I went to get a pair of skates. In this department store, they were slowly eliminating their sports department and it was full of empty paper boxes, some stuff here and there, but nobody around. I mean, not one sales guy! So I decided to do a kind of a 'hit and run'. It was on the seventh floor. I took my empty sports bag... straight in the elevator... went up to seven... got the pair of skates... back in the elevator and left. Elementary. But that is not the funny part. Next day

I decided that I ought to go back and get another pair. The sports department was swarming with sales guys. They probably found the empty box, so for next day they were 'ready' for me. I left. A week later when I got that second pair... plus knee-pads and ankle-pads everything was back to normal. The sports floor was guarded only by empty paper boxes."

UP THE SLEEVE

It's magic!

A magician's move in reverse. The magician produces a dove or a card from his sleeve. The shoplifter slides stuff up there. The maneuver works best with jackets that have an elastic or other fastener around the wrist. The item either goes from the front upwards, or slides down from the top of the sleeve. If your sleeves are bulky enough, they can even hold some larger items. Your hands will move freely, and you will therefore raise less suspicion. We've even heard that books or a bottle of wine can fit in a sleeve.

UNDER WEAR

The 'safest' concealment for clothing items. It can be done out in the open if there is no security around. Try on a shirt, a pullover, or something, and immediately dress over it with your original clothing.

It won't slip under the slip.....

Packing can be done most safely in fitting rooms or booths. In many cases you have to conceal the item before taking it in, bringing along something else for cover. In case there are fitting room checkers (unlikely), they will just see you trying on some articles. If they suspect that there are more than they allowed you to take in - it is their mistake. Tell them. There is no 'appropriate' order in which to dress yourself. You can slip a winter jacket under your shirt if it fits. Having outerwear under your underwear will keep it tight.

IN SOCKS AND BOOTS

Puss 'n Boots

Many times you have seen your favorite action hero or cowboy hiding a revolver on his ankle. The 'bad guys' had no idea he was so cleverly prepared to gun them down. Your ankle is as safe for you as it was for the action hero, an excellent concealment spot for long, small items. Tuck them into your socks or your high boots where there is plenty of room for them. Your leg movements will stay smooth. The source who told us about this procedure once 'done 'em in' completely. Security checked only his coat, pockets and upper body. How's that for dumb luck, Pilgrim?

'NO CONCEALMENT' CONCEALMENT

"Don't hide the stuff! Yeah, you heard it right. Sometimes it's better not to hide the thing you want to take for a walk... I mean literally 'for a walk'. Depends on your guts and the size of the item. The bigger the better. The more gutsy you are the bolder you act. Let's say you go and nonchalantly pick up a VCR in its box and just firmly walk out the department store. Think about it. In their mind, nobody would dare to do such a thing. They look at you from afar - here you are walking with this big box - and they think you must have paid for it! If you are convincing enough and you checked for snoops beforehand, the sales people won't stop you. And if they do, you can still pretend that you were looking for help... changed your mind... all the stories you have at your disposal..."

Breaking the enemy's resistance without fighting

The highest form of victory, according to Sun Tzu, is the one which you achieve without fighting. The most sophisticated hiding place is out in the open. If you can hide something within the ***aura*** of your self- confidence, than size and shape will not matter. If you can walk out with bold self-assurance, you have your battle won, your spoils secured.

GENERAL RULES OF CONCEALMENT

"The data on concealment methods used by apprehended shoplifters may differ from those of unapprehended shoplifters."(Baumer and Rosenbaum, 1984)

Go Baumer! Go Rosenbaum!

As you may have noticed by now, Baumer and Rosenbaum, two social scientists, are our preferred source for quotations. Sometimes they fall into the same statistical, social and psychological traps as the others, but at least they are ready to analyze, assess and evaluate the picture with some objectivity. We are not social scientists, but we did try to learn from the better ones.

In making our conclusions, we have decided to forget about all kinds of assumption-statistics. We do not discuss in this book the million more concealment methods there are. We have only dealt with the most common ones - above and in many other places. It is our intention at this point in the book to illustrate in a short, concise passage the 'general' rules of concealment as we heard and collected them from our professional sources (the smart lifters).

Go Booster!
Go Rosenboost!

"If you hide the stuff well, and nobody has seen you are home free, my friend. Cashiers, stacker boys and baggers have no time and energy to look if your hand is not hanging right, or if you have a small bulge under your upper arm or really, anything."

In spite of your mastery of all the methods and tricks of concealment, you could find yourself in front of a judge faster than you can say: 'I didn't do it!' if somebody ***saw*** you packing or lifting. The most important rule is to make sure that you are invisible to any video contraption, security personnel, or other shoppers. Make sure that you are alone. We mean, make sure ***cautiously***, and then continue. Remember that looking nervously around is a no-no. Your invisibility check can give you away fast if you don't do it right.

You have to be calm, relaxed and tranquil. Remember that you have time, and if you do not, there are other stores and other days. This is a 'general' rule of shoplifting, not only for the time of concealment but for any other portion of the act.

Keep it light and walk easy

"And just after you hide the stuff well, you have to walk out. It's sometimes hard to walk with that much stuff in your pants, on your back and in your coat pocket. Walk? No. You stroll, pacing calmly. You promenade out. You stop here and there; look at stuff right in front of a sales girl; ask a question. You know you have the stuff tight. You know nobody picked you out. Then do not screw it up by sauntering out like a herd of buffaloes."

Finally, about the proper way of concealment, here is a little Aesopiesque fable we wrote for you:

The Frog, The Fox and the Vixens

The Frog is on vacation in Florida. He is spending a lot of time on the beach, trying to score with the Vixens. Nothing. He notices, though, that many of them are swarming around this lifeguard, the Fox, like flies. He decides to get some advice from him. He goes to him and asks: 'Tell me, good friend, could you give me some advice about how to be a little more successful with the Vixens?' 'Certainly,' the Fox answers, 'You go to the market and buy a nice, well-shaped potato. You come back, put it in your swimsuit and I guarantee you that there will be some action.' Okay, the Frog does exactly as told. Nothing. Strangely, the Vixens not only look through him, but they are trying to get away as far from him as possible. The Frog goes back to the Fox and says: 'Good friend, I did exactly what you told me, and now the situation is even worse! What should I do?' The Fox smirks and answers: 'Put the potato in the front!'

Now that we have learned about the crucial importance of proper concealment, it is time to learn a little about fashion. Maybe, after all, it wasn't the placement of the potato but the style of the swim-wear.

DRESS CODE

"Fashion is architecture: it is a matter of proportions."

(Coco Chanel)

"People tend to have preconceived notions concerning shoplifters, visualizing them as punks, teenagers, blacks, bums and ethnics dressed in shabby clothes, strolling in off the street. A professional shoplifter, which I am proud to be for the past fourteen years, would never look like them. I mean you have to discriminate. I won't allow any of my guys to dress like a bum punk. My minions and I are always impeccably dressed and well-mannered - we must. We have to be the least likely suspects."

Let the glove fit!

Never wear clothing that might raise suspicion in the minds of the security people in the stores. Because of their training and experience, veteran sales clerks and security officers become immediately aware of anybody who is dressed in baggy clothing, a large coat or a puffy jacket, especially in mild weather. Do they notice such clothes in the winter, though? They cannot stop everybody with a ski jacket or large coat on. Actually, smart lifters dress like an average customer if not more so (meaning that on a cold day they will look 'under-dressed' for the weather).

Let the seasons fit!

You should never wear your coat or jacket on your shoulders or carry it on your arm. Never wear unusually loose or baggy pullovers or jackets. Dress according to season and weather. A woman raises suspicion if she walks into the department where they sell hats and purses without a hat or a purse. Carrying bags, umbrellas, or even a bunched up newspaper might present you as a potential target for trailing by the troopers. Yet, if you use such items appropriately and in a natural manner, they will deflect suspicion.

DRESS APPROPRIATELY FOR THE SEASON

"You have to dress for the seasons. Elementary. You have to be crazy to try to get away with bulky coats or pants in the summer. I do more books and CD's in the summer, less or almost nothing of the bigger stuff. Food is about the same, but in the summer you have to go twice, big

Watch Weatherman!

whoop. Anyways, I'd rather go one by one anytime. The risk is lower and if they catch you with just one stupid little thing, you come out better."

"Everybody I know considers the season. You don't want to look ridiculous when you march in your winter coat on a very warm day of the spring. And not only ridiculous but suspicious like hell. The only thing in the summer, mind you very rarely, the only thing I use is a small fisherman's vest. It has millions of hidden pockets; it's loose and in a mall where they have shops that cater to fishermen or campers and if the mall is close to a resort, campground, beach or something, it works very well."

Dress like Weatherman?

Some of our subjects told us about how they plan their appearance. They consider the season, the style (wearing less casual apparel to a more expensive store), and the practicality and usefulness of their articles of clothing.

BE COOL AND BE LOOSE

Suspicious? Who, me?

Not only in your behavior but also in the way you dress. The general rule is that the garment you are wearing has to look and be loose. Security advisors tell their trainees to look out for large, zipped-up, secured jackets and buttoned-up coats with belts (these being uncharacteristic apparel inside), but their advice won't help their students catch smart lifters! The pros prefer loose jackets open at the front or long coats worn open and loose. They secure their loot with shirts, pullovers, pants, or by other means.

"I never close my jacket, not even on the coldest days. I wear a short scarf on my neck that gives me a certain coverage. I pack either onto my back, in my crotch or under my shirt or pullover and under my shirt."

SUSPENDERS

Always old-fashioned, always in fashion

We hesitated about whether we should put suspenders in the 'Tools of the Trade' section, but finally we decided that suspenders were more of a fashion accessory then a tool. For men they are normal attire and always in fashion for all ages because a pair of suspenders expresses an attitude. You can further enhance the effect by wearing a bow-tie with your suspenders. For a woman, - about woman's fashion we know hardly anything. Who does? - suspenders might be an interesting look which will make the security studs more sympathetic toward her. This fashion benefit comes as an addition to their main function - their practicality. They help keep flat or neatly folded items securely on your back. Under your arm and shirt they keep items from wandering around aimlessly.

"You can leave your coat or whatever loose and open. You hide the merchandise under your shirt. I usually leave a couple of buttons open and wear a comfortable pullover over it. I slide in the stuff. My suspender will hold it from sliding back out. I can wave my arms freely. The less chance they will pick me out. If your arms are not in motion, rigidly holding the stuff, they will suspect you."

We have already discussed the pros and cons of working in the summer and winter. Here we offer only a couple of additional, short quotations.

IN THE SUMMER

"In the summer I wear shorts and a large T-shirt. I wear bicycle pants under my shorts. That's the trick. It keeps the stuff securely in place, and anyway... very few people look at your crotch. It's just not proper. Anyway, they won't pick me as a lifter since they cannot imagine that I'll be the one who boosts. I mean, I have a loose T-shirt on, where does the stuff go? Of course you cannot bring out the 'world' in the summer. You must go more than once, that's all."

I could do it in the buff!

Note: There were many unresolved arguments between the authors, one of the main ones was about looking at the crotches of members of different gender groups. One of us thinks that looking at crotches in general is 'just not done', and the other thinks it does not apply to women because he looks often. This conflict has never come to a head! Write to us: What do you think?

IN THE WINTER

"In the winter, you can make twice as much as in the summer. I work in clothing, and it's winter stuff. In the summer you cannot get away with jacket and coats. You would be stupid to think that they won't stick on you in an instant! It is easier to dress for work when it's cold. And other people look exactly like you, most of them never even open their coats and that, my friend is suspicious. I know that the tail will be put on them and the snoops will be screwed. There is another thing for winter. You can pick out the snoops more often! They are the ones who are not wearing winter coats or jackets!"

Snoopy is always bare-ass naked, except some times he wears a tie.

IS FAKE ID A DISGUISE?

If that, then why not crack safes?

Sometimes, it seems useful for professional criminals to carry fake identification. It makes some sense, but only if the individual's circumstances are extraordinary, his attitude is bold, and he is not flustered by the thought of long prison sentences. If a thief has a very minute record, or no record, a fake ID might work a couple of times at the beginning of his career because very rarely would shoplifting result in an arrest coupled with a thorough investigation or a trip to jail.

"I had a fake ID once. After they caught me for the second time - I was really stupid, they made my car and in it my real driver's license - I had to stop. When I used that ID for the first time, I happened to buy it in a bar from a fellow who urgently needed cash, then it was safe. I used it once. They ate it up like a donkey eats up a sugar-doughnut. They got all the data - name, address, the works. They looked them up in their files, but they didn't find anything... they might be still looking for that guy, Paul something. But I decided that after I had my record and Paul had his record, it will be better to go on my real name. To buy a new one might not be worth it. They slap you with extra for the fake ID. But I know pro boosters who use it, no matter what, I guess they have better access acquiring it than I do. But I'm not a pro."

THE MORAL OF THE PASSAGE

"Privacy is not something that I'm merely entitled to, it's an absolute prerequisite."

(Marlon Brando)

If they did not see you pack it away, they will never see it again!

What a very individualistic and democratic principle! And how practical! By all means seek privacy in all cases. Find the empty aisles, but do not behave like a thief. Behave like a customer! Keep your cool. Check your front and back before looking at an article, and after you are certain that you are in a blind-spot situation go ahead and pack away with your best available method.

It's magic!

The most crucial point of artful lifting is the brilliant, magical execution of concealment. Just remember where to put the potato!

Blend in and prosper!

When it comes to clothing, think exactly how 'they' think you look and dress and do the opposite. Looking exactly like the other legitimate shoppers is the best policy.

DEALING WITH THE ENEMY

"If you know the enemy and know yourself, you need not fear the result of a hundred battles. If you know yourself but not the enemy, for every victory gained you will also suffer a defeat. If you know neither the enemy nor yourself, you will succumb in every battle."

(Sun Tzu)

PREVENTION EFFORTS

"An ounce of prevention... worth two birds in the bush"

(Cynthia W.)

Who is the enemy here? We are very sorry, folks, but it is the store and its security staff. The enemy is anybody who works against the shoplifter. We warned you at the beginning of the book that we were writing 'for' shoplifters, the 'good-guys.' We do not apologize. If your soul seems badly shaken because of our 'support' for shoplifters, by all means comfort it by condemning us for our immorality. We do think, however, that if you have read this far into the book, you may want to hold your nose and read on.

The Goods, the Bads and the Uglies!

"...Carroll and Weaver (1986) concluded that novice shoplifters are 'sheep-like' and can be deterred by almost anything (e.g., sales personnel or cameras, signs, etc.), but that experienced shoplifters are more like 'wolves' who adjust their strategies to overcome security personnel or technological devices." (Baumer and Rosenbaum, 1984)

The problem with any kind of prevention is that it may only affect the honest people, those who can usually be trusted to fret and feel bad about being suspected. Even if they felt tempted to steal, any simple preventive measure might deter ***them***.

POLITE AND IMPECCABLE SERVICE

"In fact there was one thing - and one thing only that ever prevented me from stealing: a knowledgeable, persistent, good salesman who drives you nuts. The fool wants to try to sell you something; you can't get rid of him. He wants to make money because he's on commission."

Me no like service!

Motivating sales personnel to serve their customers well is believed to be the most effective deterrent to shoplifting. It seems like a reasonable assumption to us that their very presence on the sales floor, as well as the helpful attention they give to all customers, hinders opportunities for concealment of merchandise. Their friendly interest in the customer may also act as a psychological barrier to theft, not only by increasing perceived chances of being apprehended, but also by making the act of shoplifting

People, ordinary people!

seem 'personal.' It's easy to lift something from a faceless corporate entity but hard to steal from someone who's just helped you choose the perfect gift for Aunt Jane.

SEND THEM TO THE COMPETITION

The greatest 'drawback' of anti-theft devices is that they do not diminish shoplifting in general. If boosters cannot figure out how to defeat these devices, they simply relocate to stores which do not have them.

The ultimate 'bad guy'

"I use every possible preventive, deterrent method, my stores have mirrors, CCTV, EAS's and floor detectives. I am certain that shoplifters will go somewhere else where they will have fewer obstacles. Shoplifters are like water - they flow towards the passage of least resistance." (Food Chain Security Manager)

Live and Let (the others) Die!

The words of this security manager (he seems to be quoting an article he read [we read] somewhere) show that he really believes that different electronic devices and ink tags are the solution. We know, however, that many shoplifters quickly learn how to defeat these gadgets. They will frequent his store more often after they realize how blindly he trusts his gizmos. Moreover, he is not really trying to curtail shoplifting in the retail trade by using all that technology. He is only trying to direct shoplifters from his own store to the store of some less fortunate merchant who cannot afford his expensive toys. Is it ethical to do so? Will the overall damage done by shoplifters plummet if, as he fondly hopes, they 'flow' from his premises? The answer to both questions is 'No.' There are, of course, ethical merchants out there. One of our friends remembers telling a restaurant owner that she did not like the pizza at another place. 'Please don't think I want to hear you slam my competition,' she replied. 'We are all in this together. Try it again. Maybe you caught the cook on a bad day.' If you want to see further proof, attend a hairdressers' convention where everybody is trying to boost the other person's morale and sales even though each hairdresser is an independent businessman or woman. Retailers need to stop contemplating their own navels and band together to examine just how useful anti-theft devices are to the industry as a whole. Fair competition is smart competition.

WRITING ON THE WALL

"With my wife and kids when we first visited this Provincial Park, the first sign we saw was about forbidding nudism. That's how we knew instantly that we had found a nude beach."

Posters with slogans such as: "We prosecute shoplifters!" "Shoplifting is a crime!" , etc., have never proven to be a deterrent to shoplifting. Au contraire! These warning signs have actually been proven to increase incidences of shoplifting. You must have seen the one declaring, "Shoplifting is a crime everybody pays for." We can perfectly understand why such a sign might drive people to commit crime. It is very easy to prove that the statement is false. You only have to steal something to show that shoplifting is a crime everybody ELSE pays for.

Conjunctures and Refutations

Most stores use warning signs with messages trying to persuade the public at large and 'at large' not to steal. The signs work mostly on the innocent shopper's conscience or fear of punishment. Smart lifters, who cause the most damage to retailers, are not affected by reminders about what they already know: They are in danger. They are watched and, if caught, will have to accept the consequences.

The Lonely Crowd

SUBLIMINAL MESSAGES

We have heard that some stores use subliminal messages. They play music embedded with phrases such as: 'Do not steal!', 'Stealing is wrong,' or they just add the sound of police sirens. Actually, none of our sources ever said anything to us about feeling that some inner voice was telling them not to steal. Nevertheless, they may not have heard it right! They may have left the store feeling that their astral body was patting them on the shoulder, or that they were somehow being watched.

The Medium IS the Message

"Their effectiveness is based on behavior, attitude and pre-disposition. The subliminal message will have an effect on the person who is already predisposed to suggestion concerning his or her existing value system. The same thing probably in the case of subtle or humorous messages displayed on posters. They will have no impact on the professional, or pro-amateur shoplifters." (CHAIN STORE AGE EXECUTIVE, July 1986)

EDUCATION OF EMPLOYEES

Most larger retailers have developed programs for their employees, counting on the fact that sales personnel believe that they are the front-line defense against shoplifting.

"Bunny, your job isn't just to selling things. You also have to protect the merchandise. Alert sales people are the best deterrent to shoplifters.... Yes, you should watch the merchandise, but you can prevent theft... You should acknowledge each new customer immediately.. Don't interrupt a transaction, of course, but let the other customer know

The Loss Prevention Beaver says...

that you will be with him/her in a minute.... A shoplifter doesn't like being noticed, but a legitimate customer welcomes the attention.... Always turn to customers as soon as possible. Some people shoplift just because they have to wait a long time... We never ask sales clerks to apprehend a thief. If you observe a shoplifter, notify your immediate supervisor. And of course be discreet. Do not give any hints to the suspect about your suspicion.... If you cannot reach anybody, be firm and professional. Ask polite questions such as: 'Can I help you?' Or 'Are you paying for that with cash or a credit card?' Never accuse anyone of theft - never. In most cases the shoplifter will either buy the item or return it. Do not let anyone go with you into the stockroom. That place would give even an honest shopper ideas.... Try to keep even numbers of articles on display or on the counter. It will be easier to keep an eye on them... An empty hanger should mean only one thing - the garment has been stolen.... Customers should never be allowed behind the counters. You should ask them politely to leave the area immediately. If someone has walked behind the counter, he should be watched until he leaves the store... A person who enters a store and then stands around handling items, making no attempt to buy anything, is always suspicious, so watch out. If a person is carrying a large box, a piece of luggage - even loosely folded newspapers or a shopping bag - that person should hold your attention... Except for a small number of shoppers, who shy away with a 'just looking,' 'only browsing' comment, most customers want to be served. Customers who act nervous and try to avoid store people send a silent signal to the vendor: watch that person; he or she might be a lifter... Alert sales people and cashiers are the backbone of any store's security." (From a Security Video Training Film)

The education of employees ordinarily consists of two phases: in-the-classroom and on-the-job training. If security personnel are to be armed, a third phase is added, one concerned with weapons.

Classroom training often consists of four general topic areas: surveillance and apprehension of suspected criminals, state and local statutes applicable to the retail security operation, filling out the necessary report forms, and appearing as a capable witness in court. The goal is to provide the security operative with a working knowledge of requirements prior to entering on-the-job training.

Bachelor of **R**etail **S**ecurity **S**ciences (BRSS).

If the security officer is to be armed, his initial classroom instruction is followed by weapons training, which informs him when and how to use a weapon, clarifying for him those federal, state, and local laws which outline the legal use of firearms. Target practice is also included to allow the operative to learn to display and fire a weapon without endangering the safety and well-being of innocent bystanders. While firearms are not used extensively in retail security, operatives are armed in high-crime areas of large cities, and weapons training is a necessity in these situations.

"Programs for non-security or sales personnel are developed on the assumption that these employees constitute a front-line defense against both shoplifting and employee theft. Solid education in these complementary areas of sales and interpersonal skills, operational skills and techniques, and security is believed to produce more competent and loyal employees who are able to assist customers better and serve as deterrents to internal and external theft." (Excerpt from a training manual)

Finally, these training programs include a cursory overview of the company's security strategy. Most often, this is a single presentation by a member of the security staff, consisting of a concise talk and perhaps a movie. After all this, there is a graduation ceremony at which the officers receive their CPP (Certified Protection Professional) diploma.

Focus on **C**ertainly **P**ointless **P**rofessionals!

SCARECROWS

Planting visible hints (birdseed) that prevention is on the march is one rather subtle policy which stores are fond of. A guard who looks like a policeman (has uniform, will travel) is on the premises to suggest that other, similar authority figures are lurking about; or eternal vigilance is suggested by the cardboard cut-out of a guard. We call this the 'scarecrow' approach. While at first some of the 'birds' are scared away, as soon as they get used to the 'scarecrow,' they settle down to feed on the merchandise.

Against the Lifter Bird (Neverus Apprehendus)

"I go to this department store quite often, and in the last two weeks I noticed that they have a police car parked right at the entrance. First I thought, yooppy, they caught someone. That means that everybody, all the store detectives and security are busy filling out forms on the poor bastard. I robbed them blind that day. But, next time when I went back, there was the police car again - empty, mind you. Maybe they are renting it or bought an old police car and use it to scare away lifters..."

ACME Police Kit!

A very inventive idea, we would say. You can rent cops for a funeral, for your garden party, etc. Why not spend some money on renting a cop (or maybe just his car) for your store? Doing so will definitely scare away impulsive shoplifters! But, then, inventive though the idea is, maybe it's not a useful one. As you saw above, the smart lifter will react to your rent-a-cop (or cop car) policy with derision. We also saw, in a big department store,

Is it the painted tunnel, or the planted birdseed?

cardboard cops keeping an eye on the 'shoppers.' We looked at them and smirked. They just looked funny. We imagined one of these two-dimensional cardboard figures moving around trying to apprehend a lifter. It is not going to happen. We know that this approach might work on honest people, but they could also be offended by it. We must admit that we read a very enthusiastic article extolling the value of installing these paper cops. Shoplifting plummeted (exactly for how long the article did not say). A similarly futile method is to have a uniformed security officer standing at the door. He might be useful if a chase ensued, but lifters will not be frightened by him.

"I ran out of good pots and pans, so I decided that we need a new set. Went down the store to check out if it was in any way possible to get one. There I found a whole set (9 pieces) in a large box, scattered around. I checked them out, they probably were a return, but there was nothing wrong with them. Okay, that's what I need. I put the box on my shoulder and went straight to the 'rent-a-cop' at the store entrance. 'I brought this back' I told him, 'but they need my receipt which I either left in the car or at home.' He checked out the box, scattered pans, obviously once opened before. 'Should I leave them here, with you, until I come back?' I asked. 'No,' he answered 'it's better if you take it with you.' I did. Even if he would have said yes, I was not in danger for one second..."

EVALUATION OF PREVENTION EFFORTS

One is four the other a third of a dozen!

The security and retail industries are well aware of the advantages and shortcomings of their prevention efforts. In their survey Ernst and Young asked retailers to rank the effectiveness of their security methods and devices.

The top four contenders were:
- Training programs
- Guards and detectives
- EAS systems
- POS (point of sale) systems

The four least effective contenders were:
- Mirrors
- Observation booths
- EAS systems
- Locks and chains

Hey, Big Spender...

We hope you noticed the overlap in the assessment of the usefulness of EAS. (You will notice more overlaps - if you are interested - in a table in the Appendices). In the survey about the same number of stores ranked EAS among the worst devices as the number of stores ranking them among the best. We found it similarly cute that the same number of respondents selected CCTV (cameras) as the best protective device as the number which classified them as the worst. Naturally, these numbers are based on belief and not on any verifiable 'data'. We suspect that most of the people answering the questionnaire were also responsible for the decision to buy or not to buy those expensive gadgets and therefore were 'somewhat' biased in their opinions. Once you have talked your boss into spending half a million on installing an electronic theft-prevention system, you can hardly admit in a questionnaire that it is totally useless. Well, the jury is still out (and may never return a verdict) on the usefulness of those gizmos.

Spending on people, betting on technology

One thing is certain: nothing can replace well-educated and polite people. If you are out there working, they are the ones you definitely have to watch out for, not the gadgets. Good personnel offer the highest-rated protection. Retailers, aware of the value of 'the human touch,' spend the most prevention money on security people as can be seen in the following table compiled from the Ernst and Young survey. However, they do not seem to be aware that security's 'human touch' is less important than that of sales people. We maintain that the most effective use of prevention money, the hiring of well-paid, efficient sales people, should at least appear on the chart below. The fact that it does not points up, we believe, a defect in prevention budgeting and planning.

PEOPLE COSTS (PREVENTION)	
Employee Guards and Detectives	22%
External Guards and Detectives	11%
Other Prevention Employees	27%
Outside Services	5%
Incentives and Reward Programs	4%
Training Employees	4%
People Costs (Total)	73%

OTHER SECURITY COSTS	
EAS (lease, rent, depreciation)	6%
Other Electronic Equipment (CCTV, etc.)	9%
Physical Facilities	5%
Other	7%
Other Security Costs (Total)	27%

There are variations in different sectors of the retail world, but they tend to disappear as the size of the companies gets bigger. The bigger the retailer is, the higher is the proportion of people costs in its loss prevention expenditure.

SURVEILLANCE AND APPREHENSION

The retail acting workshop

Training courses on surveillance and apprehension of suspects often cover a wide range of materials. A personality profile of shoplifters is sometimes presented. Films that illustrate common shoplifting and employee theft techniques are shown. Various procedures for apprehending suspects, detaining suspects, and properly notifying police are reviewed.

The retail barrister training

Due to the liability of the retail outlet and the security officer for violation of a suspect's civil rights, it is also necessary that the security trainee be informed of and understand legal statutes pertaining to situations that are likely to arise. These include state and local as well as federal codes that define the officer's legal powers.

The retail witness coaching seminar

Finally, instruction on how to appear as a viable witness in court. once considered nonessential, has become an increasingly important part of security training. Most security officers are now evaluated in terms of how many apprehensions they make and how many of these apprehensions lead to a conviction.

THE MORAL OF THE PASSAGE

Deterrence is a schizoid concept. How could anyone scare you if you knew that scaring and not catching you was the real goal? When it comes to theft prevention efforts, you have nothing to fear. Worry about 'catch-prevention'!

STORE POLICIES

"I am afraid we must make the world honest before we can honestly say to our children that honesty is the best policy."

(George Bernard Shaw)

Every source, including every store security manager, told us that stores do not want to catch thieves; they just want to prevent them from stealing. The designers of security policies must have priorities. Their 'anti-criminal calculus' goes like this: 90 percent of the lifters are worthier of concern than the other 10 percent. Most of the policies, therefore, are directed against the amateurs - impulsives, juveniles, drug addicts, etc. - and not against the small number of professionals we call smart lifters. Even though smart lifters cause more damage than amateurs do, the stores suspect that measures taken against them usually prove to be ineffectual.

When merchants devise their policies for dealing with apprehended shoplifters, they have only two options. Either they prosecute or they don't. There are various methods open to them if they decide not to prosecute. In the case of juvenile shoplifters, they can notify the parents or school. Another method is simply to recover the stolen merchandise, shame, embarrass or humiliate the 'customer,' and then ban him from their store forever.

They string you up or kick you in the butt!

The other, much more difficult option is to call in the police, have the shoplifter arrested, and then prosecute him. Store-owners often shy away from that option, mainly because it is usually far more expensive than simply writing off whatever loss they may have incurred (many times they have recovered the goods and so lost nothing). They also worry about different possible accidental violations of the shoplifter's civil rights by their employees, who may not have understood or known about certain legal statutes governing the apprehension process. Some jurisdictions have passed laws making arrest and prosecution for shoplifting mandatory, but the question is: How can such a law be enforced?

If y' jail'em sheriff, y'ave to tak'em t' Tulsa!

SHOULD YOU ARREST THAT PERSON?

The arrest of a suspected shoplifter involves following many complicated rules that sometimes make the job of security forces impossible.

Before Don Pedro returns, we'll have to find the Three Amigos!

"Once a product is concealed, you can stop a person. (...) Here the going gets kind of ticklish. We try to let the person get past the check-stand. In the most blatant cases, that is probably not necessary. If he has six cartons of cigarettes stuffed in his shirt, we know he has no idea of paying for that product. (...) If they have any doubt about whether a person is shoplifting, they should let the person go. (...) That person is going to come back to your store and you can get him next time. They always come back."(Security Management, May 1989)

A store owner described his unpleasant experience in one case when an employee made mistakes in apprehending the suspected culprit.

Miss Roselyn was roughed in the five o'clock fight. She couldn't get on her back for weeks.

"One of my employees, a petite woman, once tried to grab hold of a large, burly shoplifter. Violence ensued. She was able to fight him until others came and helped her to arrest the culprit, but she broke some of her ribs and her arm in the process. She was out of work for several weeks and her hospital bills were hefty. I say, a less expensive approach is to let him go, take his description, maybe his license plate number out in the parking lot." (Security Management, May 1989)

There will be a chapter shortly describing all the legal mumbo-jumbo as well as the practical procedural defects which create huge obstacles for security personnel.

CASH FOR THIEVES

A borderline store policy prevention effort is to offer the employees incentives such as cash or merchandise to make them more security conscious and keep their eyes open for shoplifters. Like all policies, this one, too, is somewhat controversial. Listen to an expert's opinion:

Reward! Fifty dollars for the capture of Quick Finger Joe! Dead or alive!

"Some stores have programs offering cash awards to security personnel [and sales people] **for apprehending shoplifters. These well-placed intentions to increase security efforts are noble, but placing a bounty on shoplifters is risky business. An overzealous security officer may place a higher priority on financial gain than in making a correct apprehension. This could cause more false apprehensions, which may result in poor customer relations and possible civil litigation against the store. Discovery of this type of bonus**

program during a civil suit also may result in disastrous financial repercussions." (Security Management, May 1989)

MORAL OF THE PASSAGE

Although security managers may design dozens of strategies, implement policies, and invent new incentives, nothing will make a difference as long as the basic question remains: Is it worth management's time and money to prosecute?

THIEFCATCHERS

"He may be a very nice man. But I haven't got the time to figure that out. All I know is, he's got a uniform and a gun and I have to relate to him that way. That's the only way to relate to him because one of us may have to die."

(James Baldwin)

SALES CLERKS

Sales clerks are trained both to serve customers and help catch shoplifters. They are often rewarded if they provide information which leads to an arrest. They are warned, however, not to apprehend the thieves themselves. Don't worry about them much. In most places (on paper at least), they do not have the right to physically confront you (or are advised against confronting you). However, in small stores with no rules, it is a different ball-game.

At the bottom of the hierarchy

"I was a teenager lifting some silly thing - I can't even remember what - in the corner store. The shopkeeper caught me and took me back to the storage room. He offered me a chair and stood in front of me. He started with the bullshit, of how he should beat me up. He got me pissed off, I got cocky and told him that I can see that he is stronger than me but he doesn't have the right to do it. He showed me. He slapped me across the room and threw me out. He didn't 'teach' me not to steal, but I learned when not to be cocky."

On the top of the potato bags

"Couple of weeks ago I picked up a bottle of perfume and a couple of bars of soap from this little trendy boutique. They sell only health-food and natural products, and I am a healthy and natural lifter. This guy catches me at the door, empties my pockets and throws me to the wall, like in the movies, and searches me from head to toe! He is shouting something in Arabic and starts beating my head. I know he cannot do this but what am I to do! I ran as fast as I could. I should sue the !@#$head!"

The lowest of the 'blow'

SECURITY PERSONNEL

The ranks and casts of thief-catchers

Security personnel could be broadly defined as store detectives, uniformed guards, fitting-room checkers, article-surveillance monitors, and others involved in related functions. We focus primarily on the education of regular security employees, most commonly store detectives. Training programs for other types of security personnel are either beyond the control of the retail company or have yet to be so fully developed as to warrant discussion.

"Security personnel are cautioned about a multitude of potential shoplifting techniques. These include individuals palming small articles and placing them in a pocket, purse, other packages, or bags. Others put on clothing, jewellery, etc. and wear it out of the store or hide it under their clothes. Some shoplifters bring packages, newspapers, umbrellas, baby strollers, etc. into the store that can be used as hiding places. Another technique is to conceal items in another package or item that will be purchased. Price tags may also be switched to give the buyer a real bargain. Some may disguise themselves as a 'handicapped,' 'clerical,' 'blind' customer, or as someone with a broken arm to hopefully, reduce suspicions of the store personnel.

They are also advised to scrutinize customers who: shop very rapidly and those who linger; hang around back areas of the store and those who stay in crowded areas; are not carrying around or picking up merchandise and those who are carrying a lots of items; are alone and those with other people; act nervous and those who are relaxed; avoid sales personnel and those who pester them." (Lloyd W. Klemke, 1992)

Their goals and limitations

The overall goal of most security training programs is two-fold:

(1) to increase the effectiveness of security officers by increasing their knowledge of store operations, shoplifting tactics, and sales procedures, thus increasing their ability to detect and apprehend both shoplifters and pilfering employees.

(2) to increase their knowledge of their legal powers and limitations so as to minimize the risk of costly law suits against the company or individual employees.

The Head Potato

The security representative typically reviews the company's policy on employee theft and attempts to create the impression that pilferage will not be tolerated. It will be detected and followed by appropriate punishment. Company loyalty is sometimes discussed in conjunction with statements encouraging employees to report any suspicious or criminal activity they may observe.

STORE DETECTIVES IN GENERAL

The professional store detective could be considered the greatest threat to any lifter. The smart lifter may know tons of tricks of his trade and have a dozen gimmicks for packing, walking and leaving with the merchandise. He may know where to go; what to steal. How to avoid cameras or circumvent electronic devices. He can notice but cannot eliminate the threat of a resourceful detective.

The best but most expensive 'toy' of store owners

The main element of the detective's job is to catch shoplifters, but he is not always required to make arrests. Several states have laws permitting 'citizen arrests.' However, arresting culprits is usually left to the police.

Pseudo police tactics...

The main task of a store detective is to stop the shoplifter. 'I believe we have a problem here. Would you come with me to the office to discuss it?' 'I would like to have the radio that you have in your pocket.'

..irreproachable...

These are the words of a detective who is trying to avoid making a straight accusation or threat. Such carefully chosen words usually get the amateur to admit to the deed immediately and give back the stolen item. Many even return merchandise which the detective did not see being stolen.

...and polite!

The detective in the store has to be one hundred percent certain that he himself saw somebody stealing something. He does not go after a shoplifter on the basis of another person's report of theft. One manager told us that his policy is: 'If you didn't see it happen, it didn't happen!'

What you see is who you get!

Detectives search bags, pockets and the suspect's person, in most cases with permission to do so. If permission is not granted, they will probably wait for the police to do a search. Stores usually warn their personnel not to get involved in any violent action, including the hot pursuit of a shoplifter. Shoplifters are generally not dangerous, but no one (with such rare exceptions as our poor hospitalized employee in the example above) takes unnecessary risks to apprehend a petty thief. Security personnel might, of course, use necessary force to protect themselves. At the time of apprehension a detective must have some kind of proof of a criminal act.

Cautious, considerate and alert

We were often advised that the only thing you can do against detectives is to watch out for them or have a 'colleague' covering your back. A couple of circles or turns before leaving the store will usually reveal whether you are being watched or followed.

The counter-measures

Of course, security staffers, armed with a description from somebody, can hide outside and wait for the culprit (overzelousness), but that is usually done only in cases where

Manpower and money

stores have one exit - or just a few. Even large department stores can't spend the money to cover all the exits.

"It should be clear, there are few if any universal clues that security personnel can rely on. Much of this advice is contradictory and/or falls within the realm of normal customer behavior and is therefore of limited value. Perhaps its only utility is that it reinforces the view that security personnel should consider every customer to be a potential shoplifter." (Baumer and Rosenbaum, 1984)

NON-SECURITY PERSONNEL

The thousand eyes that watch you

Anybody, really, whether they work in the store or not. They can be workmen building a new ceiling or shelf. They can be other shoppers. At any point of any shoplifting procedure, your eyes must be open. You are only safe if ***nobody*** saw you! Do not trust people to be indifferent about other people's actions. Anyone who saw you might or will tell on you if prone to do so. Of course, if somebody not belonging to the store saw you, turning on the speed may get you and your 'acquisition' safely outside. Remember, measure risks and benefits!

MYSTERY AND GHOST SHOPPERS

Sometimes it is easier than you think

Smart lifters call plainclothes detectives 'mystery or ghost shoppers.' There are many clues to picking them out. Sometimes they make themselves obvious by being very friendly with the sales personnel. 'Ghosts' are not invisible while they are chatting familiarly with the sales girls.

You cannot pick out the type...

Another way of picking them out is to know their types and attitudes. Today's society denies its racist attitude quite vociferously, but it over-uses minorities to pose as normal customers. Minority people - blacks, Chinese, and Indians - are widely hired as plainclothes detectives. Security managers also use young, cool and juvenile-looking 'dudes' or normal 'housewives' as store security. Look out. Pay attention (not obviously) to what goes on around you!

...you have to study their behavior.

They will shop too. Oh, how they will shop. Nevertheless, most of the time they choose articles that give them away to the trained eyes of a smart lifter.

"In a report about shoplifting they showed (proudly) a security camera picture depicting a group of shoppers. The reporter asked the viewers if they could pick out the detective. Immediately, I picked out the guy. He was black, dressed like a street guy, a rapper-bro. He was pushing a cart with a lot of garments in it. It was obvious."

Additional clues include:

Give-aways and layaways

- They observe shoppers more diligently than the merchandise.
- They are not dressed according to the season.
- They wear running shoes (an obscure one but many of our sources talked about the young, sporty looking detectives).
- The merchandise they pick doesn't seem to suit their personalities, or the items look like randomly chosen misfits.
- A person keeps following you.
- Suddenly at the checkout line someone shows up behind you with only one item which seems hastily chosen.
- In front of you somebody pays and then keeps waiting, lingering around the exit.

Your own experience should add more clues to this list.

MORAL OF THE PASSAGE

It is always the best policy to assume that ghost shoppers are there and that they can apprehend (even hurt) you. Shoplifters are non-violent in general. Security officers are more likely to hurt a shoplifter than the other way around (at least this is the case as regards our smart lifters). In case you suspect a person, or if have doubts about him, taking your leave is in order. Pushy lifters needlessly put themselves in dangerous positions.

PART THREE

REALITY

THE LAWS AND THE COURTS

"Let reverence for the laws be breathed by every American mother to the lisping babe that prattles on her lap. Let it be taught in schools, in seminaries, and in colleges. Let it be written in primers, spelling books, and in almanacs. Let it be preached from the pulpit, proclaimed in legislative halls, and enforced in the courts of justice. And, in short, let it become the political religion of the nation."

(*Abraham Lincoln*)

THE PROCESS

"When you go in search of honey you must expect to be stung by bees."

(Kenneth Kaunda)

WHEN YOU GET CAUGHT

Every person, without exception, who decides to go the shoplifting route, will have to face at one time or another the embarrassment of being caught.

It does happen!

Shoplifters are caught often, almost every time outside the store, by one or more security officers, who have the right to escort them back inside with a reasonable degree of firmness, sometimes even making a citizen's arrest. Security can then summon the police to take their captives into custody. The rule of thumb in cases like this is: 'It was calculated in the risks, they caught me, and I accept.' If 'running' is an option, then you, the perp, might indeed do it, but it is safer to give up.

To know when to give up is also a skill!

It is, of course, humiliating to be caught, but if dealt with in a professional manner, it is never dangerous. The security officers simply parade you through the store and then take you to the back office. A brief aside: If you have something on you that is easily removable, you can try to discard it (maybe by tripping over something and falling down, at the same time sliding the stuff under a display case or dropping the item and kicking it under something) without them noticing while the parade is marching through the aisles. If the officers cannot find anything on you, they have to let you go. Although we have heard of laws that allow arrest on suspicion, without the stolen article as corpus delicti the lifter will hardly ever be prosecuted.

The parade route and the 'fall'

An apprehension takes maybe a couple of hours and usually ends with a citation to show up for fingerprinting and an order to appear in court. In very rare cases, the culprit might end up in a police station cell until his arraignment. When that happens, the police give him something to eat, maybe a coffee, let him buy cigarettes and make some phone calls (the number of phone calls allowed varies from place to place) and keep him in jail for the night. Most of the police station holding cells our 'friends' told us about don't give you anything if you have no money. If you do,

The sky is NOT falling!

you might be able to buy stuff. It is advisable to go out working with a full pack of smokes if you live by the weed.

The continuance

In the morning, the police take you in front of a judge for arraignment. The judge, according to his mood and your behavior, lets you go with or without bail (the amount of bail varies according to your record and the part of the country where you have been apprehended). The judge is very unlikely to order you to be kept in custody.

The time of arrest determines your time spent

It is advisable to go shoplifting on weekdays, early in the morning. If an arrest falls during office hours, the arresting officers are able to book court-dates and other appointments for the culprit on the phone. If they can do that, they often forego the option of taking you in - it costs money, manpower and time.

The royal beast has no sharp teeth

It is prudent to carry some sort of identification and be truthful. Unless you are really prepared to present a fake identity card, it is better to tell security personnel the truth about your name, address, etc. Also, it doesn't hurt to show remorse from the first moment you are caught. Never forget that you are only one of many people they deal with. Your case is only important to you. Although they might act in a haughty manner, don't take that behavior personally. They are just working stiffs doing their jobs.

The traveling shoplifter

In foreign countries (European), the police, after flexing their muscles a bit, usually let the lifter go with a warning. In France and Germany there is a grace period. Officials prosecute only after the third mishap. We have very little information about most of the other countries, but a bamboo-pole-caning for graffiti might characterize the possibilities. Do not break the law where they cane people with bamboo. Hippo-hide whip is a different story...

THE 'SMOKIES'

"However low a man sinks, he never reaches the level of the police."

(Quentin Crisp)

To serve and protect!

Smart lifters know that they have no reason to fear the police. Other than in rare sting operations (we read about one in Chicago) there are no units specially designed for chasing shoplifters. If you are caught, and you have definitely decided to give in, do not worry. The police are very unlikely to hurt you.

There are times when they carry the lifter as well

They are only the administrators of your crime. The information carriers. They take all the information about you, very possibly just giving you a warrant to appear for fingerprinting, They snap a lovely shot or two of your mug. They may arrange a court appearance for you. If you do not have a long record, they let you go. If your record has the requisite number of notches on it, they take you in.

ASSESSING YOUR MISFORTUNE

It can happen to the best of them. It can happen to you. What makes the difference between the amateurs and the smart lifters is the way they handle the experience.

"The time you are caught is when you have let your guard down. Unless they simply get lucky, it is very rarely 'them' Their methods, gizmos and stuff, never change. It must be you who screws up. There is a long period you keep cleaning them out, and as you grow more confident, you start losing your alertness. That's what happened to me. I kept going back to that 'safe' store, a super-market. As time passed, my load got bigger and bigger. I started to imagine that they had no snoops, no anything. They did. I paid and I left and suddenly from nowhere three of them are around me. All undercover detectives. Wasn't fun, I am telling you. I had no other choice but to walk back with them. My only break was that I had only a bottle of wine on me. Straight through the system, came out with a two-fifty fine. What can I say? You have to look at the safest store as any other and never get comfortable."

Too much comfort can quickly lead to discomfort

"I still get furious when I think of it. I was so !@#%ing stupid it's incredible. I know what I'm doing, I have my rules, then I go and !@#% every single one of them. I was working very late into the night, and I had to get up early to see someone about a script. I finished with my meeting in the early afternoon. It was a Thursday. Worst day, worst time. I was very tired and I had a splitting headache. I stopped at a mall to get a coffee. I had less then two bucks on me. I went into a drugstore to get a !@#%ing painkiller. I put the stuff away right at the shelf where I picked it up, I noticed the pharmacist looking at me when I came out from behind the shelf, and I saw him picking up the phone while looking at me. I didn't walk around, I didn't even have a basket. I walked straight out of the store. As I was passing the cash register I noticed the spook. He was an absolutely out of place black guy in a short leather jacket.(it was minus 20 degrees outside) It crossed my mind that I should slow down and look around to see what is he doing but then I said to myself What the !@#% for? He didn't see anything. I was right, but he ran out of the store after me anyway. The pharmacist pointed a finger at me. The point is you see is that I made all the mistakes and I saw all the warning signs. I was just too !@#%ing tired and ill-disposed to pay attention."

A pain in the head can quickly turn into a pain in the ass!

"You see the only moment they can catch you is when you're packing away. It's like you were an animal at the wa-

tering hole. You are vulnerable, but that is the thing you have to do. You have to pack the stuff away.

A pan in the hand can quickly turn into a pun!

The detective came out from nowhere; grabbed me. With the pan in my hand sliding under my shirt. His partner showed up; they took me to the office and searched me. If they would have caught me with only that shitty frying pan, I would have had a chance to explain myself out of the hole. But I had other stuff. A couple of knives, a coffee grinder. I am sure they never seen me with those. I just had to have another. It was one too many."

From show-off to show-down

"They caught me the worst time. I was with my wife. She doesn't approve that I do lift, and never, I mean, never does it. She never comes with me. This was this one freaky time, when she was there that they had to be on their guard. But you know, I still think it was me and not the security. They didn't score. I scored for them. Self-goal. I have no idea what came over me, most probably I was showing off to her. I was proud how easy I can do it. We were laughing. Until they caught us both. She had nothing but a T-shirt, which I told her to just keep on after she tried it. I was so full of myself, I still can taste it. What do you learn? Not much. Keep your ways, keep up your guard and never show off. Even if you are good."

Every smart lifter we know told us that getting caught was their fault. They made mistakes. They were overconfident, sloppy, lazy, tired, greedy, too quick or too slow. They were critical of their own behavior; and they painstakingly analyzed their actions and the circumstances that led to their arrest. From the attention they paid to the subject, we must assume that they learned from the experience.

If you're ever caught, do the same. Remember that the apprehension was most likely the result of a mistake you made. Find that mistake and learn from it!

MORAL OF THE PASSAGE

Robert Browning wrote: 'I give the fight up; let there be an end, a privacy, an obscure nook for me. I want to be forgotten even by God!' We do not advise that in every case you give up totally. Only if, in your judgment, as a last resort, giving up is more appropriate than 'fighting.' Shoplifting doesn't (yet) carry the death penalty. It sometimes doesn't even carry any penalty.

The process is humiliating and unpleasant but not dangerous. Nothing can happen to you that you should be afraid of. Show repentance, be apologetic, tell them that you will learn from your mistake, and then don't let them catch you again.

THE LAWS

"The due process of law as we use it, I believe, rests squarely on the liberal idea of conflict and resolution."

(June L. Trapp)

Naturally, the law deals with shoplifters in slightly different ways in different states and countries. Just a few examples:

Tidbits

In Michigan, shoplifting is a felony (on paper), punishable by up to four years in prison, not depending on the value of the stolen article(s).

Maryland punishes lifters if shoplifted goods retail for more than $50 with prison terms up to ten years(!)

A new law in Florida says that you are criminally liable if you unlawfully possess anti-theft devices (tags, tag-removers, etc.)

In California parents are made co-liable with their juvenile children in cases of petty theft. They 'shall be jointly liable with the minor to the merchant for the retail value of the merchandise unless the merchandise is recovered in salable condition.'

In Washington D.C. first offenders get probation if they admit the crime and show genuine repentance.

France has a lenient three-time limit. Only after being caught the third time does the lifter face prosecution. The first two arrests culminate in a warning, a purely administrative 'penalty.' The police do not conduct an investigation the first two times, but if you get caught the third time, it is not easy to argue that what happened was only an accident.

Canada has a system involving fines which, of course, depend on the judge. Starting at fifty dollars for a small first time offense (arrest), these suggested fines go up and up for repeat offenders. After a number of collars, the repeat offender finds himself serving a one-week to three-months sentence.

In Australia you can be charged with burglary, if the value of the lifted items is higher than what you could pay for (or so we heard.)

In some 'exotic' countries you might be caned, and in some others your very 'working fingers' could be in serious jeopardy.

The grass is not greener...

We could continue to give you tidbits of information from around the world. It would be very interesting to describe and analyze the ways in which different societies deal with lifting and petty crime, but within the scope of this book we could not do the topic justice. Even if we decided to make the subject the focus of our next book, we would be handicapped by the fact that information about shoplifting in foreign countries is very hard to come by. Record keeping is not any better in other parts of the world than it is here. And there are other considerations. Not only are the practices and methods likely to be different, but the definitions as well. Trying to make a comparative analysis of shoplifting in different countries might turn out to be just about as meaningful as comparing the domestic abuse laws and statistics of the United States and Saudi Arabia.

...but the color of the lawn-chair is shockingly different!

If you are reading this book in translation, your have found herein occasional references to, let's say, an 'adobe hacienda,' 'casa,' 'haus,' etc., depending on the target language in which you have been deeply appreciating our splendid prose, and you have felt right at home. Now and then, however, we bet you have been thrown right out of your living room chair in said adobe hacienda, casa, or haus - struck dumb by culture shock. Even if you are reading our guide to lifting in English, the language in which it was written, you may have been suddenly stunned to realize as you sat in your lawn-chair in Wales or lay in your hammock in South Africa, that things are very different in the U.S. of A. and Canuckland! Catch your breath, take a drink (or two). Okay? Now, please reflect on the fact that not everything is so shockingly different in that part of the world (Canada and the U. S.) where the information for this book was obtained. There are surely similarities with your own lifting culture which we trust have held your interest and made this book useful to you. Shoplifting does have what might be called its world-wide characteristics. Why not write to us about what in this-here handbook seemed familiar and what seemed mighty weird?

THE 'CODE'

Which war? On what crime?

To make matters simple, in preparing our analysis of what the law has to say, or might one day have to say, about shoplifting, we decided to follow the Model Code (hereinafter called: the 'Code') recommended by the National Coalition to Prevent Shoplifting. The N. C. P. S is not around any more. We wonder what happened to that organization. Really. It seemed like a good idea at the time. We do not know the reasons for its demise, but we can safely assume that it succumbed to lack of interest. The 'war on crime' attitude, so successful at electing even feeble-minded politicians who promise death to drug-dealers, mandatory sentences for certain crimes, etc., does not resonate in the public mind when the crime is shoplifting. The problem is not serious enough. Not one law-making bozo ever got elected by promising to wage a war on shoplifters.

Coalition under the bridge

The organization is gone, but the 'Code' is there, and it remains the most comprehensive attempt to delineate the crime called shoplifting. Everything else out there in 'lawyerland' is much less complete. We are going to examine it because a look at the best example of the way the other side sees you prepares you for every possibility. To define shoplifting as a distinct offense in the criminal code is a relatively new development. It became necessary to define it in specific terms in order to set it apart from the rest of the crimes under the petty larceny umbrella. Some new provisions (such as references to EAS systems) were needed, and retailers were asking for a process that would put a lighter procedural burden on them.

Coding the view

Baumer and Rosenbaum commented on every aspect of the 'Code' from the merchants point of view. At the time of the publication of their book, there were fourteen states in the US which had enacted laws specifically aimed at shoplifting. Most of these laws were very close in their formulation to the proposed law that we will look at below. The numbers have probably changed. There must be more places with specific shoplifting laws today, but these laws are very likely be similar to those in this model code:

1. Theft by Shoplifting Defined.

Viewing the code

(a) A person commits the offense of theft by shoplifting if, with intent to appropriate merchandise without paying the merchant's stated price for the merchandise, such person, alone or in concert with another person knowingly:

(i) Conceals the merchandise; or

(ii) Removes, takes possession of, or causes the removal of merchandise; or

(iii) Alters, transfers, or removes any price marking, or any other marking which aids in determining value affixed to the merchandise; or

(iv) Transfers the merchandise from one container to another; or

(v) **Causes the cash register or other sales-recording device to reflect less than the merchant's stated price for the merchandise.**

(b) **A person commits the offense of theft by shoplifting if, with intent to appropriate, such person, alone or in concert with another person, knowingly removes a shopping cart from the premises of the mercantile establishment.**

Viewing the view

This is a very broad definition indeed. A sincere attempt is made to cover every possible variation of the act including price-tag switching, repackaging of expensive items, and removal of shopping carts from stores. Also, some aspects of the definition cover employee theft. Of course in law a broad definition does not always mean full coverage. A smart lifter's smart lawyer can be trusted to find any 'lootholes!'

The invisible intent

Many amateurs do not consider price-tag switching to be theft. Because it is one of the most common 'entry level' lifts, the law naturally needs to deal with it. Although we understand the effort to do so, we must note that it is popular to claim that the switch was a mistake of the store. This assertion is very difficult to prove either way. If you do not conceal anything and are ready to pay for the article, it is hard to prove felonious intent.

We must mention that the law per se takes the retailer's and the security officer's side. It is not unusual to find these worthy folks lying quite shamelessly about witnessing the act. They also sometimes fabricate proof of possession or intent. It is very tricky to prove that they are lying because they have the repossessed article as proof. Don't forget that a judge will accept their 'truth' more readily than yours!

We have discussed several methods that are almost fool-proof. What makes them so is the difficulty of proving some aspects of the crime. We cannot help noting that the actual cost, or 'real' value, of the merchandise is immaterial. In the 'Code,' it is only 'the merchant's stated price' that matters. As you will see, the 'Code' shows clearly that its preparation was done in cahoots with retailers. Its main goal is to satisfy them, not the law.

Time after time we point out the discrepancy between retail wishful thinking and legal or social reality. If you want to have fun, replace every use of the word 'shoplifting' with the phrase 'overpricing and customer deception.' Replace the word 'shoplifter' with the word 'store-owner.' Voila! (French for 'Hey, man, look at that!') You now have a CIVIL CODE ON OVER-PRICING AND DECEPTION PRACTICES!!!

2. Evidence and Presumptions.

(a) **Knowing concealment of merchandise shall create a rebuttable presumption that the person intended to appropriate the merchandise without paying the merchant's stated price for the merchandise.**

(b) **Evidence of stated price or ownership of merchandise may include, but is not limited to:**

(i) **The actual merchandise or the container which held the merchandise alleged to have been shoplifted; or**

(ii) **The content of the price tag or marking from such merchandise; or**

(iii) **Properly identified photographs of such merchandise.**

(c) **Any merchant may testify at a trial as to the stated price or ownership of merchandise, as well as to other matters pertaining to the case.**

The two crucial pieces of evidence needed for a merchant to make his case are proof of ownership and proof of intent. To illustrate these concepts, here are two stories:

These boots'll walk all over you..

A couple went to buy a special pair of shoes. They could not find it. The husband got in line at the counter to ask for, or order, a pair. The wife wandered off and found a pair of shoes. She tried it on, liked it and wanted to show it to her husband. She kept the new shoes on, slid the old ones under a seat and went (on a shortcut) outside the store. Before she was able to return from the other side, she was apprehended. She argued that she had no intent to steal. She only wanted to show the shoes to her husband, who was inside, in another part of the store.

The merchant's headache

Proof of ownership is a rather important element in the legal process. Let's say I go into a drugstore while suffering from a headache. Suppose I pass in front of a shelf of drugs and am reminded that I have some medicine with me to numb the pain in my throbbing noggin. I take the medicine out of my pocket, swallow a pill, and then return the bottle to my pocket. Security happens to notice me only at the crucial moment when I return the bottle to my pocket. I promptly get arrested. The merchant has to prove that the bottle in my pocket is his property.

Gain knowledge on knowledge gain

If you go to a bookstore with some textbooks in your bag, lift another one, and manage to remove the store's sticker from the book before you are challenged, security will have a tough time proving ownership. Nobody can build a successful lifting career on this knowledge, but it is useful. Because the entire prosecution process hinges on these two aspects, intent (the shoe-loving lady takes a short cut) and possession (treating a migraine at the wrong moment), they are also the most likely defenses. As long as you have a chance to show that you did not have the intent to steal or that whatever the store personnel found on you actually belonged to you, you have a chance to beat the rap.

THE PROCESS

Citizen's arrest

Those statutes which give merchants the privilege of detaining or arresting other citizens are another important aspect of the laws governing shoplifting. According to most legal codes, a regular arrest can be made only by an officer of the law. Under common law, however, the retailer or his employee, acting as a private citizen, can make a citizen's arrest. The laws regulating citizens' arrests are rather complex and strict. (Hmmm. Would they be equally strict if we entered never-never land and permitted the lifter to arrest the retailer for price-gouging?)

False arrest

Furthermore, any citizen who makes an arrest that is later found to be unjustified can be liable for false arrest. You can probably see the dilemma of the merchants. If they do not arrest lifters, they have no way to protect their merchandise. If they do make an arrest, and the lifter is found not guilty, they might face a very expensive civil suit. To deal with this problem, the 'Code' included a section most commonly referred to as the 'merchant's privilege':

4. Merchant's Immunity from Civil and Criminal Liability.

(a) **General Rule: A merchant who detains, questions, or causes the arrest of any person suspected of theft by shoplifting shall not be criminally or civilly liable for any legal action relating to such detention, questioning, or arrest, if:**

(i) **The merchant has reasonable grounds to suspect that the person has committed or is attempting to commit theft by shoplifting; and**

(ii) **The merchant acts in a reasonable manner under the circumstances; and**

(iii) **The merchant detains the suspected person for a reasonable period of time.**

As you can see, even though the empowerment of merchants is quite explicit, the law is still very cautious. Merchants have three opportunities to get into trouble depending on their interpretation of what is reasonable. Their interpretation might differ from the court's. In the trade magazines, we came across descriptions of a few cases where merchants were ordered to pay up to $200,000.00 in damages to the person whom they falsely accused of shoplifting.

Expensive trouble

These issues are so important that the 'Code' has an entire section devoted to the further interpretation of what 'reasonable' means in these cases.

(b) **Reasonable Grounds: Reasonable grounds to suspect that a person has committed or is attempting to commit theft by shoplifting may be based on, but is not limited to:**

- **(i) Personal observation, including observation via closed-circuit television or other visual device; or**
- **(ii) Report of such personal observation from another merchant; or**
- **(iii) Activation of an electronic or other type of mechanical device designed to detect shoplifting.**

The notion of reasonable grounds has some rather important implications for you because store security must constantly wrestle with it. Reasonable grounds has two aspects: the first is the determination of intent; the second is the quality of the information. Although technically the very act of concealment can mean that you have committed a crime, in practice:

Ground for reason

"...The courts have held that the merchant or employee must actually witness the act of concealment and maintain constant surveillance until apprehension. The detention cannot be made purely on the basis of suspicion." (Baumer and Rosenbaum, 1984)

The key words are 'constant surveillance'. To establish intent beyond any doubt, the merchandise has to be carried past the cashier's station where it would normally be purchased. We read in an article that when a person stacks six or seven cartons of cigarettes in his shirt and doesn't pay for them while being checked out, his action could be 'reasonably' looked at as serious intent.

Lode implies intent

Detaining someone who does not have the merchandise in his possession can be grounds for a false arrest suit, and everybody knows that. Merchants are generally very conservative with their policies regarding the detention of suspected lifters. We cannot emphasize enough how important it is to take your time

Take your time!

after you pack away. If they are watching you, they are likely to be so slow and careful at it that you in turn should be able to notice them doing so.

Inferences and observations

The requirement concerning the quality of the information means that it must be reliable. The personal observation of a security officer is considered reliable, but the report of one customer is not seen as reasonable grounds for the detention of another customer. The issue becomes a little more shaky when it comes to non-security employees. A sales clerk sees someone concealing an item and alerts a store detective, who then must make a decision whether to detain the person or not. Employees have to be well-instructed on the subject and the related policies of the store, whereas the security officer needs to do his best to determine the facts and act on them, not just on the inferences of the employee. All that hemming and hawing takes time and lot of movement which is easily detectable by the smart lifter and gives him the opportunity to change his plans.

They cannot just ring you in

The third point of this section of the code refers to article surveillance devices. It was included as an attempt to protect the merchant who detains a suspect on what turns out to be a false alarm.

"Without such a statutory provision the alarm generally does not constitute reasonable grounds." (Baumer and Rosenbaum, 1984)

Now that is an important thing to know. It is yet another bit of information about the usefulness of those wonderful gizmos.

'Reasonable manner,' a term used below, applies to both the way in which the suspect is detained and the purpose of the investigation.

(c) **Reasonable Manner: A merchant or peace officer who has reasonable grounds to believe that a person has committed or is attempting to commit the offense of theft by shoplifting, as defined in Section 1 of this act, may detain such person on or off the premises of the mercantile establishment if such detention is done for any or all of the following purposes:**

(i) To question the person, investigate the surrounding circumstances, obtain a statement, or any combination thereof;

(ii) To request and/or verify identification;

(iii) To inform a peace officer of the detention of such person, and/or surrender that person to the custody of a peace officer;

(iv) To inform a peace officer, the parent or parents, guardian, or other private person interested in the welfare of a minor of the detention and to surrender the minor to the custody of such person(s); or

(v) To institute criminal proceedings against the person.

(d) The merchant may use a reasonable amount of force necessary to protect himself, to prevent escape of the person detained, or to prevent the loss or destruction of property.

Judgement call

The passage on reasonable manner is as straightforward as it can be. Since it deals with behavior, it calls for a lot of judgment. Clause (d) has as its aim clarifying reasonable manner as much as possible, but as you can see, it stretches the definition so far that a number of 'unreasonable' actions become only a question of point of view, therefore eliminating the 'strictness' found in the first three clauses.

Ball and chain

What the passage on reasonable manner does not say, but obviously implies, is that detained shoplifters must be treated in a polite and courteous manner. Abusive language, public accusation, and humiliation are not considered reasonable. Keeping you chained to a pipe in the basement until the police arrive is not reasonable, either. Regardless of the outcome of the criminal case, such treatment can constitute grounds for a civil suit against the merchant.

Till death do us apart

As we have already noted, the inclusion of the right to use force makes the merchant's privilege statute in the Model Code questionable. We could ask how much force is reasonable to prevent an escape. In a recent case a security guard shot a lifter who was trying to run away. How much force is justified if the person has not yet been detained?

The questions pile up more as we move along although the next part of the 'Code' which concerns itself with time and seems to be the most straightforward and 'reasonable' one.

(e) Reasonable Time: A reasonable period of time, for purposes of this section, shall be deemed to be a period of time long enough to accomplish the purpose set forth in this section, and shall include any time spent awaiting the arrival of a law

enforcement officer or the parents or guardian of a juvenile suspect, if the merchant has summoned such law enforcement officer, parents, or guardian.

(f) **Any detention as defined in this section shall not constitute an arrest.**

Reasonable time in most existing law books is usually well-defined. Many states have very specific limits saying, for example, that a detention of two hours is reasonable but one lasting four hours is not.

A frivolous distinction

Differentiating between arrest and detention is a crucial element of the 'Code'. This distinction has to be made to protect the merchant from false arrest suits. It is argued, however, in the legal literature, that the inclusion of the right to use force and to search the suspect renders the distinction between 'detention' and 'arrest' a frivolous one.

THE PUNISHMENT

Penalties (as we have already noted) vary considerably depending on the location, the circumstances, and your personal history. Petty larceny laws are rather soft and timid and leave much to the discretion of the judge. The 'Code' offered some serious recommendations aimed at changing that situation:

3. **Penalties.**

A person convicted of theft by shoplifting shall be punished as follows:

(a) **First Theft By Shoplifting Conviction: Upon a first theft by shoplifting conviction:**

(i) **When the merchant's stated price of the merchandise is less than or equal to $100, the defendant shall be fined not more than $250.**

(ii) **When the merchant's stated price of the merchandise exceeds $100, the defendant shall be fined not less than $100 nor more than $500, and such fine shall not be suspended; or the defendant shall be punished by imprisonment not to exceed one year; or both.**

(b) **Second Theft By Shoplifting Conviction: Upon a second theft by shoplifting conviction:**

(i) **When the merchant's stated price of the merchandise is less than or equal to $100, the defendant shall be fined not less than $100 nor**

more than $500, and such fine shall not be suspended; or the defendant shall be punished by imprisonment not to exceed one year; or both.

(ii) **When the merchant's stated price of the merchandise exceeds $100, the defendant shall be fined not less than $500 and shall be imprisoned for not less than thirty days and not to exceed three years. The first thirty days of such sentence shall not be suspended, probated, deferred, or withheld.**

(c) **Third Theft By Shoplifting Conviction: Upon a third or subsequent theft by shoplifting conviction, regardless of the merchant's stated price of the merchandise, the defendant shall be fined not less than $500 nor more than $5,000, and shall be imprisoned for one to ten years. The first year of such sentence shall not be suspended, probated, deferred, or withheld.**

(d) **In determining the number of prior theft by shoplifting convictions for purposes of imposing punishment under this section, the court shall disregard all such convictions occurring more than seven years prior to the theft by shoplifting offense in question.**

Tough, is it not? Fortunately, it looks much scarier than it is in real life. We have still to see someone who has spent ten years in jail for shoplifting unless convicted of other offenses as well. We talk a bit more about this in the next chapter.

CIVIL RECOVERY

Another one of the possible consequences of shoplifting is civil liability. Civil recovery procedures are gaining popularity, and a growing number of states have statutes which allow them. In the appendix we list the ones we know about. There are several reasons for their growing popularity. As you will see below, civil suits offer a venue that is much easier to navigate than criminal prosecution. The burden of proof is much lighter, the process is streamlined, and most cases can be pursued in small claims courts. This process is more financially rewarding to retailers. In criminal prosecution, for example, restitution does not include the merchant's cost of prosecution or punitive damages, but it may do so in civil courts. The retail community is understandably loosing faith in the criminal justice system. Hitting back at lifters financially is seen as a more effective deterrent than a slap on the hand from the criminal courts.

Here we will take a look at the questionable aspects of such civil liability and recovery offered in the 'Code'.

6. Civil Liability.

(a) **An adult or emancipated minor who, with intent to appropriate merchandise without paying the merchant's stated price for the merchandise, alone or in concert with another person, knowingly commits any of the acts described in section 1 (a), or an adult or emancipated minor who, with intent to appropriate a shopping cart alone or in concert with another person knowingly removes a shopping cart from the premises of the mercantile establishment, shall be liable, in addition to actual damages, for a penalty to the owner or seller in the amount of the value of the merchandise or the value of the shopping cart, respectively, not to exceed $1,000, plus an additional penalty of not less than $100 nor more than $200.**

(b) **The parent or legal guardian having custody of an unemancipated minor who, with intent to appropriate merchandise without paying the merchant's stated price for the merchandise, alone or in concert with another person, knowingly commits any of the acts described in section 1 (a), or the parent or legal guardian having custody of an unemancipated minor who, with intent to appropriate a shopping cart, alone or in concert with another person knowingly removes a shopping cart from the premises of the mercantile establishment, shall be liable, in addition to actual damages, for a penalty to the owner or seller in the amount of the value of the merchandise or the value of the shopping cart, respectively, not to exceed $500, plus an additional penalty of not less than $100 nor more than $200.**

(c) **Liability of parents or Guardian: Civil liability under this section is not limited by any other law concerning the liability of parents or guardians or minors.**

(d) **Costs and Attorneys Fees: A merchant who is a prevailing party under this section shall be entitled to costs and reasonable attorneys fees.**

(e) **Effect of Conviction: A conviction for the offense of theft by shoplifting is not a prerequisite to the maintenance of a civil action authorized by this section.**

(f) **Right to Demand Payment: The fact that a mercantile establishment may bring an action against an individual as provided in this section shall not limit the right of such establishment to demand, orally or in writing, that a person who is liable for damages and penalties under this section remit said damages prior to the consideration of the commencement of any legal action.**

(g) **An action for recovery of damages and penalties under this section may be brought in any court of competent jurisdiction, including a small claims court, whether or not the merchant is a corporation, partnership, etc., if the total damages do not exceed the jurisdictional limit of the court involved.**

The most obviously questionable part of the 'Code' is the section about the 'Effect of Conviction.' It in fact delegates the right of decision about guilt to a court which is considerably less stringent as regards requirements of proof. In a criminal action, the state must prove beyond any reasonable doubt that the accused is guilty. In a civil action, acceptable proof is generally a preponderance of evidence. 'Clear and convincing evidence' is much easier to provide than proof of guilt beyond any reasonable doubt.

In a civil court, the bloody glove would get you...

Try to imagine a more serious case, such as assault, rape or robbery. Delegating it to a civil court would mean that the defendant would not have any of the legal safeguards, the due process, of the criminal justice system. This section in the 'Code' negates the very need for strict safeguards in criminal cases, the need which originally separated the justice system into civil and criminal branches.

The branches of the law

Although questioning the legal nuances of civil recovery laws is definitely justified, we must admit that these laws can be beneficial to lifters. If a civil suit is an alternative, and not just complementary to a criminal case, the obvious benefit is that at the end of the process the defendant is left with no criminal rec-

No record!

ord. Because most apprehended shoplifters are not career criminals, a civil action can be both an end and an effective deterrent.

Know your courts!

In case you get caught, it might be worth your while to investigate the local laws and practices in force in your community. Always show your willingness to pay restitution if a merchant is in turn willing not to prosecute you. In 1990 there were 35 states in the US with civil recovery statutes. They are (naturally) all different. Check them out. We are no library!

Let them make the mistakes!

As a final note, we have to say that most merchants are not fully aware of the law and their obligations under it. They are uncertain what their responsibilities are during the investigation of a shoplifting incident. Many believe that they do not have to do anything before the actual arrest of the suspected shoplifter by the police. We advise you not to do anything to prevent them from making mistakes that can be used against them later on.

THE MORAL OF THE PASSAGE

The law is there, written and practiced. It might get you, but with a couple of trips to the library to gain a better understanding of it, you can learn to use its safeguards to your advantage. Still, though, the best advice we are able to give is: Do not get caught!

THE COURTS

> ***"The law isn't justice. It's a very imperfect mechanism. If you press exactly the right buttons and are also lucky, justice may show up in the answer. A mechanism is all the law was ever intended to be."***
>
> *(Raymond Chandler)*

Courthouses. Those big buildings in your city that are close to City Hall. They have morning sessions. Afternoon sessions. Night sessions. Shoplifting cases are usually bunched up with small time plea-bargains, traffic tickets, and illicit solicitation cases. In no way, shape, or form are courthouses comfortable or inviting. They have doors leading straight to holding areas with cells and really bad food. They also have those doors you came in through, staying open, most times, for you to leave.

The gate of justice is open

THE JUDGES

> ***"Judicial judgment must take deep account . . . of the day before yesterday in order that yesterday may not paralyze today."***
>
> *(Felix Frankfurter)*

Believe it or not, judges are people, too. They want to get their work done, go home, 'get in their Dry Martinis.' You cannot make them happy by asking for a grand jury. They usually have a heavy caseload and want to get you out the door (the courtroom's that is) as soon as possible.

More openings

Shoplifting cases ***are*** minor compared to almost any other, and judges quite understandably don't want to waste too much time on them. They will most likely go straight by the book, rendering a verdict which you can afford. To make waves is not worth the effort. Remember your size! You are probably the smallest fish in the tank.

Like small fish in the water

THE DUE PROCESS

"The due process of law as we use it, I believe, rests squarely on the liberal idea of conflict and resolution."

(June L. Trapp)

Kafkaesque

First you receive your notice (if they did not take you in) about showing up for 'I.D.ing' (photo, fingerprints and such) at the police station. After the cops have taken a mug shot and recorded your prints, they usually assign you a court date right on the spot. On that date, the process begins wherein you (the defendant) are charged under the appropriate laws and scheduled for trial. If you (the suspect) are not present in court on the date assigned and have not arranged for someone to ask for a continuance, a warrant is issued for your arrest.

If the suspect (you) is present, the judge determines whether the other necessary parties (store detectives; clerks) are also present. If they are not, the judge might set a new date or just dismiss the case. If all parties are present, the defendant can ask for a lawyer and therefore a continuance. If the defendant already has a lawyer, and if that lawyer is present, the lawyer himself might ask for a continuance to prepare a defense. Once everybody is ready, the defendant is asked to enter a plea. If he pleads guilty, the judge moves on to sentencing, and the process is over. Five minutes, tops. If the defendant pleads not guilty, the case will be heard.

Alabama smokes

If the case is actually heard and the verdict is guilty, any resultant jail sentence will be in direct proportion to the perceived degree of severity of this 'petty crime.' The sentence will also, of course, be proportionate to the length of the lifter's record. Nevertheless, even if the length of your record is impressive, and always provided that you have never committed a hard crime, do not lose faith! We looked at a few statistics, and they were all good news. Other than one pending case in Alabama, where they sentenced a black murderer out on parole to life for stealing a carton of cigarettes(!) we heard and read only about light punishments.

"The value of the goods stolen and the dangerousness of individual shoplifters are relatively inconsequential when compared with most of the other crimes and criminals. Therefore judges tend to view this as a petty crime and their role as one of dispensing justice and the role of the courts as providing a general deterrent function through the use of fines, probation, and occasional imprisonment. Taken together, this means that very few shoplifters are assessed any significant penalty beyond a fine or probation. Data

from the Chicago courts suggest that less than 5 percent of all cases result in such a penalty."(Baumer and Rosenbaum, 1984)

You see, your life is not in great danger. The five per cent figure mentioned above is the percentage of shoplifting cases filed in court!!

"In one large US city, only about 20 percent of all adult shoplifters were arrested during a year's period. Only 7% had their cases filed in court by the prosecutor, 3% were convicted, and less than 2 percent were incarcerated." (Kathleen B. Brossi, 1979)

We could quote other sources where the figures vary slightly, but they are all very low. We can confidently say that less than a third of the apprehensions results in arrests. Less than ten percent are tried, less than 5% are convicted, and less than 3% are jailed. These odds do not seem too bad to us. And none of our sources has received more then a couple of months (out in a couple of days, time served) in jail. The percentage figures on the lifters' 'freedom loss' seem not much higher than the percentage figures showing the losses due to shoplifting incurred by the retail industry.

Similarity is grounds for understanding

THE ATTITUDE OF THE ACCUSERS

"Money is human happiness in the abstract: he, then, who is no longer capable of enjoying human happiness in the concrete devotes his heart entirely to money."

(Arthur Schopenhauer)

The accusers' attitude is directly governed by money. Exactly how much a court action will cost in time, working hours lost, and lawyers. Cost of prosecution is the major issue for the retailers. Most of the sources we looked at say that the cost of prosecution is usually higher than the value of the loss.

Time is money

The other major cost is manpower. The security person or clerk who made the apprehension has to be in court, sometimes for the whole day, to deal with the case. Quite often continuance is granted to the defendant (or, depending on how shameless you or your lawyer is, several times), making the presence of the witness pointless.

Manpower is time

There are also times when the witness is simply not available. Employee turnover rates at retail operations are relatively high, so it can easily happen that by the time a case is heard, the witness for the prosecution is unreachable. The knowledge of all these costs and possible problems is a major factor in the retailers' decision whether to prosecute.

Testimonial is manpower

Is it not reasonable?

Although we cannot know for sure, we would venture to say that one of the reasons for the low apprehension rates in the morning hours is that all the security guards are in court assisting in the prosecution of the cases they have sent there. Apprehension rates are high in the early afternoon hours because that is the time when they get back from court eager to do something 'productive' after spending hours waiting to be heard. The point in all this is the one we have already made a few times: Retailers do not like to prosecute. They want to deter and prevent.

CIVIL RECOVERY

> ***"He is mad past recovery, but yet he has lucid intervals."***
>
> *(Miguel de Cervantes)*

Go, Rocinante, go!

Today, yes, criminal prosecution of shoplifters is a fight against windmills. Our own dear mad Don Quixote, the hapless merchant, has taken his inspiration for the battle from some very scrupulous, unrealistic statutes (chivalric texts), and decided to charge the enemy (well, give us a break in putting together our analogy and just imagine that our poor mad merchant sees the lifter as a demonic creature with lots of arms for packing away) on the back of his skinny steed (his loss prevention budget) with his lance and kitchen pot (two cops, Sam Lance, and Phil Kitchen Pot), assisted by his very own Sancho Panza (his security officer). The success he may expect at combat's end, even if he topples a windmill or two, is best described by a part of the Civil Recovery Statute from Michigan: 'Additional penalty on written demand, ten times the retail value of the merchandise, but no less than $40 and no more then $100.' Chivalry is dead.

We have already talked about the legal aspects of civil recovery. Here we will say a few words about the practices.

In the appendix we list the states that have civil recovery statutes (not at all romantic). The number of those states is growing, probably because the process is gaining popularity, but civil recovery is still far from being widely accepted or used. The statutes are an obvious prerequisite, but by themselves they do not mean large scale acceptance of the process.

In some cases civil recovery is used as an alternative to criminal prosecution (battling windmills). In most cases, however, it is used in tandem with the criminal case. The reason for the second approach is that most retailers are not sure that they can make a case before the civil courts without a criminal conviction (toppled windmill).

In some states law firms act both as solicitors and collection agents for the retailers they represent. They send demand letters, do the paperwork, and, with the possible help of a collection agency, sometimes even get some money. We note that in the list of thirty states with recovery statutes only ***one*** (Ohio) includes some kind of criminal procedure against the non-paying booster. The actual recovery rate achieved through civil prosecution is about 40-50% of the total amount of the loss, which is just about the percentage merchants and their lawyers usually demand from the court.

Sancho, take my lance and hand me a pen...

Paying damages is nothing compared to having a criminal record. Our advice to you is that in case you are asked to do so, express your willingness to pay immediately as long as they are ready to drop the criminal charges against you. Then, later, you can recover your damages from them your way.

...let me right a cheque to the miller!

SHOPLIFTING COURTS

"Optimism is the content of small men in high places."

(F. Scott Fitzgerald)

In most places, shoplifting cases are still heard in the same court as all other small-time cases. It has been suggested that having shoplifting cases heard with more serious crimes makes the sentences lighter and less likely to be handed down at all. Comparisons, after all, are odious. Having cases heard with unrelated others (different categories of lawyers, witnesses, etc., vying for time before the court) has also made scheduling unpredictable. As an answer to this problem (and as a result of the lobbying efforts of some retail associations) in some municipalities special courts have been set up to deal with shoplifting cases only.

Deflating courts

Because the decision to set up a special shoplifting-cases court is made by each individual municipality, we could not possibly find out where all of them are to be found. As we always say, check out your own area! These special courts are not really different or separate from the rest. They only represent procedural changes at the regular courts, but because they deal only with shoplifting cases, they can process cases faster. It's a sad fact for lifters that such courts tend to give out tougher sentences because cases there are only compared to each other and not to more serious criminal actions.

Inflating sentences

These special courts also help retailers to do batch processing, meaning that store security can schedule several cases to be heard at the same time, greatly reducing costs.

Conflating cases

None of this is good news for you, the smart lifter. If you have to go to one of those places, your chances of getting off are

Bad news

somewhat lower than they would be in regular courts. However, if you consider the odds in general, they are still not ***that*** bad.

COURT SITTING SERVICES

More bad news

Court-sitting services represent another alternative for the merchant who wishes to prosecute shoplifters. The idea is that a person sits in the courtroom all day and phones the witness, who is doing his regular duties at his workplace, to alert him when the case is about to be heard. The court sitter can monitor several cases at the same time, reducing the cost of prosecution for the retailers. This service is unlikely to change the outcome of a case. The only difference it makes to you is that where such a service exists, the witness who plans to testify against you will definitely make it to your trial. Too bad, pal, no easy dismissal!

CIVIL MEDIATION SERVICES

Civil mediation services were not designed to deal with shoplifting cases, but sometimes, where they exist, they are used that way. They function like a parental lecture.

"The rationale is that shoplifting can be diminished through the development of newly internalised values on the part of the offender." (Baumer and Rosenbaum,1984)

Baby talk in its infancy

Community mediation is still in its infancy. We cannot say much about it, and we have very little faith in it. It might work well in solving domestic disputes, but its value in fighting shoplifting is dubious to say the least. Just think about it. Would a lecture on behavior be likely to change the attitude of a booster who considers lifting to be his life style?

"I was caught for the first time. With a bottle of analgesic. My first court appearance I learned that the judge and prosecution will be satisfied with me paying thirty-five dollars to my favorite charity and then my case will be dismissed. No record. Sounds good. And I can choose my theater company - a registered charity, as you know - and give myself the money. I feel cheated, I expected some sort of punishment."

REHABILITATION PROGRAMS

Twelve steps walking away from crime

There are only a few. There is of course 'Shoplifters' Anonymous,' and there are a few other programs, administered by various retail associations. STOPS, the 'Shoplifting and Theft Organized Prevention Specialists' or NCTI, the 'National Corrective Training Institute' and CASA (Kleptomaniacs and Shoplifters Anonymous) are a few of them. The rehabilitation programs they organize are often designed as alternatives to criminal prosecution. They all claim amazingly low rates of recidivism while admitting that since none of the programs is run nation-wide, tracking the results is almost impossible. We think that they are jokes, but they should make you happy, because if you are referred to them, you can get off at the cost of a few hours of mutual bullshitting.

YOUR ATTITUDE

> ***"A crime persevered in a thousand centuries ceases to be a crime, and becomes a virtue. This is the law of custom, and custom supersedes all other forms of law."***
>
> *(Mark Twain)*

We decided to discuss possible attitudes in the form of a FAQ file.

Q: Should I get a lawyer?

A: Some of our sources would never go to court without one. Some would never waste the time and money on one. If we look at the results, lawyers do not seem to make much of a difference. Some of our sources actually seemed to be worse off with their help than others were without it. Forget about legal aid or the public defender. They are of little help. They will tell you to plead guilty and beg for a lenient judgment. They will probably (ill) advise you to hope for probation and ask for it in court.

Good question.

Q: Should I be cocky?

A: You should not be defiant, either. If you choose to be 'innocent,' then you may present yourself with an underplayed air of indignation, but you have to be very careful to accompany that indignation with an obvious readiness to co-operate in the process. Having an 'attitude' always works against you. You can be upset, but not angry.

Definitely not.

Q: Should I (or my lawyer) ask for postponement?

A: Continuance (called adjournment in Canada) is a very useful option. In about one third of all shoplifting cases a continuance is granted at least once. You can probably do better than that if you are lucky. The first time, let's say, you cannot enter a plea because you need counsel. The second time your lawyer needs time to prepare. The third time he might ask for a jury trial. At the last moment you can still plead guilty and pay a fine. If at any of those steps the witness for the prosecution fails to show, you have a chance for a dismissal. All this sounds very good, but we must caution you about abusing the procedure. Asking for a new date at every trial date can increase your chances for dismissal, but it can also be seen as what it is, a deliberate tactic for

Definitely yes.

achieving that very goal. You need to exercise sober judgment in deciding how far you can go.

Q: Do I have a good chance for dismissal?

Quite likely.

A: Very possibly. It is far more likely to happen than you would think. In regular courts it happens in about two thirds of the cases. If the witnesses for the prosecution do not show up, the prosecution does not have a case.

"I've got off a couple times. It happened that they just let me go. Case dismissed. I like these words. It's no different from the traffic courts. If the guy from the store doesn't show, you're home free."

There are changes in the offing, however, and they do not bode well for the lifter. In traffic ticket cases in Quebec, Canada, the court is satisfied with a sworn statement (signed in front of a notary public) from the police officer, who does not have to show up in court. Such a change in shoplifting prosecution procedure could be a severe blow to 'working' people even though it might mean a diminution in the severity of fines or other sentences.

Q: What if I do not show up?

You are !@#$ed!

A: The worst thing that you can do is not show up at court. It is a serious mistake. You may be summarily convicted, but, if not, a warrant is issued for your arrest. The court does not chase you, but sooner or later they will get you, and probably at a time when you least expect it. Most of the arrests on warrant violations happen in unrelated situations, such as being stopped for a traffic offense or being arrested for some other reason. Of course, everything depends on what you want to do with your life.

Dumb and dumber!

Warrant violations, even jumping bail, work fine for serious criminals. If you like being hard to find, never want to own a car, can get a new identity, and want to start a new life in order to avoid a possible hundred dollar fine, then go ahead and do it. We just do not think that it is very smart. In fact we think that it is dumb. No. It is dumber. And even dumber than that.

Q: Should I plea guilty?

It's your call!

A: It always makes things smoother to plead guilty. Punishment, although certain, is more lenient when you cooperate. In a way your decisions at court are not unlike the choices you make playing poker, and pleading guilty means that you are folding. It is gambling at its best. With odds, wins, losses and jackpots. Not pleading guilty raises the stakes slightly, but it does give you a chance to win.

The court is not the place to feel guilty!

If it is your first offense, you are much better off asking for a lawyer and a chance to consider your options. Most people plead guilty because they do not want to 'anger' the judge. They feel that showing repentance will improve their chances for a softer sentence. Giving advice here is very difficult because this is a personal judgment call. We cannot say what would have happened in this or that particular case if the approach of the defendant had been different. Even if we try to compare outcomes, the matter remains a judgment call. Not pleading guilty gives you a better chance to get off, whereas pleading guilty usually results in a lighter sentence. It is your call.

Q: How about acquittal?

A: If there is compelling evidence against you, your chances are slim, but if you have a really good argument, it could happen. A good lawyer can do anything. A few years ago in Ontario a prominent politician was arrested in a drugstore for lifting (allegedly!) a bottle of contact lens cleaning solution. He hired the best lawyer around (against whom one of the authors of this book lost a little legal skirmish some time back). That lawyer was able to convince the judge that the poor civil servant had so much on his mind - all the worries created by thinking about the welfare of his constituents; all the problems in his office - that he was not thinking about what he was doing. He argued that it was absent-mindedness which caused him to pick up the bottle, not intent to steal. The judge either bought the argument or just did not want a fight. The accused politician was acquitted.

Dream on! ...or get into politics!

Q: Should I bargain for probation or a suspended sentence?

A: Probation is great. A suspended sentence is better than going to jail, one supposes, but not as great as probation for reasons we'll explain later.

As we travel deeper into the information age, the distinctions concerning access to information are becoming blurred. Awhile ago information had to be obtained at the source, requiring time and effort justifiable only in serious cases. Getting information today is very easy. Keeping it is very cheap. No matter what they arrest you for and where, the police will know everything, including the number of parking infractions you have accumulated all around the country in the past decade.

The criminal record highway

Watching courtroom-dramas and cop-shows on TV you must have heard the phrase 'x number of arrests, no conviction' over and over. Whatever we think about the procedure that helps officers of the court obtain such information, we have to face the fact that it is there to be dealt with. If you have crossed an American-Canadian border lately, and they asked you anything, probably it was not whether you had ever been convicted, but whether you had ever been arrested. Responding to that question with a lie could get you an FBI record.

How to obtain an FBI record.... for shoplifting.

The term 'probation' means that after you serve the time specified in your sentence, you will not have a criminal record. A

A record is a record

'suspended sentence'. means that you will not go to jail unless you commit another crime within the period of the suspension. Your arrest record will stay with you just as if you did indeed go to jail.

Q: What excuses or explanations work?

We believe in you!

A: People can come up with the wildest excuses under pressure. We do not wish to water down your creative juices by giving suggestions. Think of something that makes sense in your situation. Just make sure that it accords with the facts. If you have walked out of a store with a single item, big or small, you can claim absent-mindedness. If you have packed away a bunch of things with obvious deliberation, then saying that you just forgot to pay for them will not really work. Be consistent in both your story and attitude. Once you have thought of something, stick to it.

Q: Should I take revenge? And how?

Are you Shmart?..

A: Revenge is sometimes possible. There ***are*** options which enable you to bare your teeth and exhibit that 'attitude' you've been squelching. First, let's talk about suing your accuser for false arrest. You definitely need a lawyer for that. You need a good case. And, of course, you must have been granted an acquittal in the case the merchant initiated against you. You would be surprised to know how many successful civil cases have been won against careless retail establishments. If you check out the 'Code' and our comments on it in the previous chapter, you will be able to assess whether your particular case might just be won. If you decide that you have a case, and if you can find a good lawyer who believes in it, too, then go ahead and bring it.

...or are you smart?

Revenge of a second sort is entirely in your own hands. If, after they have fined or jailed you, you decide to go back and punish the store, you may, or so say our sources, succeed admirably.

THE MORAL OF THE PASSAGE

Nobody can advise you better than yourself. If you are intelligent and well-informed about your own circumstances, it is you who should make the decision. The above information might give you enough guidance to enable you to discover and analyze the facts pertaining to your personal needs and situation.

MYTHS ON ALL SIDES

"The great enemy of the truth is very often not the lie - deliberate, contrived and dishonest - but the myth - persistent, persuasive and unrealistic."

(John F. Kennedy)

THE EXPERTS ADVISE...

"An expert is a man who has made all the mistakes which can be made in a very narrow field."

(Niels Bohr)

The following chapters are a collage of the mistaken ideas, misconceptions, prejudices, misplaced fears and angers of all the 'combatants' on the 'Retail Battle Grounds.' As we have already mentioned, there are persistent mistakes being made on all flanks and fronts. Now, for your edification, we collect and organize them more systematically.

There is a shopping-cart load of literature on the subject. Eventually the stuff turns out to be mostly worthless or impractical, however, because it conveys confusing information which frustrates the retailer in his quest for enlightenment.. We found only three good books and a few readable and reasonable articles.

Oh, those puns again!

The 'experts' can be put into two distinct groups, the scientists and the consultants.

The scientists: sociologists, psychologists, criminologists, and their ilk, desperately cling to the idea that the 'pathology' of shoplifting can be deciphered. They believe that they can shed some light on the shoplifter's enigmatic identity and motivation, and who are we to say they cannot? However, such sensitive and complex theories as they come up with are utterly useless to a guy who just wants to make his shop safer.

Impractical ideas...

The consultants: reformed lifters, retired cops and detectives, and their sort, shamelessly pretend to have the answers and tirelessly peddle a wild assortment of gadgets and gizmos to unsuspecting merchants. It is not as bad as we make it sound, perhaps, but it is a sad state of affairs.

Practical idiocies...

THE SCIENTISTS

"Aristotle could have avoided the mistake of thinking that women have fewer teeth than men by the simple device of asking Mrs. Aristotle to keep her mouth open while he counted."

(Bertrand Russell)

We did not start thinking and writing about the subject of shoplifting with the intent of critiquing the literature, but we could not help forming an opinion. The scientists are way off in the blue somewhere gazing at moondust. We could poke fun at them, as we did in some parts of our book, but we do not want to be unfair. In our research, we did find a few good and useful studies.

Peer to peer networking

Articles in the learned journals can be, and sometimes are, interesting, but they are so very far away from reality and a street-smart understanding of the phenomenon, that they are useless. The articles (essays) which learned folk write in their journals are aimed at each other. They are meant to be read by peers who are in on the story currently in fashion, and they seldom contain any useful information for ordinary souls like ourselves. What we have just written here seems to indicate that what the illuminati write is actually good - just aimed at a different audience. Not necessarily. Some of the research we came across contained half-cooked hypotheses, wrong-headed questions, and questionable methodology, but then again, we are not here to pass judgment on theories, assumptions and methods.

What we will pass judgment on, however, is the amazing work of the other group of the (mostly self-appointed) experts:

THE CONSULTANTS

"It takes no talent to be a shoplifter. A safe breaker, a second-story man, a bad check artist or a con man has talent - negative as it may be. But shoplifting requires no talent."

(Roger Griffin, CPP)

"It takes no talent to be a security consultant. A salesman, a window dresser, a store manager, even a store detective has talent - useless as it may be. But consulting requires no talent."

(The Authors)

Pierot to Pierot networking

The retailers' major source on practical advice is trade magazines. Before we started working on this book we would never have thought of seeking out such exalted titles as *Progressive Grocer, Security Management, or Chain-Store Age Executive.*

Trade magazines have a relatively small circulation. They make most of their money on advertising. Their articles seem to be mainly fillers. They seldom pay their writers, but when they do, it is customary to pay them with advertising space. The result is a collection of articles with shamelessly self-advertising ideas in them. Who do you think wrote these two articles?

How to Give a Head in Advertising

"The Hidden Benefits of EAS" and

"Linking EAS with CCVS Helps Stop All Types of Theft".

We learn from the articles that technology is the answer to every loss prevention problem. There are also subtle hints about which specific product one should buy, as well as the intimation that one of these sterling examples of technology is never enough. Smart retailers should buy all of them and link them. We hope that you agree with us that giving such advice probably has nothing to do with their being presidents of companies which make millions by selling those gadgets!

Gizmo manufacturers are not the only ones 'metamorphosing' into writers in order to sell their garbage. The most frequently seen writers in the magazines are security consultants selling their services. They offer amazing methods, incredible strategies, and outstanding advice.

How to Get a Head...

Read this serious advice and see if you can make heads or tails of it:

"Internal survey [in your store] **should also consist of a red-dot program. The program is a way of tracking high-theft items. Each item is flagged with a small red dot placed on the shelf next to the stock-keeping unit (SKU) coding label. If the product is merchandised from the floor, a red sign should be hung above the product. Each item identified by a red dot should have a sticker attached, with the week and year it came into the store from the warehouse or outside vendor. Placing the sticker on the item allows the loss prevention manager to track the ordering turns of that specific item week after week. The red dot helps store management recognize high-theft items being tracked without calling it to the attention of clerks and other individuals. By tracking the ordering of the items, management can determine if the ordering turns of this item are acceptable compared to the customer demand." (Security Management, 1993)**

Suck on this

Wow! What? Did you get it? Now, read it again. And again. If you still think that this wise guy has a clue about what he is talking about, write to us. This is not all, and it gets better:

"The next step is to establish a known theft test period. Many retailers have found empty packages in their store at one time or another. This is a typical sign of shoplifting in

Don't bite!

drug, hardware, and electronic stores. Many shoplifters remove the merchandise from a blister pack or other packaging when stealing. Depending on the sales volume, the loss prevention manager should develop a test period to track all empty packages found. *Although that does not account for merchandise taken with the package, it places a value on shoplifted merchandise*. During the test period, management must communicate any shoplifting to the loss prevention department and document it. The loss prevention department can then react to these issues as they arise and begin to maintain a *file* supported by incident reports." (Security Management, April 1993)

A file of what? On the value of the shoplifted merchandise taken with the package? We do think that this writer is rather convincing when he says that maintaining a file supported by incident reports is a great way to react to the issues (as they arise).

A cigarette?

This sexy little bureaucracy is every shoplifter's (wet) dream. As long as security is kept busy with little red dots and incident reports, the floors will be safe for the smart lifters. We will not insult your intelligence any longer by exposing you to the wisdom of this expert, but here is food for thought: The wise guy who wrote the article quoted above is not your average loss prevention officer. He is one of the few who is smart enough to get published.

The dotty retailer

Looking at this amazing program, we cannot help wondering which is the store's greater loss: inventory shrinkage due to shoplifting or the paycheck the give to one of these wise-guys?- Maybe it's the cost of buying little red dots?

The 'best ones' have the word 'survey' in the title

Some of the consultants test their prowess in sociology by conducting their own research and presenting their insightful results to unsuspecting readers. We saw charts with irrelevant numbers. We found tables with means and medians but without the basic variables which would give these figures any meaning! We are very tempted to show you examples of some of these brilliant works, but we are not here to embarrass people (not all of them - not all the time). If you are really curious, you can check our bibliography and find their follies in a library.

A CASE STUDY

Read it 'right' side up!

To formulate a 'useful' case study on shoplifting, go to the serious literature on the subject and turn almost any scenario that they present 'right side up.' What these writers present as typical cases are actually case studies of mistakes, a showcase of all the things a smart lifter would never do. These 'case studies' can be compiled into a check list of foolish scenarios to avoid. We all need reminding now and then to unplug the radio before we clean it.

The message of these stories is that no matter what you do and no matter how careful you are, you will surely be caught. The message they keep sending is: 'We know who you are!' / 'We know how to recognize you!' / 'We know all your tricks - and no matter how clever you are, we will catch you!'

Do you? Will you?

In a way, we can understand. Their efforts are limited by their knowledge. They recognize only the lifting styles they ***can*** recognize. If they could recognize those they do not recognize then your chances for a safe 'work environment' would not be as good as they are.

The (sh)uplifting environment (again)

We here present just one of their morality tales, annotated to point out lifting mistakes and show why those mistakes had to lead to apprehension.

"Mr. X. walks into the crowded store, perspiring strongly, since he is wearing a winter coat with large pockets on a warm spring day."

A crowded store is never an appropriate place to 'shop.' (A completely empty store is not very good either.) Whatever the size of the crowd, however, everything a lifter does depends on style, and Mr. X ain't got any. Never wear out-of-season garments. Work in appropriate attire. Smart lifters love summer weather, which is just right for their loose shorts and big T-shirts.

"After choosing the item he knew he needed, he pretended to read the label with extreme care. Then he picked up something else; another brand. As he was examining the second item, he casually slid the first into his wide pocket."

For the 'checking the label' ploy, he did not need to pick up another brand. He could have taken two of the same brand at one and the same time. Checking the label can be a legitimate method, but the core of the idea is that you pick up two pieces of the same item in the same fell swoop, and then you pack one away (not into your pocket though) while examining the other. The idea is to show anybody who might be watching you that you have put an item back in place. (They're not supposed to know you took two of them.) Working into a pocket is seldom a good idea unless the object is very small. If it is not, it will require an unnecessarily complicated hand movement. Sliding something into a shirt or your crotch is much less obtrusive.

"Then he moved on and picked up an item he was going to pay for and carried it along in plain sight until he reached another aisle. He picked up another item from the rack. Glancing furtively around to be sure nobody was watching, he slipped the item into his pocket."

Easy to pick out somebody who is 'glancing furtively around.' Besides, isn't it a little too late to start checking out security while packing his second item?

"Then he bumps into another customer and drops yet another item in his pocket. He heads to the cashier and pays for the one item in his hand. Gets caught."

Is it not a fact that his pocket was a little overloaded already when he dropped in this last item? And why the bump? He is a shoplifter for god's sake, not a pick-pocket! The function of a bump for pick-pockets is to divert the attention of the person they are cleaning out. A bumbling idiot in a store does not divert attention. He attracts it.

The way the subject of this fable executed his 'job' naturally set him up for a fall. He should have shopped around the way every civilian does and then found a point in time when he could pack away safely, making sure before and after (casually and not furtively) that nobody was watching him. He should not have walked out of a store immediately after packing away. A smart lifter always gives himself time before he leaves. If the security officers have noticed you, they have to keep watching you to make sure that you still have the merchandise when you try to leave the store. The longer the time you spend inside the store, the greater your chances are to find out whether you are being watched.

The only thing we can learn from the above fable is that if you behave like a complete idiot, you will get caught. Most of the stories presented for the purpose of education, deterrence or raising public awareness never rise above the level of the fable we presented here.

MORAL OF THE PASSAGE

Be happy that the experts don't know how to do smart lifting. If they knew how to do it, they might know how to catch you.

THE RETAILERS THINK...

"When we can drain the Ocean into mill-ponds, and bottle up the Force of Gravity, to be sold by retail, in gas jars; then may we hope to comprehend the infinitudes of man's soul under formulas of Profit and Loss; and rule over this too, as over a patent engine, by checks, and valves, and balances."

(Thomas Carlyle)

ABOUT THE LOSSES

Retailers have seriously mistaken ideas about the nature and sources of their losses. The following table should give you an idea of the extent of their errors.

RESULTS OF A HYPOTHETICAL LOSS-PREVENTION PROGRAM FOR A BUSINESS WITH $1 MILLION ANNUAL SALES

RETAIL CONDITIONS		LOSSES BEFORE PROGRAM	AFTER PROGRAM
ASSUMED:			
Shoplifting	(63%)	50,400	5,040
Employee Theft	(36%)	28,800	23,040
Non-theft	(1%)	800	800
		80,000	28,880
SHRINKAGE RATE		(8%)	(2.9%)
ACTUAL:			
Shoplifting	(20%)	16,000	1,600
Employee Theft	(65%)	52,000	41,600
Non-theft	(15%)	12,000	12,000
		80,000	55,200
SHRINKAGE RATE		(8%)	(5.5%)

(Baumer and Rosenbaum, 1984)

An internal worry

Retailers seem reluctant to admit that shoplifters are not their biggest worry. It could be a natural reflex to attribute their losses to foul play by an outsider. It is easier to put the blame on that 'mysterious monster,' the shoplifter, than on the Joes, Marys, and Janes they work with every day.

ABOUT THE LIFTERS

People?

Although the literature attempts to be objective, retailers and their employees still see shoplifting and shoplifters through a filter of prejudices and preconceived ideas. They still look at shoplifting as a problem of people rather than as a problem of behavior. It could be that it is also a natural attitude to see shoplifters as vagrants. Shoplifting is a crime, therefore shoplifters must look like criminals.

Behavior?

Even though there is data showing the social makeup of shoplifters, the people who work in the retail industry still have difficulty understanding that there are no typical lifters. When they do at last come to this realization, they must not then immediately decide to become suspicious of absolutely everyone. Instead, they should make up their minds to look for and be perceptive of certain ***behaviors***, not people.

Race?

We found articles quoting statistics showing that 60% of apprehended shoplifters are black, failing to mention that the data came from predominantly black neighborhoods. Colored and ethnic people in general are less likely to be shoplifters than anybody else because they know that a biased store security is out to get them. Old prejudices and beliefs die hard. Retailers do not spend enough on training, and when they do, the trainers do not seem to be any more open-minded than the trainees. Especially when it comes to methods.

ABOUT THE METHODS

Bad bags and booster boxes

People who know have been telling retailers for the past twenty years, but we still have to say it again: No, lifters do not use 'booster boxes' any more. They have not used booster boxes for a long, long time. Yet even today, training videos show the booster box, the wrinkly shopping bag from a previous trip, and the huge inside pockets from shoplifting's quaint past. We have described dozens of new, realistic methods, most of which rely on concealment inside clothing, not on any obvious external aid. The assumption about lifting methods is that they have to be either clumsy or elaborate, neither of which is the case. Not for the smart ones.

ABOUT PREVENTION EFFORTS

There is a four billion dollar industry out there trying to convince retailers that the gizmos they sell actually work. They do, but to what extent remains untold. Luckily for you, the belief is strong that they do catch and deter many lifters. That belief relaxes store vigilance. Retailers spend their money on the gizmos and then try to recover the cost by firing a few employees. This deterrence-oriented attitude makes the smart lifter happy because he can see what obstacles he has to overcome.

We shall overcome!

Department stores have recently fallen in love with ink tags. They ***are*** cute, but as protection they are worthless. Their deterrence value against the ignorant is high, but they make the smart lifter feel safe.

The signs stores put up can be equally worthless. It has been proven that a sign stating in one form or another that 'everybody pays for shoplifting' actually increases incidents. You do not have to be a brain surgeon to see the logic in it. Because the lifter obviously does not pay, every act of lifting is a rebuttal of the statement on the sign.

No brain surgery

MORAL OF THE PASSAGE

Due to an enormous number of misconceptions and lingering biases, retailers are in the dark about almost everything. Protection is lame. Prevention is ridiculous. They hardly have a clue who you are or how a smart lifter works. You should be delighted.

THE AMATEURS BELIEVE...

"I might say that what amateurs call a style is usually only the unavoidable awkwardnesses in first trying to make something that has not heretofore been made."

(Ernest Hemingway)

In citing the mistakes made by retailers, we have been, we hasten to admit, somewhat unfair. Some of the things they employ do work on what is the largest group of shoplifters, the 'unskilled amateurs.'

THE VALUE OF THE LIFTED ITEM

Zero to one thousand

We can confidently say that the most prevalent of all myths in shoplifting's collection of fables is that stealing something of little value is somehow a lesser crime than stealing something expensive. Not so. Theft is theft, and up to a certain point value is immaterial. The only aspect of reality in this myth is that retailers will be less likely to prosecute for a minor loss. However, if they choose to prosecute, there will be no significant difference in the outcome.

Clear conscience?

Most statistics kept on shoplifting treat discount stores as a separate category. People (amateurs, that is) are more likely to steal cheap items, probably because that way they can better put their conscience at ease. Their sense of guilt is in direct proportion to the amount on the price tag.

THE EFFECTIVENESS OF THE GIZMOS

Of course, gizmos work. If you walk through the gates with a bunch of EAS stickers in your pocket, the alarm will go off. ***If*** the system is turned on.

What's that buzz?

"Once I walked out of a music store with three or four CDs, and then I walked across the street into another store and the alarm went off as I stepped in. I was lucky, but I also learned that the alarms in the first store didn't work or were there only for decoration."

While professional shoplifters are hard to deter, amateurs can be scared off by almost anything. What can we say when even a cardboard policeman can reduce shrinkage?

THE UNREASONABLE FEAR OF THE LAW

Per diem

"When I got caught the last time, they scared me. It was my third arrest, and I was expecting at least a $500 fine. I wouldn't have had a problem with that. It is the cost of doing business. When the judge said ten days in jail, I was shocked. I got ten days! As they were taking me over to the jail I tried to cheer myself up by telling myself that it is better than a five-hundred dollar fine (which I thought I would get). I will save fifty bucks a day I said to myself, but I was kicked out the next morning. If I want to stay true to my calculation, I have to say that I made five-hundred bucks overnight."

Horror of horrors!

For most amateurs the law looks much scarier than it is. They fear the criminal record, the sentences, the JAIL! They are justifiably afraid of being seen and treated like criminals, but they do not know that it does not hurt. We exposed you to the realities a few pages back, and so now you know.

MORAL OF THE PASSAGE

You do not have to excuse yourself. We understand. However, after reading our book, you will no longer have excuses. Sorry.

FINAL NOTES

"We do not need to be shoemakers to know if our shoes fit, and just as little have we any need to be professionals to acquire knowledge of matters of universal interest."

(Georg Hegel)

THE FUTURE OF SHOPLIFTING

"Future. That period of time in which our affairs prosper, our friends are true and our happiness is assured."

(Ambrose Bierce)

The more everything changes, the more everything remains the same

We venture to say that the future of shoplifting (just like its past) will be closely tied to the future of retailing. Videos will be sold on demand through cables. Books, records, computers, flowers and whatever else are already sold on the Internet. Kitchen wares and sports accessories are already sold through infomercials. Food supplements and beauty products through multi-level marketing. Other things we cannot even think of yet will be sold through channels not yet invented.

Small picture

The options for marketing are mind-boggling compared to what was available half a century ago, but with all the advances in direct and multi-level marketing, on-line stores and sales through infomercials, mail order, and catalogues, retail merchandising is here to stay. So is shoplifting. There are certain things that are quite impractical to sell by the new methods. The methods presently used to market these items are therefore unlikely to change. Or so, at least, we hope! Clothes have to be touched, looked at, and tried on. Food needs to be checked for quality... you get the picture.

Big picture

As long as 40% of a retailer's revenue comes from impulse shopping, retailers cannot afford to put their wares under wraps. They cannot afford to make them untouchable; immovable; unavailable. EAS manufacturers often use this argument. It is either (our) tag - they say - or no impulse shopping. Although we do not think that the tags help, we must agree that impulse shopping weighs in the balance. The two sides of the equation are shoplifting and impulse shopping. Whether technology can help reduce the former without doing away with the latter is another question.

Advances in technology

It is quite obvious that present technologies are less than perfect. Well, less than good. In fact, they are less than adequate. Actually, they are crap. We hope that we have shown that everything now on the market can be defeated, avoided, or circumvented. Although we haven't written down the exact method for putting every single gadget there is out of commission, we have made clear the optimism with which the smart lifter goes after each new challenge to his skills.. The question which comes to mind is whether we can even imagine a foolproof technology. We have already done our wild chapter on the subject of 'future technologies,' and, if you recall, we pretty much failed to think of anything fail-safe. If you have done the impossible, write to us, and we'll submit your ideas to the real experts in prevention technology - the guys who defuse it.

Engage!

'Source tagging' is the buzzword in the retail industry at present, but source tagging is nothing more than an extension of the present EAS system. The only difference is that the tag will somehow be built into the packaging. As long as the product can be unpacked, the tag can be gotten rid of. As long as the tools for deactivating a tag can be 'lifted' (meaning [for the first time in our magnum opus] not being excessively heavy), they can be carried into a store to deactivate the tags. We could come up with more wild ideas, but we don't see the point. Whatever the technology is, it can be countered. Technology will never be the answer, but attitude might be.

Spending on illusions

Attitudes can be changed on two levels: in the stores and in society. An attitude change in the stores, unlikely though it is, would mean more employees, more attention to each individual shopper, and lower accessibility of products. Retailers are not ready to spend the necessary money to create shopping environments that would both stimulate shoppers and deter shoplifting. Their losses are not high enough to justify higher spending. It is very likely that the money they do spend will go for more technology, which is still, relatively speaking, the cheapest weapon in the war against lifting as well as being the one which gives the greatest illusion of protection.

Consuming our morals

Attitude changes in society would mean a change in the perception regarding the crime. Shoplifting would have to be seen as more serious; more damaging to society. We have shown you the 'Code,' which proposed rather heavy penalties, but harsh penalties cannot become reality unless supported by a societal attitude which shows no signs of changing. Although social attitudes these days support harsher sentences in every area of crime, shoplifting is still and, we hope, will continue to be, a footnote buried at the end of political reformers' list.

A FINAL NOTE TO RETAILERS

We bet you came to this section first. What did you expect? That we would give help to ***you***? Look at the title of the book. It isn't meant for you. It would be seriously immoral of us to tell you in this book how to counteract the methods of the smart lifters.

It's not for you

Can they be counteracted? Good question. The answer depends on your attitude. If you want to wage a war, you will have a war, but there will be casualties on both sides. We hope that we can get through to you the point that shoplifting should be seen as a matter-of-fact issue. The design and planning of an effective shoplifting prevention strategy should not be different from the design of effective fire prevention plans.

Don't light the fuse!

Any ***real*** expert on the subject will tell you that there are no typical shoplifters, typical motivations, or even typical methods. There are many things that can be done to prevent shoplifting, and we will (against our better judgment?) put out a pamphlet later to give you some ideas and pointers.

We are thinking...

"New training materials and increased open-mindedness have taught security professionals to be more cognisant of those whom they might not have suspected before. In short, today they suspect everyone. Retail security professionals, therefore, should not concentrate their energy on catching what was considered years ago as the typical shoplifter. Instead they should concentrate on recognising specific shoplifting techniques, enacting effective countermeasures to minimise shoplifting, and training store and security personnel on appropriate apprehension procedures. By focusing on these issues, security professionals will win the war against shoplifting and better protect their company's assets." (Security Management, May 1989)

We are sorry to say so, but you will never win the war. If you are very good, you might win some battles - more likely just some skirmishes - but you do not have even a fighting chance for a final victory!

No !@#$ing chance

Even though this book was not meant for you, if you have read it carefully, you should have learned a lot from it. Here we can only give you a few general pointers. They are all variations

Do your business better!

on two basic themes: do your business better, and treat your people better!

Spend your money on people, not gizmos.

Have more sales staff on the floor.

Pay your employees better, and create a better work environment for them.

Train your employees both to be more aware of customer needs and faster at completing sales.

Treat your customers with courtesy. Be helpful but not pushy.

Nothing will turn shoplifters away faster than the attentive, courteous service that every customer deserves. If you want more advice, read the book again.

A FINAL NOTE TO OUR READERS

What else can we tell you? We seem to have said everything.

We could warn you about the 'No-nos' again. We could 'kosher' ourselves even further by advising you against doing the wrong thing, but we do not really see the point. If you have read this far, morals are not very likely to be of concern to you, and if you have been as diligent a reader as we hoped you would be, still another warning is superfluous. If you lift, do it smart. Know what you are doing. Be smart. Be knowledgeable. Be aware. What does make some sense is to advise you where to go from here.

You made it!

All we can say in practical terms is that you should go out into the real world and 'observe' it for yourself. While we got most of the information presented in this book from very reliable sources, there is also some that is based on our own observations, or on the knowledge we gained from studying the literature on the subject. Since we started writing this book, we have not been able to walk into a store without immediately assessing it from a lifter's point of view. If we were able to judge the effectiveness of certain approaches and security measures, then so will you be. Walk around with your eyes open. Try to notice the thieves and the 'thiefcatchers' - the methods they use, the mistakes they make.

May the force be with you!

If you want to learn more about laws and legislation on shoplifting, check them out in your local library. If you want to know how the law deals with shoplifting in your area, do some research. The courts are open to the public, and they represent the best way to learn about the realities of the system.

If you are the cerebral type and have an interest in researching or thinking about the subject, there are a few questions that we find both very interesting and very much open to further research. For one reason or another nobody seems to have dealt with them. We could ask a series of practical questions, such as:

What is the value recovered from apprehended shoplifters (and employees) in proportion to the total loss?

Every article praising the value of EAS systems indicates the increase in apprehension rates and the decrease in the losses, but we have not seen any figures on the long term effects and comparative figures of similar establishments with and without EAS.

What is the net cost of prosecuting shoplifters?

Is there a net gain in civil recovery?

And more. We could also be philosophical. It would be interesting to see some good thinking about the attitude toward shoplifting and morality in general. We think that a soft crime such as shoplifting is a wonderful catalyst for the discussion of larger issues:

> What are the processes through which we 'negotiate' morality? Does permissiveness imply immorality?
>
> How do our morals relate to the law? At what point does one cease being able to rationalize criminal activity and begin to feel guilt or consider oneself immoral?
>
> What criteria do we use to determine the value of the material things in our lives?
>
> What is the relationship between cost, market value, stated value, and perceived value, and how do they influence our moral stamina?

For now, farewell. If you truly love the jungle and know what those drums are saying, we shall let you go, wishing you:

"Good hunting, little brother!"

”

...

APPENDICES

I have noticed that doctors who fail in the practice of medicine have a tendency to seek one another's company and aid in consultation. A doctor who cannot take out your appendix properly will recommend you to a doctor who will be unable to remove your tonsils with success.

Ernest Hemingway

Appendix #1

National Coalition to Prevent Shoplifting: Model Theft by Shoplifting Code

1. Theft by Shoplifting *Defined.*

(a) A person commits the offense of theft by shoplifting if, with intent to appropriate merchandise without paying the merchant's stated price for the merchandise, such person, alone or in concert with another person knowingly:

(i) Conceals the merchandise; or

(ii) Removes, takes possession of, or causes the removal of merchandise; or

(iii) Alters, transfers, or removes any price marking, or any other marking which aids in determining value affixed to the merchandise; or

(iv) Transfers the merchandise from one container to another; or

(v) Causes the cash register or other sales-recording device to reflect less than the merchant's stated price for the merchandise.

(b) A person commits the offense of theft by shoplifting if, with intent to appropriate, such person, alone or in concert with another person, knowingly removes a shopping cart from the premises of the mercantile establishment.

2. Evidence and Presumptions.

(a) Knowing concealment of merchandise shall create a rebuttable presumption that the person intended to appropriate the merchandise without paying the merchant's stated price for the merchandise.

(b) Evidence of stated price or ownership of merchandise may include, but is not limited to:

(i) The actual merchandise or the container which held the merchandise alleged to have been shoplifted; or

(ii) The content of the price tag or marking from such merchandise; or

(iii) Properly identified photographs of such merchandise.

(c) Any merchant may testify at a trial as to the stated price or ownership of merchandise, as well as to other matters pertaining to the case.

3. **Penalties.**

A person convicted of theft by shoplifting shall be punished as follows:

(a) *First Theft By Shoplifting* Conviction: Upon a first theft by shoplifting conviction:

(i) When the merchant's stated price of the merchandise is less than or equal to $100, the defendant shall be fined not more than $250.

(ii) When the merchant's stated price of the merchandise exceeds $100, the defendant shall be fined not less than $100 nor more than $500, and such fine shall not be suspended; or the defendant shall be punished by imprisonment not to exceed one year; or both.

(b) *Second Theft* By Shoplifting Conviction: Upon a second theft by shoplifting conviction:

(i) When the merchant's stated price of the merchandise is less than or equal to $100, the defendant shall be fined not less than $100 nor more than $500, and such fine shall not be suspended; or the defendant shall be punished by imprisonment not to exceed one year; or both.

(ii) When the merchant's stated price of the merchandise exceeds $100, the defendant shall be fined not less than $500 and shall be imprisoned for not less than thirty days and not to exceed three years. The first thirty days of such sentence shall not be suspended, probated, deferred, or withheld.

(c) Third Theft By Shoplifting Conviction: Upon a third or subsequent theft by shoplifting conviction, regardless of the merchant's stated price of the merchandise, the defendant shall be fined not less than $500 nor more than $5,000, and shall be imprisoned for one to ten years. The first year of such sentence shall not be suspended, probated, deferred, or withheld.

(d) In determining the number of prior theft by shoplifting convictions for purposes of imposing punishment under this section, the court shall disregard all such convictions occurring more than seven years prior to the theft by shoplifting offense in question.

4. Merchant's *Immunity from* Civil and *Criminal* Liability.

(a) General Rule: A merchant who detains, questions, or causes the arrest of any person suspected of theft by shoplifting shall not be criminally or civilly liable for any legal action relating to such detention, questioning, or arrest, if:

(i) The merchant has reasonable grounds to suspect that the person has committed or is attempting to commit theft by shoplifting; and

(ii) The merchant acts in a reasonable manner under the circumstances; and

(iii) The merchant detains the suspected person for a reasonable period of time.

(b) Reasonable Grounds: Reasonable grounds to suspect that a person has committed or is attempting to commit theft by shoplifting may be based on, but is not limited to:

(i) Personal observation, including observation via closed-circuit television or other visual device; or

(ii) Report of such personal observation from another merchant; or

(iii) Activation of an electronic or other type of mechanical device designed to detect shoplifting.

(c) Reasonable Manner: A merchant or peace officer who has reasonable grounds to believe that a person has committed or is attempting to commit the offense of theft by shoplifting, as defined in Section 1 of this act, may detain such person on or off the premises of the mercantile establishment if such detention is done for any or all of the following purposes:

(i) To question the person, investigate the surrounding circumstances, obtain a statement, or any combination thereof;

(ii) To request and/or verify identification;

(iii) To inform a peace officer of the detention of such person, and/or surrender that person to the custody of a peace officer;

(iv) To inform a peace officer, the parent or parents, guardian, or other private person interested in the welfare of a minor of the detention and to surrender the minor to the custody of such person(s); or

(v) To institute criminal proceedings against the person.

(d) The merchant may use a reasonable amount of force necessary to protect himself, to prevent escape of the person detained, or to prevent the loss of destruction of property.

(e) Reasonable Time: A reasonable period of time, for purposes of this section, shall be deemed to be a period of time long enough to accomplish the purpose set forth in this section, and shall include any time spent awaiting the arrival of a law enforcement officer or the parents or guardian of a juvenile suspect, if the merchant has summoned such law enforcement officer, parents, or guardian.

(f) Any detention as defined in this section shall not constitute an arrest.

5. *Arrest of* Theft By Shoplifting *Suspects.*

A law enforcement officer may arrest without warrant any person he or she has probable cause for believing has committed the offense of theft by shoplifting. "Probable cause," as used in this section, includes but shall not be limited to the statement of a merchant containing facts and circumstances demonstrating that he has reasonable grounds to suspect that a person has committed theft by shoplifting.

6. Civil Liability.

(a) An adult or emancipated minor who, with intent to appropriate merchandise without paying the merchant's stated price for the merchandise, alone or in concert with another person, knowingly commits any of the acts described in section 1 (a), or an adult or emancipated minor who, with intent to appropriate a shopping cart alone or in concert with another person knowingly removes a shopping cart from the premises of the mercantile establishment, shall be liable, in addition to actual damages, for a penalty to the owner or seller in the amount of the value of the merchandise or the value of the shopping cart, respectively, not to exceed $1,000, plus an additional penalty of not less than $100 nor more than $200.

(b) The parent or legal guardian having custody of an unemancipated minor who, with intent to appropriate merchandise without paying the merchant's stated price for the merchandise, alone or in concert with another person, knowingly commits any of the acts described in section 1 (a), or the parent or legal guardian having custody of an unemancipated minor who, with intent to appropriate a shopping cart, alone or in concert with another person knowingly removes a shopping cart from the premises of the mercantile establishment, shall be liable, in addition to actual damages, for a penalty to the owner or seller in the amount of the value of the merchandise or the value of the shopping cart, respectively, not to exceed $500, plus an additional penalty of not less than $100 nor more than $200.

(c) Liability of parents or Guardian: Civil liability under this section is not limited by any other law concerning the liability of parents or guardians or minors.

(d) *Costs* and Attorneys Fees: A merchant who is a prevailing party under this section shall be entitled to costs and reasonable attorneys fees.

(e) Effect of Conviction: A conviction for the offense of theft by shoplifting is not a prerequisite to the maintenance of a civil action authorized by this section.

(f) Right to Demand Payment: The fact that a mercantile establishment may bring an action against an individual as provided in this section shall not limit the right of such establishment to demand, orally or in writing, that a person who is liable for damages and penalties under this section remit said damages prior to the consideration of the commencement of any legal action.

(g) An action for recovery of damages and penalties under this section may be brought in any court of competent jurisdiction, including a small claims court, whether or not the merchant is a corporation, partnership, etc., if the total damages do not exceed the jurisdictional limit of the court involved.

7. Severability.

If any section, causes, grounds, paragraph, or part of this act is for any reason adjudged to be invalid, such judgments will not invalidate the remainder thereof but shall be confined to the part directly involved in the controversy.

8, Definitions.

(a) "Conceal" *means* to hide, hold, or carry *merchandise, so* that, although there may be *some* notice of its presence, it *is* not visible through ordinary observation.

(b) "Merchant" *means an owner* or operator of any mercantile establishment, *and includes the merchant's employees,* servants, security agents, or other agents.

(c) "Mercantile Establishment" means any place where merchandise is displayed, held, or offered for sale, either at retail or wholesale. "Mercantile establishment" includes adjoining parking lots or adjoining areas of common use with other establishments.

(d) "Merchandise" means any goods, foodstuffs, wares, or personal property, or any part or portion thereof **any** type or description displayed, held, or offered for sale.

(e) "Merchants Stated Price for the Merchandise" means the price that the merchandise is offered for sale at the time and place of offense.

9. Effective Date.

This act shall become effective ninety (90) days after enactment.

10. Repealer.

All laws and parts of laws in conflict with this act are hereby repealed.

Appendix #2

SUMMARY OF CIVIL RECOVERY LAWS

STATE	STATUTE	APPLIES TO MINORS	ACTUAL DAMAGES	RETAIL VALUE OF MERCHENDISE	ADDITIONAL PENALTY	COURT COSTS	ATTORNEY'S FEES
AK	9.65.110	YES	YES	TO $1,000	$100-$200	**	YES
AZ	12-691	YES	YES	YES	$100	**	**
CA	490.5(b)(c)	YES	NO	IF NOT SALABLE	$50-$500	YES	YES
CO	13-21-107.5	YES	YES	**	$100-$250	**	**
FL	772.11	NO	$200+	**	**	YES	YES
GA	51-10-6	NO	YES	YES	> OF $150 OR 2 X DAMAGES	YES	YES
HI	6663A-2	YES	YES	IF NOT SALABLE	SEE notes	YES	**
ID	48-701,702	YES	NO	YES	$100-$250	YES	YES
IL	16A-7	YES	YES	ACTUAL DAMAGES = RETAIL VALUE	$100-$1000	YES	YES
IN	34-4-30-1	NO	YES	**	ACTUAL X 3	YES	YES
LA	9.2799.1	NO	NO	IF NOT SALABLE	$50-$500	**	**
MA	231:85G, 85R ½	YES	YES	**	ADULTS: $50-$500	**	**
MI	-	YES	NO	See notes	SEE notes	See notes	See notes
MT	27-1-718	YES	YES	MANDATORY: TO $500	RETAIL VALUE MERCHENDISE	**	**
NE	24-523	YES	YES	YES	NO	YES	YES
NV	598.033,035	YES	YES	YES	$100-$250	YES	YES
NH	664:17a	NO	See notes	NO	NO	NO	NO
NJ	2C:20-20	NO	YES	**	3 X DAMAGES	YES	YES
NM	30-16-21	NO	NO	IF NOT RECOVERED	$100-$250	YES	YES
NC	1-538.2	YES	YES	See notes	See notes	**	YES
ND	51-21-05	YES	NO	YES	TO $250	YES	YES
OH	2307.60/61	YES	YES	YES	See notes	YES	YES
TN	39-3-1124	YES	NO	IF NOT RECOVERED	NO	YES	YES
TX	ART. 1e	YES	YES	**	TO: $ 1000 CT. AWARDS	YES	YES

STATE	STATUTE	APPLIES TO MINORS	ACTUAL DAMAGES	RETAIL VALUE OF MERCHENDISE	ADDITIONAL PENALTY	COURT COSTS	ATTORNEY'S FEES
VA	18.2-104.1	NO	NO	IF NOT RECOVERED	COST OF PROSECUTION	**	**
WA	4.24.230	YES	YES	TO $1000 JUV. TO 500	$100-$200	**	**
WV	61-3A-5	NO	See notes	IF NOT SALABLE	See notes	YES	YES
WI	943.51	NO	YES	IF NOT RECOVERED	TO 3 X RETAIL PLUS ACTUAL	YES	YES

NOTES

HAWAII: ADDITIONAL PENALTY ON WRITTEN DEMAND, $75. CIVIL SUIT PENALTY OF $50-$500

MICHIGAN: RETAIL VALUE OF MERCHANDISE IF NOT RECOVERED OR NOT SALABLE. ADDITIONAL PENALTY ON WRITTEN DEMAND: 10 X RETAIL VALUE OF MERCHENDISE, BUT NO LESS THAN $40 AND NO MORE THAN $100. CIVIL SUIT, PENALTY OF $200 PLUS REASONABLE COSTS NOT GREATER THAN $50.

NEW HAMPSHIRE: ONLY DAMAGES AVAILABLE - COST OF EMPLOYEE'S WAGES FOR ARRAIGNMENT AND PROSECUTION

NORTH CAROLINA: RETAIL VALUE OF MERCHANDISE CALCULATED AS FULL VALUE IF DESTROYED, LOSS OF VALUE IF RECOVERED OR DAMAGED. ADDITIONAL PENALTY OF 3 X ACTUAL OR CONSENQUENTIAL DAMAGES.

OHIO: ADDITIONAL PENALTY OF THE GREATER OF $200 OR 2 X ACTUAL DAMAGES. OHIO IS THE ONLY STATE IN WHICH NON-PAYMENT OF CIVIL DEMAND MAY RESULT IN THE INITIATION OF CRIMINAL PROCESS.

WEST VIRGINIA: ACTUAL DAMAGES ARE ALLOWED, BUT STATUTE SPECIFICALLY STATES THAT MERCHANT MAT NOT RECOVER THE COST OF PROCESSING THE CASE.

BIBLIOGRAPHY

The following bibliography is a limited one. It only mentions the books and articles we looked at. A rather extensive bibliography of the subject can be found in "The Sociology of Shoplifting" (Klemke, 1992)

12th Annual Pevention Survey,
Chain Store Age Executive , Jan 1991, v. 67 sec 2

A Chicago Crime Story: Score One for the Good Guys,
Chain Store Age Executive , Jan. 1991, v. 67 sec 2p. 52-3

A Shoplifter's Bag of Tricks.,
Progressive Grocer, May 1982, v. 61 p. 14

Capitols' Needy Seek Relief,
U.S. News & World Report, Dec. 1 1986, p5

Chain Focuses on Security in a Bigg's Way: Newest Store Has Theft Under Control with Quality Surveillance System.,
Chain Store Age Executive , Mar. 1993, v. 69p. 168

Crime Prevention in your Business,
Metro Toronto Police, 1995, pamphlet

Definition of Larceny,
Encarta, 1995,

Determining Deterrence by Studying Shrinkage.,
Security Management, Apr. 1992, v. 36p. 10

EAS Thwarts Shoplifters at Las Vegas Diamond's.,
Chain Store Age Executive , Sept. 1984, v. 60p. 149+

Going to Market.,
Security Management, May 1993, v. 37 p. 18-19

Is Source Tagging Possible?.,
Progressive Grocer, Aug. 1993, v. 72 p. 116

Linking EAS with CCVS Helps Stop All Types of Theft.,
Chain Store Age Executive , Aug. 1991, v. 67p. 64

Loss Prevention Can Be Profitable: Civil Recovery Procedure Demands Restitution from Shoplifters.,
Chain Store Age Executive , Dec. 1988, v. 64p. 72-3

Prevent Shoplifting,
Metro Toronto Police, 1995, pamphlet

Robery Prevention,
Metro Toronto Police, 1995, pamphlet

Security Trade: Checkpoint Systems Bets on Radio-based Antishoplift Device.,
Barron, May 11 1987, v. 67 p. 65-6

Security: EAS Cuts Giant Shoplifting.,
Chain Store Age Executive , July 1983, v. 59p. 48

Shoplifting Dynamics: Who, what, when, where and how?.,
Chain Store Age Executive , Sept. 1985, v. 61p. 79-80

Shoplifting in America: Krazy Kirk Meets Dr Shortage.,
The Economist v. 318, Jan. 19 1991, p. 65

Shoplifting Reigns Supreme.,
Security Management, Sept. 1993, v. 37p. 16+

Shrinkige Survey of Canadian Retailers,
Ottawa Retail Council ofCanada, 1986,

Snatching up the Festive Season.,
The Economist v. 322, Jan. 4 1992, p. 54

Solvents for Sticky Fingers.,
Chain Store Age Executive , Sept 1984, v. 60p. 145

Subliminal Messages: Subtle Crime Stoppers.,
Chain Store Age Executive , July 1986, v. 62p. 85+

To Stop a Thief.,
Progressive Grocer, May 1986, v. 65 p. 17

Wanamaker Approach Keeps Tabs on Loss.,
Chain Store Age Executive , July 1987, v. 63p. 102

When You Least Expect It.,
Chain Store Age Executive , Feb. 1985, v. 61p. 18

Abelson, Elaine S.: When Ladies Go A-Thieving: Middle Class Shoplifters in the Victorian Department Store,
New York: Oxford University Press, 1989,

Adamo Frank S.: Holliday Season Crime Awareness,
from the Internet, 1994,

Adler, Steven: Has Your Store Had a Check-up?.,
Security Management, Apr. 1993, p. 61

Arbetter, Lisa: Dealing with the Realities of Retail,
Security Management, Mar. 1994, v. 38

Arbetter, Lisa: Retail Theft from the Inside Out,
Security Management, Apr. 1993, v. 37p. 11-12

Baumer, Terry L., and Dennis P. Rosenbaum: Combatting Retail Theft: Programs and Strategies,
Boston: Butterworth, 1984,

Bennett, Hilary M: Shopliffing in Midtown,
Criminal Law Review, 1968, vol 4: p41335

Bennett, Stephen: To Catch a Thief,
Progressive Grocer, June 1990, v. 69 p. 30-2+

Bergin, Daniel M.: Theft: How Safe are Pharmacies?.,
Drug Topics, Nov. 19 1990, v. 134p. 30-4+

Bernikow, Louise.: Excuse Me, Miss! Did You Pay for This,
Mademoiselle, September 1994, p 280

Brenton, Myron: Women Who Steal,
Cosmopolitan, May 1985, 285

Brown, M. Lindsay: Five-Finger Discount: A Look at Shoplifting and Retail Security,
USA Today, November 1984, p64-67

Canton, Lucien G.: : Should Shoplifters Be Prosecuted?.,
Security Management, May 1987, v. 31p. 61-4

Carolin, P. James, Jr: Survey of Shoplifters,
Security Management, Mar. 1992, v. 36 p. 11A-12A

Cleary, James, Jr.: Prosecuting the Shoplifter [book review].,
Security Management, June 1986, v. 30p. 120+

Cleary, James, Jr.: Pay to the Order of John Q. Shoplifter.,
Security Management, Feb. 1983, v. 27p. 59-62

Clepper, Irene.: Cutting Your Losses.,
Drug Topics, July 11 1994, v. 137p. 62-3+

Clifford, John T.: Something for Nothing.,
Security Management, Feb. 1988, v. 32p. 57

Crawford, Mary Alice.: To Educate the Public.,
Security Management, Sept. 1982, v. 26p. 24-6+

Crowley, Thomas E.: Attention, Shoppers: Shoplifting Program in Effect.,
Security Management, Sept. 1988, v. 32p. 123-5

Davis, Melissa G.: Private Corporate Justice: Store Police, Shoplifters, and Civil Recovery.,
Social Problems, Aug. 1991, v. 38 p. 395-411

Epstein, Debbie.: Theft: How safe are your pharmacies?.,
Drug Topics, Jan. 7 1991, v. 135p. 13-14+

Epstein, Debbie.: New State Laws Protect Retailers from Sticky Fingers.,
Drug Topics, Feb. 5 1990, v. 134p. 20

Espinoza, Douglas C: Shoplifters No Sale,
Security Management, May 1989, p 65-69

Ewen, Stuart: Captains of Consciousness: Advertising and the Social Roots of the Consumer Culture,
New York: McGraw-Hill, 1976,

Farrell, Katheleen L: Shoplifting: The Antishopliftilq Guidebook,
New York: Praeger, 1985,

Farrell, Kathleen L.: Shoplifting [book review].,
Security Management, Nov. 1986, v. 30p. 87-8

Feinberg, Gary: Profile of the Elderly Shoplifter,
Cambridge, Mass.: Oelgeschlager, Gunn & Hain, 1984, pp. 35-50

French, Warren A., Melvin R. Crask, and Fred H. Mader: Retailer's Assessment of the Shoplifting Problem,
Journal of Retailing, (4) 1984, 60108-14

Francis, Dorothy Brenner: Shoplifting, the Crime Everybody Pays For,
New York : E.P. Dutton, 1980, 128 p. ; 21 cm

Gibbens, T. C. N.: Shoplifting,
British Journal of Psychiatry, 1981, 138: 346-47

Griffin, Roger.: Why the Temptation?.,
Security Management, Dec. 1989, v. 33p. 126+

Griffin, Roger.: Walking off with Billions.,
Security Management, Aug. 1984, v. 28p. 70-2

Griffin, Roger.: Supermarket Losses Estimated to Top $1 billion in '81.,
Security Management, June 1982, v. 26p. 40-1

Gruber, Christina.: My life of Crime with Operation Gotcha.,
Chain Store Age General Merchandise Edition, Nov. 1983, v. 59 p. 38+

Gusfield, Joseph P.: Constructing the Ownership of Social Problems: Fun and Profit in the Welfare State.,
Social Problems, (2) 1989, vol 36 p431-43.

Hayes, Jack L.: Who Are the Shoplifters?.,
Chain Store Age Executive with Shopping Center Age, June 1982, v. 58p. 11

Hayes, Read.: The Civil Recovery Side of Shoplifting.,
Security Management, Mar. 1992, v. 36p. 30A-32A

Hayes, Read.: Winning the Civil Recovery War.,
Security Management, Mar. 1990, v. 34p. 83-4

Hazel, Debra.: Do Retailers Take the Punishment for Crime? Rehab Programs Can Be Less Costly Alternatives to Prosecution.,
Chain Store Age Executive , Oct. 1987, v. 63p. 82+

Hoffman, Abbie: Steal This Book,
New York: Grove Press, 1971,

Kallis, M. Jeffery, and Dinoo J. Vanier: Consumer Shoplifting: Orientations and Deterrents,
Journal of Criminal justice 13, 1985, 459-73

Klein, Gerald.: The Hidden Benefits of EAS.,
Security Management, June 1991, v. 35p. 56-60

Kleist, Trina.: Theft is the Thing.,
Business Mexico v. 4, Aug. 1994, p. 8

Klemke, Lloyd W.: Does Apprehension for Shoplifting Amplify or Terminate Shoplifting Activity,
Law and Society Review, Spring 1978, 12(): 391-403

Klemke, Lloyd W.: The Sociology of Shoplifting: Boosters and Snitches Today,
Westport, Conn.:Praeger, 1992,

Klokis, Holly.: Confessions of an Ex-shoplifter.,
Chain Store Age Executive , Feb. 1985, v. 61p. 15-18

Kopecky, Gini: Shoplifting: Why Women Who Have Everything Steal,
Shoplifting: Why Women Who Have Everything Steal, December 1980, p 156.

Leonard A. Sipes: And the Answer Is........,
Security Management, May 1989, v. 33p. 69-72

Lesser, Ellen: The Shoplifter's Appentice,
New York. Simon & Schuster, 1989,

Levine, Karen.: Retailers Hit the Shoplifter with a Civil Fine.,
Drug Topics, Dec. 14 1992, v. 136p. 120

Maguire, Kathleen, and Timothy J. Flanagan, eds: Sourcebook of Criminal Justice Statistics-1990.,
Washington, D.C.: U.S. Government Printing Office, 1991,

Marx, Gary: Undercover: Police Surveillance in America,
Berkeley: University of California Press., 1988,

Minerbrook, Scott.: A Face-Off with Racism: In a Manhattan Train Station, Grappling with the Tricky Questions of Prejudice and Race Relations,
U.S. News & World Report , Aug. 22 1988, p105 57.

O'Neill, Robert E.: Giant to Shoplifters: Gotcha!.,
Progressive Grocer, Apr. 1984, v. 63 p. 129+

Osgood, Wayne D., Patrick M. O'Malley, Gerald G. Bachman, and Lloyd D. Johnston: Time Trends and Age Trends in Arrests and Self Reported Illegal Behavior,
Criminology, (3) 1989, vol27 p389-415

Pousner, Michael.: Women Who Shoplift,
Cosmopolitan, April 1988, 162.

Purpura, Philip P: Security Loss and Prevention,
Boston: Butterworth., 1994,

Purpura, Philip P.: Security and Loss Prevention [book review,
Security Management, Nov. 1991, p. 112

Purpura, Philip P.,: Security & Loss Prevention [book review].,
Security Management, Jan. 1986, v. 30p. 76

Ray, JoAnn: Every Twelfth Shopper: Who Shoplifts and Why,
Social Casework, April 1987, vol 68 234-39

Rook, Dennis W.: The Buying Impulse,
Journal of Consumer Research, Sept. 1987, vol 14 p189-98

Sam Sifton: Booster Club,
New York Press, Feb. 2-8 1994, vol. 7, no. 5

Sansolo, Michael.: Shoplifting Statistics: Seeing Is Believing.,
Progressive Grocer, Oct. 1983, v. 62 p. 101-3

Schlueter, Gregory R., Francis C. O'Neal, JoAnn Hickey, and Gloria L. Seiler.: Rational vs. Nonrational Shoplifting Types: The Implications for Loss Prevention,
International Journal of Offender Therapy and Comparative Criminology, (3) 1989, vol 33 pp 227-39

Sennewald, Charles A.,: Shoplifting.,
Boston: Butterworth-Heinemann, 1992,

Solomon, Gary S.: Irrational Beliefs of Shoplifters.,
Journal of Clinical Psychology, July 1984, v. 40 p. 1075-7

Stinson, Delany J.: Attention, Retailers: Civil Law Provides a Tonic.,
Security Management, Sept. 1988, v. 32p. 129-32

Terry Fuss, NM: Shoplifting Simulation,
1994, from the internet

Tooley, Jo Ann: Smugglers at the Supermarket,
U.S. News & World Report, March 13 1989, p73

Townesend, Michael: Shoplifting ; A Study,
Vancouver, Elizabeth Fry Society of B.C., 1972, 31 leaves

Tsiantar, Dody: Big Brother at the Mall: Retailers Go High Tech in the War on Shoplifters,
Newsweek, July 3 1989, 44

Tunnell, Kenneth D: Choosing Crime: The Criminal Calculus of Property Offenders.,
Chicago: Nelson-Hall Publishers, 1992,

Walker, Samuel: Sense and Nonsense about Crime: A Policy Guide,
Monterey, Calif.: Brooks/Cole, 1985,

Walsh, Denis Patrick,: Shoplifting: Controlling a Major Crime.,
London: Macmillan Press., 1978.,

Whitcomb, Debra.: An Exemplary Project: Focus on Robbery : The Hidden Cameras Project,
Seattle, Washington, 1979.,

Wiessier, David A: Surge in Petty Theft: Symptom of Hard Times,
U.S. News & World Report, July 19 1982, p50

Williams, Hubert, Brian Forst, and Edwin Hamilton.: Stop! You Should Arrest That Person,
Security Management, September 1987, v. 31 p 52-57

Willis, Steve.: Confessions of a Shoplifter.,
Security Management, Jan. 1991, v. 35p. 83-4

Zellner, Wendy.: Sticky Fingers are Rifling Through Retail.,
Business Week, Mar. 28 1994, p. 36

ABOUT THE AUTHORS

GABRIEL CAIME was born in picturesque Sophianae, illegitimate son of some lowly Enemies of the People. From there, everything in his life was downhill. He was raised in Budapest by his upstanding mother and loving stepfather. Being a true enemy of the people just as his father and grandfather were before him, he spent a year of his youth in the lovely prison of Kőbánya for being in the wrong place at the wrong time saying the wrong thing to the wrong people under the wrong circumstances.

He had a passing interest in the occult. Closer scrutiny of his fortune revealed to him that having conflicts with authorities is his karma. He decided to stop fighting his fate and to embrace conflict and controversy with ambitious projects such as the writing of The S(h)elf Help Guide

A recovering abstainer, he longs for the freedom the readers of this book will provide him with buying this first in a (hopefully) long line of infuriating bestsellers.

His days are spent in a red fog of fury over the state of the world, politics and morals. He is an incurable intellectual masochist, listening to college radio, and reading leftist publications. Sometimes he even reads Noam Chomsky 'till his mouth starts to foam.

He is said to be a good cook, and an excellent dancer. A womanizer wannabe, married four times (four wives in four countries,) and will quite possibly do it again. He hopes to die in the hottest moment of a passionate night with a sexy sixty years old, yet unborn. His sex-appeal is intensity and brain-power. Definitely not his hair. He is bold about being bald, shaving his head every now and then.

GABRIEL GHONE was brought to this world by Sárika, an elementary school teacher in Budapest, Hungary. He (yes, he is a he) lives and works in Montreal, Quebec with his family. He used to live in Budapest, Szeged, Paris, Toronto, Szentendre and other likewise very small places.

Most of his days are spent in depression and the performing arts. Lately, he was mainly writing dramas and scripts-- theatre and film -- and this humble but soon to be world famous work, the S(H)ELF HELP GUIDE which is his first attempt to make money with the help of his artistic skills.

He is a thinker, a tinkerer, weaver of words and devoted theatre artist who is convinced that theatre together with shoemaking are dead!

He has two ears, two blue eyes but unfortunately (or luckily) only one mouth, that he uses for food, drink and nicotine intake as well as for incessant talk and breathing. Both his legs reach the ground. Sometimes he lifts them and puts them one after the other forward -- what simple people call walking. Because of his obnoxious personality that is worsened by his incredible brainpower he falls in and out of different moods, therefore his family put him on Prozac. Other than he is a beautiful human being he is fat and bearded with a graying bunch of facial hair. He keeps himself 'well-fared' by swimming in debt constantly as well as at the YMCA regularly.